Blood and Mind

Melanie Bonnefoux

PublishAmerica

Baltimore

First printing

This book is entirely fictitious and comes from the author's imagination. Any resemblance to actual locales, events, or persons, living or dead is entirely coincidental.

ISBN: 1-59286-442-2
PUBLISHED BY PUBLISHAMERICA, LLLP
www.publishamerica.com
Baltimore

Printed in the United States of America

Dedication

I dedicate this book to my extraordinary family. I owe you all a debt of gratitude for supporting my dreams and for always telling me that I 'spun a good yarn.' This one's for you guys, I love you all so much.

Acknowledgements:

A first book is no small feat, and this work was no exception. This book would not have been possible without the support and help of so many people. Thanks to Colby Hausmann for his wonderful cover. His talent is immense and I am so lucky to have had that talent working for me. A great big thanks to the staff at PublishAmerica for their dedication, commitment and most importantly their faith in Holly and in me. Isaac, your web page is a dream, you've brought the world to me and me to the world. Ker Bear I miss you more than I can say. Your strength and friendship has carried me through many years, remember bff. I owe a debt of gratitude to Ed Gizzi, a big debt of gratitude. Ed, thank you for your time and patience. Thank goodness you understand and communicate with that hunk of 'junk' that tries to pass as my computer. Thank you Jennifer McKinney for your gorgeous and professional photos, you even made me want to smile. I need to give great thanks to Ashleigh and Michelle for being two great roomies, how does a girl get so lucky? I wish to thank all my English professors through the years, you all made me stick with it, even when I wanted to throw in the towel. A special thanks to Dr. Frost and Professor Tanksley of Fordham University, your classes were truly inspirational. To all the girls of 15B, for just being the Divas that you are. Last, but certainly not least, thanks to Margaret and Mimi. For although they are no longer with us, I am certain they had a hand in this.

Chapter One:

Okay, so it's like this; the monsters you always thought lurked under your bed as a child actually *do* lurk under your bed. Are you wondering how I know this? Well it's quite simple actually, one of them tried to eat me when I was five. My name is Holly-Anne Feather and I've been told I'd make a delicious meal, on several occasions by several beings, both human and non-human. It seems that nowadays you can't go anywhere without someone, or something wanting to eat you, literally. You'd think that in the eleven years since the 'Invitation Acts' had been passed that civilization would have grown more civilized, however, the only thing more civilized these days would be the monsters. In accordance to the Acts, the monsters have to ask before they decide to have you for dinner, and when I say for dinner I really mean for dinner. If you decline their oh-so-generous offer they very well may eat you anyways, because as you know monsters don't change. Oh, now, they may wear Armani suits and Dior dresses and own and establish successful businesses but deep down inside they are still what constitutes evil. Now I know you're thinking to yourselves, how does she know so much about monsters and the nature of evil, again the answer is quite simple, I know about monsters because I am one.

When I was five years old a big, ugly ghoul tried to eat me for dinner. It had been hiding underneath my bed, attracted to me, my mother claimed, by the similarities in our nature. I never did learn why my mother saved me that day, certainly it hadn't been out of maternal instinct; Mother didn't have a maternal bone in her body. For whatever reason three shotgun blasts later, and a scream that would make any daughter proud, ghoul guts littered the floor and walls. I escaped with my life that day but over the years I would learn that such events were not uncommon and that the fates had decided that I would always be drawn into them. It would be five more years before I learned that my 'evil' had a name, five long years of suppressing my true

7

nature and accepting my mother's abuse.

At the age of ten, Mrs. Muller, the only teacher I can remember liking, pulled me aside. Mrs. Muller had noticed my distance from the other children, my constant solitude, and it worried her. She shocked me by being able to pick up other things, like how I would cover my ears and shut my eyes whenever I was in a crowd. With much reluctance and a great many tears I spilled out five years worth of agony, frustration and fear, at the end, Mrs. Muller took me into her arms and hugged me. With a brilliant smile and tender manner she explained to me who I was, what I was, an Empath. But no ordinary Empath was I; I was an Empath with strong PSI abilities, abilities that were uncommon together. Oh, some Empaths, the really strong ones manifest some PSI abilities, but it would seem that my abilities ran the gamut from the very normal, to the very abnormal.

Mother thought I was an abomination. I went against every law of nature and was unclean in the eyes of the Lord. She knew, she had to have known what I was but she never told me. She led me to believe that I was like that ghoul who had tried to have me for dinner. I suppose to her I was like that ghoul, I suppose to her a monster was a monster no matter what the trappings. In the years following my discovery at the hands of Mrs. Muller, whom I later learned was clairvoyant; I honed my craft. By the age of fifteen I could thought-disconnect, which meant, suddenly, I wasn't besieged by other people's emotions and pain. I no longer screamed because my mind was being invaded, in truth it was the exact opposite, my mind was a steel trap, no one got in and out unless I let them. Mrs. Muller assured me that I wasn't a monster; she called my abilities 'gifts', 'gifts' which had been bestowed upon me for some higher purpose. I ran with that, I mean what would a fifteen year old prefer to think she was, a monster, or merely gifted. But deep down inside my mother's words would and do haunt me; I was, I am, a monster, no matter how pretty the package.

Chapter Two:

I wasn't impressed by the display. Oh, he was handsome enough it you liked that sort of thing. With long blond hair, clear blue eyes and a body to die for, really die, for, he was two hundred years of hard bodied male, he was also dead as a doorknob. Club 'Ecstasy' was having its 'mix and mingle' night and I, unfortunately had been conned into attending. I had been under the impression that I was attending a birthday party, it seemed that some of my 'friends' thought I was too reclusive for my own good, this was their poor attempt at socializing me. Instead I was surrounded by the undead and unnatural and from the looks of things I was already being 'tested.' Oh yes, we can usually sense our own kind. I am surprisingly skilled at hiding my abilities and shielding my nature from others, but like attracts like, and in this place there is a lot of 'like.'

"Isn't he beautiful?" This came from Vanessa Bibley of the Long Island Bibleys. Just twenty-one Vanessa has more money than Midas and the brains of an addled ox. Now I'm not being cruel, just truthful, at this rate Vanessa won't reach her twenty-second year. She's what is commonly referred to as 'dead bait' or simply put, she's an undead groupie. Yeah there seems to be a foolish amount of those around these days, oh yeah *everyone* wants to be around the undead, everyone except me, I can't get far enough away.

"You don't find me beautiful?" The voice was cool, cold and yet at the same time managed to be warm and silky. I didn't have to turn around to know it was the same blond haired vampire that Vanessa had been ogling. His 'essence' poured around me like a cool breeze but neither raised the hairs on my arm nor sent off warning signals in my brain, all of which told me that this blond beauty was low on the power scale. "You don't want to feel my cool flesh?"

Did he want me to answer? I merely swung my head around to give him a cool, level look; I immediately realized my mistake as I felt the tug of compulsion pour through my body. I didn't move a muscle, just let the tingling subside, but I knew I had made a fatal error. If I had been smart I would have played along, at least for a little while, at least until he had been certain of my humanity, now, now he knew that I was different, unnatural, one of *them*. By resisting his compulsion I had sent off the alarms. Hypnosis, or compulsion is commonly used by the undead as a means to an end, if you're going to eat, why not eat easily, or so say the dead. Under hypnosis the most acute pain can be transmitted as pleasure, and the most perverse acts can be reveled in. As an Empath I had learned to build walls and place up shields so strong as to keep the populace at bay, the shields don't discriminate; they include the undead, so Mr. Blondie's attempts at compulsion were wasted on me. I was shaken out of my momentary stupor by another tug of compulsion, it seemed Mr. Blondie sure was determined.

"All right, unless you're going to attempt to do something more than just give me a headache I suggest you give it a rest." I was sick of the macho act, it seemed that a man was a man—alive or dead.

"What are you?" Mr. Blondie's voice was cold, well all their voices are cold but his was tinged with the heat that only a vampire can get when they're angry. I wasn't sure what my odds would be if I took him on in the club, but you can be sure that I wasn't excited about the prospect of such action.

"What I am is tired." I sighed. I really, really didn't want to attract any more attention, especially not from the undead. Truth be told I had been showing off, it hadn't been necessary to erect the double walls and I needn't have mouthed off to him. You should never mouth off to something that could possibly take your head off with its teeth. "Listen, I'm sorry, I was rude. I really am exhausted and I think it's time I head home." I held out a hand and watched as Mr. Blondie's blue eyes got wider and wider. He laughed suddenly and it was a rusty sound. He took my warm hand in his and held it longer than necessary. I clenched my teeth as he continued to hold my hand. Not caring if I was rude anymore I yanked it free and gave him a curt nod. Turning on my heel, I strode briskly and assuredly towards the front of the club, ignoring the eyes and the stares that bore holes into my head. I was sweating now, sweating and scared. I had let myself go tonight, more so than I ever did. I hadn't wanted to admit that surrounded by all things unnatural I had felt the faint stirrings of familiarity and comfort. For the first time in a very long time I had dropped some of my shields and that scared me more than anything, because now I knew they were aware that I was among them, and they were searching for me.

Chapter Three:

Calculus sucks. The plain, undiluted truth is that nobody really needs calculus. I mean, if you can balance a checkbook, calculate tip and add on both fingers you have all the math knowledge you'll ever need, however, it would appear that my professor doesn't share my opinion. Sitting now in an upright desk-chair with thirty or so other unfortunate souls I can almost appreciate the benefits of being one of the undead. Hey, if you're one of the undead you need never attend a calculus class or be lectured to by a man old enough to have seen the Civil War.

Twirling the pencil around and around I was unaware that the pages of my book were turning by themselves. It was the crinkle of paper that alerted me and horrified I looked around to see if anyone had noticed my blunder. Not a face turned towards me, so, slowly I opened a pathway and was relieved when thoughts flooded my brain, none were about my textbook, *but* there was one about me. Risking a look, I craned my neck towards the opposite end of the room to cast a glance at the back of Ryan Maloney's head. Ryan was thinking very interesting thoughts and they were all about me. Not the usual thoughts about my ass, or my breasts or the unusual shade of my eyes, but about *me*. It seemed that Ryan was attempting to build up the courage to ask me out, furthermore, it seemed that Ryan had been eyeing me for quite awhile now. I smiled and suddenly calculus didn't seem so bad. I became somber quickly and I pulled into myself and disconnected. I rarely read people. It was a moral code that I tried to live by, a privacy thing. How would you feel if someone was looking into your head? What would you do if you knew that your emotions, your pain, your thoughts and fears were all subject to the open whims of someone you didn't even know?

Oh, I know, sometimes I don't have any control over what pours over me, but often, often I do. I have spent years training in thought-disconnect, years learning my personal 'switch,' that switch which can be turned off and on at my whim. And here I was reading some poor guy's mind. It didn't matter that his thoughts were about me, I was invading his privacy pure and simple and it disgusted me. I may be a monster, I may be unnatural but I try to live by a very natural code of ethics, which I don't often violate. It's what keeps me sane. And in these times it doesn't take much to turn the corner from that which is sane into that which is not.

After class Vanessa found and cornered me. Trapped between the water fountain and a throng of unruly students I gave in and turned towards her. I would find out later that I should have taken my chances with the unruly throng of students, but that is neither here nor there.

"I really need to talk to you Holly."

"So talk." No need for me to mince words with someone I didn't particularly like.

"I..." Vanessa's face flushed red, her eyes fell downward and her shoulders suddenly stooped. She seemed to shrink into herself and that wasn't like Vanessa. Suddenly I was concerned, it didn't take any empathy to realize that something was wrong, and it was impossible for me to ignore her obvious pain and discomfort.

"What's wrong Vanessa?" My voice had grown less clipped and I had relaxed my stance considerably.

"Could we talk somewhere a little more private?" She cast her eyes around and I nodded, it wouldn't do to talk about something private in the midst of a crowded hall. Following her I concentrated on blocking all open paths, I didn't want to invade her privacy, not when she was about to open up to me. I wrapped my shields around me and built up my inner reserves, it was necessary because Vanessa's emotions were battering my defenses and it was becoming considerably harder to shield myself from them. Whatever was bothering her was strong enough to break through several fortified pathways. We came to stand outside the school and I spared a couple moments to take in the night. I reached out to place a reassuring hand on Vanessa's shoulder and I smiled into her painfully tense face.

"Hey, what's wrong?" I had one moment to register the prickly sensation that scored the back of my neck before shooting pain stabbed through my head and I fell into sweet oblivion.

When I woke up I woke up to blackness, literally to blackness. The whole room was painted black and the furniture was black to match. I was lying in the center of, you guessed it, a black bed and wearing a lacey thing that was totally not my style. I groaned and tried to suppress the nausea that threatened to overtake me when I sat up. As things began to clear, my mind began to replay the last moments before I was struck unconscious. I recalled Vanessa's expression, and what I had taken for tenseness had certainly been guilt. Vanessa had known, Vanessa had known and led me out like a lamb to slaughter.

My eyes grew more and more narrow until they were nothing but small slits filled with intense fury. I was going to kill her, okay, maybe I wouldn't kill her but it was going to be a hell of a bitch fight. Testing my limbs to see if they worked I was delighted to find that nothing was broken, everything seemed to be in working order. I slid easily from the silken sheets but to my humiliation fell quite ungracefully to the ground, it seemed that my legs, though fine, were not quite ready to be stood upon. Taking a moment, I steadied myself using the bed and gently, gingerly got to my feet. I wobbled for a moment but soon found my strength come back to me. I was studying the room for a possible exit, although in the back of my mind I knew it was futile, this was not a 'normal' room, this was a tomb, no matter how nicely furnished it was. With those thoughts in my head, suddenly I heard what was unmistakably the sound of a door opening. I whirled around and saw with astonishment and not without a little admiration a large panel of the black wall open and with the opening of that wall in walked death. And I was well and truly screwed.

Chapter Four:

He was simply the most beautiful thing I had ever seen and he scared the living hell out of me. Oh, there was no doubt as to what he was; the million-dollar question was who he was. With hair that seemed to be both auburn and mahogany colored simultaneously, deep, forest green eyes and that pale, pale, pale as porcelain skin he was truly the most beautiful guy I had ever seen, dead or alive. He was wearing tight black leather pants that appeared to be painted on and a richly colored brown silk top that flowed effortlessly around his torso. He did nothing but stare at me and the hairs on the back of my neck stood to full attention, yes, oh yes, this one was old. I had never been accused of being stupid, I had been accused of a myriad of other things but never of stupidity, however, what I was about to do could definitely rank among the top ten stupid things to do when you're facing one of the undead.

"In accordance to the rules of hospitality I would like to know exactly where I am and who the hell you are, I'd also like to know why you've kidnapped me." I think at the time it had seemed like a good idea, what time that was I have no idea, but watching his face tighten and his eyes grow, if possible, more cold I knew I had probably just signed my own death warrant. Yeah it was illegal to kill someone, and the police didn't take kindly to murders committed by the undead, but the point of fact here was that you had to be caught and charged and who was going to charge this hunk of dead meat of my murder?

"You are unaccountably rude considering I have the power to end your life right here and now." His voice was smooth as cream, dark, sinister yet oddly melodic. I steeled myself mentally and it proved quite a challenge, as he was quite the strongest member of the undead I had met in a long while.

"If you had wanted to kill me I'd already be dead." I forced my voice to come out calm and collected but inwardly I was shaking like a leaf. I didn't let up my guard even when he laughed, a deep, rich, throaty laugh.

"You are quite right." His voice held a tinge of an accent, British perhaps? A British vampire in North Carolina, not unheard of, I suppose. Since the 'Equalization Articles' had been passed in 1990 with the 'Invitation Acts' hot on their heels most Vampires felt quite free. They were hardly, by human standards, considered equal, as the title of the Articles would suggest but they certainly were more free to enterprise and come and go as they so chose. Hey, news flash, the vampires don't find us to be in any way on equal terms with them either. In their minds we are either food or entertainment. Oh, I've heard stories of great trans-species romances, hey who hasn't heard of Dracula, or the lovely stories of the many romances of the Fae, but none of that stuff is real. Reality is that vampires have more strength, speed, agility, and mind capabilities than humans, and lets not forget that little thing called time. Vampires have eternity where we poor humans eventually die and rot, yeah not a pretty picture. But hey, it would seem that we have one thing in common, egocentricity. Both humans and vampires think they're the superior race. Unfortunately, if you go by the food chain, well you get the idea. Suffice to say although synthetic blood has been developed and widely distributed most vampires find that the good, old- fashioned way is still the best, and that nothing comes close to the real thing in the warm 'package.'

"Okay, so now that we've established that you're not going to kill me, could you tell me what you are planning on doing?" Forcing a laugh (I often laugh when I'm nervous) I fingered the material of the gown I was now wearing. "Looks like I'm dressed for a party, or…" I took in the black of the lace gown, "A funeral."

Again, the vampire laughed, it was a beautiful laugh, almost as beautiful as he was. I couldn't believe that I was thinking that a laugh was beautiful, but somehow that was the only word that was appropriate.

"You were hardly dressed to meet me in the rags you came in with."

I narrowed my eyes; I didn't particularly like hearing my clothes described as rags.

"If I had known I was coming to meet you, your majesty, I would have chosen something more appropriate. However, since this little rendezvous was a mystery, and by the way is still a mystery to me, you'll excuse me if I say who died and made you king of the clothes?" At that I clapped my hand over my mouth, was I looking to die painfully?

"Actually, no one has died, yet…" The word hung there and he looked inordinately pleased at my discomfort and obvious distress, "But the night is still young." He began to walk towards me, actually walk would be the wrong word, he more or less floated towards me. I, not caring how it looked began to scoot backwards on my heels. My feet were bare, my sandals having probably been discarded with the rest of my clothing.

"You look extraordinary, come to me." His voice was lower now and my skin prickled. "Come…." He stretched his hand towards me and fixed those brilliant eyes on mine. That's when the elaborate black desk hit him squarely in the chest. He landed unceremoniously on his butt. I was aggrieved that the desk hadn't done more damage but what did I expect, he could probably lift a school bus if he so desired. Not to mention the only reason he had fallen in the first place was because he wasn't expecting anything from me. I stood shivering, doing the best to mask my fear across the room from him. I never saw anyone get up so gracefully, but he, he did. He also stared at me with an unreadable expression on his face. After what seemed like an eternity I heard the familiar sound of the paneled door opening again.

"Come now, my hospitality has been lacking, let me make it up to you."

"I want to leave."

"First, let me explain." His expression was unreadable, a beautiful mask. When a vampire offers you an explanation you take it. Pulling my shields together I mentally searched for any holes in my 'armor,' finding none I nodded. I hesitantly stepped towards him and when he made no move towards me I felt some of my fear abate. If he were going to kill me, he could do so now, that he made no move towards me told me quite a lot. He seemed to float out of the room and I…I followed as only a mere human can.

Chapter Five:

It was dark, much darker than I would have liked. The halls were damp; I could feel it in my bones. I shivered and felt the reaction my fear caused in the vampire striding gracefully in front of me. We seemed to walk for what felt like an eternity, or it could just be that I was unbelievably exhausted and aching from every possible pore in my body. The hallway curved sharply left and I could see light at the end, I giggled, a light at the end of the tunnel. Stifling back my nervous giggles I followed Mr. Sexy, Strong and Silent into the light and couldn't quite contain my delight or my surprise. I was in an honest-to-god throne room, or what could have passed for one Eons ago. The room was made of stone, shocker, right, and furnished beautifully to match the setting. There was a large elaborate chair, which I guess was supposed to be the throne up on the dais. Below the chair in the center of the room was a large, long, sturdy table. Surrounding the table, on either side of the room, facing one another were smaller, engraved chairs, each one matching. My pleasure and obvious absorption in the room made me slow and I didn't notice Mr. Sexy, Strong and Silent move in behind me until his hand came to rest lightly, but possessively on my shoulder. I flinched and jerked away. He didn't move just watched me with those unblinking, beautiful eyes.

"Okay, about that explanation." I tried not to fidget as he continued to stare, why did it seem as if he were reading me? That would be impossible, right? My shields were holding, my mental guard had not been breached and I was in complete control (yeah, sure). When I realized how close we still were I backed up a little, I seem to be doing that a lot tonight, but hey, you can't put too much distance between you and the undead.

Suddenly it seemed as if my head were exploding and all those carefully constructed barriers came crashing down. Pain flooded my body as surely as if someone were standing there kicking me. I could feel the agony, the excruciating sense of fear and pain, the knowledge that you get right before you see your own death mirrored in the face of the one who is going to kill you. "NO, NO, NO" it kept ringing in my head, a litany, a chant, a prayer. I didn't realize I was screaming until I felt the sharp nails of the vampire digging into the soft flesh of my arms.

"What is wrong...what ails you?" His words were filled with urgency and strangely, I could feel, real, worry?

"They're dying.... They're going to die." I managed to croak and instantly felt myself crumple, as my legs could no longer hold me. I began to scratch my own arms in panic as I had become half crazed by the emotions that I could not control, emotions that weren't mine.

"You must not hurt yourself...who is dying?"

"Oh my God." My body began to shake and tremble and the last thing I remember was a scream, my scream.

"You are awake, good." He was staring at me with the oddest expression in those cool, clear eyes of his, was it hunger? I was suddenly very aware that I was laying on the cold stone of the floor and that my arms felt raw and sore. I looked down and could see the blood welling from some deep scratches along my forearm...now, now I understood the look of hunger in his eyes. I swallowed and took several deep, calming breaths. With fear, and hesitance I searched the open pathways but no longer could feel anything, no pain, no horror, and no death, except that which knelt beside me now. Whatever had besieged me was now gone, or dead. *That* thought was sobering and I knew that the vampire could read everything on my face; I no longer had the energy to hide.

"I..." My mouth was dry and I swallowed again, several times.

"You are more exceptional than I had thought." He spoke and his eyes gleamed, they were heated and I hated him for it. I hated the hunger, the lust the sparkle I saw in his eyes. He was a monster, worse than a monster, than why, why did my body hum with an energy that had never been present before. "Julian told me stories but not even he could have known all that you possess."

"Julian?" It was a question, and I was getting tired of waiting for this damn explanation, it seemed the longer I waited the worse my situation became.

"Blond, good looking, dead." He said this with a half smile and I was so

19

surprised that I forgot to be scared…. A joke, had he just made a joke? He grinned so wide that his fangs peaked out, he had obviously seen the shock written across my face.

"Are *they* dead?" I watched as his face fell back into that unreadable mask, cool, detached and beautiful. He knew exactly what I was asking after.

"Yes." It was all that he said but it was enough. I began to shake and shiver anew. It was too much for me; this entire night was too much for me. I had carved a life for myself that didn't include this madness and up until tonight I had thought that I had finally triumphed over the hand that was dealt to me. "The situation, however, has been dealt with." He voice held no inflection but I could feel something, something that told me that he had been and was still in a fine rage, you don't want to see a vampire when they're in a rage.

"Who are you?" I blurted it out, but damn it all I was owed this much at least. He surprised me again by smiling and offering his hand. I stared at it for several moments before accepting. His flesh was cold, cold and smooth and unyielding. He turned my palm over and stroked my warm flesh with a finger from his other hand. He seemed enthralled with my hand and I found that I was reluctant to pull away, but pull away I did, he was the walking dead, and that was a paradox in itself, one that I just wasn't going to try to unravel. He reached out and then stopped himself. He regarded me through thick lashes; lashes that like the rest of him were perfect.

"Lucien, my name is Lucien."

I rolled the name over in my head and tested the sound of it out on my tongue, it seemed to fit him, although how many Vampires did I know on a first name basis anyways?

"And what do you want with me?"

"You are a blunt little thing."

"So I have been told, I just don't find the need to mince words." I shrugged my shoulders, "I think I'm a little impatient."

"You are charming."

"That is something I've never been called before." He was still staring at me and suddenly I felt the need to try something I had not tried this evening, something that I didn't usually try at all. I purposely focused my energy my attention in on him and tried to read him. I could feel the hum, the faint crackling of energy off of his skin and the power that radiated from his body but I could not hear his mind, could not feel his 'emotions', and I was flabbergasted. Although it is more difficult to 'do the dead' so to speak, as in to 'read them', it is still possible. Sometimes it is even easier to read the dead than the living, because the dead always underestimate you, you simply aren't of any importance to them, mentally that is, physically that's a different story. "I can't read you." I reached out again, but again there was nothing, silence, complete and utter silence.

"You were trying." There was no anger in his voice; curiously he sounded fascinated by the fact that I had been trying to delve into his brain, cipher out his thoughts, so to speak.

"Yes." I was embarrassed by my intrusion, and could feel the heat crawling up my cheeks. He saw it and smiled once again.

"Charming." His eyes grew thoughtful, "And useful."

"You are going to *use* me." It was a statement, not a question; I was human, not impaired. It seemed that 'blocking' hadn't saved me from being unearthed. Then again, my little 'demonstration' at the club had been more than foolish, I had better sense, knew better. It had been obvious that the vampire Julian had felt the press of my mental block when he had tried to force his compulsion on me. No creature of the unnatural world could have been immune to me that evening, I might as well have worn a sign on my head that read 'Empath with freakishly strong PSI abilities' I had all but advertised myself in a room filled with the stuff that nightmares are made of.

"You are even prettier than the description that Julian gave me."

"Thanks." I couldn't keep the sarcasm out of my voice. I was all out of Suzy Sunshine routine. I was exhausted, sore, beaten up, bruised and completely mentally drained. And damn it all I had to study for midterms. "So what's the deal?"

"The deal?"

"You know, like, what exactly is your plan, what is going on?"

"Ahhhh, I understand what you are saying now." He paused a moment before beginning to speak, his voice was somehow both cool and hot, I could feel it, actually feel it against my skin. "You fascinated Julian." His eyes hardened when he said the other vampires name now and I wondered at that. "Julian in turn was obligated to tell me of his discovery at the club."

"Why obligated?"

"If you had not figured it out by now I am the 'Holder,' all are obligated to obey me." In vampire communities the 'Holder' was the wielder of power, the head honcho to put it simply. Like humans, there were vampires that wielded more power than others. Unlike humans, two things, two universally known things; age and ability cemented a vampire's bases of power. Usually the vampire in question could gain certain abilities the longer he/she lived, however, there were vampires that simply never would acquire, no matter how hard they tried, the ability to lead, the ability to become a 'Holder.' In cases such as these, the vampires in question were reduced to being lackeys, or yes, obligated to serve.

"So Julian told you what happened at the club that night?"

"Yes, and Vanessa confirmed the story."

"Yeah, Vanessa." My voice had become low and threatening. Vampire Lucien smiled, as if pleased by my anger and contempt at the girl who had offered me up. "Vanessa and I are going to have to have a long chat."

"Vanessa is not, however tasty, the most clever of women." Vampire Lucien said and I merely frowned at him

"No shit Sherlock."

"Pardon?"

"Forget it, it's just an expression, it's nothing." I breathed a sigh of relief when he didn't pursue the matter.

"You have little lines marring your forehead," Vampire Lucien said.

"What?"

"Lines, on your forehead." Vampire Lucien was staring at me so intently I was certain he was memorizing my features line for line.

"I'm frowning, they're frown lines." I realized that now the frown was deeper and I tried to school my features bland once more. It didn't work. Vampire Lucien was now smiling, or I think he was smiling at me. It was disconcerting. The more he smiled the more I frowned until I was sure my eyes were at the level of my mouth. I clenched my hands together and took another deep breath. "Stop it."

"Stop what my pet?"

Hands on hips I glared at him "For one, don't call me pet, and secondly don't stare at me you're making me nervous." I groaned inwardly, he was a vampire; it was inevitable that he would make one nervous. He was also a Holder, which meant where he was just scary before, he was now the master of all that was scary. "Vanessa doesn't know what I am…." I rolled my eyes I added, "She doesn't know much."

"Yes, what you say is true, however she was witness to your little, shall we say display, at the club the other night," Vampire Lucien steepled his hands, "She saw the exchange between Julian and yourself. What's more she was commanded by Julian to help him arrange this…meeting."

My eyebrow arched "Meeting?"

"Indeed."

"So what now?" I asked. "Uhmmm, this isn't the part where you tell me what's on the menu, is it?" Even I grinned at that one, I was pleased to note that vampire Lucien seemed to see the humor in it as well.

"Nay, I am here to instruct you on your new duties, think of me as a teacher of sorts."

"Whoa, whoa, whoa, I already have plenty of teachers, thank you very much, what are you talking about? What duties?"

"You are like us, I am the Holder *of all that is*, you are in my dominion, therefore you are mine by rights of law."

"What goddamn law?"

"Night Laws."

My head was beginning to throb, no; my head had been throbbing for a long time now. "I don't know of these laws."

"Of course you do not."

"And I am *not* like you."

"Nay, you are not of the dead, you are not a *night walker*, but you are *other*. Your display the other night caused quite a disturbance and it was foolish of you to think you could remain undetected for much longer." Vampire Lucien smoothed down a lock of perfect hair and turned those brilliantly clear eyes upon me. His body seemed to glow and in that moment he was everything that was beautiful, everything that was perfect and unearthly.

"I am my own person" I struggled with the words, in the face of his beauty it was hard to concentrate "I...I am only a human student."

"You are wrong, you are more than human."

"I am mortal, I'll die."

"Mortal yes, human, that is still left to be seen." Vampire Lucien was walking closer and closer to me, at least he was showing me the courtesy of walking and not levitating or perhaps merely appearing at my side. Most vampires didn't think common courtesy was necessary, they often appeared quite suddenly scaring most humans to death, sometimes that state was permanent.

"I have nothing to offer you." The moment the words were out I wanted to take them back. Vampire Lucien's eyes grew, if possible, brighter. His aura changed, the brilliance that had surrounded him seemed to solidify until he was all but wearing a blanket of moonshine. His tongue appeared at his lips and it looked as if, quite consciously he was imagining what it would be like to taste my skin, pierce my flesh and drink the warm fluid beneath and surrounding my beating heart.

"Ahhh little one you have much to offer."

"That isn't what I meant and you know it."

"I do know, but it is what I meant."

I blushed a deep crimson and that blush seemed to fascinate him more than anything else he read on my face. I was weary and sore and kept thinking about the dawn. It seemed as if I had been locked up in this underground tomb forever, how long could it possibly be until the dawn? Looking at the beautiful creature in front of me I knew that he still had time. His color was good and his eyes bright. He obviously did not feel the impending danger of the dawn and therefore felt quite safe in his meeting with me. I also knew that vampires could sense the dawn, they could feel, hear and smell it in the air. It was as if the dawn were some heady perfume that wafted through the air and lingered ominously on everything it touched.

"You've gone through a lot of trouble just to bring me here."

"That is because you are quite unique."

"Hardly unique." There were other Empaths in the world, indeed Empaths and Telepaths were not uncommon any longer. Where once people with PSI abilities were afraid to 'come out' they now owned businesses and ran freely among the other humans in their day-to-day endeavors. PSI and Psychic ability was much more 'normal' and less feared than say, oh the undead. At least Empaths could move freely during the daylight hours and thank god they didn't have to have a steady diet of blood to keep them alive.

"How many Empaths do you know in Edwards?" Vampire Lucien asked, that unreadable mask was again firmly in place.

I knew that I had made a face when he asked the question because his fine eyebrow arched, that was the only movement he made. I debated not answering the question but decided in the end that not answering would only give him more of an excuse to keep me in this lair.

"None."

"Would you repeat that please?"

I sighed dramatically and enunciated each letter "N-O-N-E." I gave him a pointed stare. "Not because it's uncommon, but Edwards is a smallish town, not like Charlotte or even Greensboro. So, none, I haven't met another Empath."

"You see Holly, you are quite a valuable asset to me."

"Asset." I dug my nails into my arm to keep a hold on my mounting anger. I was an asset. "Well, whoopee, I'm an asset. Listen I don't have time for this. I have midterms a plethora of papers to get done and a possible date in the works…so you see, no time." I made a motion to leave and instantly found myself locked in an unbreakable embrace. I swallowed hard and my entire body trembled in fear. Vampire Lucien's arms were wrapped securely around me, I hadn't seen him move, that was how fast he was. His face was only inches away from mine and his eyes were glowing with some inward fire.

"My pet, you misunderstand me, you seem to act as if you have a choice in the matter, you see you do not. Need I remind you that having my protection is crucial to your existence."

"I was doing fine without your protection before, I'll do fine now." My eyes were locked on his face trying desperately to read his cold visage. Nothing passed through his eyes, nothing filtered through his face, and he was a cold hard mask of blankness.

"Nay, you will need protection now, now that you have been discovered."

"And whose fault is that?" I countered hotly

"Your own of course." Vampire Lucien smiled slightly and his arms loosened ever so little. "If you had not resisted Julian's compulsion that evening you would not have been identified as anything different. You could have been just another simpering, pathetic University student trying to get it on with one of the undead."

"I couldn't let him do what he wanted to do with me. I couldn't let him control me like that." I went absolutely still in his embrace, I knew enough about the undead to know that struggling just excited them. I was in enough trouble already without an excited vampire on my hands.

"So you pay the price for your…chastity." Vampire Lucien smiled but this smile played about his lips as if in a dance. "Or were you protecting something other than your chastity?"

I was outraged but found myself in no position to be arguing with a vampire. Nonetheless, I let my fury show in my eyes.

"I don't want your protection, I don't want anything from you." I shivered unexpectedly when vampire Lucien ran a hand down my hair and touched the back of my ear.

"Ahhh now that is not entirely true my pet."

"I don't know what you mean." I tried to twist my head out of his hands but he held it firmly within his grasp.

"There is something you want from me." He moved his lips close to my ear and licked the underside delicately. I shivered anew and tried desperately

25

to regain control of my racing thoughts. There was no way he could know that, there was no way he could read me. I had my shields in place and my paths shut down completely, how could he possibly know these things about me. As if reading the thoughts in my brain he smiled and nodded.

"You are not so difficult to read my pet...*Holly*. Your mind may be closed but your face is transparent. Your eyes are like twin mirrors that reflect the soul and your expressions filter through your eyes one by one casting shadows everywhere." Vampire Lucien bent even closer and whispered against my mouth, "I know you want me." He licked my lips. "I know you want this."

"I..."

"Shhhhh..." Vampire Lucien claimed my lips then in a searing kiss that made all the circuits in my brain melt down and made my limbs feel as useless as melted wax. I stood on my tiptoes and wrapped my arms around him reveling in the delicious feel of his lips on mine, of his body pressed against me. The thin lace of my gown did nothing to stop me from feeling every line of his muscled physique and I felt boneless and liquefied all at once. His cold lips were hard and demanding...wait, his cold lips. I jerked away and stared horrified at what stood in front of me. This was a dead man, a vampire, a night-walker. No matter how beautiful, no matter how sensual and persuasive, he was dead, and worse still he needs blood to survive. How could I let myself fall prey to even a moment of his temptation, it was to damn myself even worse than I already am damned.

"No...no I do not want this." I swallowed and looked him straight in the eyes, "If you are not going to kill me then I want to go home." I watched vampire Lucien watch me. He didn't move a muscle, vampires can do that you know, not move a muscle, stand absolutely still as death. His eyes never wavered from mine and his body glowed slightly. How long we stood there staring at one another I do not know, but I know that I was beginning to sweat when a freezing cold wind blew into the room and vampire Lucien noticeably stiffened.

"You had no right." A new voice shattered the silence.

I swiveled around and found myself but a several feet away from the most beautiful woman I had ever seen, the most beautiful dead woman I had ever seen. With cascading black hair, brilliantly blue eyes and a pale as death complexion she was like every stereotype of a vampire that had ever been created. She was decked out all in black and if not for her beautiful features would have drowned underneath the darkness of her garments. Her eyes were blazing with fire and her hands, dear lord, her hands had stretched and pulled, until deadly sharp claws could be seen in place of fingers. Razor sharp and just as lethal her hands could kill you with one swipe. Not wanting to be in the way if she decided to swipe I moved hesitantly back, not realizing I was moving in the direction of vampire Lucien until it was too late to do anything about it.

"Are you questioning me?" Vampire Lucien's voice was taut and cold. His eyes mirrored the beautiful vampire's eyes standing in front of him. They were full of fire and ice and his mouth had stretched and pulled until you could see the fine glimmer of fangs. This was definitely not the place to be at the moment, and as always, here I was. The beautiful female vampire moved closer and closer and I moved further and further away until I found myself uncomfortably pressed against vampire Lucien's front. I felt him stiffen momentarily before he relaxed against me. I tried to move away but his one arm held me in place.

"It is not your place to question me, indeed you are lucky I let you escape without punishment." Vampire Lucien bared his fangs fully and I cringed. They were long and pointy, just like in the movies, but thank god they weren't covered in blood, yet.

"Is this your little psychic?" Female vampire sneered. "She looks tasty, perhaps I should take her in place of Justin."

"ENOUGH." Vampire Lucien's voice was chilling "You are hungry and therefore insolent, but I have had enough of your tantrums and your disobedience. You are not in a position to question, nor argue with me. Your lack of attention, well there was no excuse for it and you could have been discovered. You are lucky that I let you live after what I have dealt with, from you, this evening." Vampire Lucien moved me to one side and strode closer to the enraged vampiress. "You will not threaten nor scare my companion again, if you do I shall have your heart staked and your body burned to ashes and scattered to the winds, do we have an understanding?"

I watched as the female vampire struggled with her indignation and her rage. Her fear of vampire Lucien was obviously warring with her need to erupt and she seemed to seethe with fury. She nodded curtly and skewered me with a terribly evil look; she began to leave when vampire Lucien's voice stopped her mid step.

"Are you not forgetting something Laeticia?" Vampire Lucien gave her a bored look and the vampire Laeticia dropped to a curtsy and remained still until Lucien spoke again "You may leave, and do not bother me again this night."

I watched as she spun around and stormed out of the room. I shuddered at the memory of her sharp talons and her evil expression. The fury in her eyes when she looked at me hadn't been reassuring either.

"Oh god." I swallowed, "Okay, now I know I want to leave."

"Do not worry she will not bother us again." Vampire Lucien made a move in my direction and I held up a hand in warning to keep him away.

"No…no this is too much even more me, I want to leave. I want to leave now!"

"You are not even interested in why Laeticia was so upset?"

"No."

"Ahhh then you will take the chance of her anger."

"What are you talking about?"

"Laeticia wished to have your life for the life of her Justin, who unfortunately had to be…disposed of this evening." Vampire Lucien shrugged his shoulders, "However, Justin was a problem that would have had to have been dealt with at one time or another, he was getting too, is the word, cocky, for his own good."

"You have totally lost me."

"I interrupted her Justin torturing two young humans. He was bleeding them quite unnecessarily, for her, he claimed, but it was torture nonetheless. Laeticia does not need her vessels bled, she can bleed them herself, he was merely enjoying the cruelty of his act."

I thought back to earlier in the evening when I had felt my mind invaded by the fear, anger, and hopelessness of other individuals. I remember feeling as if my brain was going to explode and my body disintegrate. This was the moment that I knew vampire Lucien was speaking of and I stifled a scream of rage. I skewered vampire Lucien with an incredulous expression.

"Do not try to tell me that you gave a shit about those humans…we're all meat to you aren't we?"

Vampire Lucien sighed and shrugged his shoulders, "It was not the act but the place that was inappropriate. Justin seemed to lose control and he took his victims with no care to the location of his mutilation. He was too close to the lair and he was above ground, he could have been discovered and thus we would have been discovered." Vampire Lucien's mouth went taut and his eyes grew colder, "That is unacceptable, that negligence is unacceptable and it is Laeticia's fault as much as it was Justin's fault."

"I see." But the truth was I didn't see at all. This world was foreign to me, foreign and cruel, and I wanted no part of it. "I'm not dinner, I'm not dessert.

I want to go home."

"My pet, you are priceless. Yes, yes you may go home, but know this I have warned you and you know the price of your abilities and your 'carelessness', I shall see you soon. This is not the end."

And I knew from his face that he was deadly serious.

Chapter Six:

Home again. My home consists of exactly three rather untidy rooms. Bought shortly after I turned eighteen, it's small but comfortable and what's more it's mine. The small apartment has a living room, bathroom and bedroom. The kitchen stands against the wall in the living room and takes up a good portion of the space, but no matter, it's functional and practical. My bedroom is my sanctuary and has been decorated as such. Warm peach walls are lined with shelves, which are littered with books ranging from Crawford's, *The Companion for the Dead*, Harringbone's, *Incantations*, to Anne Rice's *Interview with a Vampire*, perhaps it's time to re-evaluate my book choices. I have a large queen-sized bed in the center of my room. I had made a promise to myself that when I had my own place I would buy the largest bed my bedroom could hold. It's graced with an off white down comforter and several goose down pillows. There are candles on the bay window and bedside table, vanilla and crème broulee my two favorite scents. It's a welcoming room, a room that invites one to sit and stay awhile, and a room that has become my place of rest and relaxation, a place of peace.

I caught a reflection of myself in the long full sized mirror and grimaced. My neat braid had long since come undone and strands of my hair fell in clumps around my face. There were dark circles under my eyes and I was still wearing the black lace gown. I looked like a wraith. Clawing at the small pearl buttons I tore the dress off my body and stood naked in front of the mirror. Shivering I studied my body not even wanting to think on where my undergarments had gone. There were clusters of deep gashes on my forearm and a large bump on my head, other than that I couldn't see any other damage. Breathing a sigh of relief I went to the bathroom to take a long hot shower. I would think on this evening tomorrow, right now I just wanted to get clean,

clean and forget.

My alarm woke me at exactly eight o'clock. Groaning I rolled out of bed. Hadn't I just fallen asleep? I hadn't checked what time the vampire goons had 'dropped' me off but it had to have been near dawn because I remember their anxiety and their eagerness to have me off of their hands. They had all but dumped me on my street and raced off in their sleek Lexus. My neighborhood is as dead as the vampires that inhabit our town. I had chosen it for that exact reason. This was one of the few neighborhoods that I didn't have to fight off everyone's thoughts and emotions. There were few college students here, mostly retirees and the elderly. I had raised some eyebrows when I had moved into my small apartment. There were some concerns that I would bring the 'delinquent' element into this quiet neighborhood, I had to smile at that thought. I suppose it was understandable, I was one of the few people under fifty that inhabited this complex. After several months and my attendance at way too many block parties where all the participants sat around sipping ice tea and playing bridge I managed to convince everyone that I enjoyed the solitude and silence as much as they did. Of course they would never know just how much I enjoyed the silence. When I did hear a stray thought it was usually "Martha why didn't you feed the dog?" or "Whose turn is it to host Parcheesi night?" a welcome break after all the turmoil of campus thoughts.

I had to double-check the date, after last night's activities I felt as if I had lost some time…a day or two. Nope, it was just the next morning and I was unfortunately right on time (how annoying). I was definitely going to make my first morning class, Spells & Incantations. Yeah you heard me correctly, my first class is Spells & Incantations with Professor DeWitt. On Wednesday it's an afternoon class, but unfortunately today isn't Wednesday.

In 1995 Congress passed a series of laws that would make it mandatory for Universities to 'update' their curriculum. It had been met with serious opposition but in the end it was decided upon that it was in everyone's best interest to have the current youth aware of the forces that roamed in their midst, and of course how to deal with them. Now most Universities with the exception of a few private institutions made such courses available to their incoming classes. I had immediately signed up for Spells & Incantations, Voodoo 101, and Basic Paranormal Activity in hopes that I would be able to better equip myself against certain things that I had less knowledge in. So far it was a bust, all I had learned was that shrunken heads were a myth, that most spirits did not reach out to us via the Ouija Board and that Pentagrams could indeed summon the forces of evil. However, it was better to be safe than sorry and at least Professor DeWitt wasn't a complete idiot. Professor DeWitt had just started at EU this semester. Her courses were organized and fashioned intellectually and she seemed to have a pretty good grasp on the material. Of all my 'Other World' courses Spells & Incantations was the most enlightening.

Gathering up my materials I took inventory of my appearance. My face was devoid of makeup, my hair was done up quickly in a bun and my clothing was utilitarian and functional, which meant I was wearing jeans and a ratty old university t-shirt. It would do, I wasn't out to win any beauty contests. Rushing out the door I checked my watch one more time, damn I was going to be on time.

Chapter Seven:

"Who can tell me what will bind a Demon?"

Professor DeWitt had been at this for a good part of an hour. It seemed that the world of Demons was on the agenda for today. I looked around and noticed similar expressions on everyone's faces, exhaustion and a lot of it. I understood, I was certainly not a morning person; it was actually something that weighed heavily on my mind when signing up for my 'Other World' classes. If one was the superstitious sort one might believe that the staff had planned all the classes in the daytime due to their beliefs that supernatural forces would have more power over them in the evening. Being the superstitious sort that is exactly what I believe. So here I am stuck with a handful of classes at ridiculous times, times when even the dead aren't awake, doesn't that tell you something, even the dead don't want to attend. I yawned and found my head slipping to my desk when my ears perked up and my head followed. Thoughts about me, I could actually hear someone thinking about me…it was a similar path, a path that I had felt yesterday and without seeing I knew exactly who was thinking about me, Ryan Maloney. Risking a look I was gratified to find that it was indeed Ryan Maloney staring at me, and thinking about me. His eyes met mine and for a moment I felt that spark of chemistry that lights between two people when they know they are destined to meet, or perhaps it was my damned obsession with romance novels that caused such thoughts. Shaking my head I tried to clear Ryan's thoughts from my brain, right now they were center stage and blocking all else out. I was hard pressed not to smile and jump up and say, "Yes, yes I'll go out with you." Squashing such ridiculous notions out of my brain I focused my eyes back to Professor DeWitt and noticed she was staring at me, along with about twenty pairs of eyes.

"Ms. Feather, do you know the answer or are you like the many others who haven't read their texts?"

"Excuse me?"

"You haven't been listening have you?"

"Uhmmm could you repeat the question." I watched as Professor DeWitt rolled her eyes and pointed to the chalkboard.

"I want to know why blood can call the Ancient Demon."

"Blood is an offering, it's the most precious liquid that a human can offer. Most are under the impression that a complete sacrifice is necessary to invoke a demon, especially the Ancient Demon, but that is usually unnecessary, the most important thing is blood. When you offer blood you are offering yourself up, it is as final as if you were trading your soul." I waited and watched Professor DeWitt nod and smile.

"Very good. Do you hear that class, it seems that Ms. Feather here has been reading her assigned chapters, unlike some of you. Need I remind you all that midterms are in two weeks and that all the material covered up until now will be present on the test, I suggest that you all study and study hard...I do not give passing grades to those who merely want them." Professor DeWitt gave one last hard look around and with a glance at the clock sighed and nodded, "You may all leave, however, I hope to find you all better prepared at the end of the week, remember chapters nine through eleven and don't forget the tests at the end of the sections, they'll be good practice for the midterm."

I jumped up from my seat and like the rest of the students made a beeline for the door. Once out I took a deep breath and fortified my shields, they were being bombarded again, whenever classes got out they were bombarded, it seemed that the students' relief was my headache.

"Holly."

I spun around to find Ryan's blue eyes staring down at me. I swallowed back my nervousness and gave him a hesitant smile, it was the best I could do under such circumstances.

"Hi Ryan."

Ryan Maloney was gorgeous, a far cry from the dead man I had met last night. Don't get me wrong, vampire Lucien was gorgeous, indeed, he was beautiful, perhaps the most beautiful thing I had ever seen, but he was dead. Ryan was gorgeous as only an alive man can be. With thick blond hair, blue eyes and well-defined muscles he looked like the stereotypical football player, and I loved it. His face was clean-shaven and had a healthy glow to it, do you hear, a healthy glow. His cheeks were even rosy, that was a welcome relief. He shifted on his feet and had the very endearing quality of clearing his throat when he was nervous, he was alive and I loved it. "Was there something you wanted Ryan?" I thought I had better speed things along or we'd be here through Christmas.

"I…well I heard that the new Meg Ryan film was out at the movies and I thought you might want to see it with me…on, well, on Friday?"

I tried not to giggle, "You like Meg Ryan?"

"Well, no, I mean, yes, I just well, thought you might like it."

"I do like Meg Ryan, and yes I'd love to see the movie with you Ryan. But, if you don't like her, well we can see something else, really."

Ryan's face was positively glowing. I made sure not to 'read' him, it wouldn't be fair to listen in now, and anyways his thoughts were more than posted on his face. He was beaming and trying not to show it.

"No, the Meg Ryan film is fine. Pick you up at your place?"

"Sure, 125 Westerly, I'm apartment 1B, okay?"

"Great, say around six o'clock, that way maybe we can get a bite to eat before the film?"

"Great."

"Well, okay, great, I'll see you in calculus."

"Yeah." I watched him stride away, confident and pleased with himself, actually I was pretty pleased with myself too. How many months had I been watching and listening, however, unconsciously to his thoughts about me. I had admired how cute and smart he seemed, and how well he filled out a pair of jeans, what, what it's true. I really hadn't thought he would get up the nerve to ask me out and here he was inviting me to dinner and a movie, it was positively quaint, I loved it. Even Calculus couldn't be so bad after this, at least I would be thinking of pleasant things while my professor droned on, and drone on he would. Nothing could ruin this day, famous last words, right?

It happened right after calculus, why did everything hit me after calculus? Was somebody just thinking of ways to make my day worse? I noticed them immediately, how could you not. They were either standing there waiting for me, or the coroner. Dressed in black from head to toe they were a walking stereotype. One was tall at least six foot five with a head of black hair that was cut, believe it or not in a Mohawk. He was wearing a black vest without a shirt underneath and black jeans that were torn at the knees. Tattoos in the form of giant snakes, the cobra to be precise, graced his bulky arms and dark sunglasses finished off the rather imposing assemble. His buddy was more conservative, decked out in a finely cut three- piece suit, no less black than the vest and jeans that his friend wore. He held his black sunglasses in his long, pale hands. His hair, however, was ash blond and his eyes were a light hazel, which stood out even in his pale as death complexion. They both smiled as I got near and I wondered if it would do any good to run the opposite direction, probably not. Already they were attracting a lot of attention. Vampires are rarely seen in Edwards, there are a couple of 'mixed' clubs, i.e. vampire, human clubs, including a couple of vampire run night clubs right outside of Edwards, and of course in Charlotte, well anything can be found in Charlotte. But it was rare to see vampires wandering around Edwards, and you almost never saw them on Campus. Security seemed to frown upon the undead walking around school grounds, probably thought they were looking for an easy meal. But here were two obvious vampires waiting for me, how did a girl get so lucky?

"She is pretty." Mr. Mohawk said with a leer, his friend remained silent and stared at me, obviously on edge, as if just waiting for me to run. I wasn't about to go anywhere, I mean, have you seen how fast a vampire can go? I was sassy not stupid.

"So I'm guessing you're not with the FBI." I managed to keep my hands steady on my books and my eyes level with theirs, even though they were a good deal taller than me.

"We have been sent to fetch you."

"How lovely, I'm being fetched now." I tried to keep the sarcasm out of my voice. I failed. "So, can you tell me exactly what I'm being fetched for?"

"No." This from Mr. Suit.

"Well I tend not to go off with strangers, especially strangers that could possibly be looking for an easy meal."

Mr. Mohawk snarled at me revealing his fangs. Mr. Suit put a hand on his shoulder to quiet him and turned to look at me with cold eyes.

"You have little choice here."

"No, actually, I have a couple of good choices. One of them being screaming my lungs out and waiting for Campus security to come running, what are you going to do, eat me, eat them? Wouldn't look good in the press, would it? What would your 'Holder' think, what would he do?"

I waited and watched as the skin on their faces stretched tightly as they got angrier and angrier. I could see them mulling the possibilities over in their heads and I waited. I knew that their master had to have given them specific instructions, one of them being to avoid bloodshed, else they would have taken me with little regard to the consequences. But the 'Holder,' the master of the Hive was the ultimate authority, the high power, you did not disobey the 'Holder' no, they could and would make your life a living hell. Dead was a walk in the park to being punished by your master. Most 'Holders' were quite creative with their punishments and relished them as well. *She would be easy enough to subdue, the rest of them are worthless, they, do not matter.* I swallowed and made sure that my emotions didn't show on my face. I could 'hear' Mr. Mohawk, he was trigger-happy and because of it he was an unknown element. He could very well think to rush me and fuck the consequences. I very much doubt that if Mr. Mohawk thought to take me that Mr. Suit could do anything to stop him. I looked around for anything that I could use as a weapon and found nothing. The benches and lampposts were all firmly affixed to the ground and there was nothing else, save a student or two, I could 'throw' in their direction. I was also exhausted, my mental powers all but drained from last evening, any sort of Telekinesis would be sorely difficult at this point. However, I was ready to give it the good old college try if it became necessary.

"Whomever wants to speak to me can do so without these theatrics. I am not going anywhere with you."

I jumped back the moment Mr. Mohawk made a lunge towards me, he didn't get far because Mr. Suit put one hand on his arm, effortlessly holding him in place. Mr. Mohawk's face was glowing and I could feel his hunger, anger and fury showing through his eyes even from behind his sunglasses. Mr. Suit took one step forward and I took one step back, he stopped and held his other hand up in a sign of resignation, or truce.

"My comrade is getting anxious, therefore, since it seems that we can do nothing here without attracting undue attention we will be taking our leave. However, know this, you have just made this more difficult on yourself."

"Yeah, yeah, I always seem to make things difficult on myself." I kept my eyes firmly affixed to their forms as they moved backwards they seamlessly melted back into the darkness. Moments later they were completely gone and I was left alone at the edge of the campus staring at the darkness and restless shadows.

Chapter Eight:

I stared at the television screen in horror. The anchor's voice was clear and sharp while she relayed the terrifying and horrible news: "*Pamela Courtland was brutally murdered last night only a few feet away from her dorm. A freshman at EU, Ms. Courtland sustained massive blood loss. Strangulation was ruled the final cause of death. The police have few leads. There are at this time no witnesses....*"

Her voice disappeared under the weight of my own thoughts and overwhelming feelings of guilt. If I had not refused to go with the two vampires last night perhaps she would be alive. I had no way of knowing for certain if it was really Mr. Mohawk or Mr. Suit that had killed poor Pamela but it seemed too coincidental that there had been two vampires on Campus last evening and then one of the Freshman body is found murdered in the morning. I quickly dressed and dried my hair, determined to find out as much as possible about the murder of Pamela Courtland. I would not have her death on my conscience.

Pamela's murder was the talk of Campus. It seemed that everyone was speaking about Pamela and her unfortunate death. There were whispers of serial killers and rapists, vampires and ghouls. There were even some whispers about werewolves, quite ridiculous in my opinion, as we weren't even close to a full moon. Now the vampire talk I was much more inclined to believe, in truth, I was afraid I knew more than I wanted to know about her death. It seemed that this morning there was hardly the need to shield from thoughts, everyone was speaking out loud.

I don't know how I got through the morning. Between guilt, fear and impatience for the upcoming sunset I bit off what was left of my rather pathetic fingernails. I paid no attention during classes and hurried off before anyone could talk to me, I had a mission and it didn't matter that I was scared as hell. The rest of the day passed as if it were a dream and I barely acknowledged the sounding of the final bell of my final class. I was much too busy calculating how I was going to play out the evening. This meeting would have to be on my terms and my conditions, I could not let myself be cowered and terrified. Of course when meeting the Holder of the Hive there is little doubt you're going to be terrified, the trick is not showing it, that, that was going to be difficult. However, I had, had years developing a carefully neutral face. Mother had only enjoyed scaring and terrifying me. Therefore, I had learned to carefully mask all emotions. And after years of schooling my features blank when I could have screamed from all the rampant thoughts invading my head I had become quite adept at hiding my fears and thoughts. It was nice to know that this particular talent was going to come in handy this evening.

I made it home at half past nine and quickly scanned the parameters of my home. There was nothing unusual in sight, or sound. I heard nothing but the sound of crickets and the faint call of a restless bird or two. I reached out my mental paths but could detect nothing out of the ordinary. Determining that it was safe I entered my home and scanned the interior, although I knew that it was pointless, vampires couldn't enter your home unless they were invited, and I certainly hadn't been inviting any vamps to dinner lately. I allowed myself only a moment of pause before I ripped through my closet and wardrobe looking for something appropriate to wear. It seemed that the Holder hadn't been too impressed with my attire last evening and I certainly wasn't going to go back to the lair dressed in the piece of material that could barely be called a dress that he had provided, thus, it was about finding an even balance. Twenty minutes later found me surrounded by a pile of discarded clothing. It seemed that I had acquired a lot more utilitarian clothing that I had thought. There were stacks of jeans, mounds of t-shirts and comfortable sweatshirts. Some simple tank tops and the endless supply of shorts I seemed to favor in the summertime, quite frankly there was nothing appropriate for a second meeting with a vampire leader. Cutting my losses I settled on a pair of tight black jeans and a bright red tank top that was made out of a breathable stretchy material I had found so comfortable at the time I had purchased it. I applied minimal makeup, going instead for the barely there look I so often favored. The hair however was a problem. Due to the humidity my loose curls seemed frizzy and raggedy. I decided on braids and pulled, and divided my waist length hair into two matching sections on either side of my head. Deftly French braiding my hair I studied my reflection as I did so. I looked good even I could admit that I looked good. I nervously bit my lip scowling when I noticed I had managed to get some of the lipstick on my teeth. After a touch up and last look I determined I was as ready as I was ever going to be.

I walked over to the living room table where I picked up a slim, off white card with embossed black and red writing. The card was elegant and also my key into a second meeting with vampire Lucien. Taking a deep breath, less I lose my courage I picked up the phone and dialed the number on the card, after two rings a voice answered, it was a silky voice, almost purring in my ear, "Corruption."

I took another deep breath I was already regretting my decision.

"It's Holly, I want to speak with…" I wondered how I should refer to their Holder, I had only met him last night, and I certainly wasn't on good enough terms with him to call him by name, however would it anger this vampiress if I called him her Master? "…I want to speak with your Holder."

There was a pregnant pause while I held my breath. I was about to hang up the phone when a familiar voice whispered seductively in my ear.

"Holly, how good of you to call me, what can I do for you this evening?"

"I need to speak with you in person."

"But of course, should I come to you, or do you wish to come to me."

I shuddered at the thought of him in my house; of course the thought of being brought back to his lair was equally unpleasant. As if reading my thoughts vampire Lucien laughed silkily and said,

"I am not at the Lair tonight, I am where the card indicates, 'Corruption,' we have offices."

Offices? How very civilized, I told you the monsters could be civilized. It only made them more dangerous, a wolf in sheep's clothing.

"I'll come to you."

"Brilliant. I shall send some of my people to escort you."

"No thanks, I can come to you on my own, just tell me the address." I listened as vampire Lucien read off a swanky address in a very nice little part of town. I was impressed even though I didn't want to be. "Okay, it'll take me about fifteen minutes."

"I'll be eagerly awaiting your arrival my little human."

I really didn't like the sound of that.

40

Chapter Nine:

The offices were not what I had expected. They stood out from their comrades like a prostitute in a Convent. Where all the other offices were white and pristine, the offices for Corruption were alarmingly red. There was a large sign, which read 'Corruption' in big black letters over the door. There were two large vampires guarding the door both in standard black gear, they carried no weapons, they were threatening enough on their own. As I approached I opened my mental pathways and thrust my energy outwards trying to gain as much information as I could before I put myself in such a precarious situation. I could feel the energy radiating off of the two vampires at the front door, neither one of them was exceedingly old. They were both well fed and content and seemed mildly amused by my presence here tonight. I didn't need to use any Empathic powers to know that they thought I was stupider than sin. If you want to know the whole truth I couldn't really disagree with their opinion, however, it was much to late to back out now.

Obviously they were expecting me because they opened the door without asking any questions. I felt their eyes on me even as I entered and I couldn't help but wonder if I was making the biggest mistake of my life. I fortified myself when I saw what awaited me, Laeticia, the pissed off vampiress from last evening stood at the end of the hallway looking just as beautiful and just as bloodthirsty as ever. This evening found her in a matching black top and skirt, both tight and skimpy. She had on knee high black vinyl boots with spiky heels and her hair was shiny and free falling about her waist. Her face had been made up dramatically with red lipstick and dark eyeliner. Personally I thought it was one hell of an unflattering look for her. Her pale skin made the makeup pop out on her face and she looked like the strange unearthly creature that she was. As I got closer her smile broadened until I could see the glint of razor sharp fangs. When I was about as close as I was going to get to the strangely smiling vampire she spoke.

"Have you come back to sample the pleasures I can reward to you?" Her eyes fairly gleamed and she all but licked her lips in anticipation, yeah, this was a really bad idea. I straightened my shoulders and gave her the most insolent look I could manage under the circumstances.

"I'm taking it that you're not Miss Congeniality tonight, is your boss around?" I took a step back when she began to shimmer and made a move towards me. I'm not sure what she would have done if vampire Lucien hadn't taken that exact moment to intervene.

"Laeticia, I told you to bring Holly back immediately."

Laeticia growled but lowered her head in a submissive gesture "She only but arrived."

One look behind her into vampire Lucien's eyes made it clear that he didn't believe her, and that he was in a fine temper.

"Come Holly... you are excused Laeticia."

"Until later, little human."

"Gee, doesn't she ever learn?" I muttered under my breath and was mortified when a soft, silky voice countered with,

"It would appear not."

Shit, I had forgotten that vampires have beyond natural hearing capabilities. I followed vampire Lucien back into a large room that was furnished elaborately in black and white, it was stylish and obviously expensive, it seemed that vampires made a good living nowadays. I took a seat on the comfy white leather sofa making sure there was a good deal of distance between the vampire and myself. While vampire Lucien was making himself comfortable behind the desk I took a moment to study him, he was simply a beautiful creature, more so tonight, if possible, than the last time I had seen him. His black silk shirt was cut with a deep V in the front and tucked into obscenely tight black leather pants. The pants were held together at the sides with open stitching so that you could see his nearly translucent skin beneath the leather like a pale temptation. His shining mane of auburn hair was sleeked back from his face and tied into a ponytail, which hung long and thick down his back. He was disturbingly perfect, the perfection that no mere man can achieve, the perfection of the dead.

"Do you like what you see my pet, my Holly?"

I was jerked out of my study by his warm caressing voice and my face flushed a deep crimson. "I love it when you blush like that, I can see the blood pulsing through you and warming up that beautiful body of yours. It makes me warm like nothing else does."

If I hadn't been blushing before I was certainly flaming now. My cheeks felt hot and I desperately fought to control my emotions. I was not going to let myself lose control so early in the game.

"I didn't come here to discuss how good you look."

"So you think I look good?"

I frowned at the beautiful vampire sitting across the room from me. If I didn't know better I would swear that he was fishing for compliments.

"It really doesn't matter what I think about how you look, that isn't why I came here."

Vampire Lucien's face quickly turned very serious and his eyes hardened considerably, it chilled me seeing the sudden transformation, chilled me knowing how quickly he could turn.

"Yes, why did you come to see me, my little Holly? It is a welcome visit of course, but very unexpected, I can only hope that it was to see my shining face again, although I somehow doubt that is the reason."

"I want to know what you know about the EU student that was murdered last night." I watched as his face fell into that perfectly unreadable icy mask. He leaned back on his chair and cocked his head to one side, looking at me through those beautiful deep green eyes.

"This is why you came here, you came here to question me about a human murder?"

"I…."

"You are not even an authority, what right do you have asking such questions?"

I couldn't tell if he was angry or not, his words were not reassuring but his voice was deceptively calm and controlled. I wasn't sure if that was a good or bad sign, but whatever it was I wasn't feeling so hot.

"She was a fellow student, a fellow…" I paused before adding, "human. She deserved more than she got, much more. She was bled and strangled and left mutilated by her dorm on campus. You may not think I have a right to ask such questions about her death but I know better" I waited tense moments and tried to cipher some meaning from his rigidly controlled demeanor.

"You are quite the exception Holly."

"What?"

"You came here alone and frightened." He held up a hand when I would have interrupted, "As I was saying, you came here alone and frightened and yet you still found the courage to ask me about a student that means nothing to you."

"That's where you're wrong, she means something to me, they all do."

"They?"

"All of the students I go to school with, all the humans I know…they're good people, the operative word here is that they're people, they deserve more than to be merely the second course on the menu." I paused and added steadily, "I owe it to Pamela. It doesn't matter that I didn't know her personally. I owe it to her memory. Are you going to help me or aren't you? Because if you're not going to help me than I'd just as soon get home and into a hot bath."

Vampire Lucien smiled and his entire face lit up, literally. He glowed like a super charged firefly and it only added to his unearthly beauty. "As I said you are the exception to the rule." He looked at me from head to toe and his face took on that seductive quality that he did so well, "You are also looking particularly delicious tonight."

I swallowed, I really didn't like his choice of words and I said so. He laughed, a deep rumbling laugh that was both cool like an unexpected breeze yet held the heat of a summer in Charlotte. It was hard seeing him, as he was now to remember that he was a creature of the dark. Upon seeing his beautiful face and listening to his low, melodic laughter it was hard not to imagine him enthralling anyone of his choosing.

"About that student."

"Ahhh yes, I do believe I was told something about that this evening, it sounds to me like one of your human murders."

"She was bled."

"She was also strangled, from what I hear, we do not strangle our…prey."

"But you bleed them."

Vampire Lucien smiled again "What would you like me to say my little Holly, what would make you feel more…safe, secure in your little sturdy house. We need blood to survive, it is not a pretty truth, but it is a truth nonetheless. I make no excuses for what we do, nor do I believe we need them. We are what we are. I, however, do not have such poor control over my Hive that I would allow anyone of my people to slaughter a human on such public ground…" He shrugged his shoulders. "It is bad for our image." And soberly he added, "And quite tactless."

"Then you don't know who killed her." It was a statement not a question.

"No."

I nodded, I believed him. Oh, yeah, I might be totally demented or perhaps completely deluded but I believed him. There was the ring of sincerity to his callous words. And I had felt the truth of them as he spoke. I began to mentally ring up the possibilities in my head. If this wasn't a vampire murder then it was a human one. That gave me pause and a distinct feeling of ill ease invaded me.

"Thank you, you have been more than gracious allowing me to take up your time."

"It is always a pleasure."

I shuddered and gasped when I found him suddenly behind me. His hand was smoothing its way down my head, and he fingered my braids delicately as if memorizing the texture of my hair. I found myself rendered incapable of moving away, there were delicious tremors pulsing through my body and I arched my neck and looked up at him. His beautiful glowing face was now near mine and with one movement I could have those soft, cold lips pressed against mine, just one movement. Vampire Lucien took the decision out of my hands as he held my head securely in place while he kissed me long and thoroughly. My body felt weightless and unbelievably alive. My nerve endings were screaming and I suddenly wanted to feel all that beautiful pale flesh against mine. I knew, I knew somewhere in the back of my head that I shouldn't be doing this, that I should not be allowing this dark creature anywhere near me, and yet, there was something remarkably alluring, seductive about him. It was so much more than his physical beauty, there was something about him that seemed to call to me, and at this moment I was powerless to stop him, I didn't want to stop him.

"Little Holly you taste like the finest of wines."

I pulled back and stared at those cold but beautiful eyes. "You can't drink wine." I murmured, and watched as a smile lit those eyes, it was a sight to see.

"Just because I cannot drink wine now does not mean I do not remember what it tasted like. I remember the bouquet and the tartness on my tongue. I remember how it would slither down my throat and warm my insides…much as you do at this moment."

"Slither down your throat." I smiled slightly and his eyes crinkled up in an answering grin.

"Warm my insides, you warm my insides little Holly."

"There is nothing warm about you Lucien." I gasped a little when I realized

I had called him by his first name. I found myself breathless when he trailed a finger down my cheek. He had come around the couch to stand in front of me and was regarding me with those brilliant green eyes of his. I found myself transfixed by those eyes and the promise within them. This was not a good thing.

"But there could be, little Holly. You could change everything for me."

I jerked up off the couch, big mistake. I was now standing flush against his hard frame. I fought to regain control of my breathing and not to give into temptation. They didn't call it temptation for nothing. Look at Eve and the apple, where did temptation get her?

"I appreciate your meeting me tonight. Thank you." I paused a moment and added. "And if you find out anything please…tell me."

"As I said, it was my pleasure, I shall meet you whenever you like Holly, you need only call for me. But nothing comes without a price…" His voice trailed off and I shivered anew.

"And what would the price be for your cooperation?"

"I think you know."

My eyebrows rose and I got ready to tell this perverted vampire off when he interjected, "*That* is not what I meant. However, it would not be unwelcome." He grinned and then became somber. "No, it is quite simple my little Holly, your cooperation for mine"

"You mean…"

"I think the modern expression would be, you scratch my back and I scratch yours. If I need your particular talent…" he smiled at me, "talents…I will call on you. In turn, whatever information I uncover will be at your disposal."

I fixed my eyes on his and stared at him intently for a moment or two. "Do you swear on it."

"Swear?"

"Swear that you will cooperate with me, help me."

"You would trust me if I swear as you ask me to?"

"Yes."

He looked incredulous but after a moment nodded, "It will be as you wish. I give my word that I will help you uncover that which you wish to know, in turn you will give me your talents when I need them, you will cooperate with me."

"Within reason." I added.

"Excuse me."

"I have midterms in two weeks."

"What are midterms?"

I frowned.

"Moocho big exams at my University that count for about twenty to thirty percent of my final grades. I have to study and I have to study big time, I'm totally unprepared for my Calculus exam and I'm not so sure about my Physics test either." I sighed and knew that there was a little crease between my eyes which came out of me being annoyed, "I never was one for numbers and formulas."

"These exams are important to you?"

"Uh, yes, they're totally a huge deal. If I don't do well on my midterms then I have a lot of pressure on me going into my finals, pressure I would rather do without. So you see during this study period I would prefer that you wouldn't call on me to do any…uhmm, well to use any of my powers." I was perturbed when Vampire Lucien broke out into bales of laughter. His fangs were showing and I tried not to flinch at the sight of them.

"Priceless, you are priceless." He wiped a blood red tear from his eye and I was fascinated by the red smear. I hadn't realized vampires could cry, and I most certainly hadn't realized that they shed bloody tears. I really didn't understand what I could have possibly have said that was so funny as to make a vampire shed blood red tears. "I shall do my best not to ask anything of you during this study period Holly. However, if we make this bargain we will be in debt to one another, do you understand?"

"Yeah, I get it."

"And what have you decided?"

There were so many conflicting emotions warring within me. I had spent fifteen years doing my best to separate myself from this community. I had watched and learned but kept myself apart, doing everything in my powers to behave and become normal and completely human. I had a chance now; no one at College knew what I was and what I could do. I could melt into the student body and be just one of them. My grades were strong and I had a good chance of completing College with two majors and perhaps with honors. Did I really need this now? Did I have a choice? It was a turning point here, what I decided now would affect me in more ways than one. Could I really manage, school, dating, and 'turning tricks' so to speak, for the vampire community? I suppose we'd have to find out.

"Okay, you've got a deal." I enjoyed the surprise that flickered through vampire Lucien's eyes before it was quickly masked. "Should we shake on it?" I held out my hand. I didn't have a moment to even register shock before he wrapped one strong arm around me and pulled me in for a deep and thorough kiss. Like all his kisses this one thrilled me down to my knees and made my bones liquefy. He abruptly pulled away, a smug, satisfied smile on his lips.

"I prefer to seal our deal with a kiss."

"Uh, yeah, I can see that." I swallowed, and knew that my pulse was racing. I had to get a grip. I had to have more control on my hormones.

"I think this is the beginning of a beautiful friendship," Vampire Lucien said.

"You've got to think of some more original lines." This came out more sharp than I had intended, but I was still trying to get my heart rate under control and I didn't like the feelings that this vampire invoked within me, they disturbed me, greatly.

"Ahhh, well I shall work on my lines while we are apart and perhaps the next time we see one another they will be more original." He was still smiling and I felt like socking him one in the face.

"I've got to go, I still have to study for tomorrow." I jerked my head back quickly probably giving myself a neck injury, but at least I had succeeded in pulling my braid out of his hands. I hadn't even realized he had been stroking my hair until just now. I turned to leave but a question I had wanted to ask him earlier popped back into my head. "Corruption," I paused a moment before continuing, "What sort of business do you run? And why the title 'Corruption'?"

He gave a mirthless laugh. "I have my hands in this and that."

"But what is this particular business?"

"I run a service you may say."

Big red warning lights were going off in my head.

"What sort of service?"

"I provide entertainment to clubs and to certain individuals who wish to partake in my particular field."

I gasped, "Oh my god, you're a vampire pimp."

"Hardly." Vampire Lucien was laughing again, and laughing hard. "I am a legitimate businessman. I have the appropriate documents and do everything legally. I do not pimp anything, or anyone. I am more like the manager of many different businesses. In the case of 'Corruption' we provide legitimate entertainment services. There are many clubs and many individuals who like and need the unconventional, shall we say, dancer, or waitress, or bartender, I supply them."

"So you're more like a, placement agency." I bit my lip and wasn't feeling so hot when he only grinned at me showing more fang.

"If you like."

"But 'Corruption'?"

Vampire Lucien shrugged his shoulders, "I thought it had a certain ring to it."

"It certainly has something to it." I nodded, "Okay, now I'm ready to go home."

"Would you like an escort, my little Holly?"

"No."

"Are you certain? It has become very late."

"I'm not afraid of the dark."

"Ahhh, but aren't you afraid of other things, perhaps things that like you, aren't afraid of the dark."

I cleared my throat and hid my fear. "I can find my way home just fine, thank you anyway."

"It is your choice of course." When he made a move towards me I stepped back and shook my head, stopping him effectively in his tracks. I was pleased to see that he didn't push the issue.

"Goodnight…Lucien."

"Goodnight Holly, and…pleasant dreams."

I hurried out of the office and in my rush to leave I didn't see the dark shadow that slithered into the office right after I left.

These hours were a bitch. I was exhausted. I parked my Volvo, which had seen better days in my private parking space and just as I was about to leave the car I stopped. I concentrated and the sound, which had been just a faint buzzing in my ears a moment before was now a pattern of scattered thoughts. I could 'hear' faint words, *now, do it now, speak now, action*. I focused but the words did not form coherent sentences. Whoever was speaking was close though, the thoughts were strong in my mind and I knew that he or she was close. I exited my car and remembered to lock up, not that there was anything that anyone could steal. I had a broken stereo a temperamental air conditioner and everything else put together would barely make next months maintenance check on my apartment.

I walked hesitantly towards my apartment. I enjoyed being on the first floor. I didn't like walk-ups and I didn't trust elevators, so my current situation was ideal. I hadn't gotten more than four steps when a figure emerged from the shadows. I have to say I probably would have preferred seeing the Loch Ness monster to the thing that was in front of me. Laeticia in all her evil glory was standing firmly in my way. She had added a cloak to her little ensemble, rather unnecessary in my opinion. The weather was mild and now she just looked like something out of a bad B movie.

"Oh boy, I really don't have time for this." I gestured towards my apartment "Listen I am totally beat. I need to get up early tomorrow for classes, and well you have a time limit and expiration date too, don't you? I mean you don't really want to be deep fried vampire do you?" I waited but she still didn't say anything. I tried reaching her mind but her thoughts were carefully guarded and there was nothing to pick up. "I know you aren't here just to stare at my face, are you?" I waved my hand back and forth, probably not the smartest move, but I was too tired to care right now, "Are you going to tell me what this is about?"

She was absolutely still, nothing moved, not an eyelash, not a finger, not a toe. She was still as death; that was sort of funny, considering. After some uncomfortable silence she spoke, softy, almost in a hiss.

"You should not have dealings with Lucien."

"What?"

"You are so small, so…human, he will roll over you and discard the remaining pieces."

"Oh for God's sake, this is why you're here? I am going to bed now, okay?"

"I would not ignore my warning, human."

"I won't ignore it, but I need to get up early and well, I'm tired."

Laeticia eyed me up and down and her eyes took on a feral light, a light, may I say that I was not happy to see. I skirted sideways and tried to calculate the distance from her to the front of my apartment, could I make it in time? Could I make it to my door, unlock it and get inside before she either ripped my back to shreds or took a chunk out of my neck? Who the hell was I kidding? I stopped where I was and waited to see what she would say, or do next.

"You are a small female for such fuss. I suppose your blood could be sweet, your body and face are pleasant, but I still say you are a liability. Why the interest I do not know."

I tried to follow the conversation but I didn't like where it was going.

"If you can shake your Holder's interest in me, well that will be just fine and dandy with me, really. But I don't plan on donating any samples of blood tonight." I really didn't like the gleam in her eyes. It was hungry, anxious. I was certain by the translucence of her skin and the delicate blue veins that were more than apparent underneath the surface that she hadn't fed this evening. I knew that it was late to feed, and that she must be starving. I certainly didn't like being the red flag in front of the bull. "Is that all?" I waited and watched as her eyes seemed to suddenly clear up and she seemed to shake herself out of her stupor.

"That is all, for now, little psychic…but you would do well to heed my warnings."

"I appreciate the concern, thanks." I gritted my teeth as she continued to study me, how the hell long was she going to do this?

"I could take you now, you know." Her tone of voice was conversational and I tried not to yell out my frustration.

"You'd have some explaining to do." I took a small step forward and watched her eyes follow me the minute distance. "I'm going in now," I continued walking and when I passed her and didn't feel her talons or her teeth I breathed a sigh of relief. I knew she was still there, still there watching me, smelling me, imagining what I would taste like on her tongue, but she hadn't made a move towards me. I unlocked my door, stepped inside closed it firmly behind me and fell back in relief against the thick oak.

Chapter Ten:

Friday came fast. I sat tapping my pen repeatedly against my binder. I was wired. I had been on a steady diet of Coca-Cola and caffeine pills for the last four days. I hadn't slept, ate only when I could manage to remember and was a regular at Waffle House at six in the morning. Edwards might not have a twenty-four screen Cineplex, but Waffle Houses, Waffle Houses we had plenty of. The good news was I had memorized the three chapters for my Spells & Incantations class and was pretty sure I could handle the necessary formulas for Physics. I cast my eyes around the room and caught several of my fellow students cracking their knuckles and tapping their fingers against their desks, oh yeah, they were on caffeine pills too. It was amazing how wired you could get from one tiny pill, usually I cut the damn thing in half, but I was desperate this week. I had a schedule to keep. I had to finish up the last two chapters for my American History class and then it was time to hit Calculus, which I obviously had left for last. I was falling behind and I couldn't let myself...

"Ms. Feather, Holly."

I jerked my head up, startled by the voice that interrupted my frazzled thoughts. Professor DeWitt was watching me with those soft gray eyes of hers. "Yes, Professor?"

"If you could stay after class, I would appreciate it."

"Of course." I ignored the murmurs from the other students and concentrated on the complex doodle that was forming in my notebook.

"I've noticed that you have turned in superior work Holly."

"Uh, thank you Professor." I was surprised. Was this why she had wanted to see me after class?

"Your papers have been well developed and carefully constructed. Your exams have been the highest in the class and you have a good attitude."

"Thank you Professor." I was getting more and more embarrassed, I really didn't take compliments well. And this was high praise from the Professor many had dubbed the "ice queen." Professor DeWitt couldn't be more than forty-five, but she had one of those faces which age was impossible to tell. Her features were fine and delicate. Her eyes were dove gray her cheekbones high and she had a lovely full mouth. Her skin was perfect. Actually she had the skin of a woman half her age. Her hair was a white blond and was usually pulled back in a lose bun which only accentuated her graceful features. She was a strikingly beautiful woman who wore her age very well. If only I could be so lucky when I got older.

"I would like to know if you'd be interested in doing some research for me on the side?"

"Research?"

"Of course you would be credited, and if the research is well collected and documented you'll have your name printed in the journal that I intend to submit the work to. The school will also consider crediting you for your hours."

I was stunned but happily surprised. Of all my classes this was by far my favorite, which could be the reason I was doing so well in it. I enjoyed the work and I most certainly would love the experience, not to mention doctoring up my resume. As an added bonus, class credit would be great. It wasn't a difficult decision to make

"Yes, that sounds terrific. Thank you so much for giving me the opportunity."

"Please, there is nothing to thank me for. You've done all the work" Professor DeWitt smiled, revealing two rows of perfectly white teeth. "By the next class I will have a list of topics I would like you to look up and you'll have access to the library archives, I've cleared it with the library attendant."

"Okay, great. Thank you Professor."

"Oh, and I certainly don't expect you to start before you have finished your midterms."

I breathed a sigh of relief. I had been worried about that. "Okay."

"All right, then it's settled. I'll see you next class Holly."

"Goodbye Professor, and thanks again." I skipped out of the class positively glowing. This was a fabulous opportunity for me. I could really bolster my resume, not to mention get in some good reading.

By eight, I was just finished applying lip-gloss. I had settled on a denim skirt, t-shirt and cardigan. Boring, I know, but practical. I had decided to leave my hair down, and had applied a small amount of styling gel to the sides to keep it out of my face, the end result was pretty damn good. Low sandals completed the outfit and now all I needed was the man. As fate would have it the doorbell rang at that very moment and I quickly checked my appearance one last time before answering it.

Ryan looked handsome as ever. He had combed and styled his hair but hadn't used all that goop that men use, I prefer it that way. He wore a white t-shirt, checked shirt over it and slightly baggy jeans. He was smiling and I felt an answering grin spread across my face, I guess it's contagious.

"You look great Holly."

"Thanks Ryan, you're looking pretty great yourself." I liked the fact that he blushed. I thought it was very endearing.

"Uh, should we go?"

"Sounds good." I grabbed my keys and locked up. "Are we having dinner first?"

"Well the movie is at ten fifteen so I thought perhaps we could eat before."

"Great, where?"

"Applebee's all right with you?"

"Love it."

He grinned and I grinned, we were both looking pretty foolish.

"Uh, okay, great, I'm the blue truck." Ryan ushered me towards his car still smiling and I could tell already that this was a good guy, a keeper.

"So where are you from?" I was munching on some boneless buffalo wings and trying not to get sauce on my chin.

"Burnsville."

I smiled, I knew Burnsville. I told him as much, he looked surprised.

"I didn't know that anyone had heard of Burnsville."

Burnsville was about forty miles from Edwards and thirty-five from Ashville. It was a small quaint town named after Captain Otway Burns a naval hero of the war of 1812.

"My mother took me through when I was very little. She ended up with a carload of crafts that she displayed all over our house, we looked like a spread from an arts and crafts catalog."

Ryan was laughing and nodding "My mother ran a crafts store in Burnsville for a while, she's retired now." He paused before adding, "Our house looked like something out of Country Living. God, can you believe I even know that magazine."

"I take it your mother subscribed to it."

"Yeah. She was, she still is pretty obsessed with those home and craft magazines and catalogs. You're not a real citizen of Burnsville unless you subscribe." He said this last part in a pretty fair imitation of a woman's voice. I found myself laughing along with him.

During our dinner our conversation never dragged. I learned that Ryan was the eldest of three children, two boys and a girl. His mother was retired and his father was the manager of one of the two processing plants in Yancey County, oh, and during winter he sold Christmas trees. Ryan hadn't wanted to move too far away but he hadn't wanted to attend Mayland Community College, so he cut the difference and had attended EU, which had given him a full scholarship. He was a math major and that impressed me. I didn't know many math majors and I told him so.

"Don't you find it dull?" I blurted out before I could stop myself. Ryan laughed.

"Nah, actually I find it really interesting. It's amazing how things depend on one another. There are all these intricate formulas which are necessary to figuring out why things are the way they are." Ryan paused before continuing, "You're a double major, right?"

"Yeah" I grinned, "I'm a masochist, I have to be to take on the load I'm taking on."

"English...and..."

"English and Modern Mysticism & Magic."

Ryan digested this piece of information.

"Do you believe in that stuff?"

"What stuff?"

He looked embarrassed but pressed on. "Well, magic and that sort of crap."

"Yeah I believe in it." I tried not to frown but knew that I was failing. How could he not believe in magic? "What about psychics?"

"What about them?"

"Do you believe in psychics?"

"Well, I don't know really. I think that there are people with heightened senses, however, I don't know if I believe you can really predict the future and that sort of shit."

"I see…"

"What? I suppose since you're majoring in Mysticism that I sound pretty damn lame to you."

"No, I just think that it's amazing that you don't believe in it. How do you explain…oh, say, vampires for instance." There was very real distaste in Ryan's face now.

"I've never seen a vampire before."

I was shocked, oh vampires might be rare wandering around Edwards and Burnsville but he had never seen one before?

"Not even in passing?"

"Nope." Ryan tried to contain a shiver but failed "From what I hear they're pretty horrible monsters. They're the walking dead, it's a perversity."

"Monsters." I dropped my gaze down to my food and tried to process what I had just learned. I jerked my eyes up towards his face and shot him an accusatory look "What about 'Spells & Incantations'? Why did you take Professor DeWitt's course if you don't believe in magic?"

Ryan shrugged. "Just because I don't believe in it doesn't mean I'm not interested. Professor DeWitt is cool, her course is one of the more interesting ones in the department and well I really think that I've learned a lot so far."

"I agree, about her class being interesting." I sighed. I was trying not to feel annoyed about what he had just told me. I couldn't fault him his opinion. He was not expressing anything new, in truth, his sentiments much echoed by dead mother's opinion of the monsters. Perhaps that was why it was bothering me so much.

"…But we're lucky, we don't have to worry about them."

"Excuse me," I hadn't been paying attention to him and I felt a tad bit embarrassed.

"The vampires. We don't have to worry about them at EU."

"What about the student who was murdered, doesn't that bother you, worry you?"

"Yeah, it was terrible, but I don't believe it was committed by a vampire, do you?"

"No." And that was the truth, disturbing, but the truth nonetheless.

"Yeah we're lucky at EU, we don't have to deal with the dead."

I felt the chicken getting stuck on its way down. My throat was tight and my heart was pounding quickly, and uncomfortably in my chest. "Yeah, lucky."

I took a sip of water and forced myself to smile.

I waved goodbye to Ryan and watched as his car disappeared out of sight. The evening hadn't been a total bust, the movie had been fun and dinner had been…enlightening. I still thought he was a total cutie. He had been charming and a complete gentleman, not pressing for a goodnight kiss. He had smiled and laughed during the movie even though I knew it hadn't interested him, and he had bought me a bucket of extra buttered popcorn and the bag of 'Sour Patch Kids' I had been craving before the movie started. It was a perfectly enjoyable Friday evening and for the first date in oh, eons, it had gone really well, and yet I was still feeling discomforted and disquieted by what he had said earlier in the evening. What would he think if he knew what I was? Would he consider me as bad as the vampires, or would he just think I was a perversity?

"Is it so much to ask to hope that my date wouldn't think me a total freak?"

"I do not find you a freak my little Holly."

I let out a little screech and spun around to find myself practically face to face with vampire Lucien. I planted my hands on my hips and gave him the evil eye.

"What are you doing here?"

"Why I came to see how you are my Holly."

"Don't do that!"

"Don't do what?" there was a smile gracing his perfect face

"Sneak up on me…do not sneak up on me…can't you just, well…I don't know, just don't do that."

Vampire Lucien's smile widened and he bowed smartly to me. "I will endeavor to make more noise when I…come to see you."

"That brings me back to my first issue…what are you doing here?"

"I told you I…"

"No, no, don't give me that. What are you really doing here?" I took a step back when I saw his fine, green eyes begin to glow. He seemed to radiate energy, his body hummed with power and I didn't like it, something was up.

"That…boy," he spat out, "What were you doing with him, my Holly?"

"Not that it is any of your business but I was on a date, you know, a date."

"Ahhh, and did you let him touch you as I have."

I blushed, "No."

"Good" He was nodding "It is good that you don't lie to me."

"How do you know I wasn't lying, what if I had slept with him." I was baiting him I knew it, but he was annoying me.

His eyes grew seemingly brighter and he answered tightly, "I could smell him in the air, if he had…touched you I would have known, his scent would have clung to your skin and seeped into your pores. That it didn't tells me that you did not let him touch you, and that you did not lie to me."

I rubbed my eyes wearily. All this vampire power crap was beginning to get really tedious. Smell him on me, jeez, how icky could you get? "How did you know where I lived?"

"Ah my Holly, do you really think so little of my power, my holdings?" He laughed, "Am I so insignificant that you do not think I could find out your address easily if I wanted it."

"Yeah, yeah, ask a stupid question…" I let my words trail off. I stood staring at him, not quite certain what else to do. There was a beautiful dead guy in my parking lot something you don't see every day. He was wearing a white shirt with lace spilling down the front very circa 1800's. His velvet pants were black and had a bright sheen to them that was unusual. He had an onyx brooch almost the size of an Easter egg clasped at his throat effectively bringing ones attention towards his neck, and the delicate features of his beautiful face. He looked like he had raided a costume shop. He looked…perfect it totally annoyed me, no one should look that good, not even the dead.

"Are you going to invite me in?"

"No." I said it abruptly and without thinking. I watched as surprise danced across his face and then the beginnings of another smile.

"Why not, are you afraid of me?"

"Hell yeah I'm afraid of you."

"You would prefer it then if I had my conversation with you in the parking lot? You do not think the neighbors would mind my presence here? Because if it does not bother you then we can speak here and now, indeed, why do you not invite them to join in…"

"Fine, oh, all right. Damn you." I spun around and knew he was following even without hearing his footsteps behind me. When I reached my door I found myself fumbling for my keys, my shaking hand wouldn't cooperate. Suddenly a cold, perfectly formed hand settled over mine and effectively stopped my shakes. I swallowed, finding it totally disconcerting that his hand could stop my trembles, shouldn't it be the other way around? Unlocking my door I hesitated only a moment before speaking. "Please, come in, you're invited." It was like walking out into a blustery day, an invisible and silent chill raced around my body and seemed to energize the air around me. Vampire Lucien nodded and bowed slightly before entering my apartment. He smiled at me good- naturedly and closed the door behind him.

"Thank you."

"Don't thank me, you practically blackmailed me into letting you into the apartment." I grumbled, I didn't like to think that a small part of me had wanted him in my apartment. That if I had really wanted him to stay out I could have made it so, but the fact that he was standing here now was a testament to my diminishing will power where he was concerned.

"If it pleases you to think so." His expression told me that he knew exactly what was racing through my mind and that he found it amusing and fairly complimentary. "I like your apartment."

"No you don't, don't lie."

His expression was priceless, his mouth opened in a surprised O and he seemed to gape for a moment before masking everything behind a carefully controlled bland expression.

"Did you read me Holly...feel me?"

"Nope, didn't have to, your face told me everything I needed to know." That seemed to surprise him more, knowing I had been able to read him merely by looking at his face. I assumed that he wasn't used to people being able to read his emotions and his feelings from his face. Vampires over the centuries they were alive became really good at hiding what they were feeling. I, however, out of necessity, obviously I couldn't go around reading everyone's minds, had become very good at reading people's faces, alive or dead.

"You are right, I do not...agree with your tastes." His eyes swept around the room taking in its interior with one glance. He seemed particularly offended by the mismatched pillows and knit throw on my old, ratty sofa.

"Well whoop dee doo." I rolled my eyes. "I really don't care if you like my apartment or not, you're lucky I invited you in."

Vampire Lucien nodded his beautiful head. "You are quite right Holly, I am being unmistakably rude. It was very decent of you to invite me in and I am criticizing your taste, I apologize."

"Fine, thanks." I could tell from the hint of warmth in his voice that he wasn't sorry at all, that actually he found the situation and my annoyance amusing. I wasn't about to let him know that that annoyed me even further. He would probably get perverse pleasure out of that bit of information as well. "Okay, so talk, what are you doing here?"

"Could it not be to see your lovely face."

"If I believed that I would have left you in the parking lot." I shook my head. "I want the real reason and I want it quickly."

"Patience Holly, patience."

"No, I don't have much patience left. Listen I'm not a patient person by nature, and with you, well I think you're taking up what patience I have left, plus the reserves." I was aggravated probably more so by my reaction to having him in my living room than anything else. He looked comfortable and strikingly gorgeous even in my mismatched and cluttered space. It annoyed me. "So spill."

It was like watching a ripple in the water. His face seemed to take on an almost 'human' like quality for but a moment before turning back to that still as death look that made me shiver every time I saw it.

"All right then Holly. I have need of your particular talent."

"No, you told me not until after midterms."

"Nay, you told me. And if I remember correctly I told you that I would try to hold my needs until after your…exams. However, a situation has arisen that needs my particular attention immediately and your expertise, so to speak. It is important to rectify the situation immediately and to dispose of the problem quickly." He was regarding me with intensity that I found unsettling.

I plopped down on my couch and dropped my head into my hands. I was getting one of those killer headaches again. When my head had stopped ringing I looked up to find that he hadn't moved an inch, an iota. He was still staring at me, but there was something in his eyes, something that almost resembled…concern, could a vampire care?

"It is that important?"

"Yes, and I, in turn have information for you, Holly."

That interested me. I perked up immediately. "Oh?"

"Tonight I will send two of my people to come and fetch you." He silenced me with a look when I would have interrupted and argued. "No, this time you must have my people with you, you will be brought to the lair, our resting place, and my people must be content that you do not know of it's location. Because of this you will be blindfolded, I tell you this in advance so that when the time comes you are not scared or angered in any way, it is necessary, a precaution if you will."

I didn't like it but I understood the necessity. The resting place of a vampire was the most important secret of them all. If you knew the vampire's resting place you could destroy them. And it was commonly known that vampires slept near or in the lair. Therefore I understood the blindfold, that didn't mean I wasn't crabby about it. I knew I was sulking and I tried to contain my obvious annoyance over the fact that the vampire didn't trust me, why did I care so much, it shouldn't matter to me.

Vampire Lucien was regarding me with a placating smile on his perfectly still features. I really didn't like the fact that it always seemed as if he knew what I was thinking before even I did. It totally bothered me that this thing of death could know so much about me, or have so much power over my life. Or perhaps what bothered me was the knowledge that it didn't bother me half as much as it should. What the hell did that say about me?

"Tonight?" I checked my watch and groaned; it was already past one. "Have you fed?" I tilted my head to one side and looked at him curiously. His eyes gleamed and he made a move towards me.

"Are you offering Holly?"

"Absolutely not, just wondering. Your pallor suggests that you haven't...fed tonight, and I just didn't want to be in your way if you decided to 'snack' a little."

He laughed and his hair fell forward catching the light in its ruby red strands. "I will not 'snack' as you so quaintly put it, on you. I believe that you could never be merely a snack, my Holly, you would be the full course."

I frowned. "I think you should go now."

"What, no goodnight kiss?" His expression was full of innocence and devilment at the same time. I caught a giggle just in time and put on a stern face.

"Goodnight Lucien."

"Goodnight Holly."

And just like that he was gone, now that, that was really disconcerting.

Chapter Eleven:

Saturday afternoon found me at the strip mall trying to find something to wear for my meeting tonight. I wanted something appropriate and yet something that would wear well, that meant something that would stretch, give and be suitably comfortable, you have to be prepared for every possibility. I discarded several skirts, which would have bared all if I even bent over. I tossed out shorts, too informal, didn't want the vamp Holder to think I was insulting him. And then there were dresses, none of them seemed to work, not enough movement. I found what I was looking for on the discount rack in the back of the store. I think it was there because no one could possibly have the nerve to wear it. It seemed to think it could pass for a pair of pants but truly it was just two strips of material one in front one it back which were precariously attached on the sides by imitation leather cords. The material was a shiny, stretchy poly-blend that would probably go up in flames if anyone even thought to light a match near me. The pants were fire engine red and showed more leg than it covered, due to the fact that the pants were completely open on the sides and held together, literally, by the lose weaving of the cords. However, all the important places of my anatomy would be covered and the material was soft and stretchy enough to allow a lot of movement, if needed. I liked the fabric and I loved the price.

I spent the remainder of the day wracking my brain for reasons vampire Lucien could possibly need me to utilize my 'abilities.' I didn't like being so in the dark about things. It was like walking into a throng of mosquitoes without repellent, except these mosquitoes had large fangs, razor sharp claws and could kill you before you could say 'bite me.' I was further annoyed by the fact that he hadn't clued me into the time in which his goons would be coming to fetch me. I decided to play it safe and just about sundown I began my 'beauty' regime. I soaked for about an hour in honeysuckle bubble bath, indulging myself with the newest Marie Claire and a Kit Kat bar.

Afterwards I meticulously applied my makeup, I usually didn't bother with stuff like mascara and eyeliner but tonight I didn't want to take any chances. I went all out. I enhanced my eyes with shiny light red eye shadow, which with my coloring worked fabulously. I added a touch of cream blush and finished the look with double gloss red lipstick that was so bright you could probably spot me coming a mile away. My eyes were dramatic lined with kohl liner and my lashes were thick and apparent lathered with mascara, I looked totally vamp, and completely not like myself. I had chosen a knit black top sans bra and added a black faux leather belt to the red pants. Four-inch wedge boots completed the outfit. I swallowed audibly when I saw my reflection in my full-length mirror. I looked sexy, intimidating and dangerous, I looked like a stranger. I hadn't ever met a dominatrix but I wondered if this is what one would look like? No, they probably would be wearing more rubber. At least I wasn't carrying a whip. I wondered if I should change, was this making too much of a statement?

Whatever thoughts I might have been having were stopped with the ringing of the doorbell. At least they rang the bell. I opened the door and I wasn't sure who was more surprised, the vampires in my doorway, or me. Standing there were the two same vamps who had tried to corner me on campus. Mr. Mohawk and Mr. Suit. Tonight they were both decked out similarly to the first time we had met. Mr. Mohawk was wearing worn leather pants and a black leather vest without anything underneath. His hair was still an eye catcher perhaps more so since he had added white streaks, much like a zebras to it. Mr. Suit was wearing, of course, a suit. This time his suit was charcoal gray with an expensive pinstripe tie and perfectly creased white tailored shirt. They had similar expressions of shock and surprise on their faces, and I enjoyed seeing it. It wasn't every day that you got to surprise a vamp.

"We're to bring you to the Holder." This from Mr. Mohawk who seemed to be practically salivating, this reminded me why I hadn't liked him when I had first met him. Mr. Suit was more reserved, but his expression was no less heated. It was going to be a really long night.

I was back in the throne room. That same stone room with its intricately carved chairs and sturdy table. The room was impressive but totally gave me the creeps. I had been suitably curious the first time I had seen it but now, now it was just a cold, damp and way too intimidating room. I also didn't like the fact that Mr. Mohawk and Mr. Suit had dropped me off in the room and left me there alone, though perhaps I should be happy about the alone part, it was better than the surrounded by vampires part. What was I supposed to do now, sit Indian style on the floor? I certainly wasn't about to sit in any of the chairs, and the table was definitely out. I was making up my mind when vampire Lucien strode in. He stopped dead, do you get it, dead. Anyways, he stopped dead in his tracks and just ogled me. At least it looked like he was ogling me. His desire, and his heat, was obvious from even where I was standing. He had a fine sheen on his skin and his body was glowing that soft, perfect glow. I was beginning to get nervous when he didn't say anything. I began to wonder if I had gone to far with the outfit, yeah I'm sure that even a vampire knows what the word 'slutty' means. I was fidgeting and trying my best not to bite on my fingernails, not like there was much left to bite, when he spoke. His voice was silky and hot, but blew over me like a cool wind. I had the feeling of sizzling warmth spreading through my body along with feathers tickling up and down my spine.

"You are looking magnificent, dare I hope this is for me."

"Uh, this old thing?" I let out a nervous laugh and wasn't reassured by the smile in his eyes. I ran a hand down my top to smooth it, totally unnecessary but at least it soothed my nerves. "So, are you going to tell me what this is about?"

"Pardon?" Vampire Lucien jerked his eyes back to my face, it seemed as if he was just coming out of a trance.

"Tonight, me, here, are you going to tell me what this is about?" I sighed, "Why I'm here."

"I told you."

"No, you told me that you needed my 'abilities' you didn't tell me why, or for what. You also didn't tell me what distinct ability you needed." I tried not to let my annoyance show. "How can I do anything if I don't know what I'm supposed to be doing." I watched as vampire Lucien became completely still and his face took on that unreadable mask. He seemed to be concentrating, and sure enough within moments another vampire entered the room. This vampire was also stunningly beautiful, but younger, significantly than Lucien. He was ethereal in his beauty, almost angelic, which was painfully ironic, considering what he was. He was dressed in black from head to toe and his waist length blond hair was lose and falling around him like a cascade of gold. He was beautiful perhaps more beautiful than Lucien, although I preferred Lucien's looks to this delicate, feminine young vamps.

"This is Christian."

I winced at the name, Christian? Well, a vamp's name was a vamp's name.

"Hello," I said and noticed that he seemed surprised that I acknowledged him. He nodded his head curtly in my direction but stayed obediently close to Lucien and silent.

"Christian's companion was murdered."

I didn't say anything, it wasn't uncommon for a vamp's human companion to be slain by some hate group or another. "His vampire companion." Lucien added. Now that surprised me. Frankly it is like totally difficult to kill a vampire. Besides the fact that you have to take out the heart and cut off the head if you make one mistake, one, itty, bitty mistake it'll cost you your life. You can stake a vampire but that doesn't guarantee death, actually that's where a lot of humans make their big mistake. Most humans think you can neatly stake a vampire and walk away, no mess, no bother, right? Wrong, completely wrong. First off it's really hard to stake a vampire, they're strong, they're resilient and they move faster than you can usually see. You have to hit them dead center, there are no second chances. If you don't stake the heart then there is no kill. Secondly, the vamp can continue to 'live' with a staked heart, the only thing that will truly kill a vampire is if you remove the heart completely along with the head. Then if you really want extra insurance you can burn the remains. When everything is smoking nice and easy then, then you'll truly know the vamp is dead, otherwise, well otherwise you're risking a really pissed off vamp. There is nothing like a staked heart to irritate a vampire.

"Christian was the last to see William alive."

I nodded. Vampire Lucien had my complete attention. "I have brought Christian here to tell you what he knows."

"Master...I have told you I do not know what happened to William...I wish I did." Christian's voice was oddly lyrical and also desperate. His eyes were filled with sadness and fear, both of which I understood. Vampire murders were rare, and I'm sure that Christian was afraid that Lucien, his Holder, would blame him for his companions demise. Lucien silenced him with a slash of his hand. He turned his blazing green eyes towards me and continued.

"I wish you to sense out Christian, I wish you to tell me what you can cipher out of his thoughts, if indeed you can read him."

"And if I can't?"

"Then you cannot. You will not be blamed for something you cannot do."

"That's a relief." I answered sarcastically and chewed my lower lip nervously. I had found lately that the vampires I had been meeting were all particularly difficult to read. I wasn't sure if it was waning ability on my part or if all these vampires were really good at erecting shields against intrusive probes, probably a bit of both.

"Christian will cooperate," Vampire Lucien gave Christian a pointed look "Won't you?"

"Of course Master." Christian stood obediently still and waited for me to do whatever I was going to do to him. I only took a moment to gather up my scattered thoughts before I proceeded. The quicker I completed this task the quicker I could get home.

"Okay, relax, don't be nervous." I said to the young vamp. He gave me an incredulous look.

"I am not nervous."

"Oh, all right, well then just relax…scratch the being nervous part." I felt, rather than saw his defenses go down. His whole body stopped. There was nothing remotely human about him now. I probed gently at first and was suddenly assailed by thick waves of guilt and remorse. My tongue suddenly felt thick and my brain cloudy. I couldn't feel my limbs and I sank to the ground, to my knees. I held up a hand when Lucien would have made a move to help me and I fortified myself. I tried to see through the emotions, to cipher out some coherent thoughts but the guilt and anger was too thick, too painful. I felt beads of sweat pop out on my brow and I made no move to wipe them away, so deep was my concentration. As suddenly as the emotions swept through me they were gone and I was finally able to take a deep breath. The air was welcomed into my starving lungs and I took several moments to compose myself.

"Did you see anything?" Lucien was looking at me expectantly and Christian was staring at me with equal amounts of dread and horror written all over his perfectly sculpted face.

"He doesn't know who killed his companion." I got to my feet and my eyes widened when vampire Lucien handed me a monogrammed handkerchief, I hadn't even seen his hand move. I accepted it and wiped my sweaty brow. "He does however know more than he thinks."

"What?" The young, blond vampire seemed frantic and angered. "I do not know anything, I did not see anything."

"No you didn't see anything, except his body, after the fact, but you did hear something." I noticed that both vampires were now staring at me with something akin to fascination and awe. "It was buried pretty deep, but it was a definite memory"

"Christian you may leave us."

"No, I wish to know what she has to say."

"You will leave now, I will decide what you are to know and what you do not need to know, leave." The look on vampire Lucien's face was dark, menacing and completely feral. Christian hesitated only a moment before striding angrily away. "Now, now you will tell me what you learned."

"It was pretty horrific." I shuddered, trying to separate myself from Christian's memories. "The heart was of course removed, along with the head. All the blood…" I winced as I remembered, "…all the blood had been drained out of his body, and his skin, his skin had been removed." I couldn't keep the horror off of my face and Lucien placed a pale, cold hand on my shoulder, surprisingly it was reassuring.

"Yes, Christian told me the state William was in when he found him. You said there was something he heard?"

I nodded, "He didn't see who did it but he heard something, or he remembers hearing something right before he left him. They were, uhmmmm, you know, together, afterwards, Christian left, he was in a hurry to get back to the Hive, his companion, William, was not. William was hungry and wanted to feed, Christian said that they could feed when they got back to Edwards. William didn't want to wait and told Christian that he should return without him. Christian was reluctant but understood William's hunger. Right before he left he remembers hearing a voice, another voice."

"Someone else was there?" Vampire Lucien said in a contemplative manner. I nodded.

"But the person wasn't speaking, he or she was chanting. Christian can remember the voice, he thought at first the person was singing, but the person wasn't singing the person was chanting." I was exhausted. Probing Christian's memories and then probing my memories of Christian's memories had exhausted me. I wanted to rub my eyes but knew that if I did I'd smear my carefully applied eye makeup.

"Is that all?"

"That is all he can remember, that is all I was able to get. Christian didn't think much of it. He came back to Edwards and waited for William's return. When William didn't return…" My voice trailed off, "Well you know the rest."

"Yes." Vampire Lucien regarded me intensely "What do you make of it my little Holly?"

"What?"

"What do you think?"

"You're asking me?" I was shocked. "I'm not a detective or a police person, you should go to the authorities." I was annoyed when he broke out into laughter. It was a deep, rolling sound and it moved across my skin like silk.

"I am sorry my Holly, but you are precious. So naïve. Do you truly think that the authorities would care about one dead vampire?"

"They should. The same laws that protect humans protect vampires."

"No, little Holly. The laws that protect humans are made to protect them against vampires. They care little about our kind."

"You're all legalized."

"Legal, yes. Equal, no."

I wanted to dispute what he said but I couldn't. He was right. The human authorities often did not get involved in vampire politics or the vampire community. Which was why Holders were so necessary in the vampire world. One of the exceptions, however, was 'The Savannah Slaughter.' Several years ago a group of extreme right-wingers, those who believed that vampires should be extinguished had wiped out three hole hives in Savannah. The authorities had stepped in when C.O.H.L., standing for Coalition Of Human Life, had admitted to killing the vampires and more. It seemed that C.O.H.L believed that unless you were completely, totally human (which meant you couldn't possess any inhuman powers) you weren't fit to grace the earth. They had admitted to murdering psychics, witches, or wiccans if you prefer and, of course, anyone with proven PSI abilities. Truthfully groups like C.O.H.L. scared me a lot more than the vampires, and vampires were pretty damn scary.

"What are you thinking about my Holly?"

"Just thinking how strange society is."

Vampire Lucien smiled, "It is that." He regarded me with what I now knew was fondness. "I often believe that human existence is much more complicated than that of our existence."

"How so?"

"Strangely, we exist simply. We are creatures with basic, primal urges and we sate them, satisfy them and continue on. We have laws, rules, and they are handled without question. If someone defies us, breaks a rule we punish that person swiftly, rightly. There is no 'trial' there is no democracy."

"But that in itself is a sort of lawlessness." I interjected. Lucien shook his head and regarded me with an expression much like a parent gives to a child.

"Our rules are upheld by a leader, a 'Holder.' Such hierarchy is not questioned and has always been and always will be. Why humans deal with courts and trials, prisons and penal systems have always been a source of confusion and amusement for us vampires. Justice can only be served and sentenced by a swift and merciless hand. Anything less is unjust, for anything less is weakness."

"I listen but I don't agree. Mercy is not a weakness it is a good and noble quality. To be merciful and to be able to impart mercy shows only strength of character. It is the best of human characteristics."

"Ah, there is the crux, my little Holly. It is a human characteristic. I am not and never will be human again. Those who follow me and obey me do so with the knowledge that I am stronger and more powerful than they. I do not show mercy because I do not need to. To show mercy is to show vulnerability and a Holder cannot be vulnerable." He gave me an unreadable expression "But you know this Holly you know the truth of my words. There are humans that know nothing of our world, but you, you know."

"No." I shook my head trying to block out the truth of his words

"Just because you do not wish to admit the truth to yourself, does not mean that you are any less aware of it. You are an exceptional human, my little Holly. What you are capable of is tremendous but you impede your abilities by wrapping yourself up in fear and confusion."

I was thoroughly annoyed. His words rang too true for my taste and bothered me more than I wanted him to know. I had ignored the part of me that made me different for so long now that perhaps I had even begun to believe I was normal. But the fact that I was majoring in Mysticism and that I still knew way too much about vampire politics for even my tastes was an obvious indication that I would never be normal. It seems that no matter how much you run, the demons, or in this case, the vampires, always catch up to you.

"So tell me what you see?"

"What?"

"I asked your opinion before, I am asking again, what do you think my little Holly?"

I was bone weary and mentally and physically drained. It took an enormous amount of energy to read someone, or something. If the person had half a mind and could erect half decent defenses the process was even more difficult. This evening had been trying. Vampire Christian had let me into his mind but his natural inclination and his natural defenses had not wanted to be breached. Therefore, the process of digging into his memories had been particularly thorny. What did I think? I thought that finally I had dug myself into a hole I could not get out of. I lifted my eyes to his bright green orbs and said quietly.

"I think that whatever killed your vampire is more than human, or has more than human powers." When I saw vampire Lucien nodding I continued with a little more confidence. "It's not that difficult to reach that conclusion. Your fledgling…" I stopped when vampire Lucien held up a hand.

"How did you know that Christian was a fledgling?"

I grinned at that, "You tell me that I have all these powers and then you ask me a question like that." I shrugged my shoulders before continuing. "He…he had the look of a young one. Not to mention that when I delved into his mind I was able to construct a fairly decent picture of his life, or in this case, his death. He hasn't been dead for more than, what, fifty years or so?"

Vampire Lucien nodded. Oh, you may be wondering why I keep referring to him as vampire Lucien. Well it's a classic separatist technique. If I can keep thinking of him as a vampire leader, as a Holder, then perhaps I won't be tempted to do the 'dirty deed' with him.

"Yes, Christian is a fledgling."

"Yeah I sort of figured that one out. Well, as I was saying, your fledgling heard chanting before he bailed out to return to the Hive. At the time he didn't think much of it, but I believe that's because he wasn't trained to know what to look for."

"Explain."

"Well you vamps think you're pretty much invincible." I ignored the look of pained annoyance that filtered across his beautiful previously still features. "Therefore, you are vulnerable. Often it is your ego that does the most damage. Vampire Christian didn't think anything of the chanting because there isn't anything he thinks of that is stronger or more dangerous than he is…except probably you. But, well, the truth is probably that a spell was performed, or perhaps it was a ritual. But the outcome was to bind, or immobilize your slain vampire. That is the only way I can think of that he could have been taken."

"Can you tell me what spell was performed?"

I shook my head and ran a hand through my hair. "Without seeing the site…" I shuddered "Or the body…I can't really tell you with any assurance what spell was performed. But whatever spell it was it was really powerful.

How old was Christian's companion?"

"Older than Christian by one hundred years."

"Like I said it would have had to have been a really powerful spell to have immobilized him. Now, have I answered all your questions?"

"More than adequately."

"So tit for tat."

"Pardon."

I smiled. His voice had become terribly stuffy all of a sudden, very, very British. "You told me that you had information for me."

"Ah, I wasn't sure if you were still interested. You told me yourself, you are not a detective."

"Come on, lay it on me."

"I spoke with the Holder from Charlotte, he imparted some interesting news in my direction. It seems that last year there were a couple of murders committed within the city limits of Charlotte."

"Yeah, so…"

"Do you wish to hear this or do you wish to interrupt?"

I blushed. "Sorry."

"These murders had a similar MO and the conclusion was that they were committed by the same killer. The MO is similar to your little campus murder."

"The murders were committed a year ago? And you just learned this from the vamp Holder in Charlotte now? Why didn't he let you know what was going on before, didn't he think it was important?"

"Why should he? He is the Holder for Charlotte, as I am for Edwards. He was not obligated to tell me what occurred in his city. And furthermore, it was not his concern, the victim was human, not vampire."

This put me in a fine fury "That is so like you guys, if it's not one of your own it doesn't concern you. Well here's a newsflash…you're the Holder of the damn city, the representative, everything that happens within the city concerns you, or isn't that what the council is touting these days? Do you have so little control that you can only guard your own Hive?" I was breathing hard and still not done with my tantrum when I noticed vampire Lucien beginning to glow. His body shimmered and his eyes took on a brilliant sheen. I swallowed hard. I had seen vampires glow before, I had even seen vampire Lucien glow but this time the energy around him fairly crackled.

"Are you questioning my authority?" Vampire Lucien's face shifted slowly, the transition was startling and horrifying, it was like watching a movie in slow motion. The bones in his face seemed to liquefy and melt and then reform in a terrifyingly beautiful reconstruction. What I saw next was like nothing I had ever seen before. His face elongated and his mouth stretched obscenely wide to reveal double rows of teeth, in which the incisors were wickedly sharp and appallingly long and pointed. It was like having all your worst fears confirmed all at once. This was a monster. I took a terrified step back and did my best not to flinch or wince at the gruesome sight. I knew what he was, why then did seeing it make me cringe? "Are you afraid Holly?"

"Yes." I ground out, but I'd be damned if I let him see it.

"Good, because this is the truth. What you see here is the reality. We are not human, our humanity was long lost to us." Vampire Lucien sucked in a deep breath and closed his eyes. It was like watching rippling water. That was how 'natural' how seamless the transition was from monster back into beautiful dead guy. "Do you believe the theories that we are another species all together, my little Holly?"

"I believe you act like another species, yes."

"Then believe this. Species assemble and gravitate towards others of their kind. They are not obligated to care, nor to provide for anything other than their own. It has been that way since the dawning of time. We are an odd mixture of man and beast but our code of ethics our honor and traditions sustain and nurture us. We all have authorities that we must answer to, but tell me this…is the predator to feel sorry for the prey?"

Having seen his transformation with my own eyes it was difficult to deny the 'beast' that lurked beneath his supposed calm and casual exterior. There was truly nothing left of the human that had once been within that cold, dead shell. Instead, in residence now there was a power that was bestial and foreign to me, but a tremendous power nonetheless. I grudgingly had to admit that vampire Lucien was right. Human authorities cared nothing for the vampires. Did I truly expect the vampires to care about the humans? Even with all the problems society spawned vampires and humans seemed to be able to share a fragile co-existence. Sure it was due mostly in part to the fact that humans for the most part ignored the vampires and the vampires in turn kept to their Hives. But it was an existence nonetheless.

"I am sorry, I have no right to judge you."

Vampire Lucien merely nodded his beautiful head. His face was perfectly serene now, serene and still as death. He had a small smile playing about his lips and all traces of his previous fury and anger were erased. It was totally unnerving. "But judge us you will, as we judge you."

"I can do nothing but apologize. I have been under a lot of stress lately what with exams and, well, Pamela's murder, not to mention my little indoctrination into this 'dead society' of yours. But that doesn't give me the right to preach to you."

"Again, so unusual you are."

"I'm not so unusual."

"Yes, yes you are, and at this moment very human. Only a human would apologize so very easily."

"I'll take that as a compliment."

"As you should, I value you Holly, even your humanity." His eyes glittered like twin jewels, "…Mostly your humanity."

And with those words my meeting with the Vampire Holder of Edwards was concluded.

Chapter Twelve:

There was nothing around but dust, a stack of really old books and me. I'd been here in the mystic wing of the Library for over three hours and I was exhausted. I had, however, located a fabulous volume of books by Dr. Hasaan Zuri. Three volumes dedicated solely to unraveling the mysteries of the 'Dead Sea Scrolls,' they were fascinating. I cross checked the volumes to Professor DeWitt's list of references and important notables and found that I seemed to be on the right track. In the second column of necessary information on her list was the 'Dead Sea Scrolls.' I hadn't been able to sleep, what was worse I hadn't been able to study. Since returning from my meeting with vampire Lucien I had been completely unable to focus on anything, that included school- work. Finally I had decided on immersing myself in the library to start Professor DeWitt's research, I had hopes that this would start me back on the road towards focusing on my academics.

So far I was feeling good, yeah so I hadn't been able to concentrate on my midterm studying but what I had learned so far about rituals and the 'Dead Sea Scrolls' more than made up for everything. Checking my watch I was shocked I had been in the library for so long. I gathered up my books and shoved all my lose papers into the pages. Once everything had been packed away, including my laptop, which had been a serious investment when I began College I made my way out of the library. I nodded my head and said goodnight to the security guard on duty and began to make my way across campus. I was going to have to have a serious talk with the administration about street-lights on campus, right now the vampires would have a field day it was so dark.

I had almost reached Friedmont Hall, the main campus dormitory when something caught my attention, or caught the attention of my nose. The scent was pretty subtle, but apparent nonetheless. It smelled like sulfur and the

74

wafting scent became stronger and stronger as I got closer to the dorm. That's when I noticed it, about two feet from the north side of dorm. Engraved into the pliable dirt was a large circle with an inverted pentagram. Lying twisted like a broken doll in the center was the remains of what had once been a human body. Now, there wasn't much left to identify it. I took several deep breaths and managed not to scream, although it took a great deal of strength not to do so. I was not going to hyperventilate, I had faced worse than this, okay, no, I hadn't. I had never seen a mutilated body before. I backed up doing my best not to disturb the scene and made my way to the campus emergency phone. It was strangely ridiculous that we didn't have enough campus lights but we had more than enough phones in their bright red cases. I quickly dialed campus securities number and waited for the authorities to arrive.

Detective Marcus was a giant of a man. Measuring at least six foot four with broad shoulders and tree trunks for legs all he had to do was stand there to look intimidating. Right now with pad and pencil in hand and a censuring look in his eyes he was positively frightening. I had garnered more than my fare share of strange looks. I suppose it was because I wasn't hysterical or crying. Listen, I could be hysterical at home, it wasn't acceptable to show my scared face to strangers.

Detective Marcus had surveyed the scene with a detached face and demeanor. The look in his eyes was cool and calculating and somehow I knew without reading him that this was a man, unlike me, who had seen worse. I had already given my statement to a young rookie cop when Detective Marcus strode my way. The body had long been bagged, tagged and taken away, and all that remained was the insignia in the ground and the now sickening smell of sulfur in the air. I looked around to see if the scent was affecting anyone else but me. I was startled to see that no one else seemed bothered. The sulfur was a key point I knew it was, but I couldn't yet place why it was important.

"Miss. Feather." Detective Marcus was staring at me expectantly.

"Detective."

"I'd like to ask you a couple of questions."

"That's fine, I did however give my statement to that cop over there." I pointed in the direction of the rookie who was now chatting with a cute campus security guard, one of many, who had answered the emergency call.

"Now you can give it to me." His voice was gruff, like two pieces of sandpaper rubbing against one another.

I repeated what I had told the fair-haired rookie cop and looked for any change in expression on the detective's face, there was none. Out of curiosity I let down my barriers and focused in on Detective Marcus, I was shocked to feel the definite push of a mental persuasion from him. So shocked that it must have shown on my face. For the first time in the evening Detective Marcus's expression changed. The corners of his mouth lifted slightly, into a rather sardonic smile and his eyes narrowed significantly. He regarded me through those slit eyes of his and paused before saying quietly, intently.

"I don't appreciate people trying to butt into my business."

My mouth dropped open, he knew, he knew what I was and he had repelled me. It was obvious that he was PSI talented and no ordinary detective.

"I'm sorry." I felt the heat creeping into my cheeks and knew that I had to be a lovely shade of red by now. "I really am, I don't usually read people, but, well, this is a completely strange situation for me. Again, I'm sorry."

Detective Marcus relaxed his stance and tapped his pencil against his pad. Suddenly I felt it, the slight pull in my head, the humming in my body. I gritted my teeth, took a deep breath and double fortified myself. It wasn't difficult, not really. It was like imagining yourself surrounded and locked within four wooden walls, and those four wooden walls were surrounded and locked within four concrete walls. I had a lot of practice in fortification, this wasn't anything new, however, I hated being tested and this wasn't an exception.

"You're good." Detective Marcus wiped his forehead with his hand. I noticed he was perspiring and it pleased me. If he was going to play these little games with me I hoped they wore him the hell out.

"I don't like people butting into my business either." I stared him squarely in the eyes and challenged him with a look to try it again. He surprised me by chuckling.

"Don't worry, I won't try to delve again. Once was enough, you're a steel trap, aren't you?"

"You've got to be around here."

Detective Marcus looked around the campus grounds and nodded "Must be a bitch trying to lock all those intrusive paths away while you're going to school"

"That's putting it mildly." I looked at him, he didn't look so terrifying now. "Telepathic?" I said. It was a statement not a question.

"Only a level three."

I nodded. There were eight common levels of Telepathic range. Being a level three meant that he was relatively low on the scale but still had enough ability to mentally probe, if not piece together the thoughts coherently.

"And what are you little girl?"

I fought the urge to stick my tongue out at him, now that would be inappropriate. He actually didn't look that old himself, thirty, thirty-five at the most.

"Empath." That's all I said. It was enough. His eyes widened slightly and he nodded appreciatively, at least I think it was in appreciation.

"You noticed the scent didn't you."

Now my eyes widened, it was my turn to be appreciative.

"I didn't think anyone else noticed."

"I didn't, can't smell it, but I picked up a stray thought from you when Donovan was taking your statement."

"That's impossible." I shook my head in disbelief. I did not let stray thoughts go. "You couldn't have breached me."

Detective Marcus indulged in a smile and got a cocky look on his face. I think I liked it better when he looked like the immovable mountain. "What can I say I'm good." He stared at me a moment longer before adding "You were shaken, preoccupied. I know you didn't mean to let it go, but you weren't concentrating as hard as you could. Therefore it wasn't a difficult probe."

"I can't believe you probed me." I wasn't used to people taking advantage of my mind like that, usually it was the opposite way around.

"Hey, I'm a detective kiddo. And whether you like it or not, it's a useful ability to have in my line of work."

I relaxed but I still wasn't pleased about his admission.

"Fine, you probed me."

"I want to know about the sulfur."

"What about it?"

"You actually smell sulfur?"

I wrinkled my nose "Hey, it could be something else, but it sure smells like sulfur to me."

"When did you notice the smell?"

"Actually I noticed the smell first, it was the smell that drew me over here. I smelled it a good distance away from Friedmont Hall."

"Why didn't you tell Donovan about the sulfur?" He was looking at me suspiciously and I didn't like it one bit.

"No one else seemed to notice. I didn't know if I was imagining things.

You yourself said that you couldn't smell it."

"But you can. That's what matters." He seemed deep in thought and I wondered if they were about me. "I take it that you have other PSI abilities."

"How do you know?"

"You have heightened senses, you're obviously not just Empathic, you sensed and smelled the sulfur, even I didn't notice it. You resisted a probe. I might not be that strong but I'm pretty good at what I do. What else are you?"

"I don't want to get into that now. Are you done asking me questions?"

"Why sulfur?"

"What?"

"Why use sulfur to draw the ritual circle?"

Detective Marcus wasn't an idiot. He knew that the circle was drawn in part for a ritual. He obviously had encountered such things before, and being a telepathic detective must have its up side in his line of work. But here, the telepathic detective was asking my opinion. That was twice in so many nights that someone, something, with more authority, and more power had asked my opinion in the matter of murder, and I didn't think I liked it. I wasn't Nancy Drew, and this was no novel, I was plain old Holly Anne Feather, Empath extraordinaire, EU student and reluctant murder witness. This was out of my realm.

"I don't know."

"You know."

I shook my head. "Listen, I really don't know. It's in the back of my mind somewhere, it's bothering me that I don't know what the sulfur is for, but truly I don't know." I stared at him and I knew that he didn't need to probe. He could read the truth in my eyes.

"All right. That's all I need for tonight. You should go home and get some rest, you've been through a lot."

"Gee I didn't know you cared." It came out more sarcastic than I had intended and I apologized immediately, just because I was tired and scared didn't give me the right to be rude. He didn't take offense but his parting words gave me cause to worry.

"A talent like yours could be harnessed in many ways. You might want to give some thought to which direction you'd like to take before someone chooses for you."

I was still thinking of those parting words when I climbed into bed for the night, just around the time the sun was coming up.

Chapter Thirteen:

Why are people so fascinated with death? There was no way around it. All day I had been bombarded with questions from curious students about the body I had discovered. Everyone wanted the gruesome details and seemed unperturbed about the fact that some poor student was brutally murdered not four feet away from where they were standing. This 'little' episode only confirmed what I already had decided. When I die, it's cremation for me, burn baby burn. There is no way I want someone painting a happy face on me and dressing me in my Sunday best just to be buried six feet under. Not to mention cremation is the little fail-safe against any other unorthodox events occurring, like becoming one of the legions of the undead, or perhaps even a flesh eating zombie, hey it happens, ever seen Romero's *Night of the Living Dead*? Being cremated, eliminates the possibility of people gawking at you, no one finds ashes exciting.

Professor DeWitt was more than sympathetic to the fact that I didn't have my homework done. In fact she felt terrible that it was her research that had kept me late at the library. I assured her that it wasn't her fault that someone had mutilated a body and nearly left it at my feet. All the same she had me promise that I wouldn't go to the library until the case was solved, or until midterms were over, whichever came first. Truthfully that suits me just fine, I don't want to pass Friedmont Hall anytime in the near future. Not that I think lightning strikes twice, but I'm not taking any chances. Dead bodies aren't really my forte, now open minds…well that's a whole different story.

It hit me sometime between English and Voodoo 101, the answer to the question I had been asking myself all day. Why was sulfur used in the ritual slaying? I could have kept the information to myself for a while, or at least until after classes but somehow I felt it couldn't wait, and somehow I knew that Detective Marcus would gladly see me locked up if I didn't call to impart the news to him. Finding a pay phone nearby, no I don't own a cell phone, who wants an extra phone bill? I called Detective Marcus's direct line. After two rings a deep, curt voice answered

"Marcus."

"Detective its Holly Anne Feather, from last night."

"Yeah I remember you Miss. Feather. What can I do for you?"

"I have something to tell you."

"Yeah?"

"It's about the sulfur…" Silence met me on the other end and I tensely waited for him to say something. When the silence stretched out for over a minute I plowed on "Are you there Detective or should I try ESP?" I let out an audible sigh when an answering chuckle resonated from the phone.

"Can you come in Miss Feather?"

"I have classes now."

"When are you finished?"

"Not until six today."

"Do you know where Espresso World is?"

I rolled my eyes. Any self-respecting college student knew where the nearest coffee joint was. "Uh huh."

"Is that a yes?"

"Uh huh, I mean yes." I knew he couldn't see me frown on the other end of the phone but I wished he could, who did he think he was anyway, my mother?

"Meet me there at six fifteen." He hung up the phone and I heard the disconnect signal ringing in my ear.

"Ah, yeah, and you have a nice day too." Boy somebody woke up on the wrong side of the bed. Or perhaps it was some unwritten rule; all Detectives must be grouchy and curt. I stood frowning at the phone for a couple more minutes before I realized that I was late for class.

At six thirty I walked into Espresso World and ordered myself a double espresso with a shot of caramel flavoring. I was just paying when a voice over my shoulder said, "You're late."

I didn't turn around just fished out the remainder of my money. "Yeah by fifteen minutes, you do realize it takes fifteen minutes just to navigate the halls after class right?" I finished paying and swung around, not at all surprised to see Detective Marcus glaring at me, actually he was glaring down at me.

"Ever heard of the phone?"

"You were already here, and I don't have a cell."

Now it was Detective Marcus's turn to look shocked, "You don't have a cell phone? What sort of modern girl doesn't own a cell phone?"

"Oh for Pete's sake I don't own a cell phone because I don't want to pay two darn phone bills. And would you stop making me feel like I'm twelve years old." I gritted my teeth when he merely grinned at me.

"Am I doing that?"

"Yeah, you keep calling me kiddo, and kid and *girl*."

"Well you are."

"Even so, you don't have to make me feel that way."

He brushed me off and started walking towards a table near the far window. I had no choice but to follow him feeling extremely inane and very young. When we were both seated Detective Marcus started right in.

"So, what was it you had to tell me?"

"Demons."

"What?"

"It's about Demons."

"Goddamn it." Detective Marcus ground out and I nodded

"That's about right."

"Shit, I fucking hate Demons."

"Well I don't have a lot of experience with them, Ghouls yes…" I shuddered, remembering how I had almost become a late meal for one so many years ago "Demons no."

"So what about the Demon?"

"That's what the sulfur was for, to bind the Demon to the ritual spot. The ancients believed that sulfur could bind the summoned Demon to the spot it was called to with sulfur. That is why I was having so much trouble recalling what the sulfur was for, I kept thinking it was used to ward something away, to keep it out, but it was being used to keep something in, the Demon." I smiled triumphantly, somehow feeling flushed with the success of my knowledge, that was until I saw the grim expression on Detective Marcus's face and wiped the smile off of mine. He looked like a piece of carved granite, hard, stoic and completely still. His eyebrows were drawn down and his forehead was knitted with creases, probably caused by worry. His mouth was one tight, grim line and his hands were unconsciously tapping the table before him. He looked up suddenly as if just remembering I was there and gave me an impossible to read look before speaking.

"You're certain?"

"About the sulfur?"

"Yeah."

"As certain as I can be. Like I said, I don't have any experience with an actual Demon, never encountered one, but I know my research, and I know my history…sulfur is commonly used to bind a summoned Demon, just as salt is commonly used to ward off evil."

"Ever used salt?" Detective Marcus asked veering off subject. I stared at him from over the rim of my coffee mug and nodded curtly. "What were you warding off?"

"I told you…"

"No you told me why it's used, you didn't tell me what you, yourself were warding off at the time."

"It doesn't have anything to do with what we're discussing now."

"No it doesn't, but it does have something to do with who you are, I like to know who I'm working with Miss. Feather."

"We're not working together."

"It rather looks as if we are."

"You've got to be kidding Detective." I laughed nervously, "Why on earth would you want to work with a University student. Not to mention your Captain can't possibly have given you clearance to discuss this case with me"

"Actually she did. Actually, she would like you to work with me towards solving this case."

I think I spit my coffee out then. Or at least it looked that way when Detective Marcus took a napkin and deftly swiped some liquid off of his cheek. I wiped my mouth not caring if I was discreet or not and gave him a wide-eyed, horrified stare. Was he kidding? He had to be kidding.

"You're not kidding are you?"

"Nope."

My only consolation was that Detective Marcus didn't look any happier than I was to know that I was supposed to work with him.

"You can't possibly think I'm going to be your…uh, partner?"

"Hell no."

I glared at him. "You don't have to be so emphatic about it."

"Well you're only a kid, and you have no experience in law enforcement. What I meant to say was that you're supposed to uh, do research for us."

"Research?" I didn't like the sound of that, why was I always stuck doing research for people?

"Well, think of yourself as an informant, sort of an informant." He rubbed his eyes wearily and frowned deeper. "Sorry, this isn't coming out the way I want. Here's the deal. Besides me, there isn't any other PSI ability on the force. Most of the Edwards Police Force has never seen a vampire, let alone encountered a Demon before. They don't know shit about the supernatural. When I was transferred here it was an adjustment."

I knew I was staring almost rudely at him, but I couldn't help it. I couldn't believe that he was revealing so much to me. Then again, he probably didn't want me rooting around his brain for the information he could impart to me by tongue.

"Transferred from where?" I asked

"Chicago."

"Oh my…"

"Yeah you said it. Anyway, like I said, it was an adjustment. My Captain had been briefed on my abilities. It was actually why she had requested me. Edwards is small but has a decent size Police force, but because it's not a city they've never really thought about integrating."

I nodded, encouraging him to continue. He did. "I'm the first Detective with paranormal abilities and frankly it scares the rest of the men to all Hell, personally I think the Captain regards me with a little bit of distaste as well, but she knew that it was time to integrate and she knew that her force would be 'looked' at if she didn't get with the times, so to speak. Back to the subject on hand, you." He looked at me intently while he said this, "I've seen some pretty horrible shit. Chicago was the playground for the undead from eighty nine to around ninety five."

This I knew. It was common knowledge that Chicago had lax laws when it came to vampires. But it had been seriously bad in the late eighties to the early nineties when more humans turned up dead than the census could make sense of. This had forced Congress to look long and hard at the dilapidated city. And although they had modified their laws and tacked on additional 'Acts', much like the 'Invitation Act' it had not changed the fact that the vamps found Chicago quite homey, and very much to their tastes.

"I can't tell you how many vamps we killed on a daily…" He laughed and continued, "Excuse me, nightly basis. And of course psychics, witches, and the odd sorcerer or two came with the territory. But the Demon was the worst."

"So you've had experience with Demons before."

"Yeah." He pulled out a pack of cigarettes from his inside pocket and began to light one up when he asked "You don't mind if I smoke, do you" By this time he was already taking a puff.

"You know those things will kill you."

"Yeah, and so will a lot of other things, probably faster than these will." He took another drag and regarded me through now solemn eyes. "I wouldn't drag you into this goddamn mess for anything, you're only a kid." He held up a hand when I would have argued and continued. "You are. Listen, the point is this. I've shot them up, and cut them down but the fact remains that I know jack shit about them. Oh, I can kill them easily enough, but I don't know the rudimentary things…you know, like that sulfur shit."

"So you need me…so you can pick my brain?" I tried not to laugh at the irony of the situation.

"Basically, yeah." He cracked his knuckles and I winced. "You're different kid, I knew it the moment I met you."

"It's the eyes, I know it's the eyes." I said half jokingly. He took it as such.

"No, it's not the eyes, although your eyes are creepy."

"Ha, very funny." I knew my eyes were creepy. My mother had spent years tell me so. They were a strange half gray, half violet color, which was completely abnormal. They grew a deeper purple when I was upset or angry and faded to a light gray when I was calm and collected, it was completely creepy. I didn't blame him for thinking so. I just didn't like hearing it said out loud.

"You're an Empath. I've never met an Empath, no, not even in Chicago. Telepaths we have an abundance of. Level ones, up to level fives, I've encountered my fare share of them. They run everything from pretzel stands to psychic phone lines. But Empaths are different, and you know it." Detective Marcus was now staring at me so intently I was sure he could probably count the number of pores on my face. "You can feel, not just find what a person is thinking. You experience it with them, live the moment. Your ability allows you to become whomever you read, more or less."

"Listen Detective I live with it, I know what I can do, I don't need a lesson here." He ignored me and pushed forward.

"But you're special, it's obvious you have heightened abilities, your awareness level is almost off the charts. It can only mean one thing…you have more PSI abilities than you are sharing. I want to know what they are."

"Why?" I shrugged my shoulders "I'm nothing special Detective, I don't care what you say. I'm a student, that's all. So I'm an Empath, you're a Telepath, so what?? What difference does it make to you? I've already told you what I know. You know I'll help you however I can. I don't like the thought of a Demon on the loose anymore than you do. But one PSI ability or more isn't going to tip the scales any, and it doesn't help this investigation"

"I'll decide what helps or doesn't help this investigation. I could just look you up in the database."

Now I was getting angry. I hated mind probes, I didn't like this any better. He had no right to demand anything of me. I didn't work for him, I didn't work for his damn Captain and I didn't have to answer any of his stupid questions. So why was I still here? I couldn't possibly have a guilty conscience. It wasn't my fault that the Edwards' Police Force was practically an antiquity, that they didn't even have the sense to hire one Wiccan to help them with basic knowledge of spells and rituals. Yeah, it wasn't my fault. I stood up and looked down my nose at him, trying for my best haughty expression.

"So then look me up in your database Detective. What with your abilities you might even find what you're looking for by the next millennia." I tossed my hair over my shoulder and strode right out of the coffee shop content that I had almost mastered the bitch routine, now if only I didn't feel so guilty about it.

Chapter Fourteen:

I was halfway through a pint of Ben and Jerry's 'Rocky Road' ice cream when there was a knock on my door. I looked up from my English text-book debating whether or not I was going to answer. Sooner or later whomever was at the door would get tired and go away, right? I went back to trying to memorize all the obscure footnotes at the bottom of Beowulf but the knocking continued.

"Ahhhhh, can't a girl get any peace around here?" I was mumbling under my breath as I went to answer the door. I hadn't believed there would come a time when I was actually looking forward to my schoolwork, but that time had definitely come. After, Demons, detectives, slayed students, and vampires I was just craving normalcy…well speak of the devil. I shook my head, telling myself over and over what a bad decision it would be to open the damn door, but when was I ever known for making good decisions.

There he was, looking just as delicious and just as dangerous as ever. He was standing there in all that beautiful dead flesh…Vampire Lucien. He looked gorgeous, but then, was there a time when he didn't look gorgeous? He should come with a warning label. This evening found him decked out in an entirely black ensemble. His black shirt fit him to a T. The lace was gathered all up the front and bunched in a careless manner that somehow managed to look both reckless and arranged at the same time. The high collar accentuated his slender neck and the wide sleeves drew attention to his delicate hands, and tapered fingers. His legs were encased in black velvet pants, which were tight as all hell and unbelievably shiny and smooth looking. To finish it off he had curled, yeah, curled, his hair and it fell in soft loose curls down his back. I just shook my head in bewilderment and, lets face it, a little awe.

"Do you own anything that doesn't look like its been pilfered from a costume shop?"

"Don't you like my outfits?"

"I think you look like a cross between D'Artagnan, from *The Three Musketeers* and some Raver chick I met freshman year."

"Is that bad?" Vampire Lucien looked a little confused and I couldn't help but laugh a little at his expense. I mean, come on, how many times can one laugh at the Holder? Or should I say, *safely*, laugh at the Holder.

"No, not bad, just...unusual."

"I am glad you like my clothes Holly."

I frowned at him, "I didn't say I liked your clothes."

"No you didn't say it, but it was what you were thinking." Before I could contradict him he added, "I can see it in your face Holly...You are not guarded tonight."

I didn't contradict him this time. He was right. I wasn't guarded tonight, I was tired, but hey, what else was new. I hadn't had so much activity in my life since my ninth grade dance recital, when I was the sugar plum fairy in the very, very amateur production of The Nutcracker.

"So what, you waiting for an invitation?" I was grouchy and I wasn't in the mood to play nice to the vamp Leader. He had been invited before. He didn't need a second invitation to enter my domicile. I watched him smile, that eerily erotic smile which curled my toes and made my heart beat a little faster. He gracefully dropped into a half bow that was part mocking and part pure old world courtesy. He glided, oh yeah, glided into my apartment and stood stock still in my living room. I eyed him wearily, whatever he wanted I could pretty much assure I wasn't up to it.

"You look tired my little Holly flower."

I scrunched up my nose, I didn't like this endearment any better then the others he had tried on me.

"I am tired, so can we cut to the chase?"

"Pardon?"

"What do you want?"

He smiled widely, this time his fangs peeked out and I watched in fascination as my overhead light caught their tips. "Does this not strike you as deja vu?"

"What?"

"I believe you have asked me this question before, my little Holly."

"Yeah, and I believe you've dodged it before, buster." I groaned, "I really, really am tired. And I have an entire four more chapters to read of Beowulf."

Vampire Lucien's eyes gleamed and his smile, if possible, grew even wider. I tilted my head to one side studying him curiously. He seemed, almost, enthusiastic.

"Are you reading it in Old English, or perhaps Finnish?"

Great, he's a literate vampire. "Oh yeah, right, whatever, Finnish? Are you out of your mind? Listen, I'm lucky I can keep all the characters straight in my head, there are like, thousands."

"Closer to hundreds my little Holly."

I rolled my eyes, "Yeah, who's counting?" I shook my head in disbelief when I saw his face, "You're kidding, right? You didn't count, did you?"

"I have a lot of time on my hands." Vampire Lucien said this with no change in his expression

"Obviously. Jeez. Okay, so what do you want? We've established you know your Beowulf, and you definitely aren't here to help me with my homework, so what's up?"

"I could help you with your homework, my little Holly. I could help you with a lot of things." The cadence of his voice changed instantaneously and it flowed over me like silk and within me like fine wine. It sent shivers down my spine and caused the hairs on my arms and the back of my neck to stand on end.

"Now you stop that right now. Really! That's all I need, a horny vampire on my hands" I ignored his bellow of laughter and the following suggestive comment. "Please…" I hated sounding so desperate or so needy, but the truth was that I was desperate, desperate for study time and a good nights sleep. I was surprised to see vampire Lucien's expression sober so quickly. But then again, it isn't surprising, they're vampires, they can move quicker than human eyes, and that goes for their faces too.

"Again, I am sorry Holly." Vampire Lucien sighed and a lock of deep red hair fell into his face. I fought the urge to reach out and push it back. A deep flush stained my cheeks when I saw his eyes and the hint of smile on his face. He knew what I was thinking, again. "I seem to always be apologizing around you, Holly." This time his expression was unreadable and his stance stiff. "You should know that I do not do that…apologize."

"Ah, yeah, somehow I knew that already." I tucked a couple of stray hairs behind my ears, for some reason every time I was in his presence I felt like a complete hag. "Lucien…" I said his name quietly, without the tag on that I usually added to separate myself from my feelings for him, my very complicated feelings for him.

"What is it Holly flower?" His eyes grew deeper, and his pupils seemed to grow enormous as I slowly swayed forward. When I was flush against his body I stretched up on my tiptoes. I moved my mouth until it was a mere inch from his perfectly sculpted ear. I felt his body tighten and saw him shiver as my warm breath wafted over him. I leaned even closer and said.

"Don't call me Holly flower." I moved back quickly and watched as his face registered first shock, then obvious glee.

"Would you prefer I call you something else? Perhaps I should call you little one, or are you someone who likes to be called darling?"

"Holly will do just fine."

"But, darling, there are so many fine endearments…so many ways to describe you."

"Jeez, it's not too hard to remember, this isn't brain surgery. Just call me Holly." I looked at him through hostile eyes and wasn't amused when he laughed.

"As you wish."

"Okay, so we've wasted, what, uh, half an hour with these no-so-pleasant, pleasantries. Can we get to the point already? Why are you here? And don't try to give me any of that bullshit about coming to see my radiant face and all that crap. Why are you really here?"

"For one, to see your radiant face. It is the truth, whether you wish to hear it or not."

I was totally tuning him out. "And secondly, to tell you that I wish you to come and examine a scene with me."

"Oh no. No, no, no!" I threw my hands up into the air and began to pace furiously around my living room. I knew I looked like a harridan and I didn't care, I was totally fed up with this. At this rate I was going to get kicked out of school and end up having to beg for a living. "Forget about it. I refuse. What are you going to do, eat me?" I continued to babble endlessly "I'm sick to death with all of this. First that nonsense at the damn club, then you abduct me, oh let's not forget the part where you hit me over my damn head, I think I still have the knot. Then I'm discovering bodies left and right. Being questioned by the police, dodging Demons and possible witches, or sorcerers, you take your pick. I haven't had good nights sleep since I've met you and I have poor skin tone and limp hair due to all the stress and long nights. I even have a zit, I never get zits…are you laughing at me? Don't you dare laugh at me."

I began to wag my finger at him and realized what a stupid thing that was to do. Didn't want him to get any ideas. I stomped my foot, I knew I looked foolish and was acting possibly half my age but I was at the end of my rope. He was actually laughing at me, the big, bad vampire was practically rolling on the floor he was laughing so hard. Large, fat, blood red tear drops ran down his face and dropped down to stain my cream colored carpeting. He was wiping the tears away with a lace handkerchief that he had pulled from who knows where and was presently staring at me with a mirth filled face.

"Precious, you are precious."

"And you are a royal pain in the butt" I ignored his indignant look, could Vamp Leaders get indignant, of course they could, they had centuries on their side, bet no one had defied them in all that time.

"Do you remember our deal Holly?"

"Of course, do you?"

"But of course."

"Then you'll remember I told you about midterms, I only have a half a week left to study!"

"And you'll remember I told you I would do my best to accommodate these little exams of yours. But you see I do not make the murders…I merely investigate them, it is my duty as a Holder to do so" He grew very serious. "I do not take kindly to those who slaughter on my lands. My people and my holdings are mine to command and do with as I so desire."

"More murder." I felt myself growing colder and colder. Within moments my hands felt like blocks of ice and my toes were following suit. I might know an inexcusable amount about the supernatural and the undead but everything I know is confined to books and my endless years of study. Nothing I had ever done had prepared me for my first hand confrontation with death and dismemberment. Oh, and the gross out factor of blood draining and removed skin. It didn't help that I had kept myself locked away from this for so long. Oh perhaps is had helped at the time, but I was learning, and learning fast that you can't run from who you are, and if you do you're in for a very rude awakening.

"Holly, my Holly flower. Are you all right? You look so very far away."

I shook my head, I would not cry. I was stronger than this. It wasn't so long ago that I had stood up to Detective Marcus and told him just what he could do with his high handed demands. I gathered myself together and held my fears back, there is nothing the dead like more than fear, except for a pint of blood.

"You said there was a scene."

"Yes, and you said you had encountered death."

"Yeah, he's standing right in front of me."

"That is not so funny, my Holly flower. Now tell me what you meant."

I knew by the look in his eyes that he would not be swayed. He would stand here until the sun swallowed up the sky if that is how long it took me to tell him what he wanted to know. And lets not forget that he had all the time in the world. I sighed and haltingly told him about the body I had discovered on campus. I explained about the circle, and the pentagram and added the information about the sulfur I had discovered. I tried to gauge his expression but there was nothing to gauge. I let go the remaining resistance in my mind and slowly, gently tried to breach his fortified mental pathway. At first I felt nothing. Then I felt the slow ebb and flow of what could only be described as tightly coiled emotions. But do the dead have emotions, can they? That was certainly something I didn't want to try to understand, not right now at least.

"You were probing me?" Vampire Lucien's voice was now taut.

"I was." Why deny it?

"Did you learn anything interesting?" There was the silky edge of anger to his voice.

"Nothing worth sharing." I waited to see if he would say something, when he said nothing I felt my body relax slowly. But I was definitely not completely relaxed. It isn't such a good idea to ever relax fully in front of a vampire.

"You will stay out of my mind…unless I give you permission." His voice was iron, and I found myself nodding quickly. It had been rude, the least I could do was to try to make amends.

"Okay, so let's go."

"Now?"

"Isn't that what you wanted? You wanted me to come and see the scene with you. So, okay, we'll go." I started towards the door when a cool, bloodless hand reached out and touched my bare shoulder. "Uh, yeah, what?"

"Are you not forgetting something, little one?"

"What? And don't call me little one." I checked my hair, messy, but all right. I was wearing a perfectly acceptable tank top and my boxers were brand new, no holes or tears…wait, boxers? I groaned and refused to look at his face and see that tell tale 'I told you so expression.' "Okay give me five minutes and I'll be right out."

"I could help you change, my little Holly."

"No thanks." I glared at him. "I'd say make yourself comfortable, but I wouldn't mean it." I left the laughing vampire in the living room while I went to change into something that wouldn't produce stares when I went outside or have me arrested for indecent exposure.

Chapter Fifteen:

It was shockingly sadistic, and eerily familiar. I examined the circle that had been dug out of the ground and the inverted pentagram, which was carved into its center. The smell of sulfur lingered in the air and this time made my eyes water. I accepted the monogrammed handkerchief that vampire Lucien waved in my face and swiped my eyes with it. I leaned closer to the ground ignoring the pain in my head and the watering of my eyes and reached down to touch the soil. I recoiled instantly the second my finger touched the surface. My hand throbbed from where the small patch of skin had touched the circle. I looked down and grimaced, my hand was already swelling, the throbbing was getting worse and it looked as if my skin was peeling. I clutched my hand and continued to study the scene. It was horrible and yet also fascinating. This time there was no mutilated body to distract me from my observations and I didn't feel the need to vomit, at least not yet.

"Show me your hand, Holly."

"It's nothing, don't worry about it." I said distractedly as I moved around the wide circle. This circle was definitely bigger than the one I had found on campus, why was that? Was it the size of the sacrifice that determined the size of the circle, or perhaps it was the size of what was being called forth…I didn't like that idea one bit.

"Hey…" I bit back a curse when vampire Lucien grabbed my hand and began to study it. I thought about trying to yank it free, but what would the point be? He could lift a bus, or rip open a metal door, holding my hand in place was ridiculously easy. No point in struggling with something that has teeth like a steel trap and can lift small vehicles.

"Burned, you've been burned," he hissed, his eyes glowed and his fangs appeared. I hid my mounting anxiety and tried to smile.

"It's nothing, really, I hardly feel it."

"What caused this?" He was still holding my hand and staring at me with blood filled eyes. I could almost taste, scent the change in him. He was furious.

"The circle. The sulfur. I should have realized, it's my fault, really, for being so stupid."

"Tell me."

"The sulfur was to keep whatever was summoned within the confines of the circle. But it was also a ward against intruders." I shook my head in amazement. If it weren't so psychotic I could almost be impressed. "Whoever did this has an amazing amount of power. A double ward, one to keep in and one to keep out, it's genius really."

"And it was the sulfur that burned you."

"Yeah, usually it couldn't do that. But like I said, in this case it is different. The sorcerer obviously thought of something I didn't…jeez, a double ward." I continued to stare at the circle.

"A sorcerer, is that what caused this then?"

I shrugged, "It's the most common theory. Usually it's the sorcerers who work with Demons. For some reason no one else has a reason to summon one, nor the capacity to keep one in line. Demons are really, really difficult to control…" I swallowed and then said quietly "Or kill."

"Yes, I am aware of that Holly."

"You've, uh, encountered a Demon before?"

"Unfortunately"

"What, uh, happened?" I began regretting asking the question the moment vampire Lucien got that scary, thoughtful look on his face.

"It was quite a long time ago…If I recall correctly, the Mansidian demon took out two entire villages before it was…contained."

"Contained?"

"Yes. I do not believe it was destroyed. A local coven bound the Demon to the earth and kept it there, I believe so they would have it at their disposal if the need ever arose for such a creature again. They were not the ones who summoned it, but they saw an opportunity and they took it. In the interim they kept it from eating any more villagers."

"I can't believe they didn't kill it, you didn't kill it."

Vampire Lucien tossed me a hard look and then turned thoughtful again, it seemed as if he were deciding whether or not to tell me something.

"We cannot kill demons, Holly"

"What?"

"We haven't the necessary, equipment, to kill a demon. Hurt, yes, but kill, no." He watched me and took in the filtering expressions on my face. I thought for a moment long and hard. All my conclusions were disturbing. One conclusion was that vampires couldn't kill demons because they didn't have souls. But if they didn't have souls…what animated them during the nighttime hours? Another conclusion I drew from what he said was that perhaps vampires couldn't kill demons because they were a like being? Didn't my mother always say that like attracts like? Not that I think anything my mother said has any truth to it, she was always full of shit. But what if vampires can't kill demons because they are made from the same source of evil? What then? Staring into vampire Lucien's beautiful deep green eyes I didn't even want to try to process that thought. If he was the source of all-evil and I was consorting (and, okay, lusting, a little, uh, a lot) with the source of all-evil, what the hell did that make me? God help me.

"So you see now why I didn't, couldn't kill the demon." Vampire Lucien said, suddenly breaking the silence. I didn't answer, I couldn't. "But I remember, even after all these years, the destruction and the carnage it wrought. Even a vampire could do no worse."

I wasn't sure how much of that I believed. But after seeing the look on both Detective Marcus's face and vampire Lucien's face when they spoke of the Demon perhaps I should begin believing and fast. What the hell, and it really was hell, had I gotten myself into?

"Where's the body?" I asked, changing the subject

"It was disposed of."

"You messed with a scene?" I saw his disbelieving look and sighed. Of course he had messed with the scene. Vampires, no matter how mainstream they were nowadays, still didn't broadcast their activities. There was still a great deal of mystery and an enormous amount of privacy required in the lives of the undead. Over the centuries vampires had gotten better and better at covering up their shady, uh, dealings i.e. murders. If there had been a body here, and I was sure there had been, of course vampire Lucien, the Holder, would not have wanted it left out in the open where any hiker or camper might discover it. It would obviously draw too much attention to the supernatural, and raise questions better left unanswered.

"So what did you do with the body?"

"Do you truly wish to know?"

I didn't hesitate, "No."

"I thought not. Suffice to say, the body was found much in the same condition as Christian's companion, William. It was mutilated, of course, and the blood was drained completely." He frowned, "But this time it was found lying in the center of this accursed circle."

"Like the body found on campus." I murmured.

"Yes, but this victim was vampire."

I nodded. I was becoming less and less surprised as the days went on. "So, we have two vampire victims and two human victims."

"You have had only one human victim, my Holly."

I ignored the my part and continued "Pamela Courtland and then Portia Whitney."

"But this first human you speak of was not killed in the same manner as the three other victims."

"No, true, there wasn't a ritual…one that we could see. But she had massive blood loss. And you, yourself said that a vampire would not, uh, waste a victim on a strangulation."

Vampire Lucien nodded his agreement but still looked pensive. "It is as I said, we do not strangle our prey."

I was beginning to hate that word, prey.

"So what we're dealing with isn't a vampire. Okay, we've figured that much out. First off a vampire wouldn't strangle his or her victims. Secondly, there have been two vampire victims. Vampires don't kill vampires, do they?" I didn't like showing my lack of knowledge, but in this area I wasn't sure.

"Nay, we do not kill…our kind. However, however, exceptions are made."

I decided to ignore that last bit.

"So, what we probably have here is one pissed off sorcerer, or some such powerful human."

"It sounds feasible."

"So glad you agree." I sighed, "So now what are you going to do about it?"

"Me, Holly? Why would you think I would do anything about this little situation? Perhaps now that I know what the situation is I will decide to let it be. What is a little 'life' measured against a lot of death?"

It took me several moments to decide if he was serious or not.

"You're the Holder. Your Hive is all-important to you. And you reign in Edwards" I didn't like to admit it, but he did. He was after all the damn Holder. "So, yeah, what are you going to do about it?"

Vampire Lucien chuckled and nodded his head. "You are correct. I cannot let the situation, as it now is, stand. I will decide what is to be done. You, little Holly, have been most helpful, indeed, I would like to press upon you the possibility of your changing vocations, and locations."

"Huh?"

"You are presently a very overworked student. Your powers are such that you could do much with them, you could go very far, my little Holly Flower. If you would but consider coming with me, living with me, working with me, for me…" He left the rest unsaid but it was all implied. I glared at him.

"No frigging way!"

"Your language Holly."

"Fuck that. No way am I dropping out of school to become your little wind up toy." Ick, gross, live in the vampire vault and put on 'shows' like some trained monkey.

"Ah, Holly Flower, it was but a suggestion."

"Yeah, a really, really sucky one." I shuddered again just thinking about it. "So, no more suggestions all right?"

"If you wish."

"Yeah" I took one more look around the scene and could feel chills, actual chills rushing up and down my spine. "I need to go home now." I could feel bile rushing up my throat and I fought valiantly not to hurl.

"You are not feeling well Holly?"

"No, I'm definitely not feeling well." I couldn't help but imagine, and feel how horribly the victim had died. That's another downer about being an Empath. I can recreate scenes in my mind. It's like being a profiler but without the added benefit of detachment. Yeah, I was definitely not feeling well.

"Home, I need to go home now." My mind was being bombarded with violent images. I felt like I was being nuked with an overload of information, all of it bad. Feeling the ground spinning beneath my feet I swayed and reached out my hand. Vampire Lucien accessed the situation quickly and ignoring my protests swept me up easily within his arms.

"Shhhhh, I am going to take you home Holly flower. It was wrong to keep you out here so long."

"But…" I tried to form a coherent thought but could hardly keep my eyes open. My head felt like it was being trampled over by a herd of buffalo and the migraine was only getting worse. "I…don't…need…your…"

"Help?" Vampire Lucien placed a gentle, cold kiss on my forehead and murmured "You will have my help whether you wish it or not. Now, rest, Holly flower, rest."

I couldn't help but do what he said. My eyes felt heavy and my head hurt.

I was only going to sleep for a moment, and when I woke up I was going to have to tell him again how much I hated that endearment.

It was dark and something soft and smooth feathered over my cheek. I turned to my side and encountered two beady eyes staring at me. My mouth opened up in a scream, which died suddenly when I realized that it was only Bunny my stuffed rabbit. Burrowing deeper into my down comforter I realized that I was most certainly back in my apartment, in my own bed. I felt another feather brush my cheek and I flicked it away, a little annoyed. Perhaps it was time to fluff my coverlet. When feathers continued to rein down on me I reached over to my bedside table to turn on my light. What greeted my eyes had me gaping like a schoolgirl. There were orchids, orchids everywhere. My bed, my pillows my floor were strewn with multi-colored orchid petals. On my window seat were five, no, six full orchid plants in purple, pink and white. The feathers I had thought were tickling my face were actually petals. I sat staring at my bedroom in complete, and utter shock. I had never seen anything like this before. On my bedside table was a huge orchid plant, it was a light violet shade and the flowers drooped down, full and graceful. I saw a shockingly red card with bold black lettering perched in front of it and reached over to pick it up. The message was simple; *Flowers, for a flower. This one reminded me of your eyes. Dinner with me on Friday, I shall have someone fetch you. – Lucien.* How had he known orchids were my favorite flower? And I hoped that he didn't think I was going to be the appetizer. I knew that I should be shocked and outraged that he had taken such liberties. Tucked me in, scattered my room with flowers and had the gall to tell me that I was having dinner with him. I knew I should feel outraged, but all I felt was flushed and a little excited. When was the last time I had an actual date with a vampire? Never. And did I have the nerve to go through with it? You'd better believe it.

Chapter Sixteen:

Professor DeWitt was particularly bright eyed this afternoon. Her complexion was flawless and her cheeks rosy, her smile was contagious. She had a light step and perky voice, and was at this moment describing the necessary ingredients to have by your side in an exorcism. The pool was going fast and furious and was now six to one odds in favor of the fact that DeWitt had gotten laid. I rolled my eyes and ignored the whispers and the money changing hands. I didn't have any use for these childish antics and I most certainly wasn't going to participate in some stupid bet. However, Professor DeWitt was in a surprisingly good mood this afternoon. She couldn't have missed the laughter and note exchange in the back of the room but she was obviously choosing to ignore such facts, something that she never did. Her lecture was just as organized and prepared as ever but her mind seemed to be somewhere else, perhaps she *had* gotten laid.

Something hit the back of my neck and fell to the floor. I looked down and saw a piece of eraser at my feet. Turning my head to one side I saw Ryan's smiling face beaming at me. I pointed to the eraser and then in his direction and tilted my head, he nodded and I rolled my eyes, mouthing, *really mature*. He grinned and I grinned back. Why was it that every time I saw Ryan Maloney's smiling face I felt sixteen again? Professor DeWitt's singsong voice interrupted my thoughts.

"So, y'all can leave."

I looked around to see if the rest of the class was as surprised as I was, Professor DeWitt never, absolutely never let us out early. It was one of her pet peeves, teachers who released their class before the assigned time. Sure enough my fellow students were as stupefied as I was. We all sat there like zombies until Professor DeWitt's tinkling laughter rang through the room.

"Really, go, before I change my mind."

You didn't have to tell us twice. We raced from our seats and rushed the door. I think I stepped on someone's toe and perhaps jabbed an elbow into someone's eye in my hurry to make it out of the class.

"Hey, hey, Holly."

I knew that voice. "Ryan."

"Hi, wasn't that weird."

I nodded, I knew what he was talking about and I agreed. "I don't think Professor DeWitt has ever let a class out early. She's like some programmed robot. And what was with the Suzy Sunshine routine in there?"

"I know." He looked pleasantly bewildered. "I've never seen her so happy before. Did you put money down?"

"That's totally disgusting Ryan" I screwed up my face and shook my head.

"Hey," he shrugged his shoulders, "what can you do, it's a guy thing"

"Well it's a stupid guy thing. I can't believe you would bet on whether or not Professor DeWitt is getting…" The words stuck in my throat.

"Uh, if she has a gentleman friend?"

I liked how he phrased it better.

"Yeah."

"Well, I've never seen DeWitt so jovial before…either she's up for a grant or she's seeing someone"

I nodded…but somehow thinking of DeWitt with a boyfriend seemed…wrong. What? Professors didn't deserve a love life? I guess it was just that she had always seemed so coolly reserved before. And I had definitely never seen her with anyone, although how much time did I spend around DeWitt out of class and off campus?

"So how much did you put down" I asked with a sly smile and resigned sigh.

"Only twenty."

"*Only* twenty?"

"Yeah, hey, Rogers put down fifty." Ryan let out a laugh and then looked at me with those incredible baby blues of his. He was such a cutey; even his eyes seem to smile. They crinkled up in the corners and he had honest to god dimples. Who had dimples these days? I swallowed hard and closed my eyes. I could feel my temple throbbing with the weight of his projections. Today the thoughts were coming in my direction particularly strongly and I had to smooth over another layer of mental fortification to keep myself from eves dropping in his mind. "You all right?" he asked.

I nodded, "Fine, sorry about that, slight headache." I smiled at him and tossed my hair carelessly over my shoulder in a practiced flirtatious move. It worked. His eyes followed the movement intently. He was still looking at my hair when he spoke.

"I would really like to see you again Holly." He moved his attention to my face and looked deeply into my eyes. I felt my belly quiver and flutter. "I'd really like to take you out for dinner on Friday evening if you're free."

I began to nod and then suddenly remembered my previous 'engagement.'

"I'm sorry Ryan, I can't on Friday. I...I already have plans." I was flattered by the look of genuine disappointment that filtered over his face.

"Oh, well that's all right. How about Saturday?"

Saturday was completely okay, no vampire engagements on Saturday. "I'd love to go out to dinner with you on Saturday Ryan."

"Great, that's great." He flashed me those million dollar pearly whites of his and I tried not to swoon. "Eight o'clock?"

"Eight's fine."

"Okay, I'll call you later?"

More talk time with Ryan? Yippee. "Okay." I knew there was a sappy smile on my face but it was hard not to smile when you were talking to Mr. All American. "You still have my number?"

"You bet."

"Okay." We stood there for a while staring at one another, smiling and looking like a pair of geeks. Finally I looked towards the other end of the hallway and said "I...I should go, or I'll be late for Latimer."

"I had Latimer last semester."

I groaned, "Did he get really into your face? So close that his spit hit you when he spoke?"

"Oh yeah, we called him 'Spittle man.'"

"Unfortunately I didn't choose my seat strategically. I'm front row center. I feel like I'm taking a second shower every time I have his class." I joined Ryan in laughter. "Well I really should go." We were both reluctant to move.

"Uh, I'll call you tonight?"

"Yeah, I'd like that. Bye." I smiled and rushed off before I could be tempted to throw myself at him in the hallway. For some reason I think the administration would frown on that sort of thing.

I bumped into Professor DeWitt on my way to Espresso World. She was still bright eyed and bushy tailed. Her smile widened when she saw me.

"Holly?"

"Professor." Uh, this was awkward. "Getting an espresso?" God that was lame, really lame.

Professor DeWitt laughed. Again, that tinkling laughter, for some unknown reason her laughter irritated me.

"Oh, no, I don't drink coffee...I don't like artificial stimulants in my system. Bad for the body you know."

"Uh, yeah, I know." What? Was she crazy? She didn't drink coffee? I saw her clutching a thick volumed book and recognized it instantly.

"Zuri's book." It was a statement not a question.

"Yes, fascinating, really fascinating. Thank you for locating it for me, it has been unbelievably helpful in my research so far."

"I hadn't realized we were able to check those volumes out." If I had, you had better believe I would have.

"Oh, we're not. But Hascall and I have worked out a particular arrangement."

I nodded. Hascall was the University's library attendant. A small, balding, hawk nosed man with bad B.O. and a worse attitude. He made most of the student body quite miserable but he was widely acknowledged as one of the more brilliant occupants of E.U. Why he worked in the library instead of teaching a University class was one more mystery that E.U. could claim to have. Could Professor DeWitt and Hascall be...dating? I dismissed the notion almost immediately. Professor DeWitt was a beautiful woman, intelligent, and chic. She couldn't possibly be dating that troll of a man, could she?

"I'm glad I could be of some help to you Professor." I thought that came out well.

"Oh you have been a great help to me Holly, really. And I do hope that you'll continue the research, perhaps, after midterms?"

"I'd love to."

"Good, good. Then I must be off. Have a million things to do, you know."

"Of course. It was good speaking with you Professor."

"You too, Holly. I'll see you next class."

I watched Professor DeWitt stride away. She was almost bouncing. Yeah, something was definitely up with her.

I had a record five messages waiting for me on my answering machine when I returned home. They were all from Detective Marcus. In the last message he didn't make any attempt to mask his annoyance and frustration that I wasn't home to take his calls. I picked up the phone four times, each time with the intention of calling him, but each time I hung up. I really didn't want to speak with Detective Marcus. I didn't particularly like being used by the vamp Holder of Edwards, and I didn't like being used by the Edwards police force either.

I dumped my backpack unceremoniously down on the floor and went to the bedroom to change into my sweats and ratty old t-shirt. As I was changing my attention kept being diverted towards the window seat and the countless orchid plants still sitting there. I had left the violet orchid plant on my bedside table where I could see it every time I crawled in or out of bed. It was stupid, I know, but somehow that didn't stop me from keeping them around, and stroking their downy soft petals each time I passed. It was completely foolish, even dangerous to harbor any feelings for a vampire and it was positively suicidal to have feelings for a vampire Holder, but again, I couldn't seem to help myself. Ryan made me laugh and giggle like a schoolgirl. Vampire Lucien made me think wicked thoughts every time I saw him. I knew what the smart decision would be, but lately I seemed a few sticks short of a pile, and that certainly didn't make for smart decisions. The telephone rang.

"Hello?"

"Hi, Holly?"

"Ryan." I was smiling before I finished saying his name.

"Uh, is this a bad time?"

"No, not at all, I just got in." I settled down on my bed with the receiver to my ear. I could almost feel Ryan's nervousness on the other end of the phone. I waited. "Ryan? You there?"

"Uh, yeah, sorry."

"Not a problem. I'm glad you called."

"Yeah, I just wanted to uh, confirm our date on Saturday, and well I wanted to hear your voice."

Again, that fluttery feeling invaded my belly and settled low and deep. He truly was something special, so what was the problem? No, I wasn't going to answer that one.

"You're sweet Ryan."

"Aw shucks, ma'm."

I laughed at his terrible good old boy impersonation. Suddenly I had a brilliant idea. "Ryan. Have you begun to study for DeWitt's midterm?"

"A little. Some of the demonology is getting to me though. I think I must have tuned out for that section, I have some shitty notes."

"Do you want to get together to study for it?" I held my breath and waited.

"I'd love to! Please tell me you have better notes than I do." His voice was light and filled with humor. I made a happy face and held myself back from making a high five in the air. I'd have more one-on-one time with Ryan, more personal time. So we'd be discussing exorcisms and ritual slayings…it might spice up our dating life. Then again, lately my life didn't need much spicing up.

Chapter Seventeen:

I couldn't believe I had actually accepted a date with the vampire Holder of Edwards. Well, I hadn't really been asked on a date, I'd been told. And I hadn't really accepted, I'd been summoned, more or less. But that was neither here or there, I was meeting vampire Lucien for a *date*? The whole idea was positively ludicrous, so why was I attempting to find something appropriate to wear? It was obvious I had made up my mind a long while back. I was going on a date with vampire Lucien.

I chose a simple white dress. The heart shaped neckline was neither too revealing nor too prim. There was eyelet lace on the bodice and on the hem, which fell just below my knees. It was a sleeveless dress and the ties criss-crossed behind my neck and formed an X on my back. It was a delicate and lovely dress, one that I had purchased several years ago and hadn't had many opportunities to wear. I wasn't sure what possessed me to wear it on my first date with vampire Lucien, but it had caught my fancy and there wasn't time to change now. My hair was left loose this evening. I hadn't bothered with much makeup. It's said that less is more. In my case it certainly seems true. The doorbell rang and I forced back my jitters. I was horrified and pissed off when I opened the door; The vampiress Laeticia was standing there with a very familiar evil expression on her face.

"What are *you* doing here?" I didn't care that my voice was snippy. Of all the vampires in the world that Lucien could have sent to pick me up this one would not have been one of my choices.

"I have been given the assignment of taking you to our Holder, to Lucien." Vampire Laeticia didn't seem any happier about this turn of events than I was. "Come, we are already late."

Did I have a choice here? I could decline her assistance but would Lucien take offense? What was I thinking? Of course Lucien would take offense. This was so obviously a test, and I wasn't about to be the one who failed. I paused a moment before I gathered up my courage and nodded at her.

"All right, lead on." Vampire Laeticia gave me an inscrutable look. She probably hadn't thought I'd call her bluff. More likely than not she'd believed I wouldn't come with her. But I was certain she wouldn't hurt me...or at least I was sort of certain she wouldn't hurt me.

There was a sleek silver Lexus in the parking lot. Somehow I just knew that this was her car. You didn't see many silver Lexus's in the parking lot of my apartment complex. Sure enough vampire Laeticia stopped in front of the sparkling vehicle and unlocked the doors. She didn't hold my door open for me. I hadn't really expected her to. I climbed into the luxury car and marveled at the butter soft leather interior, you could tell I didn't get out much.

The ride was made in relative silence. But I could feel, sense the waves of emotions coming from Vampire Laeticia. Next to Lucien, vampire Julian and even vampire Christian she wasn't very good at mentally barring her pathways, at least not on this night. I began to block her thoughts when I decided just to listen a little bit. When riding in cars with hungry, malicious and potentially violent vampires it's always safer to know what they're planning. *So pretty, just a little taste, so easy. If he would only allow me a little taste...he owes me this one, just a small nibble to tied me over. Plague take him, what does he think I am, the fucking chauffeur?* I quickly disconnected when I saw her face staring at me in the mirror. Obviously, vampire Laeticia was still harboring a grudge and still lusting after my blood...literally. I wondered how much longer it was until we reached our destination, we couldn't get there soon enough if you asked me.

I think the fates were being kind, because vampire Laeticia parked the car soon after her rather undiplomatic thoughts. If I was surprised that we were back in the parking lot of 'Corruption' I didn't show it. I was too grateful to finally be out of the car. I didn't like riding with the 'snack happy' vampiress.

Once inside the unforgettable offices of 'Corruption' vampiress Laeticia took me down an unfamiliar flight of stairs in the back of the building. The corridor was long and lit with red filtered lights. I thought it was campy and really cheesy but who questions a vampires taste and actually lives? At the end of the hall there were double black doors, which vampiress Laeticia led me to. When we had reached it she knocked solidly and waited with what I realized was a permanent frown on her beautifully, pale face.

"Enter." The voice was silky smooth and husky. I noticed that vampire Lucien's voice seemed to have the same effect on the vampiress as if did on me and I found that oddly curious. I suppose that not even vampires were immune to their Holder's voice, or perhaps it was just vampire Lucien's voice that did all the damage.

"Go...he is waiting for you." Vampiress Laeticia did not seem pleased by this fact, but she kept her claws and fangs retracted, always a good sign. She pushed open the doors and held them open for me as I entered. I felt her eyes staring into my back until the doors slowly, reluctantly closed behind me.

Vampire Lucien was in rare form this evening. Resplendently decked out in black, from his velvet top to his tight leather pants. His shining hair was straight and falling free like a waterfall and his complexion was uncharacteristically tinged with pink. He looked excited and well fed, but had the look of someone who was craving more. He was draped suggestively over the arm of a large black leather sofa and he was smiling widely, anticipatorily. Not three feet away from his reclining figure was a large table set for two with expensive China and crystal goblets. There was a food server set nearby with huge silver serving plates filled with sumptuous treats; quail, caviar (which I had never acquired a taste for), chicken with what appeared to be a thick mushroom sauce, and numerous other dishes that I couldn't quite place. I felt my belly clench with hunger and two seconds later it rumbled loud and clear. I felt heat crawl up my neck and knew I was stained a bright red. Vampire Lucien only laughed and with remarkable fluidity seemed to melt off the sofa. He walked over to where I was still rooted to the spot and reached out to finger the lace on the bodice of my dress.

"You must be starving, come...you shall eat." He took my arm then, very gentlemanly and led me over to the table set for two. "Did you choose your attire with specific purpose tonight? You look suitably, chaste...very innocent."

Innocent? Me? That was a first. I guess I did give off that vibe in my present dress choice. No one had told me I looked innocent before, my mother had thought me anything but.

"And you look very Darth Vaderish." I smiled teasingly and laughed at his befuddled expression.

"Who is this Darth Vader?"

"I take it you haven't seen a lot of cinema?" I laughed, "Either that or you've been in a vacuum for the last oh, twenty five years."

"I find most films made after 1950 to be a waste of time. Although, the recent surge of popularity and interest in vampires, and the subsequent films made on our subculture have been amusing. I found *Blade* particularly…stimulating, however, Wesley Snipes is nothing like a true Dhamphir."

I nodded, somehow I doubted that Hollywood, would ever get their facts about vampires straight, or make a movie that truly and satisfactorily portrayed vampires, especially to the vampires' satisfaction. Vampires were way too guarded and took their privacy much too seriously to ever let the truth be known, it would be dangerous to their lifestyle and I believe much more than the human race could handle. I sat and eyed the food eagerly. I hadn't thought I'd be hungry, especially in the presence of vampire Lucien…Lucien. But I was starving and no one had ever accused me of having a bad appetite. I found it quaint and rather charming that vampire Lucien served me himself…but it was obvious that he wanted privacy, and it would not do to have servers coming in and out of the room while he was oh-so-obviously trying to make an impression.

Once we were both seated and there were generous portions of almost everything on my plate I looked over to where he was sitting, stock-still and very pensive. Of course there was nothing on his plate. The dead did not eat…well, nothing that he was serving me anyways. He did, however, poor himself a glass of wine and I noticed that he twirled the contents around while he eyed me intently.

"You don't mind that I eat…in your presence?"

Lucien shrugged his velvet-clad shoulders and gave me a benevolent look. "I invited you to dine, I would expect no less from you."

"But it doesn't, uh, bother you?" I hesitantly cut into a piece of chicken. "Since you can't, uh, eat."

"It has been longer than I can almost remember since I have tasted, or smelled 'human' food. The sight no longer pains me, indeed, it is a rare pleasure to see the preparation of beautiful food, almost an art form, don't you think?"

I nodded and bit into the chicken, it was completely divine. Whoever had prepared the food was a genius, I wondered if vampire Lucien had vampire chefs working for him?

"Mmmmmm." I couldn't help the look of ecstasy that crossed my face anymore than I could stop the rising of the sun. Vampire Lucien seemed positively engrossed with every little expression that filtered across my face, it was almost unhealthy. Then again, this date could be very bad for my current state of health…I was eating dinner with a dead guy. That was one for the books.

"I receive joy from watching you…your face is so very expressive, it is a rare treat for me." He seemed very solemn as he spoke. "It is also very rare for me, to see, expressions. I am not accustomed to it around here."

"I could see why" I murmured under my breath and blushed when I saw vamp Lucien's smile. Oops, I forgot, sensitized hearing, my bad.

"So, please, enjoy your meal…I will enjoy it through your enjoyment."

I raised my fork to him, no reason why I shouldn't finish the meal after he had given me his oh-so-kind permission. I quickly devoured everything on the plate and was hard pressed not to lick the plate afterwards. I raised my eyes upwards and found vamp Lucien staring at me with bemusement written all over that lovely face of his.

"Hungry?" he said quietly with feeling.

"Uh, yeah, just a little." I smiled then, widely. "I've always had a big appetite."

"Yes, I can see that my Holly flower. How do you keep so very trim?"

I shrugged, "Good metabolism? Or I might just be incredibly lucky."

"Please, have some more."

I looked over at the deserts and smiled sheepishly. "Actually I think I'll move onto…is that cheesecake?" Vamp Lucien said nothing. Simply and gracefully he stood and served me a large helping of cheesecake, which he topped off with a large dollop of fresh whipped cream. I could love him for this alone. I effectively finished off the cheesecake in record time and leaned back in my chair absolutely stuffed and more than fulfilled.

"Are you sure you would not like something else."

I shook my head and grimaced. "I have a big appetite, I am not, however, a bottomless pit."

"You could have fooled me."

"Did you just make a joke?" Every time vamp Lucien actually made a joke it stunned me. Vampires were not known for their sense of humor.

"I do believe it was a poor attempt at a joke, was it funny?"

"Since it was at my expense, no. However, you have potential in the joke department."

"Thank you Holly flower."

"No problem. Don't call me Holly flower. But if you ever need help with your material just let me know. I've been told I have enough sarcasm for two."

Vampire Lucien laughed and I let the sound roll over me in a great, giant, sensual wave. I was beginning to get used to these sexual tactics of his. And I couldn't, much to my dismay, say that they didn't turn me on.

"If you are finished, *Holly*." He made a great deal out of just saying my name. And I gave him a dirty look, which he only just laughed at. "Then, come, sit with me."

"Sit?"

"Yes, sit and talk to me."

"That's all?"

"You are highly suspicious Holly."

"Around you? Always!"

That earned me another grin. He held out his hand to me and I reluctantly accepted. He took me over to the leather couch and sat us both uncomfortably close together. He took my sweaty, fidgeting hands within his cool, dry ones and I went absolutely still. He was looking deeply into my eyes when I felt the uncomfortable tugging sensation in my mind. The tingling ran up and down my spine and I had to steady myself for a moment before meeting his gaze once again, this time with plenty of anger in my eyes.

"Don't do that." I glared at him. "Not only does it give me a headache, it doesn't work, and you know it."

Vampire Lucien sighed and smiled. "I had to see for myself. Your powers do you credit Holly. I have hardly known anyone, vampire or human who could resist my compulsion, it is very strong."

"Yeah, I know, I feel a little nauseous, and that never happens."

"I am truly sorry if I made you ill. I was only, shall we say, testing."

"I thought you asked me here on a date, not to give me a mental third degree."

"Again, I am sorry." Vampire Lucien smiled coyly at me, "You can try to probe me if you wish, it is the least I can do to make up for my blunder."

I looked at his still face and sparkling eyes and wondered if I truly wanted to know what he was thinking about.

"Thanks, but no thanks."

"Afraid?" Again, that mocking tone filled his voice.

"Of you, always."

"I believe you fear more than just me, Holly."

I narrowed my eyes. "What is *that* supposed to mean?"

Vampire Lucien gave an exaggerated sigh. "I did not mean to get into this right now Holly, you must believe that. I truly wished for us to have, a…date, much like the one you had with your human beau."

"You've got to be kidding. You're nothing like Ryan."

"Ryan." Vampire Lucien spit his name out as if it was something foul on his tongue. He unconsciously gripped my hand tighter and I winced a little. He must give a hell of a handshake. "You like his human boy?" His eyes glowed brighter and I bit my lower lip nervously…what should I say to diffuse this situation? The hell with it, the truth was always the best, right?

"Yeah, I like him, he's a good guy."

"And do you like me, Holly?"

I rolled my eyes "I'm here aren't I?"

"No." Vampire Lucien leaned closer and my belly clenched. "I wish there to be truth between us Holly. Do you like me, or do you merely lust after me?"

I wanted to tell him to go to hell, that he had a heck of an ego, but obviously I couldn't. The truth? The truth was that he was sinfully gorgeous and yes I would love to run my hands down his cool dead flesh, yeah, sick perhaps, but true nonetheless. Did I like him? Now that was a difficult question. How many people, who aren't groupies and donate blood on a daily basis, actually like vamp Holders? How safe is it to like a vampire anyway?

"Why do you care?" I tilted my head and stared at him through my darkening violet eyes "Do you really care if I like you? Can you care?"

He jerked back as if I had slapped him and withdrew his hands from mine. I felt oddly bereft and tried not to show it. I watched him through wide eyes as he slid from the couch and began to pace slowly back and forth. I found my attention wandering to that beautiful backside of his and quickly shook my head to clear it. We were trying to have a 'serious' conversation…it wouldn't do to have less than serious thoughts. Lucien stopped in his tracks and spun to face me, his eyes looked troubled and it was a disconcerting thing to see.

"I cannot remember the last time I cared about anything or anyone…" His unblinking eyes never left mine. "At least not the way you humans care. It troubles me…I do not need to care, merely control, it is my way, the way of my position, a matter of survival Holly flower."

I gasped when he suddenly appeared at my side. He didn't often use his vampire tricks on me, but when he did they were impressive, and startling.

His body was pressed against my side and he ran a slender hand down my hair, which conveniently hid my face from his. He leaned forward and my breath caught in my throat, I couldn't believe how his nearness affected me, like some potent drug that invaded my system in ten seconds flat. "But you produce the strangest feelings within me." His hand continued its journey, and traveled to my bare arm, stroking my warm skin, I shivered, and it wasn't from cold. He laughed and it was a dry, mirthless laugh. "Feelings...what shall I do with them? I had thought I had forgotten how to feel. But when I see you, when you are around me I feel my body react."

I gave a nervous laugh. "That's just lust, a chemical reaction."

"You know as well as I...that is not true. Oh, I want you, yes, but with you I find myself drawn to do, and say the strangest things. You have the strangest effect on me...but it is not unwelcome, merely disquieting."

I swallowed. What was I supposed to do with this information? I was sitting next to the most beautiful dead guy I had ever seen and he was telling me that he had strong feelings for me. But he was dead. And he was the Holder of Edwards, the badest badass of them all. He may or may not have a soul, and what the hell happened to my soul if I gave into my desire for him? I had only wanted to go on a simple date, but whom was I kidding...nothing was ever simple in my life, and nothing was ever simple with the dead.

"I don't know what to say." That was a first for me.

"Do you have human feelings for me, Holly flower?"

I swallowed. Oh boy, I was between a rock and the hard bodied vampire. What was I supposed to say?

"Uh, I guess wanting to feel you doesn't count?" I laughed a little, but it was forced. His hand stopped petting me and I groaned...I guess that was the wrong thing to say. "I was making a joke...Lucien, you know, a joke."

"Do you have feelings for this human boy?"

I really didn't like the way he kept saying *boy*, when referring to Ryan.

"I don't know him very well Lucien" At least that was the truth. "But, yeah, I like him, and I'd like to get to know him better."

Lucien snarled and I quickly held up my hand. "But I'm here with you for a reason Lucien, obviously. I want to get to know you too." This was not one of my smarter moves. But could I really give vamp Lucien up right now? Now when it was beginning to get really interesting?

Lucien's face melted back to that beautiful mask so quickly that it had me shaking my head. "So, you wish to see us...both?" He narrowed his eyes. "I could always make the decision easier on you Holly flower...I could remove this Ryan from the equation."

I really, really did not like the sound of that. "If you are hinting at what I think you're hinting at, you had better not be serious. Do you understand? Are you listening to me?"

Vampire Lucien nodded his head and his thick hair fell forward. He shrugged his shoulders. "It was merely a suggestion."

"I'm beginning to really dislike your suggestions."

"Does this Ryan know who, what you are?" Lucien must have read the guilt written across my face and he let out a dry laugh. "You have not told him."

"That's my business."

"Have you read his mind my Holly flower?"

Again, I blushed bright red and felt my face burn before I could stop it. I felt shame flood my body and it only deepened when Lucien snorted and smiled widely, revealing fangs.

"Did you like what you learned Holly?" He tickled my ear with his hot breath and I shook my head quickly.

"It was a mistake, I didn't mean to."

"Ah, of course, you have such high morals my Holly."

My blood was beginning to boil. Who the hell was he to judge me? He sank his fangs into flesh and drank blood for a living. I opened my mouth to speak, to tell him exactly what I thought of him when the door to the room blew open and a cool rush of air filled the space. Lucien lifted his head towards the door. His eyes were burning bright, never a good sign. He had tensed and one hand was still wrapped around my waist, tightly.

"Laeticia." Lucien spit the name out and disengaged himself from me. He moved slowly, gracefully towards the door. I kept my eyes trained on vampire Laeticia's face. She was scared shitless. Oh, she did her best to hide it beneath a mask of contempt, but like her thoughts, her face was easily read. Before Lucien could do anything, well bloody, Laeticia spoke.

"Yarbrow is missing."

I felt, rather than saw Lucien's anger, fury and hunger for blood. His defenses were down, he was working purely on rage and for once his mental paths were open and easily organized into thoughts and sensations that I could feel and gauge. Oh, yeah, it wasn't fun being in Lucien's thoughts. I could almost taste the bloodlust on my tongue. His mind was consumed with vengeance and retribution. The bile began to rise up my throat as the images became stronger and the sensations overwhelming. I could feel his rage and it consumed my body like a fire that was burning me from the inside out. I held out a hand and choked out his name. I was not going to pass out, bad enough to do it in front of Lucien, definitely not something I was going to do in front of Vampire Laeticia. "Lucien...please..."

Lucien snapped his head back in my direction and instantly I felt a coolness damper the fire burning in my body. My nausea subsided and my head and vision became clearer. He had tempered his reactions to Laeticia's news and calmed himself, therefore calming my overwhelming empathy, which had surprisingly reared its ugly head. "You felt, me?" He asked questioningly. I nodded, and he looked thoughtful, before turning back to Laeticia and asking,

"How long?"

"Colleen reported him missing tonight, when he did not show for his shift at 'Thermal.' He has never missed any of his shifts."

"Yes, I am aware of that. I will deal with it...shortly."

Laeticia cast those cold eyes in my direction. "Perhaps your pet psychic can locate him for you."

"Enough." Lucien turned burning eyes in her direction and held up a slender, cool hand. Vampire Laeticia instantly seemed to shrink and cower. I soon realized that she was indeed shriveling, her glow faded and died until she had the look of an old, wizened woman. She dropped to her knees and the horror didn't stop there. Her luxurious black hair seemed to thin and I noticed small clumps beginning to fall around her hunched over body. Small rivulets of blood began to drip down her face from wounds that magically, horrifically appeared out of nowhere. I brought a hand up to my mouth in terror. I had never seen anything like this. She reached out a bloody gray and withered hand and began to shake. Her eyes beseeched Lucien and she begged him without words to stop his torment of her. Lucien cocked his head to one side and took another moment before he lowered his hand and smoothly made his way over to her.

When Lucien was standing at her side he ran a hand down her coarse and dry hair. He knelt down and took her chin in his hand. Lifting her face to meet his cool and dispassionate gaze he said loudly enough for me to hear. "You will cease with your pettiness towards Holly." He stroked her cheek, evidently not bothered by her haggard and shrunken skin. "I have had enough. I am very patient, too patient where you are concerned Laeticia. But you have become a liability, which can easily be dealt with. However, I would, after these many years, prefer not to...dispose of you. I will hope that you have realized this evening that I have no patience for your...disposition where

Holly is concerned and that your good 'health' relies upon my good will. Do we understand one another?"

Vampire Laeticia nodded slowly. Her face turned sideways and I could see her eyes, which were still blue and bright in that old, shrunken face. The hate that blazed beneath them was terrifying to behold, but now, now I saw something besides hate, I saw undiluted dread and fear. Now I believed that she feared what Lucien would do to her more than she wanted her revenge against me. And for the first time since meeting her, I felt calm in my position. Ironic, since she was the vampire and I was the little human. And next to her I really was little.

"Now, you will feel better momentarily, as you know." Lucien smiled and continued to pet Laeticia's hair as if she were some disobedient dog, which had been suitably punished and chastised. "Send Colleen in…momentarily." Lucien stood and Laeticia was dismissed. I watched as she pulled her shriveled body upright and stood trembling on her two feet. My mouth must have been gaping open like an oxygen-starved fish when her features slowly, like rippling water regained their previous beauty and youth. Her body followed suit and was soon right and well. She bowed stiffly to Lucien and exited without even one more look in my direction.

I turned my horrified gaze onto Lucien and saw that he was watching me with intent eyes. I tried to collect my thoughts. My mind kept replaying the question vampire Lucien had asked me in a previous meeting "Do you believe the theories that vampires are a different species all together?" After that little display I'd have to say, you betcha. I hadn't witnessed Lucien using his full powers before, and it was basically starkly terrifying. I was going to try to date, *this thing*?

"You fear me now Holly, more than before. But I have just protected you from one that would do you harm."

"By torturing her?"

Lucien shrugged and his face remained passive and still. "She healed, I did not apply full force. And torture is merely disregarded by humans because your bodies are so…fragile, breakable. Vampires take much abuse and it is expected, often warranted. Do not worry." He stepped towards me and I quickly scampered back. Again, his beautiful face did not move, not a muscle not an inch. But his eyes, his eyes darkened and seemed to smolder with an inward fire. I couldn't help my reaction, and I wasn't going to nurse his possible hurt feelings. Hell, we hadn't even established if he had feelings. "Does this change our…arrangement?"

"What?" I looked at him, so beautiful, so dead and tried to form a coherent thought, one that didn't involve either throwing myself at him, or throwing myself away from him.

"Do you wish to reconsider your involvement with our...community, with me?"

I gaped at him. "You would let me...out?"

He laughed. "No. I just wished to know if this changed how you felt about us, me."

"Well, hell, yeah, it was freaky. But where am I going to run to?"

"Very well put, Holly flower." He moved towards me and this time I forced myself to remain still and passive. He reached a hand out to touch my hair. He really seemed to like my hair. "Know this, there is no where you could run, where I would not find you Holly. I can scent you in the air, you are like a heady perfume, which has settled in my head and will not be released. I crave you, almost more than blood...do you know what that means to me Holly flower?"

I swallowed. He craved me more than blood? Uh oh, was that possible? Probably not, did it still make take stock of my situation, definitely. Oh god, I had really dug myself deep here. Disastrous, dating a vampire is completely disastrous, but it seemed my life was becoming one big disaster. I hope in my next life I'm reborn as an oyster, how difficult could being an oyster be? But with my luck I'd be a piece of lint, isn't that what Buddhists believe? If you're bad in your present life you're reborn as a piece of lint in someone's belly button. As long as it wasn't vampire Lucien's belly button I'd be fine.

"I'm flattered that you...uh, crave me. However, this is kind of intense for me Lucien. I mean...you invite me over for, uh, dinner and the next thing I know you're telling me that you want some sort of relationship with me? Are you kidding me? I mean, well, how do I put this kindly, you're totally dead, what sort of relationship could we possible have?"

Vampire Lucien laughed, and looked down the front of his body. "Not totally dead."

I blushed and shook my head. "Stop that. You know what I mean."

"Unfortunately, I do know what you mean. However, I believe that this little 'quandary' does not bother you as much as you profess it does. I believe it is a little bit of 'the lady doth protest too much.' Do you truly not long for a taste of my cool flesh Holly?" Lucien had unbuttoned the top three buttons of his silky soft velvet shirt. I hadn't even seen him do it. He ran one smooth, pale hand down the equally pale flesh of his chest and my heart began to pound so loudly I was surprised he couldn't hear it, then again, perhaps he could.

"Uh…" I felt as if my tongue was plastered to the roof of my mouth. I wanted to speak but I knew that nothing would come out except a couple of garbled sounds. Not a way to make an impression, or to prove to someone your fortitude and willpower.

"The cat got your tongue Holly…?" Lucien came closer until he was merely an inch away from my now truly heated body. "…Or is it the vampire, who has your tongue" All my thoughts fled and scattered as he pressed those cool, dry lips to mine.

Sensations bombarded me; pleasure, guilt, triumph, hope, joy and most of all victory. I knew that not all these sensations and thoughts were mine. Being melded with Lucien had caused our thoughts to bond and fuse. I kept getting flashes of both our thoughts and feelings. At this moment, I could truly believe that a vampire could have feelings…if not feelings, emotions. I wrapped my arms around him and pressed myself deeper into his embrace. How could I not? When my entire body yearned to feel him, taste him, and to be with him. For the first time in my life I didn't flinch, nor did I feel repulsed by the melding of minds. Somehow the knowledge that Lucien wanted me as much, if not more than I wanted him filled me with a sense of power I had never thought to possess. I felt exhilarated, and very, very turned on.

I pulled back slightly so that our faces were mere inches apart. I ran the tip of my tongue across my now damp lips and watched the hunger burn in his eyes. I leaned closer and brought my lips to the cold flesh of his neck. I pressed small, nibbling kisses to his skin and then suddenly without warning bit him, hard. Lucien shuddered and quicker than a blink of the eye I was brought back into an immovable embrace. His mouth seemed to be everywhere at once. He nipped, nibbled and licked at my skin. I clung to him as if my life depended on it and he drank me in as if his life depended on me. I felt his hand at the small of my back and his mouth at the soft and vulnerable pulse of my neck. I brought drugged eyes up to his and was suddenly alarmed by what I encountered there, not turned on. His eyes had bled to red. His deep forest green eyes were no longer apparent under the strange film of red that covered them. His mouth was opening wider and his face elongating I felt panic rising and fluttering within my stomach. I had just enough strength to murmur a strangled 'no' before trying to wrench myself free of his embrace. He would not be swayed and his head was moving forward. I was no longer just panicked I was terrified and really, really freaking out…oh, this was so not good. I moved my hand up to hit him as hard as I could on his shoulder. I stopped flailing when I realized that I was exciting him, I did not want to add to my problems.

I did the only thing I could think of in my panicked state. I dropped my shields quickly and completely. I let my mental paths push out and scatter. Instantly, almost shockingly fast vampire Lucien released me. It was so quick that I stumbled back. I looked at him and found that his eyes were still a frightening shade of red and he was panting as if he had run a long distance. But thank god his face had returned to its normal shape and he was several feet away from me.

"You felt as a trapped mouse feels when it is staring at the cobra…" He clenched his hands and I was gratified to see that his eyes were beginning to bleed back to a 'normal' shade, not that his deep green eyes were anywhere near normal, but as normal as a vampire can be.

"Well, I was thinking more on the lines of a trapped bird, but, yeah, a mouse will do."

"You dropped your shields." He was standing there just as beautiful as before. But the truth was that he was a contained force of violence and death. And how does one contain violence and death?

"I had to, it was the only thing I could think of. You were going to eat me." I looked at him belligerently.

"Not eat, never Holly. Merely taste."

"Uh, yeah, whatever…same difference."

Lucien's look could only be called predatory. "Nay, there is a big difference."

Oh, yeah, time to take a big, big step back. "Okay, back off fang boy." I held up a hand. "I think we've had our date kiss."

Lucien smiled. "We can only have one?"

"If it includes transformation into scary, fang-toothed being, uh, yeah."

"I suppose I must then content myself with the one, until, of course, the next time."

"Whoa…what makes you think there is going to be a next time big boy?"

Lucien licked his lips and I shuddered. He smiled. "There will be a next time." He was suddenly alert and he turned towards the door. "Enter Colleen."

I, too, turned towards the door. A lovely vampiress entered. She was petite and sprightly looking. With long corkscrew red curls and a splattering of freckles across her very pale face she looked like an ad for 'Irish Spring' does death, an interesting combination. She was obviously a fledgling, sixty years or less. She dropped into a graceful curtsy in front of Lucien and I tried to contain another roll of my eyes.

"Colleen...you reported Yarbrow missing."

"Yes master."

"When did you first notice his disappearance?"

Colleen looked towards me quickly, surprise flashing over her surprisingly innocent looking face. "I..." she hesitated.

"It is all right Colleen. Continue." .

"I saw him briefly yesterday, right after sunset, master. But when I arrived at 'Thermal' tonight he was not there. He has never missed a shift before, master." Colleen chewed her lip nervously and once again I was surprised at how 'normal' how strangely innocent this vampire seemed.

"The rest Colleen." Lucien had seated himself on the couch and was staring at vampire Colleen with unblinking eyes. I felt rather lame standing so I sat Indian style on the floor, making sure to carefully arrange the folds of my dress to cover everything necessary.

"When he did not show I became worried...I knew that you would..." She stopped as if she had noticed she had said something inappropriate. She paused and then catching the look in her Masters eyes continued quickly. "I knew that you would not be pleased if Yarbrow missed his shift..."

"You are right...I would not have been pleased."

I turned my head to look at Lucien's face. It was filled with quiet stillness and I knew that he would have been more than not pleased if any of his people missed their 'jobs.' Obviously Colleen knew that well, perhaps through first hand experience.

"But it was not like Yarbrow to do such things. I paged him and there was no answer. I then had Marie cover my shift so that I could look for him...we have become rather close..." Again, Colleen stopped herself.

"I know about you and Yarbrow, Colleen."

"Oh. Well I searched for him in all the places he frequents, but he was at none of them...I then decided that you had to be notified."

"You did well Colleen. I will find Yarbrow and I will deal with this situation."

I watched relief flood vampire Colleen's face and could feel the weight that lifted from her shoulders. She nodded and dropped into one last curtsy before she departed the room. Lucien was staring pensively into space and I didn't need to use my skills as an Empath to know what he was thinking about and how he was feeling, yeah feeling.

"You think it was the same Demon." It wasn't a question.

"Yes, Holly, I believe whatever killed two humans and two vampires has now taken a third vampire victim." Lucien's face was inscrutable but the fury was barely contained under that cool, pale surface.

The murders were occurring closer together and were now more frequent. The Demon and whoever was controlling the Demon was becoming stronger or perhaps just cockier.

"They have to be stopped." I murmured.

"Ah, yes, what to do?"

"What do you mean? You just stop it from killing anymore…" I halted and Lucien looked at me mockingly.

"…Humans? That is what you were going to say is it not, Holly flower?"

"No, I…oh, all right, that is what I was going to say. But I didn't mean it that way. I want you to stop it from taking anymore people, human or non-human." I regarded Lucien through wary eyes. I didn't like my prejudices, but hey, I have hang ups, don't we all? Just because I was becoming involved with one of the dead, didn't mean that I had to warm up to them all, right? It was hard enough to warm up to one.

"And how would you propose that I accomplish this feat?"

I frowned at him. He was the Holder of Edwards, the goddamn Hive Leader wasn't he supposed to have a plan or something…a contingency? "I just assumed that you would know what to do."

"I am flattered by your faith in me. However, would it shock you if I told you that at this moment I do not have a course of action."

I knew I was staring at him mouth agape, but hell, I *was* shocked. Here was big, bad, vampire Lucien admitting vulnerability. He was just as in the dark as the rest of us were. The vampires didn't have any more of a clue than the humans did. Now wasn't that a shocker. "Well this has been a heck of an interesting date." I laughed. I tend to laugh when I'm nervous, or when I'm just plain out of ideas.

"Ah, Holly, yes, interesting." Lucien materialized next to me and I blinked, I'd never quite get used to him doing that. "I hope you shall grace me with your presence again, perhaps next time we shall go out…"

"Out? Where?"

"Ah, I own several establishments. One of them is five star *dining*" Lucien grinned. My eyes widened. A vampire run and owned restaurant? What the heck did they serve, a pint of blood and a pound of flesh?

"We'll see," was all I said.

"You shall need an escort home."

I began to argue, but Lucien raised a slender hand up and said. "You were brought here, how else would you get home?"

Oops, I hadn't thought about that. "Yeah, okay, an escort. Just not Laeticia."

Lucien gave me an innocent look. "I thought Laeticia was an excellent choice to bring you here. She is quite competent."

"Yeah, she's also completely psychotic."

"Ah, well, not Laeticia then."

"Great." I stood up and stared at Lucien without knowing quite what to say. Had this date made anything clearer for me? Uh, no, if anything I was more confused now than when I had first entered. So we had established that there was a clear physical attraction between us. He had let me in on some deep, dark personal issues and we had gazed at one another over a sumptuous dinner...but what had we accomplished, anything?

"What are you thinking about Holly flower...unlike you, I cannot delve into your mind or feel your...emotions."

"Uh, nothing."

Lucien laughed. "Now that is a blatant lie...why would you lie to me? What are you protecting in that steel trap of yours?"

Now that really was something I didn't want to get into right now. "It's getting late Lucien, I think I should go."

Eyes closed, Lucien seemed to scent the air. He nodded. "You are right Holly flower, it is getting late. You may go now. I will contact you shortly and we will see one another again." He tilted his head to one side. "You do wish to see me again, do you not?"

Obviously. It was ridiculous I knew that, but hell, I was attracted to the dead guy. And he did serve the best food this side of heaven. So, what did I say now? "Goodnight Lucien."

"And to you my little Holly flower." He smiled, a wide fang tooth smile. "If you exit the same way you entered there will be someone awaiting you."

I nodded. Gave him one parting look and quickly exited the room, heart beating and stomach fluttering madly, it always seemed to do that when I was around him.

Chapter Eighteen:

Mr. Mohawk and Mr. Suit dropped me off. I wondered if they were a set pair, I had never seen one without the other. Now, they were an improvement over Laeticia, but not by much. Mr. Mohawk had stared at me in the mirror the entire way back to my apartment, it had just plain old given me the willies. Mr. Suit, ever the civilized one had driven without comment or a single look in my direction. Once back in my quiet parking lot they had released the locks on their black BMW and had let me out. I had all but rushed to my apartment…not caring if I was rude or not.

Dumping my keys on the hallway table I noticed my answering machine blinking, nine messages, now that was just abnormal. I pushed the button and listened. One after the other, all but two were from Detective Marcus, and he obviously, was not a happy camper. I suppose after the five messages he had already left me with the addition to these seven that he had a right to be annoyed, after all, I hadn't returned any of his calls. I checked the mounted clock on my wall and groaned, three o'clock, it was already three o'clock in the morning. If I continued to date vampire Lucien I was going to need a serious supply of coffee and caffeine pills…these late nights were going to kill me…in more ways than one.

I stripped on my way to my bedroom, I'd pick up later. Right now I was too tired. Finding my favorite pair of pajamas, a cotton twin set featuring Tom and Jerry I slid into my newly laundered sheets and breathed a sigh of relief. Right now I needed sleep, I'd call Detective Marcus tomorrow. My last thought before I slid into a deep slumber, was what could possibly be so important that Detective Marcus would call me over ten times?

I was feeling pretty perky Saturday morning, even though I had only gotten a disastrous five hours of sleep, I tended not to be able to function with any less than eight hours. I sat at my living room table and began to make up a list of things that I had to do. I hated lists, but I found that they tended to de-complicate my life, and with all the recent complications in my life I could use all the help I could get. I was polishing off a bowl of Cheerios and had just completed my to-do list when the phone rang. I answered cheerily.

"Hello, Holly here."

"Holly? It's Ryan."

Ah, my day was only getting better. "Hey Ryan."

"I hope it's not too early."

"Not at all." He didn't need to know that usually, if he called me at this hour I would still be buried under a mound of covers, goose down pillows and content in dream land.

Let him think I was a morning person. It was obvious that he was.

"I wanted to call and work out the details of tonight." There was a pause and he continued. "How about I pick you up..."

I interrupted. "What are you doing this afternoon Ryan?"

"Uh, nothing, why?"

"Why don't you come over at one, I'll pack a picnic lunch and we can study in the park." I held my breath, had I been too forward? What if he hated picnics? What if he hated parks?

"That sounds terrific Holly."

I breathed a sigh of relief. Not only would I get to spend more time with Ryan, I was also getting to see him during the day, now that was fresh, I loved it.

"So I'll see you at one?"

"Yeah, definitely. Do you want me to bring anything?"

I grinned. "Just yourself." I could almost feel Ryan's smile on the other end of the phone.

"I think I can manage that."

"Great, until one."

"Okay, bye, see you soon."

"Bye." I hung up and felt myself glowing. There was something so endearing about Ryan, so different from...Lucien, I frowned, Lucien...oh boy, was this going to work? Just thinking about the college boy and vampire in the same sentence was enough to give me a raging migraine. Jeez, if I really wanted to de-complicate my life I would just ditch the vampire, so why then didn't I do it? Simple, I sort of lusted after the vampire, and okay, probably liked him a little too…dim-witted but totally true. The telephone interrupted my furiously raging thoughts.

"Hello?"

"Miss. Feather, Holly, its Detective Marcus."

Uh, oh, wasn't that at the top of my list, call Detective Marcus? Oops I'd let myself get sidetracked by the cute boy, shit. "Hi Detective Marcus."

"Where the hell have you been Miss. Feather? I almost sent a unit over to break down your damn door."

"I'm really glad you didn't." I said in a cheerful voice, trying to lighten his mood, he obviously wasn't having any of it.

"Well…"

"Well, what?"

"Where the hell have you been?"

"None of your darned business." It wasn't any of his business. I bit my lip. I could hear him breathing on the other end of the phone and could envision the annoyance and anger written all over that hard planed face of his.

"I need to talk to you." His voice was cold and he was obviously making an attempt at holding back his exasperation.

"Okay." I waited.

"Not over the phone. Do you know the Danbury hiking trail?"

"Yeah." Danbury hiking trail was one of the least popular hiking trails. Overwhelmingly long, it winded through some of the thickest and most dense parts of the Smokey Mountains. Hikers had disappeared from the Danbury trail, many suspected vampires, but humans suspected vampires of almost everything, including the Kennedy assassination…you understand what I'm trying to say, don't you? Basically if something bad happened, vampires were blamed. Personally, if you ask my opinion, people can be just plain stupid. It doesn't take a vampire to cause a disappearance. Most people can disappear by themselves. In the Smokies all it takes is one slip, one fall, a broken leg and no way to call for help, and voila, you're effectively dead. So, yeah, vampires don't cause all death, just the painful bite inflicted ones.

"Okay, meet me at the edge of the Danbury trail…"

Whoa, what? I cut him off. "No."

"What?"

"Absolutely not. I am not going to meet you at the edge of the Danbury trail. This isn't like…meet me at Espresso World in fifteen minutes. The Smokies are like…over an hour from here, I am not spending my Saturday afternoon tromping through the woods with you, Detective, no offense."

"What? You have something better to do."

I thought of Ryan and his big, wide, sunny smile. "Oh, yeah, I definitely have something better to do."

"What? A hot date?" There was no inflection in his voice and I frowned. Again, it was none of his business.

"And what if I do have a hot date?" I waited, nothing. Finally I spoke. "Detective Marcus?"

"So break it."

Was he kidding? Break a date with the unbelievably hot and sweet Ryan Maloney, as if. "No way."

"Listen here, kid."

"Don't call me kid, Detective."

"Holly. This is important. I don't have time to deal with your damned love life, I'm in the middle of a murder investigation, one, that unfortunately I seem to need your fucking advice on…so get rid of your boy and get your ass over here."

"Since you asked so nicely…NO!" I slammed down the phone. Could you believe the gall of the guy? Actually telling me to break a date? In addition he wanted me to drive out to the damn Smokey Mountains on my weekend to go tromping through the woods with him, that was so not my idea of fun. I ignored the phone when it rang again. Mr. Damned demanding, hot shot Detective could just go to hell and take his orders with him.

I found a clean pair of jeans and paired it with a nice striped red and black lightweight sweater. I quickly ran fingers through my loose curls and tied it back with a black ribbon, it wasn't fancy, but would keep my hair from falling into my face. I applied a cherry red lip-gloss, cream eye shadow and a tinge of blush and took in my appearance. Not bad, especially since I didn't want to look as if I had tried too hard. Couldn't have Ryan know how much I was actually looking forward to this date. Hurriedly I did the dishes and straightened up the living room, just in case Ryan actually came in. I stuffed the to-do list in my purse and headed out, I had to make sure I finished all my errands before Ryan came.

It was quarter to one when I pulled into my parking lot. I pulled the groceries from my trunk and headed to my apartment when I noticed a figure standing several feet from my welcome mat. I frowned and prepared to do battle.

"The answer is still no, Detective."

Detective Marcus was simply dressed. In navy slacks, a white polo shirt and freshly shaved he looked surprisingly well groomed and dressed. Of course that granite expression of his hadn't changed one bit, including the perpetual frown that marred his face. "I'm afraid you don't have a choice in the matter Holly. We have a crime scene that we need your help with."

"Of course I have a choice Detective. I'm not on the police force and I don't have any obligation to you or your captain. I mean, really, do you treat all your witnesses this way? I don't think so."

"How about the victims?"

I was befuddled. "What?"

"Do you have an obligation to them Holly? Do you care about the victims?"

"That's a low blow Detective, of course I care. But I'm only a college student." I held up a hand when he would have spoken and continued. "Okay, albeit, an unusual college student but a student nonetheless. Tell your captain that you need to make use of a psychic or perhaps even a Wiccan. They'll be able to help you just as well as I could."

"They won't be Empathic."

I shrugged. "Probably not. But you don't even know if you need the skills of an Empath on this. So far all you've utilized me for is my book knowledge on Demons and spells."

"You have a range of skills that would be helpful, you know it Miss. Feather."

I sighed. I'd noticed that Detective Marcus had a tendency to call me Miss. Feather when he was annoyed or angry with me. It was becoming very apparent that Detective Marcus wasn't going to budge on this subject, nor was he going to give me any peace until I agreed to help him, in that respect he was very much like another annoying 'man' I knew. "Can we compromise here Detective?"

"Explain."

"If you will just lay off my back for this afternoon then I'll come with you tomorrow, whenever you want, okay? I'll blow off studying tomorrow to come tromping through the Smokey Mountains with you, will that work?"

"As much as I'd like to accommodate you Holly, this scene will probably be as worthless as a piece of shit by tomorrow."

Jeez, I just couldn't seem to win. I was thinking about another way to persuade him to go away when a familiar truck pulled into an empty parking space. I groaned, great, perfect fucking timing. Ryan stepped out of his truck, dressed casually in jeans and an Edward's sweater. Slung over his shoulder was a book bag, no doubt it was filled with his study materials and textbooks. His blond hair gleamed in the sunlight and he looked like he had stepped off an Abercrombie and Fitch bag. I noticed the slight crease between his eyes when he noticed the groceries on the ground and Detective Marcus standing next to me. Okay, think, how to explain this one?

"Hi Holly." He stopped a foot or two away from me. He gave me a warm smile but was looking puzzled when he met Detective Marcus's direct stare.

"Ryan, uh, you're prompt." I winced. God I sounded stupid. I think I detected a small smile gracing Detective Marcus's face and I really wanted to smack him.

"Yeah." Ryan waited.

I clenched my hands into a fist and forced a smile onto my strained face. "Ryan, this is Detective Marcus, Detective Marcus, Ryan." I watched as both men shook hands, neither one said anything. As if it weren't awkward before. "Detective Marcus and I were just…"

Detective Marcus interrupted me. "Discussing how sorry we were that Holly is going to have to skip her appointment with you this afternoon. But we have really pressing business that has to be addressed immediately."

My mouth gaped open. I knew I looked ridiculous but I was shell-shocked. "I…I…"

"We're both sorry about the inconvenience Ryan, but you understand, don't you?" Detective Marcus was speaking to Ryan but looking at me smugly. The bastard. He knew he had just backed me into a damn corner.

Ryan was looking back and forth between Detective Marcus and myself. His handsome face was creased with lines of confusion and I felt heat flood my face, I just wished the ground would open up and swallow me whole. "Uh, yeah, I guess I understand." Ryan looked at me expectantly and I forced myself to find my tongue.

"I'm so sorry Ryan. It's really important." I made a motion towards the groceries on the ground and continued. "I had everything ready, I was totally looking forward to this afternoon. This just came up really suddenly and well, I don't have a cell phone and I didn't have any way of getting in touch with you…" I finished off lamely. I wouldn't blame him if he never wanted to speak with me again.

"It's all right Holly. I understand." He tossed detective Marcus another look before adding. "I'll uh, just go now. Listen, give me a call tonight if you want."

I nodded. I couldn't even speak I was so mortified and disappointed.

"Goodbye Mr. Maloney, have a nice rest of the weekend." Detective Marcus said, still smiling. Oh, I was going to kill him.

"Uh, yeah, you too." Ryan turned and without a backward glance got into his truck and drove away. The moment his truck was out of sight I turned, enraged, towards Detective Marcus.

"You sonofabitch!" I clenched my hands so tightly that my nails dug into the palms of my soft skin. "You deliberately sabotaged my date with Ryan. Not to mention he's probably wondering what the hell I'm doing with a damned Detective."

"I thought I handled the situation admirably." Detective Marcus was still wearing that smug as all hell expression.

I don't know what came over me but I could feel my body hum and throb with excess energy, all from my fury towards him. I tried to suppress it but it kept building and building. I knew my violet eyes were blazing with fury and I hardly registered Detective Marcus's startled expression before I threw a hand forward and Detective Marcus flew off his feet and hit the front door of my apartment with a sickening thud. He slid down and fell unconscious down to the ground. My heart stopped. I stood, shocked and horrified at what I had just done. Unsteadily I made my way towards him. I leaned down and checked his pulse, it was strong and steady, and he was going to be fine. That didn't make me feel any better. It was a strange cross between telekinesis and teleportation and it was the power I had the least control over, even after all these years. I had worked so hard to contain and control all my abilities but sometimes, sometimes I forgot that there were some things that could not be contained.

Detective Marcus groaned. He was coming out of it. Opening his eyes he stared at me unblinking for several moments. I reached down and offered him my hand. He stared at it for a moment before accepting and pulling himself back to his feet. He swayed and steadied himself. I looked at his head and winced. He was going to have a hell of a bump on that hard head of his. "I suppose we can add telekinetic to your list of abilities." His voice was gruff.

I stepped back, I did not want to be in the way if he decided to exact a little retribution. He was like over a foot and a half taller than me and probably outweighed me by a little over a hundred pounds…it wouldn't do any good to stand in his way. However, for some reason I believed that Detective Marcus had more control than me. Hadn't I just demonstrated how little control I actually did have? "That wasn't telekinesis."

He nodded. "Yeah, you tossed a person several feet, not an inanimate object…but it's close enough."

"I…I am sorry. You pissed me off. But I didn't have a right to do that. My only excuse is that I really didn't have much control on my emotions right then."

"Yeah, I knew that too." He smiled grimly. "You hit me with them like a ton of bricks, in addition to my little encounter with the door."

I felt shame render me speechless. What I had done was inexcusable. Detective Marcus sighed. "What I did was pretty shitty…" He rubbed his head and bit back a small groan. "Will you come with me Holly?"

I nodded. My date was ruined. I had hit Detective Marcus against a door with a strong mental shove and I had done it in a public place, did I have anything better to do? Or could I do worse? I really didn't want to know.

Chapter Nineteen:

Another day, another icky crime scene, this was just beginning to become a bad habit. I swallowed. It was grizzly and completely repulsive. And unfortunately this time the body had not been removed prior to my arrival.

I walked around the now very familiar ritual circle and tried not to gag. The smell of sulfur wafted through the air, but today, today I smelled something different, something mingled with the sulfur…perfume? I forced myself to look at the body within the circle and my eyes narrowed, definitely a vampire victim. How did I know? Well for one the head and heart had been neatly removed, along with the skin and, oh, gross, the hands. This was a different twist, but just as disgusting as all the rest. The blood had obviously been drained from the body, like the rest of the victims and I wondered if this was Yarbrow, the missing vampire from Lucien's Hive. I mean, how many missing vampires were there around with their heads cut off and hearts removed? Not to mention Vamp Leaders kept a really close watch on their Hive occupants, more likely than not, this was Yarbrow. For a moment I felt genuine remorse and sorrow for the slain vampire…no one, no one deserved to die this way, not even the dead.

I noticed something laying a foot or two away from the mutilated vampire…skin? Nasty, it looked like a chunk of flesh. I began to reach my hand forward when I remembered the last time I had attempted to reach into the circle and stopped. I motioned Detective Marcus forward. "Detective?"

"Yeah?"

"Can you get an officer over here, I think there is a chunk of, uh, skin, next to the vampire, and I don't believe it's his."

Detective Marcus began to move forward and I stopped him with a quick tug on his sleeve. "What?" He said.

"No, its got to be someone without any PSI abilities." I sighed when I noticed Detective Marcus looking at me questioningly. I didn't really want to get into Lucien with Detective Marcus, and how, it seemed that the vamp Holder of Edwards and the Edwards police force were after the same demonic creature. How to explain without bringing in Lucien?

"The sulfur I told you about before, well it's a double ward. A ward to keep the demon in and a ward to keep people out, really clever and difficult to manage." I shuddered and continued. "The sulfur will burn like all hell if you touch it, and you can't cross into the circle if you've got PSI abilities…not sure what'll happen, but I don't think it'll be good."

"How do you know this?"

I sighed. "Just trust me on this Detective Marcus." I held out my hand and motioned towards the circle. "Or if you want, go on ahead, test my theory for yourself…but don't blame me if something really bad happens." I watched the indecision filter across his face, and in the end practicality and intelligence won out and Detective Marcus called over the same fresh faced Rookie, Donovan.

Donovan stepped into the circle easily. However, his face was an uneasy and unwelcome shade of green by the time he had reached the slain vampire. He swallowed and I wondered if he was going to hurl, and hoped, for his sake that he didn't vomit in the circle and mess up the scene. I looked over to Detective Marcus and could tell he was having similar thoughts. Detective Marcus called out.

"Donovan. Just bag the chunk of flesh and bring it out, now."

Donovan nodded. He unsteadily made his way over to the shed skin and hesitated before he reached down. I sighed. Yeah, it was gross, but better to get it over quickly. If I wouldn't get second-degree burns from walking over the damn circle I'd retrieve it myself. Finally Donovan reached down and with gloved hands bagged the chunk of flesh. He quickly made his way out of the circle, handed the bag to Detective Marcus and went to the trees to throw up. Well at least he hadn't contaminated the scene.

"May I see?" I asked Detective Marcus. I examined the chunk of flesh in the bag and swallowed, yeah, pretty gross. My eyes narrowed and I hit on it. "It's human, Detective."

"You think."

"Yeah. You've seen vampires after they're dead" When I saw Detective Marcus's amused expression I rolled my eyes. "Really dead."

"Oh, yeah…" Detective Marcus's eyes gleamed and glowed.

I didn't like the look in his eyes. Detective Marcus had the look of someone who was remembering a particularly great moment. Almost the look of lust, it was really disquieting, to say the least. "Well, then, vampire's skin turns a grayish hue when it's dead, dead." I motioned towards the really dead vampire in the circle. "Just take a look. When the heart and head have been removed and the vampire is really, uh, gone, the skin turns a really pasty gray." I looked at the contents of the bag again. "This skin is obviously not vampire skin. And uh, as gross as this may sound, it's fairly smooth and well, really unblemished."

"Female?" Detective Marcus stated

I shrugged. "Maybe. I don't know. You'll have to take it to your labs and see if you can verify that. But, yeah, I'd say it's a possibility" I wondered if I should mention the perfume. "Do you smell anything Detective?"

Detective Marcus didn't hesitate. "Perfume, some fancy kind."

I smiled. "You smell the perfume?"

"Can't fucking miss it, I fucking hate perfume, never understood why women want to dowse themselves in the stuff."

I was amused. "Because it smells good?"

"Take a damn shower." Detective Marcus grumbled, "…Soap smells good too." He paused before adding, "You still smell sulfur?"

"Oh yeah. It's very strong this time. I'm thinking it has something to do with the vampire or the demon…you know, like it's taking more sulfur to contain the demon, or perhaps the sulfur is to contain the vampire. Jeez, I'm really going to have to look this up." I cast my eyes around the circle one more time. "But the pentagrams, well that's classic demonology."

"Yeah, even a schmuck like me knows that." Detective Marcus said.

I smiled. "The perfumes a new twist. I haven't smelled it at any of the other scenes, haven't picked up a trace of it. But it's really heavy here, and you're right, it's definitely a 'fancy' brand…maybe Chanel, or possibly Dior."

"Hell, I don't know much about woman's perfume…just know the difference between the stuff that smells like dishwater and the stuff that smells like rose. Don't happen to like either one, but the rose is a sure sight better than the bathwater."

I was really amused by the fact that Detective Marcus was so adamant about his dislike of perfume. Then again, after getting to know him a little better, he didn't really strike me as the perfume sort of guy. "I don't think our victim was wearing perfume."

Detective Marcus shrugged. "You can't tell these days. Woman wear cologne, men wear perfume…who's to know who is wearing what."

"Well. That's true enough." I sighed. I was all out of grand ideas. It was oh-so-obvious that the sorcerer was getting more and more powerful. He was able to subdue a vampire with what appeared to be little effort and he had now claimed five victims, for what purpose was still unclear, but I'd bet you a buck that it wasn't to go dancing.

"Can you tell me what sort of spell was used here, Holly?"

I sighed. Again, not the first time I had been asked this particular question. And once again, I didn't have the answer. "I'm sorry Detective. I thought that by now I would be able to tell you, but I'm just as stupefied now as I was before. It's obvious some rendering spell…but which one I don't know. It has to be a strong one to incapacitate a vampire. I promise I'll look into it for you."

"Yeah, you do that." Detective Marcus rubbed a hand over his eyes and for the first time I noticed how truly exhausted he looked. I had been so busy whining and moaning over my lost date to really notice how tired he was. I'd bet that he had been dedicating all his time to this case. He just struck me as that sort of guy. And he was right. Nothing, not even a date with the unbelievably cute Ryan Maloney was more important than figuring who had committed this horrendous murders and stopping them before they could commit any more.

"I'm sorry Detective." It just came out before I could stop it.

Detective Marcus looked at me with suspicion. Probably wondering if I was going to throw him into any trees. "What for?"

"For being a bratty college kid." I sighed and continued, "I've been a royal pain in the ass, hey, you've been pretty unreasonable, but I've been worse. You're right, there isn't anything more important than finding the killer and if that means I have to break dates and skip some school, well, hey, I'll live with it. I…I…don't know when I became so selfish. I guess it just sort of snuck up on me." I lowered my eyes and when I raised them Detective Marcus was staring at me with something akin to respect.

"You're wrong Holly. I don't think you're a bratty college kid, actually I think you're quite a brilliant and kindhearted person. I should be the one apologizing. Sometimes, often, I forget that you're so young, and well…inexperienced. I think it's the way you handle yourself. I come across rather like a bulldozer and my only excuse is that I want to catch this sonofabitch so badly I can taste it. I've been willing and I am willing to use anyone and every method available to me to catch this psychopath. I'm afraid that you're one of those people. You have a rare gift, a talent. People may regard us with suspicion but we're the ones that truly keep them safe Holly. We're the ones that can see into their souls and I suppose that scares them, hell, it scares me sometimes. But where I'm gifted, you're blessed. You have abilities that put the most gifted to shame. What you have to offer is immense, I suppose that I should be chastised for thinking that I could just take what you have without even taking time to consider your feelings." Detective Marcus finished gruffly and fell into silence.

I stared at him openmouthed. Just when I thought that he was nothing but a Neanderthal he surprised me with sincerity, emotions and real humanity. Damn, but that made it hard to detest him. "Apology accepted, as long as you accept mine."

Detective Marcus smiled slightly. "Of course."

"Great." I grinned. "Isn't it great to have that off of our chests."

"Yeah, great. So how about this case Holly?"

I knew what he was asking. But now, now I wasn't so scared about my answer. It seemed that I was getting a broader education than I could ever have hoped for, and truly it wasn't such a bad thing. There was only so much that four walls and a stack of books could teach you, in the end, the best education seemed to be whatever you learned in the field. And, boy, I'd been getting a lot of fieldwork lately. "However I can help you Detective…you need only ask." The moment I said the words I felt better. It was as if a great weight had been lifted off of my shoulders, to steal a popular phrase. I felt lighter and definitely better. Perhaps it was time I stopped hiding from my abilities? I looked at the circle one more time and shuddered, and perhaps I still needed a little more time.

"Well, whatever you can tell me about the ritual, the spell, that stuff would be great. And, well, I'm going to call on you if I need anything Holly." Detective Marcus dug into his pocket and tossed me a flat small square box thing.

I looked at it and cast him a befuddled look. "Uh, what is this?"

Detective Marcus tried to contain his surprise. "It's a beeper, you know, so I can page you. You told me that you don't have a cell phone, and since I don't have one handy for you…well this'll have to do." He wagged a finger at me and I tried not to roll my eyes. "They're simple and effective. I want you to use it."

I studied the thing, god I hated this thingamabob. I didn't have a cell phone for a reason. Oh, okay, I know I had said it was the extra phone bill, but the truth was that I didn't have a head for all this technical junk, yeah, even something as simple as a cellular phone. I looked at the buttons and the scrolling letters and sighed, this didn't look simple. It looked like some device off of *Star Trek*. "I'll, uh, try."

"No, you'll do." He continued to stare at me until I blinked and nodded.

"Yeah, all right, I'll use the damned thing."

"Great, now that, that is settled I'll drive you back home."

"Thanks a lot." I said sarcastically. It was so nice to him to drive me home, since he was the one who had driven me out here to the middle of nowhere in the first place. Of course he wasn't listening to me, he was already walking away, I should have figured. He always seemed to be walking away from me…was it something I said?

I picked up the phone for the one-hundredth time and slammed it back down. I had been trying to get up the courage to call Ryan back.

Detective Marcus had been as good as his word and had gotten me back to my apartment in record time. He had left me with the promise that he would be in touch, oh, and I knew he would be. Once back home I hadn't been able to stop thinking about Ryan and the look on his face when he had left my parking lot. I wanted to call and explain, but, hey, even I have insecurities. What if he hung up on me? What if he told me to go to hell? Would I be able to deal with that? Uh, hell no, this was Ryan we were talking about, he was the all American dream, was I about to let that slip through my fingers? I picked up the phone and dialed his number, forcing myself to remain calm and not hang up the damned phone. My heart raced when the phone picked up after two rings.

"Yeah." The curt voice was husky, masculine and totally sexy, I knew this was Ryan.

"Uh, Ryan? This is Holly." My heart stopped when silence met my opening words. I waited and when he still didn't say anything I rushed on. "I'm really sorry about this afternoon. It was really important, but that isn't an excuse for blowing you off like that. I…I really wanted to spend time with you, and I know you had to study for Professor DeWitt's class. I, well I was hoping you'd give it another go and come over tonight? We could study, I'll, uh, make dinner." I waited and prayed. If I could just get another chance with Ryan I'd make sure all my prayers from now on were serious and secular.

"I really like you Hol. But I have to admit that I was little put off by that Detective, what the heck was he doing there anyway?"

Oh, okay, a tricky question. "Detective Marcus and I had some stuff to talk about. He's still interviewing me due to that murder case I sort of witnessed."

"Yeah, I heard about that. Sorry."

It wasn't a surprise Ryan had heard of the body I had stumbled across on Campus, I didn't know a soul who hadn't heard that story by now. "Well, yeah, so Detective Marcus needed some stuff cleared up. And it really couldn't wait, at least he didn't think so."

"Yeah, tonight's fine." Ryan's voice was a little lighter and definitely more like the Ryan I knew. "But if you blow me off again I'll be tempted to call it quits." He said this laughingly and I took it as such. God, he was good sport. How couldn't you like this guy?

"Great. Uh, eight?"

"Eight's great."

"Okay, I'll see you at eight." I hung up the phone and stared at it with a smiling face. I had another chance with Ryan and this time it wasn't going to be with any distractions. I walked into the kitchen and suddenly stopped in my tracks. Make dinner? Fuck, I couldn't cook.

"No…damn, oh, baby, don't do that." I screamed. I was frantically waving a towel underneath the wailing smoke alarm but it didn't seem to be helping any. After five more minutes of ear piercing noise I began to hit the thing with the butt of a broom handle, well, when in doubt…use force. I studied the blackened mess on my little stove and groaned. Maybe if I scraped the bottom? Or perhaps I could run it under water. The doorbell rang and I let out a few more colorful expletives. Damn him and his prompt ways, wasn't anyone late these days?

Ryan was dressed casually, handsomely in a pair of jeans and a checked shirt. Again, his knapsack was slung over one muscular shoulder, and he wore a friendly grin on his handsome face. I hesitated, should I really let him into my apartment while it was still smoking? Did I have a choice? I couldn't very well let him stand on the front step, could I?

"Can I come in?" Ryan said good-naturedly.

I felt like a lame brain. "Of course. Sorry, yeah, come on in." I watched him take in my living room and sighed when I noticed his expression. He didn't seem to like it anymore than Lucien did. Pathetic, don't you think? Both the vampire and the college guy didn't like my interior decorating skills. Nice to know they have something in common, other than the fact that they could both get my sex drive working into overtime.

"Uh, you have a nice apartment, Holly."

"Thank you Ryan." I turned. "Considering you totally hate it." I muttered under my breath.

"Did you say something?"

"Uh, no, did you hear something?"

"Thought I did, guess it was nothing."

"Guess so…" Oh, god, was I going to burn in hell for all these lies I was telling lately? I really didn't want to ponder over these thoughts. "Something to drink?"

"Any beer?"

I smiled. "Amstel Light, and well I've got Guinness"

"I'll take the Guinness."

Oh, dark beer boy. "Sure, just a sec…" I retrieved a Guinness from my fridge and offered him a glass, which he declined. I handed him the beer bottle and watched as he took a swig. "So, you like the dark beers. I didn't know, which is why I picked up both Amstel and Guinness. Personally it's cool, I'll end up drinking the Amstel, it's one of the few beers that I actually like…oh, that and Corona."

"So like a girl."

I put my hands to my hips and looked at him in fake anger. "What the heck is that supposed to mean?"

"Nothing, except that eighty some percent of the woman I've met in my many years living on this planet has made me an expert on woman's beers. Woman seem only interested in Corona and Amstel Light, it's a universal fact. Strange but true."

"That's not true…" My voice trailed off. I scrunched my nose and sighed. "Well, I'm sure that isn't true…and when I can think of a way to refute what you just said, I'll, well, say something." Oh boy, why was it when I got around a cute guy my I.Q. dropped to, like, fifty? I bit my lip when I noticed Ryan looking around again. He had something that looked suspiciously like a smile on his face when he saw the still smoldering ruin on my stove.

"Did you uh, burn something?"

"Oh, no, I…well it's fine…" I finished lamely. I motioned to the couch. "Make yourself comfortable. Dinner is uh, ready. I just have to get it onto the table." I scurried over to my stove and poked at the burned mass in my pan, big black flakes fell off of it. Shit, shit, shit, now what? "I hope you like your meat well done."

Ryan smiled. "Well done is fine."

"Great, because that's what you're getting." I muttered. I assembled the plates and glasses on my small table and brought the food, or what thought it could pass for food, over. "Uh, I think we're ready to eat." I said with a bright, strained smile. I sat across from him and served him up a helping of meat, potatoes and some collard greens, my personal favorite. I watched Ryan with intense interest as he attempted to cut into the meat on his plate. I winced when the knife made contact with the plate and the meat remained unscathed. He looked up, a large grin on his face and then went back to cutting into his food.

"This is, uh, great Holly." Ryan said through a mouthful of really blackened food. With each crunch I felt my face burn brighter and brighter, I was mortified. And just when I thought it couldn't get any worse he began to cough, continuously, even the water didn't seem to help. Okay, that's enough…how much torture can one-man stand.

"Please, stop Ryan, you'll die of food poisoning if you continue trying to eat that." I tried not to cry. "It's terrible, I know it is, you don't have to lie. I can't believe you even got down two bites." I got up and quickly removed his plate before he could eat anymore.

"Holly, really, it's not that bad."

I stared at him disbelievingly…was this guy for real? "Ryan, the pigs down at Mooney's farm probably eat better food from the trough."

Ryan began laughing and within moments I was joining him, it was hard not to. This was one joke at my expense that I didn't mind. So I wasn't a culinary genius, I had made the cute boy smile.

"It was nice of you to try. Did you forget about it or something?"

"I could lie and say yes, but I won't. No, I didn't forget about it. Did you try they potatoes, they're just as bad."

"Uh, those are potatoes?"

I groaned, great. "Yeah, well, they're supposed to be potatoes sautéed in a garlic butter sauce." I looked at the mess on the plate. "But I don't think they came out quite right. Nope, I'm just a terrible cook. I wanted to make it up to you, you know for my behavior this morning, I wanted to make an impression."

Ryan grinned, revealing those two perfect rows of pearly whites. "Oh, you made an impression."

I swatted him with a potholder. "Listen, I really tried. I've never been a very good cook."

"So what do you do?" Ryan curiously asked.

"Well, you know there is a new invention out today called the microwave." I grinned. "Lean Cuisine makes a surprisingly good lemon chicken. And, well, if you're really starving, there are always Hungry Man dinners. They make great chicken tenders. And hey, you get corn and a brownie with it." I noticed Ryan's bemused expression. "You cook?"

"Well yeah, otherwise I'd starve."

Oh great, it figures that of all the men in the world to date I'd choose the one man who actually cooks. "Complicated things?"

"What do you mean?"

"Well, like, do you cook stuff other than grilled cheese."

Ryan laughed and cleared his throat before he answered. "Well grilled cheese isn't really considered cooking, but, yeah, I cook things more complicated than that. One of these days I'll cook something for you."

"Yeah, okay." I looked at him and then at the plates. "Uh, I have some crackers? Do you like crackers?"

By this time Ryan was positively crowing. He was trying not to show how funny the situation was, and he was failing miserably. "Do you like pizza? How about we order a pizza."

Yeah, I could live with that. "Pepperoni and mushroom?"

"Sounds great to me."

"I could kiss you." I blurted out and then blushed furiously. What on earth had possessed me to say that? I think the heat was going to my head, or perhaps it was the fumes from my toxic food. I swallowed, watching Ryan's handsome face shift, god he was cute.

"So why don't you?"

My eyes widened. Could it be this easy? Well, yeah, he was a guy, I was a girl and we were alone in my apartment discussing what we wanted on our pizza, perfect timing. I put down the plates and walked towards him. He stood up from the chair and stood perfectly still, waiting for me. When I was merely an inch away from him I stood on my tiptoes and leaned in, Ryan closed the distance between us.

I waited. His lips were warm and gentle. He kissed me softly, sweetly. He gently parted my lips with his tongue and continued his exploration of my mouth. I pressed myself into his hard body and opened my mouth wider, meeting his tongue with my own. I waited. His body was warm against mine. Pressed together I could feel the heat generated by our bodies. His hair was silky smooth, almost too smooth for a guy, but textured like silk, golden colored silky wheat, he was perfect. And still I waited. Finally I pulled away and raised my violet eyes to his bright blue ones. He eyes were glassy and he was breathing heavy. He had a sappy smile on his face and his looked perfectly adorable. I wanted to wrap him up, stick him in my storage box and just keep him with me. I wanted to tell him that his kiss made me forget the want for cold flesh that continued to haunt me...I wanted to tell him all this, but I couldn't.

I had waited. I had waited for the explosion that would occur when he kissed me, when I felt his body pressed against mine for the first time. I had waited and felt a hard, twisted knot form in the pit of my stomach when it didn't happen. There was no explosion, no fluttering, and no attack of butterflies. It was warm and sweet and...nothing. I looked into his face and saw his flushed cheeks and happy smile and wondered if I had perhaps not given it the chance it deserved. He had obviously felt something.

"That was wonderful Hol." Ryan leaned forward, as if to kiss me again and frowned when I took several steps back. "Uh, is everything all right Hol?"

"Yeah, everything is fine Ryan. I think we should order that pizza and get studying. Didn't you tell me you had crappy notes for DeWitt?"

Still that frown marred his handsome face. "Yeah, I do." He nodded slowly. "Uh, okay, so we'll start."

I smiled tentatively, but inside I was fuming. Damn that vampire, well, shit, that was already a given. It was all Lucien's fault. Lucien's fault entirely that I couldn't truly let myself go with Ryan. I would have enjoyed—no, *loved*—Ryan's kiss if I hadn't remembered a certain pair of cold, dry lips that had laid siege to mine. Damn him, what right did he have invading my thoughts even when he wasn't around...that was doubly intrusive.

"Hol, you okay?"

"What?" I was jerked out of my angry thoughts by Ryan's sweet voice.

"You looked kind of distracted."

"Sorry, I'm fine. I was just thinking about something." I went to pick up the telephone. "So, pepperoni and mushroom?"

Ryan still looked confused. I didn't blame him. "Yeah, great."

I forced a smile. Yeah, everything was great. I really needed to get a new life, or maybe I'd just trade in the vampire boyfriend for a newer, fresher, more alive model. Then, well then, my life would be perfect, right?

Chapter Twenty:

Midterms sucked even more than Calculus. It seemed that no matter how hard you tried, no matter how hard you studied you still didn't know the answers. All that caffeine wasted, because at the end of the day you couldn't remember the difference between the diameter and the circumference of a circle. And what was with the little blue books? Did like, a group of college professors get together around a large table and discuss which colors would be more practical, or perhaps more soothing to the student body during times of unbelievable stress? Well, here's some news, the blue doesn't work, in fact, I spent more time wondering about why blue, than actually writing in the darned book. I know, my mistake, but I still think it's a strange choice, and completely arbitrary.

Professor DeWitt's midterm was surprisingly slim. For all of her talk about how much was being covered on the test, very little was actually covered, odd. There was the multiple-choice section, and then several essays, mostly covering rituals, spells and demonology. I whizzed through the test and looked around quickly to see if I was the only one who had found the exam rather simple. I found several other heads being lifted from over their exams and I heard someone let out a sigh. I double checked my answers and made my way to the front of the room. Professor DeWitt was sitting, legs crossed on the desk. Her eyes met mine and she smiled.

"Finished?"

"Yeah, I think so." I handed her the exam. She placed it next to her.

"How did it go?"

"I think it went pretty well."

Professor DeWitt laughed. "Things always go well for you Holly."

Uh, what was that supposed to mean? "Huh?"

"Just to say that you're a very smart young lady. I didn't think that this would be much of a challenge for you." She tilted her head to one side. She seemed to study me, much as a scientist would study a specimen under a microscope, it was that intense. "Are you still going to do research for me Holly?"

Was I imagining it, or was there an undercurrent of something in her voice? "Uh, yeah, I haven't forgotten Professor. I thought I'd begin in a couple of days. I have two more days of midterms and then, well then I'll have a little more time."

"Excellent." Professor DeWitt's smile widened. "This research means a lot to me…and I think you'll find that it will fascinate you almost as much as it did me. Who knows, perhaps you'll think about going into the field."

I smiled wanly and nodded. Okay, creepy. There was something distinctly creepy about Professor DeWitt these days. "I, well I'd better go…I have another test before the end of the day."

"Oh, of course, I didn't mean to keep you."

I tossed a look over my shoulder. Ryan was still taking the exam. I nodded to Professor DeWitt and hurried out of the classroom.

It was waiting for me when I got home, a huge vanilla orchid plant on my living room table. Vanilla orchids, god I loved them, and they were very rare and difficult to find. Not to mention they were totally not in season. A familiar blazing red card was propped up against the plant, but I didn't need to open it to know whom it was from. Who else would send me an orchid plant? Not to mention whom else owned fire engine red cards. I was torn between rushing over and ripping open the card or throwing a massive hissy fit because the vamp Holder of Edwards had come into my home while I was out. I was really going to have to un-invite that fang tooth fiend. Not that the orchids weren't beautiful, but I really couldn't have vamp Lucien wandering around my place while I wasn't around…talk about giving me the creeps. I jumped when the phone interrupted my thoughts. I really wasn't in the mood to answer, but remembering all the trouble I had gotten into lately, what with Detective Marcus I picked it up.

"Hello?"

"Holly flower."

Oh boy, big trouble. "Hello Lucien."

"Holly, I hope you like the gifts."

"Gifts? As in more than one?"

"Have you not checked your bedroom yet, Holly flower."

My temper began to flare. "You were in my bedroom?"

"Now, now, why do you not go and see what I have left you."

I clenched my hands, oh yeah, I was totally going to have to un-invite that bastard. I walked into my now invaded sanctuary and noticed a large black box on my bed. Nice, black, it figures. I hesitated.

"Are you frightened of my gift Holly?"

Damn, how did he do that? Why did the bastard always know what I was thinking? "No, not afraid." Liar, liar, pants on fire.

"Then, will you not take a look."

I sighed. I opened the box and pulled back the black tissue paper. My mouth fell open and I was speechless, but not for long. Was he joking? "Are you joking?"

"Whatever do you mean Holly flower?"

I stared at the contents of the box and shook my head, who did he think he was, the fashion police? Was he trying to tell me something? Well, whatever it was I didn't like it. "I told you no more suggestions, not even subtle ones."

"Is this a suggestion?" Lucien's voice was filled with mirth. Strange, it was strange hearing mirth in his voice.

"Well, what else could it be, you've sent me a dress."

"Could it not be that I merely liked the dress and thought it would look positively beautiful on your luscious body?"

The gown was filmy, nearly transparent and absolutely gorgeous, it was also totally not my style, I didn't often do gorgeous. Comfortable was more me. There were two layers to the gown, one bright red and one a smoky almost charcoal gray. Two such colors were not meant to blend but blend they did, seamlessly. The gray layer was a knit weave, detailed, meticulous, it looked like a finely woven spider web. The red layer was chiffon, soft and silky to the touch. There were small red and gray seed pearls lining the low bodice and the spaghetti straps were dripping with them as well. I fingered the delicate material and let out a low sigh of pleasure. The dress was beautiful. It was also presumptuous. "I can't take this."

"But of course you can." Lucien's voice had dropped and was now caressing my ear. I shivered, which was nothing new when dealing with the head vamp. He just seemed to have that effect on me.

"No, I can't. And you are not invited into my apartment."

"I have been invited."

"Yes, you were invited. But you are not invited any longer. You can't just come into my space when I'm not around, that is totally rude." I frowned when I heard him chuckle on the other end of the phone. "It's not funny."

"Yes, it is, Holly flower. A rude vampire, have you ever heard of such a thing? We vampires are always so very polite." He said this last mockingly.

"I don't care what you are, but I do care about my privacy. You are no longer invited into my house." I waited and several moments later I heard a deep sigh.

"It will be as you wish. I will no longer come into your domicile. However, you will keep the gifts, they were meant as such and cannot be returned."

"Tough, because I'm returning them." I bit my lip. "Well at least I'm returning the dress." I looked at the tag and rolled my eyes. "What do I need a Yves St. Laurent gown for anyways?"

"You will have many occasions to wear the gown my little Holly flower. Keep it."

"No."

"Must you always be so stubborn?"

I didn't hesitate. Never hesitate when you're speaking with a vamp. "Yes. I don't want or need the gown Lucien. So are you going to take it back or not?"

"And what will you wear to dinner tonight?"

"Excuse me?"

"Holly, Holly, Holly, what will I do with you? Did you not read the card, my little flower?"

"Don't call me your little flower, and no, I didn't get around to reading the card."

Lucien laughed. "So, read it."

I was not amused. He had me running back and forth from my rooms like some damn courier. I opened the card and read the elegant embossed writing. *Dinner, tonight, I will meet you at your apartment at ten. – Lucien.* "Thanks for asking me."

"I am asking you, that is the purpose of the note my Holly."

"That isn't asking, that's telling, you jerk."

"Jerk?"

"Yeah, as in idiot, ass…" I stopped because he interrupted me.

"I see." He paused before adding. "I will meet you at ten."

I rolled my eyes. You can't teach old dogs new tricks (and this was respectively a very old 'dog'). "There you go again, telling me. Why not ask me for once." I waited. He seemed to ponder this new development.

"Will you come to dinner with me tonight Holly?"

"No, I have too much studying to do, but thanks for asking." I was grinning. I could just imagine Lucien's annoyed and befuddled expression, I knew he had expected me to accept his invitation. Well, tough luck. I had too much work to do and he didn't have any right just ordering me out at the last minute. Not to mention I was still pissed at the breaking and entering thing.

"You will not come?"

I detected the warmth of anger in his voice and sighed. I really didn't want to have an angry vampire on my hands. But I was relatively safe since he was there and I was here. I groaned. Even I didn't believe that shit. If a vampire wanted to hurt you, well time or space wasn't a deterrent. "Lucien…" I softened my tone, "I really don't have time tonight. I had three midterms today I'm exhausted. And on top of that I have two more. You don't seem to understand how much pressure I'm under right now. I can't have dinner with you."

"I will have you home at an acceptable time."

I scoffed. Yeah right. "Who are you kidding? You never have me home at an acceptable time. I'm always waltzing into my apartment at like three in the morning. I can't afford to do that tonight Lucien. I have so much work to do and I'm physically and mentally drained. Because of you and all these damned late nights I haven't had a good night's sleep in ages. And, well, if I ever needed a good night of rest it's now. So, no, I'm not coming to dinner tonight." I ran out of breath and waited for the vampires response. It was forthcoming.

"It has been many days since I've seen you, my Holly flower."

Did the vampire miss me? Wow, what a novel thought. "I still can't see you Lucien."

"Holly…"

"No, no, no, no, no…"

"I take it your answer is no."

I smiled into the phone. The vamp was also developing a sense of humor. "My answer is no."

"And after your human exams."

"Are you asking me for a date after I finish my midterms Lucien?" I was still smiling.

"Yes, I believe I am."

"After midterms I'll have dinner with you Lucien."

"I have news for you Holly…" Lucien's voice was soft, seductive and caressed my ear. I felt like purring but, well, that would probably be inappropriate since I was giving him the brush off.

"What news?"

"News that must be imparted to you in person, I do not like the phone."

"Okay, well we'll talk after my midterms."

"All right then Holly. I am sure that any information I have on the murders can wait until you're done with your human exams."

My heart stopped. I gripped the receiver tightly in my hand. "Information on the murders?"

"Is that not what I just said? You really must listen more carefully Holly."

That blood-sucking bastard! "I hate you."

"Oh, Holly flower, you know that isn't true. You might wish that you hated me, but you most certainly do not hate me…I know the truth."

"You manipulated this entire conversation."

"That is also false. I did not manipulate anything. I merely told you the truth of it from the beginning. You were the one who complicated matters when you insisted on breaking our date."

"We didn't have a date you jerk." My eyes were blazing and I felt really in the mood to break something, preferably over Lucien's beautiful, dead, head.

"We most certainly did. But I am a reasonable man. If you do not wish to see me tonight, well then you do not have to. I will keep what information I have until the next time we see one another."

Oh, oh, damn! He knew I couldn't wait that long. It was obvious that he had set this up knowing I would cave in. The solving of this case was too important to leave whatever information the Vamp Holder of Edwards had in his head. I needed that info. "Okay. I hate your guts, but okay." I may have to go on this date, but I sure wasn't about to make this evening pleasant for him. He might be stone cold, but he didn't know the true meaning of it yet.

"Excellent. I am most pleased Holly flower. You shall wear the dress of course."

"Now wait a minute. I said yes to dinner, I did not say yes to the dress."

"But it was understood. The dress is appropriate. We are going to a very fine restaurant tonight, you must wear it."

"Now listen…"

"No, Holly, you do not have a suitable wardrobe. Your clothing is merely pleasant."

I wanted to hit him. He said pleasant like it was a bad thing. "My clothing is comfortable."

"Yes, comfortable. It is suitable for your human university. However, it is not suitable for dinner with me. Do not try to lie to me, I know you do not own a gown that is appropriate for this evening."

If he had been through my clothes I really was going to kill him. Right now a steak through the heart sounded terrific. How does French-fried vampire sound? "Did you go through my things you…you…?"

"No, I did not need to. I know you Holly, you may not like the thought but it is true. I have seen what you have worn to meet me. You have tried valiantly, but it is obvious that you own very little that is…fashionably correct. I do not understand why you would begrudge me gifting you with a lovely gown."

Okay, now he was the fashion police. He had some nerve. I can't believe he was telling me that I didn't dress well. He was dead, what did he know about fashion? Well, okay, so he always looked gorgeous. I think that was a vampire rule. If you're going to be dead, at least be well dressed. "I'm going to look ridiculous." Okay, I wasn't caving. I was merely playing around with the idea…it was a beautiful gown.

"You shall look like the beauty that you are. Do not worry about your escort, I shall pick you up myself, at ten."

I looked at the wall clock. That didn't give me too much time. "Are you going to be on time?"

Lucien chuckled. "Why are you asking? Are you planning on standing me up?"

Stand up a vampire? Did he think I had a death wish? Uh, don't answer that. "Just wondering if I had enough time to get ready, it is getting late."

"You will have enough time. Until later, Holly flower…" Lucien hung up the phone and I banged my head against the wall. I was definitely a sucker, a big time sucker.

I hated when the vampire was right. The dress was perfect. It fit my body like a glove and the colors complimented my skin perfectly. The glass beads shimmered in the light and the material felt like a slice of heaven. I had arranged my hair in a loose chignon and added some shimmery makeup that I thought finished the look quite nicely. I had fished out some high heels, which had probably not been worn since my early high school days. I had to blow off the dust and polish them a little, but, hey, it's a good thing I don't throw anything out. I tied a piece of black velvet around my neck to act as a choker and pinned a small cameo that I had inherited from my mother. Yeah,

I don't usually wear anything that belonged to my mother…mostly because she dressed like a missionary and didn't believe in adornments. However, the choker had belonged to her mother and for some strange sentimental reason, she had kept it. Funny, my mother had never struck me as the sentimental type. I studied myself in the mirror again and once again wanted to hit the vampire. Yeah, okay, I looked great. The doorbell rang and I carefully made my way over to the door, don't laugh, I wasn't used to the heels. What greeted my eyes could only be classified as the tenth wonder.

"You look terrific." I muttered. I didn't want to say it, but when you have the tenth wonder at your door you kind of have to acknowledge it.

"You take my breath away Holly flower." Lucien was breathtaking.

Garbed in a tuxedo, his auburn hair pulled back from his patrician face he was almost too beautiful to be true. I took him in, from his head to his toes and I think he only got more beautiful with each look. "Yeah, you kinda take my breath away too." I sounded like an awestruck teenager, but, hey, that was how I felt right now.

"Are you ready to go my Holly?"

"I'm not your anything Lucien."

Lucien sighed. "Are you ready to go?"

"Yeah." I took Lucien's hand hesitantly. I was always hesitant around Lucien. One wrong move and I was going to have to say a thousand Hail Marys. There was a sleek black limo pulled up to my curb. I didn't want to be impressed but I was. The closest I had been to a limo was when my friend Gwen had dropped off to say hello to me in hers before she had gone to the senior prom, yeah, the same prom I had missed.

Once seated in the back I let myself luxuriate for a moment. I took in the plush black leather interior, the mini bar, the small television and telephone and wondered if there was anything else I was missing? Perhaps there was a dancing bear that jumped out and entertained us while we waited. This was too much. I turned to see Lucien staring at me bemused. His green eyes were filled with light laughter and his mouth was curved upwards in a smile. I shut my mouth and crossed my arms across my chest. Remember, I was not going to give him an easy time at this. He had all but blackmailed me into coming to dinner tonight and he wasn't going to get any pleasure out of me. I tossed him an insolent look and wasn't reassured when his smile grew wider.

"You have never been in a limo before Holly?"

"So?"

"I was merely asking. I am glad I can give you your first experience."

Oh no, I really didn't like that suggestive tone of his. "Stop it."

"Stop what Holly flower?"

"Stop that."

"What is it that you are referring too?"

"You know very well."

"I am afraid you have me at a disadvantage Holly. I do not understand what you are saying."

Lucien's face was dancing with laughter and mirth. Oh that smug bastard. Why was it I was surrounded by smug, arrogant men? Is it so much to ask that I find a man who is sensitive, kind and modest? I found myself frowning. Hadn't I already found that man? Wasn't Ryan exactly that type of guy? Sensitive, kind and modest, not to mention that he cooked to boot. What more could I possibly want? Why then wasn't it working out between us? Oh, the study session had gone well. We had compared notes about Aztec and Judeo-Christian demons over several slices of mushroom and pepperoni pizza. Yeah, it had been just jolly. We had shared that lovely kiss, the kiss that he had wanted to repeat at the end of the night. I gave him my cheek. Effectively stopping any repetition of 'the kiss', oh yeah, I had sabotaged it. I was like one of those people who don't vote. But then want to bitch to you on the current demoralization of our nation. Here I was bitching about there not being any good, decent, alive men, when I kept sabotaging a relationship with one of those exact men.

"Your mind is working frantically little Holly."

"Uh, what?"

"You are thinking very hard. I could almost see the wheels turning."

"No."

"No what…"

"No, I wasn't thinking that hard." It came out in a rush and I gave him a look as to say, drop it. He took the hint and nodded. "Where are we going?"

"To dinner."

"Yeah, you told me that, where?"

"Ah, the restaurant is called 'Nectar' it is five star dining."

My eyebrows wrinkled. "Is this your restaurant?"

"I own it, yes."

"The one you told me about before."

"I believe I did say that next time we would dine out, yes."

I sank back into my seat. Well I had been talking about broadening my horizons, what was more broad than eating at a vampire restaurant?

"Do not worry my Holly flower, you shall find the food magnificent. I own only the best." Lucien smiled and I frowned.

"About this information."

Lucien laughed. That beautiful, sensual laugh that invaded my dreams and my waking thoughts. "Ah, I think not. No, I shall tell you how it will go this evening my Holly flower. We will enjoy a lovely dinner and then after, once all is finished I shall tell you what I know. This way we can enjoy the experience." Lucien's smiling face suddenly turned dark, like a quick storm over the sun. "For after I tell you what I know I can guarantee you will not be in the mood to eat."

Great, an ominous warning, I loved those at the onset of a meal.

Chapter Twenty-One:

I wondered if anyone could see my boobs. The light from the chandelier kept reflecting off of the bodice of my dress and I had the most horrible feeling of exposure. The tables were all set with fine crystal and china. The food smelled divine and the wait staff was all dressed in appropriate black and white, why then did I feel so uncomfortable? Well, perhaps it was the fact that the patrons were all vampires and their 'pets.' Each table held an array of vampires and humans. But not just any humans, 'dead bait,' or if you want the more PC term, 'human companions.' It wasn't any secret, the humans seemed quite proud of their 'war wounds.' The eclectic blend of men and woman wore skimpy, tastefully revealing outfits and had an array of bite marks upon their very exposed flesh. I shuddered.

The couple across from us consisted of an older vampire and his very nubile, young human companion. She was obviously barely the consenting age. Her wheat blond hair was cut ala Jennifer Aniston and her body seemed courtesy of Pamela Anderson. She was sporting several red swollen bite marks on her neck and on her wrist. The wrist wounds were exposed every time she lifted the glass of champagne to her shimmering lips. Her vampire keeper kept eyeing her as if she were a particularly delicious meal he was about to consume, and perhaps he was. She in turn giggled and batted her eyelashes, I wondered if she had more brains than poor dead bait Vanessa...probably not. Was this what I was? Was I just a vampire's pet floozy? Was my acceptance of vampire Lucien an acceptance of this lifestyle of evil and perversity? And did I truly think this lifestyle was perverse and evil?

"You are not she."

I turned my eyes back to Lucien's deep green ones. "What?"

"You are not the young girl across from us. You are nothing like her."

"How do you do that?" I was beginning to think that Lucien had been keeping secrets from me, how else could you explain the knowing what I was thinking all the time.

"I can read you Holly. I told you from our first meeting that you are exceptional. I see things filter through your eyes and across your face much like rippling water. The emotions and thoughts and feelings are so intense that you shatter me at times. I can read what I can see, but rest assured that I cannot read your mind."

I was not assured. How could I be? I had spent years fortifying my mind and now I learned that I had to learn to fortify my face as well. I thought I had mastered it, obviously I hadn't. However, I had never come across a vampire Holder before either. Maybe he was just more intuitive than the rest. "Is it always like this?"

"Like what Holly?"

"Uh, well…" I swept my gaze around the room. I gritted my teeth, I was getting stray thoughts and the odd emotion or two, I didn't like it. I really, really didn't want to get anybody's stray thoughts in this place, and I especially didn't want anyone else's emotions. God that was just what I needed. Dead bait emotions.

"If you mean do we have many vampire clientele the answer is, yes. We are a very exclusive establishment and we serve only the best. I have always believed in the best." Lucien smiled at me before he continued. "It is expected that our unusual clientele would bring their…companions with them. We do not discriminate. We offer excellent service, excellent cuisine and excellent…benefits."

Did I really want to know? Yeah, I did. "What benefits?"

"The restaurant is attached to a very discreet, and specially serviced hotel."

My eyes widened. I hadn't realized that the restaurant was part of a hotel. And I most certainly hadn't been aware of any vampire hotels in the area. But then again, we had driven out of Edwards and closer to Charlotte. "You, uh, house vampires?"

"Most certainly. Which is why the security is so tight. You can never be too careful of the fanatics nowadays my little Holly flower."

"Yeah. I guess you're right." My mind was reeling. The vampire Holder of Edwards was an entrepreneur.

Just then the food arrived. I stared at the food. I hadn't ordered anything. Actually I hadn't even seen a menu. I looked up at Lucien's still face and frowned. "I didn't order anything."

"Nay, I did though."

"Excuse me?"

"I am sorry. I took the liberty of ordering your meal for you Holly flower."

"And why did you do that? Didn't you think that I would like to see a menu? You know I am perfectly capable of ordering for myself"

"Unfortunately not in this restaurant" Lucien motioned towards a waiter. "The servers are all…"

"Dead, yeah, I noticed that."

Lucien grimaced at my curt tone. "Yes, they are all night walkers. We do not have any menus here Holly. We communicate mind-to-mind." Lucien finished.

I stared at him impassively. Which was to say I was deciding if I was going to get angry at him or not. So this really was a vampire restaurant. Owned, operated and functioned in vampire capacity. I didn't know how I felt about that really. I looked down at my plate. The meat was cooked to perfection. The aroma was already tantalizing my senses. The little red potatoes on the side were smothered in butter, chives and garlic. And the asparagus looked heavenly. I winced. So this was how meat and potatoes were supposed to look. I thought back to that disaster I had prepared for Ryan and almost choked on my wine. Pathetic, it was pathetic that vampire chefs could cook better than I could. God? Were there vampire chefs? "Lucien?"

"Yes Holly flower?"

"Uh? Who prepares the food?"

Lucien laughed. "Are you afraid that there are vampires cooking your dinner little Holly?"

"No, uh, yes." I winced. "Yeah, all right, yeah." I couldn't stop a little shudder that ran through my body. "I can't help but find that thought a little bit icky."

"Well put your mind at ease, the restaurant may be vampire, but the chefs are most certainly of the human persuasion. If you recall my little Holly flower, we cannot eat human food, nor, are our senses so keen when it comes to…human cuisine. I could not employ vampires to cook in light of that fact."

"Why do you guys even come to restaurants then?"

"You guys?" Lucien cleared his throat. "If you mean, why do we in the vampire community go out to restaurants it is because of something I revealed to you before. When I told you that I receive pleasure from seeing you consume food I was not lying. Your enjoyment is thusly my enjoyment. I am not alone in this pleasure. Many vampires like to watch their companions eat. They enjoy the experience of dining in a human capacity, we are no longer human, and we may not all remember the 'old' ways, but that is not to say that we do not wish to." Lucien sighed. "Something this simple means very much to very many."

Strangely, I understood. How must it feel to be living for so long but not alive? To have all this strength, power, and near immortality but not to be able to have something as simple as the enjoyment of food.

I gingerly cut into the meat and sighed in contentment. The meat was cooked perfectly. The outside was brown and crisp and the inside was a tantalizing pink. The moment I popped it into my mouth I could feel my whole body react, god it was good. I closed my eyes and savored the taste, now this was meat. When I opened my eyes again Lucien was leaning on the table staring at me so intently that I felt a blush creep into my cheeks. I knew now why he stared and I understood his need to 'see' me, but that didn't stop the weirdness I felt having him do so. It wasn't a normal thing, to stare so while someone ate, but then again, vampires were so not normal. And I was so beginning to realize that.

Half an hour later I had consumed everything and was stuffed like a capon. I was certain that if I stood the seams would pop out of my dress. I took several deep breaths. If there were a god he would let me digest fast. Okay, I really needed to get my mind off of how stuffed I was.

"Okay. So I've missed like hours and hours of studying to accompany you to this restaurant and…" I grimaced. "Eat the most delicious food I've probably ever tasted in my entire life." I ignored Lucien's smile. "I want the information now."

Lucien shook his head. "I believe we should wait."

"Wait for what?"

"Until we are in a more private setting. And you are feeling a little less…full" He said this last with a grin.

I stuck my tongue out at him. Yeah, real mature, and really smart, stick your tongue out at the vampire. It would serve me right if he bit it off. Thank god he couldn't read my thoughts, I really didn't need to give him any ideas. "A more private setting?"

"Yes, I have a room prepared for us."

"Uh, what?" I knew I sounded lame and that I was staring at him like a moron, but I really just thought I had heard him say that he had a room prepared for us, prepared for us and for what?

"I own the hotel, do you not remember Holly? Perhaps you should have your ears checked."

"Shut up. Now what the hell do you mean you have a room prepared for us"

"We need a place to talk, we cannot very well talk in the restaurant. I have a delightful room, we'll talk there."

I shook my head. "Oh no, absolutely not."

"It has already been arranged. I use this room when I need it, when I stop through. It is ideal for us."

"You're absolutely too much." I said.

"Come." Lucien held out his hand and waited.

"Uh, what about the bill."

He looked at me indulgently, again, that parent to child look. "It has been taken care of, come now."

I took his hand and let him lead me out of the restaurant via the back way. The first sign of anything, well, anything fishy and I was out of there. Just because he was dead didn't mean he didn't know the meaning of funny business. A man was a man, right?

The room was beautiful. Unlike Lucien's black, white and red scheme ala his offices at 'Corruption' and his tomb, this room was light, airy and very, dare I say it, feminine? The walls were a creamy sea shell pink and the carpeting was made to match. The furniture was delicate, detailed and very, very old. I let my eyes take it all in and the more I saw the more impressed I was.

"You find this room very different?"

"Uh, hell yeah. I mean, look at this place." I laughed. "You're sure not the decorator."

Lucien frowned. "And why not?"

I began to giggle. My giggles then turned into laughter. "If you decorated this place then I'm the Queen of England."

"I could have."

"Ah, no, you couldn't have." I smiled at him. Now it was my turn to look at him indulgently. "You didn't, did you." It was a statement not a question.

Lucien gritted his teeth and after a long pregnant pause answered. "No, I did not decorate."

"Ha, I knew it." I knew it was petty to take such pleasure in my being right but well then…I was just going to have to be petty.

"Laeticia decorated." Lucien said.

My mouth gaped open. Lucien was staring at me with a huge smile on his face. He was obviously enjoying my stupefied shock. I was trying to figure out if he was lying or not. But somehow I just knew he was not lying. Somehow I just knew that scary ass, 'I want to eat you' vampire Laeticia had designed and decorated this beautifully feminine and peaceful room. Now, wasn't that a scary thought.

"She has quite a talent for these sorts of things. She particularly enjoyed doing this room." Lucien smiled, it was almost wistful, his expression. "I did not think I would like it, but I have found that I do, like it very much."

"Well, it's, nice."

Lucien could barely contain his glee, I could tell. He just loved to shock me and he loved how uncomfortable he made me. "So, the info." I chose an ornate chair to sit in. I wondered for a moment if I would break it under my weight, but then decided that well, they didn't make things like they used to, and that it was safe to sit in.

"So forward, my little Holly flower."

"Yeah, you already know this about me. And I already know that you love to stall, and that you love to manipulate me you annoying jerk. So let's get this over with."

Lucien sighed melodramatically. "I had thought, that after all this time we would have been able to dispense with all of this…"

"All of what?"

"This little charade."

I stiffened. "I don't know what you're talking about."

"Oh but you do, Holly flower." Lucien came to stand in front of me. He parted my legs with his and came to stand between them. I calmed my racing heartbeat. "You are very good at this charade Holly. You do not wish me to *rush* things, anymore than I wish to." The way he said rush made it sound obscene, and with Lucien it probably was.

"This is important." I swallowed. Lucien's head was dipping down. In one deft movement he had released all that long, silky hair and it was falling free around his face. It hung like heavy silk around him and brushed my face, I shuddered, and he smiled.

"Yes, very important." His voice was deep and beckoning. It wrapped itself around me like the ebb and flow of the tides. It pulled at my heart, my soul, and at my mind…my mind?

I jerked and pushed backwards out of my chair so hurriedly that it fell to the floor. I barely registered the thump it made as it contacted the ground. I turned furious eyes to Lucien's and tried to contain my mounting anger. "You tried compulsion you bastard." I took several steps back. "You know how I feel about compulsion and you tried it anyways." I clenched my hands into fists. "I can't believe that for a moment I trusted you." I laughed bitterly. "That's a joke, god, trust…trust a vampire? I must be completely insane." Lucien made a move towards me; a single thrust of my hand stopped him, that and the fact that there was now a large desk between us.

Lucien stared at the desk with surprise. It hadn't been there a moment before. He knew by now that I was adept with telekinesis but it obviously continued to startle him. The desk hadn't been much of a challenge. I hadn't had to move it far.

"Holly flower…"

"Don't you Holly flower me, you, you…dead person." I was so angry I couldn't even think of a better comeback. "I'm going home, now."

"How?"

"I'll walk." I began to stride to the door, in the blink of an eye he was in front of me and his arms were effectively blocking my escape.

"All the way back to Edwards, Holly flower?"

"If I have to walk to Edwards then I'll walk to Edwards." I glared at him. "I need the exercise, it'll be good for my girlish figure."

Lucien pulled me closer, and I began to struggle in earnest. I did not want this. I was not going to be swayed this time. He had done an intrusive, and inconsiderate thing, and he had done it for the last time. "You are not being reasonable my little Holly. You are trying to put distance between us and you are using whatever means you can think up. It was not compulsion. Do you blame me for the cadence of my voice."

"Oh, oh, yeah right, the cadence of your fucking voice. What sort of bullshit is that? You know I'm angry when I begin to swear. "You were using compulsion, even when you know how I feel about it, how it makes me feel." I would not cry. Who was I kidding? I was way too angry to cry. "Now let me go you asshole."

"No."

"What?"

"We will discuss this."

"There isn't anything to discuss. I want to go home. If you won't take me home, well then I'll walk home. Or perhaps I'll hitchhike, how do you like that. Ten to one I'm safer hitchhiking than I am with you, you, you…" I couldn't think of anything else, I had used up all the bad words in my vocabulary.

Lucien's face had become still and quiet once more, I knew he was angry, hell I knew he was furious. He had not let me go, but he hadn't tried to pull me closer, actually his arms had stilled around me completely. The silence stretched out between us for what seemed like an eternity…obviously, though, it wasn't an eternity, I wouldn't be alive then, and well, Lucien, that was debatable. When he finally spoke I felt as if a north wind was eating my skin alive with cold.

"I will not have you out alone. If you wish to go home, then I shall take you." With that he exited the room.

I stared at the door, which he had just exited out of. Had he just left? Had he actually just left without arguing with me more? I needed the ride home, that's what I told myself. Therefore, that was the reason I ran out of the room to catch up with him, for the ride, yeah, nothing else.

Chapter Twenty-Two:

The vampire was out of my life. That was what I had wanted. I should congratulate myself for so effectively dealing with the problem of Lucien. I would not let myself believe that I was melancholy. I was definitely not melancholy.

I had finished midterms and turned in all my papers. I had cleaned my apartment, done my laundry, sent off all my bills and even gone shopping, and there had not been one call from Lucien during that time. There were no more orchids or gowns or letters and no more calls in which his smoky voice would caress my ear, and other parts of my susceptible body. I was pleased by this fact, obviously. I mean, he was a pain in the royal behind, not to mention dangerous as all hell. Continuing to date him would have meant a serious possible deduction in my lifespan. I finally had the vampire out of my hair, so to speak, I could finally get good nights sleep…and I couldn't sleep.

I tossed in my bed. I woke up with the sweats. I found myself looking at shadows and seeing faces where there were none. I had to get a grip. I was a strong, intelligent, young woman and I did not need dealings with the dead. Indeed, my life had been un-complicated, pleasant and perfectly normal before that gorgeous, lying dead guy had abducted me. He was the cause of all my problems. And now that he was removed my problems would be removed, well obviously. It was the logical conclusion. *Beep, Beep, Beep, Beep, Beep, Beep,* I jumped. Damned beeper. I checked it, all though, who knows why I did, I already knew who was paging me, Detective frigging Marcus. Great, just great, could my week get any better? I was cursed, that had to be it, I was certainly cursed, what other reason could there be?

I picked up the telephone and dialed the blinking number on the pager.

The phone picked up after one ring.

"Marcus."

"It's Holly."

"We have to talk."

I knew better than to ask him about what. "Where do you want to meet?"

"I'll meet you at your place in fifteen."

"All right...but..." I didn't get to finish. He had already hung up the phone.

"You look like hell." I told a gray faced, dark eyed, Detective Marcus. He did. He had deep, dark circles under his eyes and look like he hadn't slept in forever, he probably, most likely, hadn't. His clothes were wrinkled and obviously not clean and his frown was even more prominent than usual.

"Thanks, it's good to know that I look how I feel."

"Uh, come in, have a seat..." I gestured towards the room. "Anywhere."

Detective Marcus chose the couch. He slumped down and rubbed his eyes with the back of his hand. He put down the folder he had been carrying on the coffee table and it was just then I noticed a slim book beneath the folder. "So...we've got something." Detective Marcus sighed. "The only problem is that we're not sure what we've got"

I was bewildered. "What do you mean?"

Detective Marcus opened his folder and pulled out a photo which he handed to me. "What do you see?"

I looked at the photo and shook my head. Suddenly something caught my attention and I went in for a closer look. What? Okay what was going on? "Detective that looks like Pamela Courtland."

"Yeah, you think so?"

I looked up from the photo and saw his tired face. I nodded and looked again. "Yeah. I mean I didn't know her too well and we didn't hang out, but that really looks like her. I clearly remember the picture they showed on the news, and well she was easily recognizable around campus." I turned curiously to Detective Marcus. "I don't understand."

"Yeah, well that makes two of us, kid. This picture was taken at 'Thermal' and it was taken after Pamela Courtland was murdered."

"That doesn't make any sense Detective."

Detective Marcus stood up suddenly. He began to pace and he continued to rub his eyes. "You think I don't know that. Fuck, most of the department thinks its some sort of hoax." He slammed his fist down on the photo. "This is not some fucking hoax. This is a photo of a supposed dead girl drinking at a bar inhabited by vampires. And it's a photo taken after her death. The pictures don't lie."

"I see what you're saying Detective. But something obviously isn't adding up. I mean Pamela Courtland is dead, isn't she?"

"Yeah. The coroner examined her. She was deader than dirt. Jeez there was even a mass and service for her."

I remembered the service. There had been two. One service was for the family and the other was a service for the students of EU. Suddenly I had a really, really, awful thought.

"Oh, gross." I muttered.

Detective Marcus heard me and stopped his pacing. "What? You've thought of something, tell me."

"It's, uh, really, well not a pleasant thought Detective."

"I don't give a crap, tell me."

"Have you, uh, checked her grave."

Detective Marcus's eyes grew wide and he fell back onto the couch with a thump. "You think her body is gone?"

"Weirder things have happened" I shrugged my shoulders. "It's all I can think of, the only thing I can think of to explain this."

"You think she's a zombie?"

I shook my head. Boy, it was really time to educate the Edwards police force in the ways of the occult and unnatural. Basically it was time to bring them into the twenty first century. "No, zombies don't have rational thoughts, actually they don't really have any thoughts. They are pretty much just the shell of what once was. They have urges and needs, depending on what brings them back. You've probably seen zombie flicks before, haven't you Detective?" When he nodded I continued. "Well they are not like the zombies in movies, but then movies usually don't portray anything correctly. Zombies are pliable, thusly, easily utilized because they have motor skills, basic ones, but motor skills nonetheless. The most amazing thing about zombies is, the fact that they are really strong. They will continue until they reach their goal. Like I said, they're used a lot because they're pliable. A lot of amateur voodoo priestesses or priests will bring back a zombie. Usually they're not very effective though. I've found that not many can bring back a really effective zombie. Not powerful enough, or not enough knowledge about the dynamics of the materials or spells needed." I finished and gave Detective Marcus an intent look. "So, do you want the good news or the bad news first?"

"Give me the good news."

"The good news is that it's easier to kill a zombie. Basically a zombie is just a reanimated rotting corpse. You can dispose of a rotting corpse, bones are just bones, skin is just skin…etc. You can shatter bone and well you can break skin. So, you see, a zombie is not indestructible."

"Okay, now what's the bad news?"

"That girl in the photo…" I paused. Even I didn't like what I was going to say. "She is definitely not a zombie…I can't believe I'm saying this, but I wish she was." I pointed at the photo. "She's perfect. Look at her. Her skin is unblemished, her complexion, healthy, I mean she looks healthier than you do for goodness sakes."

"Thanks a lot."

"Sorry. What I mean to say is that she is way too…well alive to be a zombie. Zombies don't come back in good condition Detective. It is a long, hard way back from the grave and they don't stand the wear and tear well. Your girl would not look that good if she were a zombie."

"What the hell else can she be?"

"I don't know."

"I'm not hallucinating, am I Holly? I mean that is the dead girl."

I nodded. "I see her too Detective. That is definitely Pamela Courtland, or else, it's her evil twin sister. And I think that only happens in Soap Operas." I put down the photo and pulled out the book beneath the folder. *Modern Mysticism* by Dr. Desmond Winthrop. I held the book out to Detective Marcus. "So, what are you doing with this Detective?"

Detective Marcus shrugged his massive shoulders and sighed. "I thought it was time that perhaps I did some research."

I grinned. "So what made you choose Winthrop?"

"I think I saw him on Oprah."

I laughed. "Yeah, okay, not a bad referral. You may want to try Richardson's *Devils, Demons and Gods*.

"Good?"

"Yeah, actually it is. It's basic but good."

"Thanks, I'll look into it. So…what do you think about taking a trip with me to the cemetery."

What did I think? It was the only place that housed the dead that I hadn't been to lately.

After getting permission from Pamela's parents and going through the appropriate channels, Detective Marcus and I made our way to 'Edward's Memorial Cemetery.' Pamela's grave was easily located, it was the one covered with flowers and with the headstone that featured her photo smack dab in the center.

I watched uneasily as they began to dig up Pamela Courtland's grave. There was something very wrong about disturbing someone's resting place. When the crane had lifted the coffin from the moist dirt and lowered it down to the ground, I, along with Detective Marcus made our way over. "Does it bother you Detective?"

"Does what bother me?"

"Digging her up."

Detective Marcus sighed. It was a heavy sigh, one filled with remorse and weariness. "I don't have the time to let it bother me. I have a case to solve, and well, if this is the lead we need, then I'll do what I must." With those curt words he took a crowbar and pried open the top of the coffin.

"Shit." I muttered.

"My sentiments exactly." Detective Marcus said.

I stared into the empty coffin and felt my stomach clench painfully. This was one time I had really hoped I was wrong. The smooth satin interior was shiny and seemed to wink at me mockingly. Pamela Courtland wasn't a zombie. But if she wasn't a zombie and she wasn't dead, then what the hell was she? "Well, uh, look on the bright side, Detective."

"There's a bright side?"

"She won't be difficult to locate." I forced a smile onto my tight face. "I mean, just tell your units to keep a watch out for...a sort of, maybe, dead girl."

"God, no one is going to believe this shit."

I was frustrated and most certainly annoyed. What was wrong with everyone? First Ryan told me he didn't believe in magic, and now Detective Marcus reaffirmed the fact that the entire Edwards Police Force was completely ill informed when it came to modern mysticism and the supernatural. Not to mention that most of them were obviously disbelievers. But what did I really expect? I was living in the town where the most exciting thing that happened was the Pumpkin Day Parade in October. "We need to find her Detective. We need to find her fast. Whatever she is, it can't be good. Nothing comes back from the dead good." I pushed thoughts of vampire Lucien out of my mind. I didn't have time for them right now. "The longer she is animated...well, the more damage she could do."

"She can't get far. Everyone recognizes her."

I thought for a moment. "Did you say that photo was taken at 'Thermal'?"

"Yeah. It's that vamp bar right outside of the Edwards city limits."

"I know the place you're talking about Detective." I ignored his look of curiosity. If I wanted to tell him I'd tell him later. Right now I was thinking. "She was spotted at a vampire bar having drinks. If she's truly dead she can't drink Detective."

"So what?"

"So, obviously she was there for another reason." I thought about Lucien's missing vampire and frowned. Were both things connected? Were they related to one another, Pamela's missing corpse and Lucien's missing vampire, well, and his likely, dead vampire? "I need to go check up on something Detective."

"All right."

"Just like that? No argument?"

Detective Marcus shook his head. "Too tired right now for an argument."

Okay, I could accept that. "Can you take me home?"

"Certainly."

"Thank you."

I left Detective Marcus with a promise that I would call him later. The moment his car was out of sight I rushed into my apartment, picked up the telephone and dialed the dreaded number.

"Corruption."

"I need to speak to Lucien."

There was silence and I could only detect heavy breathing. I was not amused. I had not called for phone sex. "I know he's...under for the day, but tell him Holly called for him. I need him to call me back, it's very important" I tried to curb my annoyance when I was put on hold and terrible 'elevator music' assailed me. It seemed like an eternity before a voice came back on the line.

"Hello."

"Hi, it's Holly, I'm calling for Lucien..." I rushed on when she would have interrupted. "I know, I know, he's dead to the dawn, but I need him to call me pronto, the minute he wakes up, it's really important."

"Give me the message, I will relay it to our master."

I laughed. "I'm sorry, it's just that I don't know you from Adam...I'm certainly not going to talk to you. Just tell Lucien Holly called." I hung up. He'd call back, I was certain of it. Well I was fairly certain.

I spent the day a bundle of nerves. It had been awhile since Lucien and I had spoken and we hadn't left on the best of terms. Actually, I sort of think we broke up. Broke up? Jeez, what was I talking about? I, occupied my time with more research, yeah it was becoming apparent that I was good at this sort of thing.

I double checked my references and confirmed that the sulfur was a binding mechanism for the summoned demon, not the slain vampire. I also had a little fight with my computer, yeah we fought often, it, just came with the territory, the 'I'm totally inept with technology' territory. Obviously my computer didn't respect me, and how did one have a relationship without respect? I was still glaring at the glossy screen when the shrill ring of the telephone startled me. I picked up instantly.

"Hello?"

"Holly."

I knew that voice. I sunk gratefully into the nearest chair and almost wept with relief. I had never thought I'd see the day when I was relieved to hear the vampire's voice.

"Lucien, thank you for calling me back."

"What can I do for you Holly?"

I swallowed, so, he was still angry. It was pretty obvious. His voice was cool and the chill reached me even over the phone. Well, I didn't have time to deal with the nuances of our very twisted relationship…too many things to settle and get straightened out. "I really must speak with you Lucien."

"So, we shall speak."

"Where?"

"My offices, twenty minutes." He hung up the phone.

Great, I'd pissed off the vampire.

Chapter Twenty-Three:

Lucien's offices were still stark and meticulous. But tonight I wasn't really in the mood to take in his decorating abilities. Lucien was dressed all in black, from his silk shirt to his now trademark leather pants. His long, thick hair was hanging free, and fell like a cloak around his body. I swallowed nervously. There was nothing human, nothing, soft, about Lucien tonight. His face was so pale I could see the fine blue veins in his cheeks. His mouth, those lips I remembered so well were now, at this moment, an almost unnatural shade of red. His eyes were startlingly pale green tonight, and it scared me. He had never looked more the predator, except perhaps, for that time he had nearly bitten my head off in the throes of what he would obviously like to think was passion. His cool countenance bothered me, I wasn't used to it. I had seen the many faces of vampire Lucien, but tonight, tonight was new.

"So, you wished to see me. I am here, you are here, what did you wish to see me about Holly?" Lucien tilted his head to one side and studied me. "I had thought after our last meeting you would have wanted to distance yourself. You seemed quite intent on ending our...liaison. Intent on running."

I looked him directly in the eyes. "You once told me that there was nowhere I could go that you wouldn't find me...nowhere I could run that you wouldn't hunt me down." I walked closer. "Has that changed?"

"Nothing changes, especially not nature." Lucien stood and rounded the desk. He came to stand a foot away from me. His appearance scared me, but for once I wasn't running.

"So you know that I am not running."

"But you were." He closed the distance between us and took my warm face in his cold hands. I didn't flinch. His cold, dry hands felt good on my now heated skin. "You erected barriers between us that night that not even I could breach if I wished to. You fortified yourself so strictly that you would never be breached."

I sighed. "I have done it most of my life Lucien. It is nothing new."

"And you lied."

"What?" Now, I was surprised. I hadn't lied to him. "I haven't lied to you Lucien."

"But you have lied to yourself."

"I don't know what you mean." I was still looking him directly in the eyes. He knew better now than to try compulsion on me, I wasn't worried that he would try to sway me with his eyes. His mind, now that was another story, but one worry at a time.

"Have you not lied to yourself Holly about your feelings for me?" He pressed those beautiful lips to my ear and caressed the outside skin with the tip of his tongue. I couldn't suppress a shiver of delight. "No, I will not ignore this issue any longer Holly flower. We will address this now, or we will address nothing."

I wanted to tell him this was too important to wait. That our little dating foibles weren't anything compared to the loss of lives that were being sustained in Edwards. But with him looking so hungry and his face pressed so tightly against my neck I wasn't sure that this was a good time to argue with him. "Okay, we'll talk then."

Lucien smiled against my neck. "What, no arguments little Holly flower…are you not feeling well."

"Ha, ha, very funny. I just thought since you were so kind as to take this meeting that I could take the time to listen to what you want to say to me"

"Very well." Lucien released me suddenly and I stumbled. I righted myself quickly. Gave him a quizzical look. Something was definitely up. "I have no use for this distance between us. I have given you more of myself than anyone over the recent centuries, but you, you continue to pull away from me." Lucien swept a lock of hair away from my face and walked away, back to his chair, and the sanctuary of his desk.

He continued to surprise me. Who would have thought that the vampire would miss me so much? Missing someone was such a human emotion that it had never occurred to me that he would have such thoughts. I really was at a loss for words, but it seemed that Lucien was not.

"I have become soft dealing with you, my people see the change…I see the change" Lucien sat and tapped his slender fingers on his desk. "I have wanted to give you the space that you seem to crave, but this space that you seek is used for ill purposes." His eyes glowed suddenly. I didn't like it when his eyes glowed. "Used for seeing other men."

"You mean Ryan?"

"Ah, yes, the boy. But have you not been seeing another man Holly flower?"

I wracked my brain, what the heck was he talking about, the only other man I had seen lately was…I laughed. "You can't be serious. Are you talking about Detective Marcus?"

"Yes, the detective. You spend a lot of time with this detective, Holly."

"I have to."

"Because of the murders, or for another reason."

Okay, didn't like what he was presuming at all. "Detective Marcus is a dedicated man. He wants to find this looney and stop him before he can kill anyone else, before he takes anymore victims…vampire or human." I held out my hands. "The two of you are working towards the same goal."

"Which would be?"

Okay, now he was just being dense. "Stopping the killer."

"Do you believe that is his only goal, Holly?"

I didn't hesitate. "Yes, I do."

"Then I will not question your infallible instincts. However, you and I must come to some sort of arrangement."

Why did I really, really not like the sound of that? "What sort of arrangement Lucien?"

"One where we will see each other more often, one where you will have more of a hand in our…community."

I gritted my teeth. I already was knee deep in the vampire community, what more could he want from me? I thought for a moment and then my eyes widened in horror. He didn't mean? "I'm not giving blood, Lucien. That is absolutely out of the question"

Lucien's face went passive but his eyes were still gleaming brightly. "I would never dream of suggesting that you give blood to anybody else but me Holly flower."

"I'm not giving blood to anyone, not even you Lucien." Jeez, what did I look like a blood bank? "Just because we're dating doesn't mean that you get to make use of my neck for nightly feedings."

"Oh, but there are much more pleasant places to take blood from than the neck."

I shuddered. This was just getting worse and worse. "You're not biting me Lucien."

Lucien shrugged. "Not yet." He smiled then. "I wish you to attend some...meetings with me, Holly flower, that's all."

"What sort of meetings." I asked suspiciously.

"Meetings, that as my...companion, you should attend." Lucien narrowed his eyes. "Meetings that my people expect you to be at...and you are expected to be suitably, meek." He said this last with a chuckle and I clenched my hands into fists. Meek, was he kidding me? Meek my ass!

"Hey, listen here buddy. There are a lot of things I am, but meek isn't one of them."

Lucien sighed. "Yes, I know, mores the pity." He smiled at my annoyed expression. "However, your attendance will be a start."

"Why do I even have to go?"

"You are my companion."

"We're dating Lucien...I mean...I'm not even certain if we're really even doing that. This whole thing is pretty fucking weird."

"You have spent time in my company in a less than casual capacity. My people recognize you as someone that means a lot to me. You have my protection and my care. This all adds up to the fact that you are now considered a vampire's companion. The fact that you are the Holder's human is even more crucial. I cannot allow defiance in my Hive, Holly, you know that."

I nodded. I did know that. The Hive was the most important thing to a Vampire Holder. As Lucien had told me before you cannot show weakness as a vampire or you will be forever ruled. The only way to survive is by strength and by the fear you impart on others. That is the rule of the Hive. "I understand that Lucien, but I don't see what this has to do with me."

"I have been too lenient with you thus far Holly. You are a sign of weakness to my Hive. They believe that I have grown soft, fragile, that you make me an unfit...leader."

"That's ridiculous," I scoffed. "You're like the badest badass of them all."

Lucien smiled slightly. "I take it to mean that you believe I am a capable leader, I thank you." His face took on that serious expression again and he continued. "However, I will not tolerate challenges to my authority. And I will not tolerate those who believe that my...affection for a human render me incapable to lead them."

"Is someone challenging your authority Lucien?" It seemed so implausible. Who would possibly have such a death wish?

"In the future, possibly. It is for this reason that our relationship to one another must be made clear. It must be acknowledged by the Southern Night Leaders, so that all may know that you belong to me."

"I don't belong to you." I really hated how vampires thought that humans were their pets. I wasn't anyone's pet. I was hardly anyone's girlfriend.

"You belong to me Holly."

Jeez, it was like talking to a brick wall. "Listen Lucien, I don't have time to argue this point with you. I understand what you're trying to tell me, but I don't agree with it. I don't see how our dating has made you weak in the eyes of your Hive. I don't see why they would give a crap who you date."

"I am the vampire Holder of Edwards."

He said this like it explained everything, and I guess it sort of did. The vampire Holder was the acknowledged leader. Everything he or she did was inspected and analyzed. The Hive's well being depended upon a strong leader, and that explained why Hive members took such interest in their leader's life, or in this case, death. "I'm not going to be anyone's property Lucien." I didn't care what he said. "I will come with you to a meeting or two…" Okay, so I was curious, didn't a girl have the right to be curious? "…but I am not going to be anyone's property and I will not let anyone cow tow me, it's not in my nature, you know that."

"I do. And I believe that the meetings will be quite…enlightening for you."

"Don't say things like that." I ignored his smile at my plaintive tone of voice. "You only make me worry and think that I should change my mind."

"Do not worry, no harm will befall you at these meetings Holly flower."

"Oh, great, I'm so reassured now." Oh, god, surrounded by a bunch of blood sucking beasties, that was all I needed to make my life complete.

"So, now, the reason you came tonight."

"Are we done…bonding?" I asked sarcastically. Lucien chose to ignore my tone of voice and nodded before answering to the affirmative. "I came because I need your help."

"My help? Well, well, have we changed so very much then Holly flower?"

I snorted. "Not, hardly. No, what I have to say will also affect you. I think it's time we pooled some resources here. I mean, ever heard of the saying, 'the partners that play together, stay together'?"

Lucien laughed. "I am not familiar with that saying, are you sure that is how it goes?"

I shrugged, "Does it matter?"

"No."

"Good, okay. So Detective Marcus showed me something really unsettling."

"Yes."

I could hear that undercurrent of anger in his voice and it was really beginning to annoy me. I can't believe the beautiful vampire is jealous of a grizzly detective and a college boy. Will wonders never cease. "It was a photo, a photo of Pamela Courtland. It was taken after her supposed death and it was taken at 'Thermal.'" I watched his face trying to detect expression, but there was none. I waited for him to speak and when he did not I shifted uncomfortably, why wasn't he saying anything. "We exhumed the body Lucien, just one problem…there wasn't any body to exhume. Pamela Courtland has effectively disappeared from her grave, there isn't any trace of her."

"Zombie?"

I shook my head. "No, you didn't see this picture Lucien, she looked perfect, she, looked healthy. It was not a zombie. I would have known if it were."

"The photo you say was taken at 'Thermal.'" Lucien's eyes bore into mine. "Are you certain?"

"Yeah."

"Yarbrow was at 'Thermal' on his day off," Lucien said. I had pretty much figured this out already, considering I had seen the body of the slain vampire and put two and two together. However, it was good to have it verified. "He was approached by a young woman, pretty, compelling."

Now this was new. My ears perked up and I gave Lucien my full attention. "Pamela?"

"I am assuming, yes, that it must be your missing girl. After some persuasion…the workers were eager to tell me what they knew, what they had seen that night at 'Thermal.'"

"When you say persuasion you mean torture, right?"

Lucien shrugged, and the look in his eyes was hardly remorseful. Actually he seemed to be telling me to get over myself. "We have been over this before Holly."

I sighed. Yeah, we had been over it before. And we'd go over it again, just not right now. "Go on."

"He was seen speaking to a lovely young girl. And many recall them leaving together."

It made sense. Yarbrow having been approached by Pamela, or at least by whatever Pamela now was, had been more than eager to leave with her. She was pretty, young and it seemed more than willing to donate a little blood (that was what I was guessing). But how did this all connect in with the Demon? And had Pamela killed Yarbrow, was that even possible?

"There are other possibilities."

"Excuse me?" I looked at Lucien curiously. His expression was still the same, big surprise.

"There are other possibilities for your young girl. She need not be a zombie, to be lost to the human world"

I nodded. I knew this. It was what I feared most. If Pamela was not a zombie and obviously not a vampire it left few choices. None of them, I feared, were any good. "That is what I'm afraid of Lucien. Whatever Pamela has become she is somehow linked to this." I rolled my eyes. What was I talking about? She could crack the case wide open. "She couldn't have killed Yarbrow...could she?" I was more speaking to myself but Lucien answered anyways.

"It is doubtful. Yarbrow was a little over two hundred of your human years. He was not a great power, but he had power nonetheless. He was also physically very strong. I cannot see that young girl overpowering Yarbrow, it would be laughable."

I wasn't laughing. "Perhaps Pamela couldn't have killed Yarbrow, but whatever she has become might have had the strength to overtake him."

"Again, doubtful."

I put my hands on the desk and leaned over. I was done with this ego trip, vampires really needed to put things into perspective, especially this one. "You are not the only strength out there. Vampires are strong, yes, but they are not invincible. Y'all prance around as if you are the only things out there that wield any power, well, hey, guess what...you're not. And if you need an example, I can't think of a better one than this damn demon and this psychotic sorcerer. They've taken out both vampires and humans and they're still going. Obviously there are still things that can intimidate you." I sighed before I continued. "And kill you, really kill you."

During my little speech, Lucien had sat and listened, with a small frown marring his perfect face. I was just glad he hadn't interrupted me. I really needed to get that all off of my chest.

"I have already taken steps to locate this girl." Lucien said.

Well this was news to me. Again, it seemed that Lucien was more than happy to keep secrets from me. "Have you?"

"I did not know that this girl you spoke of, and the girl that was spotted by my people at 'Thermal' was Pamela until you told me so tonight. However, I did know that a young woman had left with Yarbrow, and immediately alerted all my people to keep watch for her. I have also alerted the workers at all the night establishments I own to look for her."

I nodded. It was what I was going to suggest. If this dead alive Pamela had been soliciting at 'Thermal' it was more than likely that she would pop up again at another vampire establishment. It seemed that vampire was on the menu, and what better place to serve them up than in their own habitat. "We're getting closer, I know we are."

Lucien smiled, and I smiled in return. It was that same enigmatic, beautiful smile that sent shivers through my body. I couldn't help but smile. I hadn't realized how much I had missed him, sick, I know. But I was beginning to realize that perhaps being sick wasn't so bad. And was Lucien right? About me erecting barriers between the world and myself? That I wouldn't let anyone get close to me? Well, duh. I had done so most of my life, and it had become stronger during my adulthood. I had to protect myself from having a nervous breakdown every moment of every day. And Empaths often did, have nervous breakdowns, that is. They couldn't balance their life and others. Every feeling, every emotion would become so intertwined with their own that eventually most Empaths couldn't tell the difference between who they were and who the 'others' were.

I had found a solution to this problem. Just don't feel. If you could detach yourself from everyone else then you did not have to worry about 'feeling' those people's feelings, or becoming them emotionally. You could have the normalcy you craved, and the only thing you gave up was your ability. It was ability I had never wanted, thus, the decision hadn't been difficult. But now, now everything had changed...and it seemed that I had to change too. If I didn't I would be consumed. Better to control than be crushed. This was about power, a play of power and strength. And if I knew anything I knew how to be strong, and well, the power...that just came naturally.

"Good."

I jerked my head up. I had almost forgotten he was there, staring at me, watching me with those dead eyes of his. "What?"

"You are beginning to accept."

"Please, lets not go there."

"Is it not the truth though? Are you not beginning to accept the nature of things? How things must be. I believe I once said that yours is a rare gift and how you choose to wield it will be just as important as the power itself." He smiled wide, his fangs were not retracted, and they glinted in the light of the office. "Now that time has come. How will you wield your power, and for whom?"

He wasn't saying anything that I didn't already know. However, he was voicing it, where I had always just preferred to live in a nice land called, denial. Hey, it had worked for me…well until recently. "I will do what I have to, to stop this thing. Whatever I must."

"Ah, Holly, You sound more vampire everyday."

Now that wasn't something I wanted to hear. Lucien must have seen the disgust on my face, he laughed. "I've got to tell Detective Marcus about Yarbrow." I sighed when I saw Lucien shake his head. I had known this would be his reaction.

"It's out of the question Holly flower."

"He has to know, he has to be informed." God, everybody was so damn stubborn. "Listen, whether you like it or not, the two of you are after the same thing. You both are inadvertently working together. Wouldn't this be easier if you were both informed about one another's activities?"

"Ah, but I am informed on Detective Marcus's activities."

A spy, it figured. "You have someone on him, don't you?"

"It was inevitable. Detective Marcus is transgressing into my territory, therefore I have every right to keep, 'someone on him' as you so quaintly put. I am the Holder, it is my job to be informed."

"So why not just let Detective Marcus in on this?" I laughed, there I went again, it was obvious I was nervous. "If you know about Detective Marcus, then you know about his…abilities."

"He's a low level telepath, yes, I know." Lucien laughed, and it was that low, rolling, sound that spread warmth through my entire body. "Edward's Police Force's own answer to modernization. I believe Captain Porter was under some pressure to bring in PSI talent. Charlotte, Greensboro, Raleigh and the surrounding cities have already integrated their task forces. Indeed, Charlotte has, two psychics, one telepath and a rather shy witch on their police force. They are quite ahead of everyone else."

I had to agree with Lucien. Most police forces were completely backward when it came to the paranormal. This was mainly because of ancient, very conservative politicians who were disbelievers. If modernizing the force meant they had to acknowledge the fact that powers existed out there that couldn't be explained by science, well then, they would choose to keep everyone in the medieval ages for as long as possible. It was a travesty, but it was the truth. And we would all suffer, together.

"How am I going to explain the Pamela situation to Detective Marcus without bringing in what you've told me this evening about Yarbrow?"

"But you are a bright university student. I am sure you will think of something." Lucien's face was filled with mirth and god I hated that smug expression of his.

"I'll do what needs to be done Lucien."

Lucien's face went absolutely still and his eyes began to glint. I knew that glint. I backed up a couple of feet and braced myself. I swallowed when he began to shimmer and I saw his hands stretch and pull, fingers elongating and sharpening to points. Oh boy, talons, I hated talons. There was something about razor sharp, pointy things that always seemed to turn me off. This was no exception.

"You will not disobey me Holly."

"This case is more important than your stupid secrets Lucien."

"Nothing is more important than privacy, especially for the Hive. I will not have you endanger my people by bringing in the human authorities. Even one that you have become so fond of…" He said this last with a sneer and I shuddered.

"Would you really have me keep this information from Detective Marcus. He can help Lucien, really, he can."

"There is nothing that he can do, that I will not accomplish faster without his interference."

"You are such an egotistical bastard."

Lucien smiled slightly. "Thank you."

"That wasn't a compliment."

"However, I took it as such."

It annoyed me when I couldn't irk the vampire. "He can travel in daylight, or have you forgotten that you have a slight problem with something called…the dawn?" Now it was Lucien's turn to be irked. "Detective Marcus has to be informed. He will be able to get to things that you can't. We'll all be more productive if we don't keep secrets from one another."

"But is that not what you do Holly? Keep secrets?"

"Keep talking that way and I'm out of here."

"As you wish. However, I have not changed my mind. Detective Marcus will know nothing about my involvement in this…problem. Nor will he know about my Hive. If he is such a good detective, and as capable as you have said he will discover all he needs on his own. Perhaps he'll even get lucky and stumble into it."

Jeez, this was frustrating. But if you have dealings with a vampire prepare to be frustrated. There is nothing easy about vampires.

"Fine." It was obvious that Lucien wasn't about to change his mind and I didn't have all night to stand around debating this point with him. I had more important things to do and definitely a long night of research and retrieval ahead of me.

"I am so glad that you see my point Holly flower. You will be a great asset to me at the meetings. And I am sure that this new willingness to admit your faults and when you are wrong will only enhance our relationship"

Oh no, no, no. Who the hell did he think he was? There was no way that I as just going to shut up and hang on his dead arm. Just because I was tired and not willing to open a can of worms right now, did not mean I had lost any of my abilities to bitch and moan. He had gotten a companion tonight, not a coma patient. I would not let him dictate to me. I opened my mouth to tell him all this when I saw the glimmer of mirth flickering in his eyes and I realized he had been toying with me, obviously trying to get a rise out of me…sadly I had to say that it worked. I was much too sensitive when it came to Lucien, and I was definitely going to have to work on that. "Thank you Lucien."

"For what Holly?" Lucien asked curiously.

"For meeting with me."

"I will always meet with you Holly, whenever you wish, you know that."

"Yeah, I'm beginning to see that."

"You are tired." It was a statement not a question.

I nodded. "Exhausted. I'm really exhausted. It's been a trying week. Midterms are over but well I haven't quite been able to process that fact. I'm still lacking crucial sleep hours and now, well now I have some strange dead alive girl to deal with." I rolled my eyes. "So, yeah, I'm exhausted…wouldn't you be?"

He didn't answer. I hadn't really expected him to.

"Well, I think I've got to go, I have a huge amount of research to do."

"Always running to work." Lucien said with another enigmatic smile.

"Yeah, well there is always work to run to." I held up a hand. "No, you don't have to provide an escort, I've got it covered."

"Do not forget Wednesday…I will send someone for you at ten."

"What's on Wednesday?"

"Your first experience with the Southern Night Leaders."

"Uh, again, what?"

"The first of many meetings, Holly."

There he went again, not asking, just telling. "So soon?"

"It is necessary. And I do not believe you will find it as tedious as you think."

I had agreed to attend these meetings with him, so I couldn't back out now. I nodded. "All right. I'll be ready at ten."

"Good, good. I will keep you informed of the activities of the night...especially if they deal with your, Pamela."

"Thanks. Same here." I stood staring at him, still seated behind that massive desk of his. He was gloriously perfect and invoked the most dangerous and suspicious feelings in me. I knew I was sinking deeper as the days went on, but I seemed quite powerless to do anything about it. And perhaps scarier still, was the fact that I didn't want to do anything about it.

"So, shall we say goodnight in proper fashion?"

"What do you...?" I didn't get to finish the sentence. One moment he was behind the desk and the next he was in front of me, his arms supporting my drooping figure. I felt faint as those cold lips pressed against mine. My body thrummed, suddenly alive. It was pointless to deny the fact, that with the dead guy I felt amazingly alive.

When he released me I felt lightheaded. I opened my eyes to see him standing a foot away from me with a large, hungry expression on his face. His eyes were bleeding red, and that was never a good sign. I began to back away slowly and Lucien nodded.

"Yes, go, I...feel the need."

I didn't know what the 'need' was, but I bet it wasn't to play Parcheesi by moonlight.

"Goodnight Lucien." I said, right before I fled out of the door and down the shadowed hallway as fast as I could.

Chapter Twenty-Four:

I was awoken out of a semi-sound sleep by scratching on my window. Rolling right over stuffed Bunny I fell in an unceremonious heap by the side of my bed. I was attempting to pry my eyes open when the glass pane of my window was shattered and pieces went flying, some becoming entangled within my sleep tousled hair. I gasped and scurried around to the other side of the bed, ducking down quickly. I barely dodged what appeared to be the strike of a claw in my direction. Okay, now I was scared.

"Come out, come out, pretty."

The eerie voice was faintly feminine but horribly grotesque at the same time. I peeked up over the side of the bed and was shocked to see a pretty blond head poking through my window. When the moonlight struck and the wind blew drapes to the side I was shocked when I recognized Pamela Courtland's cherubic face smiling evilly into my bedroom. What the fuck was going on? Damn, damn, damn, if ever I needed a cell phone it was now.

"Why are you hiding pretty? I just want to talk to you." Pamela was attempting to crawl through my window but the broken pieces of glass around my pane were impeding her progress. She braced herself with one hand and I shrunk back when I saw that she indeed had claws for fingers. Her hands were humongous. The nails were hooked and appeared to be a good four inches long, like a cross between a bird of prey and a bear.

I suddenly had an idea. Reaching up to my bed stand table I felt around for the beeper that Detective Marcus had given to me. I had figured out, quite by chance, that one of the buttons on the shiny black surface automatically would contact Detective Marcus by flashing my telephone number on his matching beeper. I had just located it when a horrible pain shot through my hand and I screamed as it began to tear through my body. I

178

began to stand up but found that my hand was being held in place by what felt like a spike driven through the skin.

Pamela was on her hands and knees on my bed, her claw was pinning my hand to my bedside table. Blood was running quick and red down the side of the table and I was already losing feeling in my hand. I was stifling back screams of pain and trying to keep my eyes fixed on Pamela's widening color changing eyes.

"I don't like people running from me pretty."

I narrowed my eyes and tried to concentrate on anything other than the pain that was assailing me. "Don't...call...me...pretty!" I ground out.

"You are so strong, I can smell the power that surrounds you."

"Well goodie for you" I was trying to come off arrogant; it was all I had right now.

"Now, now, pretty, do not be afraid. I only come to talk with you."

"So talk." I was swallowing back the pain but was beginning to feel light headed.

"You have been very, very busy my pretty." Pamela, or whatever Pamela now was, was staring at me with very un-humanlike eyes. Her face was still beautiful, unblemished and faintly flushed but her eyes, her eyes were wild and beastly. They were a terrifying mix between gold and pale yellow, the same eyes I had once seen on a wolf. She smiled at me and ground her claw in deeper, I let out a shriek. With a large smile she took her other hand, which was also now clawed and dug it into my pinned arm. I tried not to hyperventilate. The gashes on my arm were wide and deep and hurt like hell. I tried not to think on them to deeply, if I did I'd probably pass out. And I couldn't pass out, I couldn't.

I took several deep breaths and tried to regain some of my concentration. I opened my mind fully and instantly felt nausea assault me. There was nothing here but hunger and rage. I could feel nothing but evil attacking my senses and quickly pulled up some fortification. I could not risk passing out, not now. I had, however, been able to scent some change, this was not a werewolf, she was definitely not a Lycanthrope, but the smell of death lingered in the air. Whatever she was, she was no longer Pamela. Pamela was lost to us. "What do you want?" I breathed a sigh of relief when she released my hand. I retracted it quickly and drew it to my chest. Blood was flowing heavily from the wound and running in a steady stream down my body. My nightclothes were most certainly ruined, unless Clorox bleach would take out bloodstains.

"You do not look happy to see me pretty. But I have heard that you have been looking for me." She was smiling at me and licking her lips with her pink tongue.

I had taken the beeper with me when I had drawn back my hand, and was grateful to see that she didn't seem to notice. I pushed all three buttons, and prayed that the telephone number would go through, hoping that Detective Marcus would get the idea. "I haven't been looking for you." I said. Pleased that my voice came out steady and calm.

"Oh, but I have heard that you have been looking for me. Well you've found me. Or perhaps I should say, I have found you." She laughed evilly and the sound chilled me through. I really, really wished that she would stop licking her damn lips. She was eyeing the blood pooling down my front with the same hunger I had seen many times on Lucien's face. And like when Lucien looked at me with those bleeding red eyes I felt the same dread and disgust gather within me. I felt like I was about to become a meal.

I was shivering and trembling. I felt cold and hot at the same time, neither of which was a good sign. We continued to stare at one another for what seemed like an eternity, an eternity in which I was losing a terrible amount of blood. Finally I spoke, choking out the words.

"I've...been worried about you, Pamela."

Pamela giggled. "Pam, Pam, Pam, what a silly little name. But humans have such silly little names...silly little creatures that they are." She sat on her haunches and watched me while I tried to come up with a plan to get the hell out of my bedroom...in one piece. "I would suggest you stop prying into business that doesn't concern you...pretty."

"I...I don't know what you're talking about."

"Oh, but I think you do. If you don't, I am sure that tonight will have given you the idea. It isn't safe to be a curious kitty." She cocked her head to one side. "Do you know what I am yet...pretty?" She giggled. "What I am, what I am, what I am..."

I swallowed as she continued to chant. What did I think she was? She was a scary bitch, that's what I thought she was. Other than that...well there was only one obvious answer. "Shifter." I swallowed a shudder when she reached out with what looked like an attempt to pet my hair. I was backed up against the wall. There was nowhere to run.

"Smart. I knew you were smart, pretty. Ah, but you still don't know the truth, do you? Perhaps you're not as smart as you think."

"I...I don't understand." I desperately was trying to keep conscious. But my hand was throbbing and I felt as if my entire body were on fire.

"You will..."

With the last remnants of my strength I opened my pathways and let the walls in my mind fall away. I concentrated on the bed and tried to push it backwards, but all I managed was to make it tremble. Pamela didn't even seem to notice the disturbance. Considering how intent she was on watching the blood drip down my body, I wasn't surprised. I couldn't hold on much longer. I felt sweat popping out on my forehead and my breathing was accelerating. I knew the signs. I could easily fall into unconsciousness and fast. I had little strength left and was totally out of options.

It was then that I heard the faint sound of sirens. I began praying harder than I ever had before that they were for me. Beastie Pamela must have heard them too, because she straightened up, her shoulders squared out and she lifted her head and seemed to sniff the air.

"You will remember what I have said this night. And remember how easily you bleed." She spared me one more glance before vaulting with extraordinary speed out of my bedroom window.

I sank to the ground. My back to the wall my hand held to my chest. I tried to keep my eyes open but found that my vision was blurry. I knew that I had lost a lot of blood. But I also knew that I wasn't going to die...not from this.

"Hey, hey, stay with me Holly."

My ears perked, I recognized that voice...thank god, it was Detective Marcus.

"Hey Detective." My voice was weak and slurred. "What...what took you so long?"

"Sorry kid. I'm here now. Shhhhh...just stay with me."

"I...I don't feel so well."

Detective Marcus laughed. It was a raw and forced sound. "I'm not surprised kid. The paramedics are here...they're going to take good care of you."

"Tell them..." I swallowed trying to force out the words.

"What?"

"Tell them...tell them to watch out for infection." I felt my lids drooping and Detective Marcus's face was fading out. I could hear his voice faintly, but it sounded like it was coming from a long distance away. Sleep, I would just sleep for a little while. My last thoughts before I slipped into unconsciousness were Pamela's parting words...'Remember how easily you bleed.' Yeah, there is nothing to remind you of how human you are like major blood loss.

The walls were stark and white. There was a small screen television in the upper left hand corner of the room and an equally small window, which boasted a view of a brick wall. I was propped against several white pillows in what had to be one of the most uncomfortable beds I'd ever had the misfortune of sleeping in.

My hand was bandaged heavily and affixed to my chest by a large, extra durable sling. I was still hooked up to an IV and it was dripping what appeared to be some sort of saline like solution into my arm. I was trying to recall all of the nuances of last night when the door to my hospital room opened and Detective Marcus strode through holding a bunch of daisies. I smiled.

"Hi Detective."

Detective Marcus's face was grim. "Holly."

"Why so grim, Detective? I'm alive aren't I?" I said this in a joking manner, but by the look on his face he wasn't in a joking sort of mood.

"You could have been killed last night Holly."

I snorted. "Could have been, but I wasn't, Detective."

Detective Marcus's attention shifted from my face to the sling and IV. He shook his head and pulled up a seat next to me. "You lost a lot of blood. They had to replace it with Synthex."

I nodded. I had figured as much. Synthex was the most commonly used manufactured blood in the United States today. It was generally of a high quality and it was supposed to be just as good as the real stuff. However, most vampires would probably disagree. They seemed to have a discriminating palate. I had a rare blood type. I wasn't surprised that they had to use Synthex on me. "Infection?" This was the part I was dreading. You could never be too careful with wounds inflicted by an abnormal being.

"You were running a high fever...the doctor gave you some antibiotic and it subsided by early this afternoon."

"So...I'm a-ok?"

"I want you off this case Holly."

My eyes widened. "What?"

"It's too dangerous. You've done all that you can."

"The hell I have. No, I'm not stopping now. That thing that attacked me last night used to be Pamela Courtland. Somehow she found out that I was researching the murders and she came over to...warn me off the case."

"I suggest you take her warning to heart. She could have killed you."

"But she didn't!"

"Are you going to take the chance that she'll come back and finish the job she started."

"It was important that I saw her last night Detective. I learned things that I only could have if I saw her in person."

"Great. So that's it."

"No. That isn't it. Not by a long shot." I held up my sling. "I did not sustain this for nothing. You need me Detective, you've said so yourself."

"Yeah? Well I don't need you anymore. We've got enough to run with this." Detective Marcus ran a hand through his hair and looked me dead in the eye. "I once told you that I was willing to use any means, and anybody to achieve my goal, to catch this killer. Well, I lied. I'm not willing to use any means…because I'm not willing to use you. Not any longer."

"But I want you to use me Detective."

"Doesn't matter. I won't." Detective Marcus stood up and began to walk to the door.

"She's a shifter Detective. But she's not a lycanthrope."

He pivoted on his heel and stood staring at me from the doorway. He seemed at war with himself. It was obvious that he wanted to grill me, but just as obvious that he truly did not want to involve me further in this mess. Finally, his instincts as an officer and his devotion to his job won out. "Not a lycanthrope?"

"Absolutely not. I sensed her before you arrived. She isn't a lycanthrope. But that creates new problems…because she's obviously a shifter."

"Is that even possible?"

I was frowning. "I hadn't thought so. I hadn't thought it possible. But last night I saw evidence to the contrary. That thing in my bedroom was definitely bestial and very, very evil. But I didn't sense lycanthrope."

"Could it be that your senses were damaged?"

I knew what he was asking. Could the fact that something had tried to take my hand off have anything to do with my conclusions? Could major blood loss be the reason I had concluded, shifter, but not lycanthrope? No, I shook my head. "Whatever was in my room last night was not a lycanthrope Detective. But she has all the attributes of one. She was partially shifting last night. Her face was perfectly normal; except for her eyes and her hands…well you see what her hands could do. They were claws, detective. Her fingers were hooked and very, very sharp. They effectively pinned my hand in place, it was effortless."

"Shit."

"Well said. Yeah. She was delivering a warning."

"Wanted you off the case." Detective Marcus said with that dour expression once again apparent on her face.

"Yeah. She had heard some rumors that I was looking for her, that I was digging into her business as she called it and wanted to deliver a little message."

"God."

"She wouldn't have killed me. Although I wasn't sure about that at first."

"How do you know she wouldn't have killed you Holly. She damn well near succeeded last night."

I shook my head. "Like I said, that was a warning. If she had wanted to kill me Detective she could have done it easily enough. I had sustained major blood loss and was nearly passed out. My powers were as useful as a pinprick and well, one good gouge and she could have killed me...she didn't." I looked at him. "It makes me wonder why she didn't."

"You would have preferred otherwise?"

"You know what I mean Detective. Why didn't she kill me? If she had wanted me off the case, she could have taken me off the case...permanently. But she didn't kill me Detective. It's suspicious."

"Just be glad of it Holly." Detective Marcus came to stand by my side. He reached out and brushed a strand of hair out of my face. I stared at him with my eyes wide and mouth open. "I'm not quite ready to lose you yet Holly...not yet."

"Uh, yeah, well I'm not going anywhere Detective."

"Good. Get some rest Holly. I'm going to the office to compile some paperwork. I'll be back later and we'll talk some more."

"Detective..."

"No. Get some rest. Like I said we'll talk later, it'll wait."

I nodded. "All right. Thanks Detective." I watched as he left the room, closing the door softly behind him. Peculiar, everyone was acting so very peculiar.

"How are you feeling Hol?" Ryan asked. His eyes filled with concern. Ryan had stopped by almost after Detective Marcus had left. He had brought with him a large bouquet of flowers and a stuffed bear. The bear was currently sharing my uncomfortable bed with me.

"Better…I feel a lot better Ryan, thanks for coming."

"Nowhere else that I want to be, Hol."

"Not even studying for our calculus exam?" I said with a smile. Ryan laughed and shook his head.

"No, I definitely prefer to be here with you." Ryan's face turned somber and he reached out to take my one good hand in his. "I can't believe a bear attacked you last night Holly."

I swallowed, yeah, a bear. God I hated lying to Ryan, but I really didn't think he'd understand this. What was I going to tell him? 'Oh, by the way some really scary ass shifter came into my apartment last night and tried to kill me…oh, and don't forget she used to be a fellow student of ours…but that was before she went and got dead.' Oh, yeah, he'd get that. "Well…it is North Carolina Ryan."

"Yeah, but we hardly get bear attacks anymore Holly. Not to mention, it's a pretty populated area that we're in."

"Uh, yeah, I know." I shrugged my shoulders. "Well, what can I say…weird stuff happens."

"Yeah, I guess so. God, you're lucky you weren't killed."

"Don't I know it." I said under my breath.

"You're sure you're feeling all right?"

"Really, I feel so much better. I'm sure I'll be in class."

"Do you think that's a good idea?"

Couldn't tell Ryan that the real reason I had to get back to school was because I had to get back to the library. "It'll be fine. I'm fine. Healthy as a horse, minus a pint or so of blood." Ryan didn't look amused. I sighed. "That was a joke Ryan."

"It wasn't funny Hol. Listen, you've got to take care of yourself. If you're not feeling up to going back to school yet, well don't go. Jeez, it's not like you're missing anything. Latimer's class will still be as dull as dirt. And, well, Professor DeWitt has been in such a good mood lately I'm sure she'll understand the situation."

I sighed. "Thanks for being concerned about me Ryan, but really, I'm fine. I don't want to accumulate too much late homework."

Ryan laughed. "You're nuts Hol. Never knew anyone so dedicated to school."

"Well, you know me…I'm just a nerd at heart."

Ryan stroked my hand and tenderly brushed my cheek. "You're great. I'm so sorry this happened to you Hol. If you need anything, well, you have my number. Don't hesitate to call me, okay?"

He was such a sweetheart. "Thanks Ryan. I will." When Ryan left I slumped back into my bed, exhausted. I was going to get to the bottom of this if it killed me. I winced as my hand began to throb again…and it very likely would kill me.

I don't know how late it was when I felt pressure exuding itself on my body and in my mind. I rolled onto my side but the pressure didn't abate. It was like a large migraine had hit me in my sleep. I grudgingly opened my eyes and the first thing I saw was a dark shadow in the corner of my room. Oh, the whole room was full of shadows, it was nighttime, but this shadow was large and rippled softly. I propped myself up and leaned forward trying to get a better look.

A shaft of moonlight from my open window illuminated the side of a perfectly sculpted face and I whispered. "Lucien."

"Good evening Holly flower." He glided effortlessly out of the dark corner and moved, as if floating to my side. Perhaps he was floating. "Are you well my Holly?"

I nodded. "Yeah, I'm okay." I looked at his face, so still, smooth and beautiful and I whispered. "Thank you for coming Lucien. Thank you."

Lucien leaned over and brought his face a mere two inches from mine. He brushed my hair off of my face and then leaned over and placed a cool kiss on my forehead. "You know I will always come to you my Holly flower." He pulled back and studied me. "I smell blood…were you wounded greatly?"

"No. Not too bad."

"Are you lying to me Holly flower?"

"Just a little Lucien." I smiled along with Lucien. "Really, it's so much better now. It was painful as all hell when it happened, but I'm feeling pretty good right now." I grinned. "The drugs help."

"Ah, my little addict."

I laughed. "Hardly. Hell, I deserve some drugs."

"That you do my Holly flower." Lucien ran a hand down my face and I shivered. He smiled at my reaction. It wasn't as if he didn't already know that he turned my legs to mush and produced goosebumps all over my body by just looking at me. "It was she?"

I knew what he was talking about, could see it in his face, and hear it in his words. "Yeah, well I was right about one thing."

"And that would be?"

"She's no zombie." I sighed. "I didn't, however, expect her to be a shifter." Lucien hissed. His fangs were clearly visible now and his eyes were glinting with a dangerous light. "Shifter? They wouldn't dare."

"What?" I was confused.

"No shifter would dare to attack you. They know who you are to me, and what attacking you would mean to them, in lieu of what I would do. The vengeance I would exact for such audacity."

"You don't understand…"

"It will be dealt with." Lucien narrowed his eyes. "I had not thought of the possibility that she could have be transformed into a shifter. But it makes sense."

"Lucien, she's not a lycanthrope."

"What?"

"She's not of the lycanthrope community."

"That is not possible."

"I know. But I also know what I saw last night. She's definitely a shifter. And what's more she was only partially shifted."

"I say, again, that is not possible. I know every power in my territory, and that power belongs only to the lycanthrope or the vampire."

"Lucien…she attacked me." I held up my sling. "She dug her claws into my hand and her face was unchanged…except for her eyes, they were bestial. Believe me, I know what I saw."

"I must look into this." Lucien's face was puzzled and there were faint creases between his perfect eyebrows. Frown lines. I smiled, remembering how I had explained the lines to him once. What would he do if he knew he had them now? "I will converse with S.A.F.E."

"Who?"

"Shifters Authority For Equality."

Oh? Well I should have known, right? "Okay, sounds like a plan."

"You look bewildered Holly flower."

"No, I just didn't realize that the shifters had their own little, uh group?" What were they, like a union?

Lucien laughed. I let the sound roll over me and sighed in pleasure. "Do you not realize by now Holly that we all gravitate towards our own? Thus, it is safer for all involved to be organized and…in some cases to be led."

"Yeah, I guess so." I thought I knew it all, obviously I didn't.

"How long will you be spending in this human hospital?"

"I'm discharging myself tomorrow."

"Do you think that wise?"

I rolled my eyes. He was only, like, the third person to ask me this question. "I know what I'm doing. I'll be fine."

Lucien nodded his head. "I will of course defer to your judgment."

"Thanks so much." I said sarcastically.

"Do not forget that you must be in attendance at the Southern Council meeting."

Damn. I had forgotten about that. Being attacked in your own house and having your hand almost clawed off really put a strain on your memory. "Shit."

"I take it from your delightful response that you had forgotten"

"Uh, yeah." I smiled. "Listen…"

"No."

"But it…"

"No."

"I could…"

"No. You will not get out of it this easily Holly."

I held up my arm again. "You call this easy?"

"Nonetheless. You made a promise to me, a promise that you must keep. Everything has been arranged. You cannot back out now."

I pouted. "Why not?"

Lucien smiled at my disgruntled look, clearly enjoying my discomfort at the prospect of being surrounded by a bunch of dead people. Dead people with razor sharp fangs and wicked talons. "It shall not be as bad as you think. Merely consider the fact that you are becoming even more educated in the ways of the Night Clans."

Yeah, yeah, great, what if I didn't want to be more educated in their ways? I don't suppose I could attend via satellite. "I'm not getting out of this am I?"

"No."

"Fine, all right. Send your goons and I'll be prepared. However, don't be surprised if I show up, sling and all. The doctor said I would have to wear it for a little while, insurance you know…"

Lucien's eyes glowed brightly and he licked those delicious lips of his. "Do not worry…the wound will only heighten the display."

"Uh, pardon?"

"You sustained injury and you are still standing…it is a mark of courage. And the council will take in the display. It is good Holly. I could not have asked for anything more."

I wanted to stick my tongue out at him, but I was afraid he would take it as a suggestion. "So…all I need is to lose a pint of blood to gain respect?"

"In a word…yes."

"That was a joke, Lucien."

"I was not joking, Holly."

"Yeah, I can see. Well, I don't plan on bleeding anytime soon for everyone's pleasure."

"You have done enough. It will be sufficient for the time being Holly flower."

"Great, just great. Because, of course I want to make y'all happy…you know I live for it."

"Are you being sarcastic Holly?"

"No, of course not." I grinned and Lucien studied my face intently.

"You are being sarcastic Holly flower"

"Just a little."

"I see." Lucien continued to stare at me and I sighed. The vampire might be gaining a sense of humor, but he certainly still didn't understand, well, sarcasm.

"Can I get some sleep now Lucien?"

"But of course…I am sorry to keep you Holly flower. I will check up on you and shall see you at the Southern Night Council." Lucien placed a chaste kiss on my lips and cupped my face in his hands. "And do not forget…you must dress appropriately."

"What does that mean?"

"It means that your jeans will not suffice for the evening."

"You want me to wear the Yves St. Laurent?"

"I am sure when the time comes you will find something that shall suit."

I closed my eyes and rubbed my temples. God, it was like pulling teeth. I opened my mouth and my eyes, I was going to give the wise cracking vamp a piece of my mind, but of course he was no longer there. Yeah, great, and he was accusing *me* of running.

Chapter Twenty-Five:

I stared frustrated at my notes. I just couldn't cut it as a leftie. I was completely useless with my right arm in a sling. My notes were slanted and barely legible...it is definitely not a good sign when you can't read your own writing.

"Having a problem?"

I recognized Ryan's voice and turned my surprised face towards his. "What are you doing?"

"I believe I'm taking class."

I rolled my eyes. "You know what I'm talking about Ryan. What are you doing sitting by me?"

"You need a hand." He started to laugh and then swallowed it back. "Well I just thought I could help you." He pointed to my arm. "It's obvious that you can't write like that, I'll take the notes and if you have anything to add, well just shout it out."

"Well, I'll try not to shout." I said with a smile. "Thank you Ryan."

"Hey, no problem. Anything to help out a...friend." He smiled at me and ran a hand down my arm slowly, suggestively.

"Ah, yeah, a friend."

"Mr. Maloney, Miss. Feather, are you listening to me? Or do I need to separate you?"

Ryan and I jerked our heads up at the sound of Professor DeWitt's voice.

"Professor?" I smiled at Professor DeWitt and pushed Ryan's wandering hand away.

"We were discussing how Egyptian mummification plays a part in the myths dealing with zombies. Would you care to add to this discussion?" Professor DeWitt narrowed her eyes. "Or perhaps you'd rather play footsie."

Oh boy.

"I was only helping Holly out, Professor DeWitt. She can't write with her arm in a sling and well...I just wanted to make sure she had adequate notes for your class." Ryan flashed her one of his million dollar smiles and I was shocked when I saw her demeanor change. She seemed to melt, her frown subsided and she nodded.

"I see. All right then Ryan. However, please make sure that you keep your attention on me. I do not want to see it...wandering again. Not in my class."

"Of course Professor."

"And you Holly?"

I nodded. "I'm sorry Professor. It won't happen again."

"See that it doesn't." She turned back to the chalkboard and began to map out a complex diagram.

The moment her back was turned I leaned over in Ryan's direction and whispered. "I can't believe you."

Ryan gave me an innocent look. "What?"

"You just blink those baby blues and flash that pearly white smile and well...you're golden."

Ryan laughed. "That's not true."

"Oh, yeah, whatever." I turned back towards the front. "We'd better pay attention to this lecture or she'll put a hex on us."

Ryan smiled and turned his attention back on his notes. He whispered under his breath. "Remember I don't believe in that stuff."

God, yeah, I remembered. This could definitely be a problem.

I was gathering up my things when Professor DeWitt called me over. Slinging my backpack over my shoulder with one arm I made my way up front. Ryan was waiting at the door and I shook my head and waved him away. He made the motion to tell me that he'd call me and I nodded, turning my attention back towards the Professor.

"You wanted to see me Professor?"

"Yes, I wanted to say how sorry I am that you were attacked in your home...how horrible."

"Yeah, it was."

Professor DeWitt smiled slightly and smoothed back a piece of her hair. "You're so lucky that you survived...I'm shocked that this happened."

"Yeah, I was pretty surprised too."

"And in your neighborhood no less."

"I'm just happy that everything turned out okay."

"So am I." Professor DeWitt narrowed her eyes and braced herself against the front desk. "Are you certain that you're strong enough to continue this research for me? I wouldn't be upset if you decided to quit, give yourself some much needed rest and relaxation."

I nodded. "That's really considerate of you Professor. But I told you I would do it and I will. It's really very interesting and this…" I held up the sling. "Won't stop me from doing top of the line research."

"No, I'm sure it will not. Well, please, let me know if there is anything you need. And do not hesitate to call me and tell me that you need to stop working for me, I will understand, truly I will."

"Thank you. But I'll be fine, and I'll do superior research for you."

"Yes, I'm sure you will." Professor DeWitt nodded. "You are an exceptional young woman, Holly." She reached out and then seemed to catch herself in time. She drew her hand back to her side and gave me another of those strange smiles of hers. "So pretty, you are very pretty Holly."

"Uh, thank you Professor." I stared at her for another moment longer before I smiled slightly and said. "Well, I'd better be going or I'll be late for my other class."

"Of course, of course. I always seem to be keeping you from your other appointments. By all means, you must go. But remember if there is anything you're curious about, or anything you need verified, then please come to me, I will answer all your questions."

"Okay, thanks Professor." I waved to her when I reached the door. "I'll see you Wednesday."

"Yes, until Wednesday."

Wednesday came way too fast for me. I had agonized over what to wear all day. I hadn't registered anything that Ryan had said to me and basically behaved like an antsy bitch all day. Even now I was at a loss to what to wear to the meeting this evening. It was past eight and I was wrapped in bath towels. One around my middle and one over my head like a turban. It was hopeless, not only did I not have anything appropriate I was still sporting the ugly sling. Double whammy. The doorbell interrupted my thoughts and I debated whether or not to run and put on some clothes. The bell sounded again and I decided to fuck it. I strode over to the front door and looked through the peephole. My eyes widened in obvious surprise when I saw who was standing on my front step. I took another moment to compose myself before opening the door.

Vanessa was decked out all in black, from her black leather halter-top to her tight black jeans with rhinestones on them. Her hair was pulled away from her face and secured on the top of her head with a black scrunchy. She had applied heavy black kohl lining around her eyes and used a dark, dark, burgundy lipstick on her lips. Her feet were encased in black platform boots and wide black leather bands on her forearms completed the look.

This had to be punishment. Lucien had to be trying to aggravate me, and obviously get a rise out of me. Why else would he be sending, like, my least favorite person to fetch me? I was immediately suspicious when I saw the long white box that Vanessa held underneath her arm.

"May I come in?" Vanessa asked politely.

I frowned. "Are you going to knock me over the head again?"

Vanessa blushed. Well at least she blushed, did that mean she was an okay person? Uh, I don't think so. "I have come as a courier." She gave me a look and continued. "And *I* didn't knock you over the head."

I'd deal with it later...right now there were more important things to deal with "A courier to whom?"

"Lucien, our master."

I rolled my eyes. I couldn't seem to help it. And when did Lucien become Vanessa's master? She wasn't even a vampire. "What did you bring? Anything explosive or weapon like has to be left outside my door."

Vanessa was obviously wondering if I was serious or not. "Lucien feared that you would not have the appropriate clothing for this evening."

God I hated that word...appropriate. "Yeah, so?"

"He sent something over for you."

My mouth gaped open. "Is he nuts?"

"Are you questioning are master?" Vanessa asked coldly. "Our Master knows the way of things. He says that you are to wear this tonight." Vanessa continued on when I would have spoken. "I would suggest that you be grateful for all that the Holder has given you. Come, invite me in, you won't be disappointed, this gown is a slice of paradise."

I sighed dramatically. I obviously wasn't going to get anywhere by letting her just hang out in front of my apartment. She wasn't going anywhere. "Oh, all right, fine. If you want to come in, come in."

She smiled. "Great." She cast her eyes around the room and I didn't even bother feeling annoyed anymore. It was obvious that whatever she felt, she felt. And she certainly wasn't alone in her opinion on my decorating skills.

She took a seat on my sofa and placed the long white box on the coffee table. She gestured to it. "Aren't you going to open it?"

"Maybe not," I said with an answering smile.

"But you have to."

"Why?"

Vanessa grimaced and shifted uncomfortably in her seat. "You must wear it Holly."

"Listen Vanessa. I don't have to do anything I don't want to. Maybe I'll just sit here for awhile with you and let Lucien stew for a bit." I was really pleased when I saw Vanessa turn a strange color of green, somewhere between pea and puce. She has this and a lot more coming to her for her little stunt awhile back…I still owed her a bump on her head and a migraine the size of Alaska.

"Our master will…"

Now I was just amused. "Will you just shut up Vanessa?" I laughed when Vanessa opened and closed her mouth like a fish. It was fucking hilarious. "I will open this box and look at what's inside if you promise to keep your mouth shut for like, a minute."

Vanessa nodded and I breathed a sigh of relief, thank god. I reached over and flipped the lid off of the white box. I pushed away the red tissue paper and now I was gaping like a fish. "Uh, no."

"Is it not positively…unique?"

I swallowed. "It's certainly something. It's also something I totally am not going to wear."

"But you have to." Vanessa's voice was plaintive.

"What did I say before?" I gave her a narrowed eyed look.

Vanessa seemed to think on that. I almost just told her but before I could she blurt it out. "That you don't have to do anything you don't want to."

"Yeah, that was it. And I meant it."

"This is a beautiful dress Holly."

"It's a dress…I don't know about the beautiful part." I lifted the 'dress' out of the box and continued to shake my head in disbelief. "What the hell was he thinking?"

"The council will be very impressed." Vanessa seemed to preen a little. "And it is all about appearance."

"Well I won't be making an appearance in this…thing. It's totally indecent."

"You've worn worse."

I gave her a look. "Really? You think so?"

Vanessa wrinkled her nose. "Well perhaps not. But this dress isn't indecent. It's fashionable, and tasteful. It's all the rage in New York City. I should know, I just visited my cousin in the city and, well, everyone is wearing dresses like this now."

"Where to? A brothel? And, hey, I don't know if you've noticed, but this is not New York City."

"You have to try it on."

I eyed the dress suspiciously. Would it hurt to try it on? "I…don't think so Vanessa."

"Please."

I was shocked. Did Vanessa just say please? I didn't even know that she knew that word. Then again, I remembered the last time I had tried to help her. I had gotten a bump on the head and a very unwanted first introduction to the vamp leader of Edwards. "Vanessa…"

"Listen Holly. Let's not kid ourselves. I don't like you, and it's obvious that you don't like me."

Well, hey. "You don't say."

"But if you don't wear this dress our Master is going to hurt me."

I laughed. "Think you're being a little dramatic?" I looked at her and saw the flicker in her eyes. She was really frightened. She really meant it. "Did he threaten you?"

Vanessa gave a harsh laugh. "The Master does not have to threaten anyone. He just tells you how it's going to be."

"I can't believe this. And you stand for this?"

"I love them."

Okay, now I knew she was crazy. "Holy shit…" I stared at her with horror in my eyes. "You're a vessel?" I knew she 'gave' blood every once in a while, but this was something completely different. Vessels were daily blood donors. They could belong to one or the entire Hive. Vessels considered their 'mission' sacred, they provided life for the dead (yeah, freaky, right?) and the vampires in turn considered them a step up from slave. Wasn't it obvious who was getting the better deal here?

Vanessa nodded. "Yeah, I am."

"Why?"

Vanessa looked at me as if I was the crazy one. "Because they're everything. They're life."

"They're dead Vanessa, or haven't you noticed? You and I, we're alive...they're just reanimated flesh." I looked at her.

"Eternal life Holly."

"Yeah, but I don't see you getting it." I looked at her pointedly before asking, "How much are you losing?"

"If you mean blood, they only take what they need."

"And you don't think that one of these days they're not going to get a little overanxious and suck you dry?" I stared at her wrists, now that I was looking I could see bite marks on both of them, not to mention the ones prominently displayed on her neck. "God, you're stupid."

"You're the stupid one Holly. You have our Master's attentions but you flout their ways and you take unnecessary risks."

"I'm no one's vesse,l" I spit out. "No one's biting me!"

"You don't know what you're missing Holly."

"No, I know what I won't be missing...blood. I plan on keeping all of mine."

"It is the most intense pleasure...better than sex."

I rolled my eyes. "It's called hypnosis Vanessa, or didn't you know." Jeez, some people. "They use compulsion and they put you under. Otherwise it would hurt like a bitch."

"It doesn't matter, they do what they must to live, and I...I will live with them."

I stared at her glinting eyes and her flushed expression and knew that it was futile to argue with her. She was a vampire groupie, and there was no reasoning with vampire groupies, they were that way for a reason. I didn't even like Vanessa, why did I care? Who was I kidding; the thought of any person being an appetizer to a throng of hungry vamps was enough to make me sick to my stomach. "I'll try on the dress." I said resignedly. I ignored Vanessa's thankful look and went to the bedroom to put it on. She was losing pints of blood a day, all I was losing was a little of my time. I could give her this.

Half an hour later I stood in front of the mirror wondering how I let myself get talked into these sorts of things. I was wearing the 'dress' Lucien had sent over and it had taken Vanessa's deft little fingers to tie me into place. The back of the dress was completely open except for criss crossing black leather ties which held the dress in place but left little to the imagination. The front was much the same. The bodice plunged all the way to the navel and was, like the back, held in place by leather ties. There were slits up the side of the dress, hell; they revealed most of my leg. What in god's name was I wearing, or in this case, not wearing.

"You look sensational Holly." Vanessa was staring at me with undisguised envy.

I shook my head. "I look ridiculous." I held up my arm, which was still in a sling, "And not just because of this. I can't wear this dress…I mean, look at me."

"I am. You look great." Vanessa narrowed her eyes. "Julian never gave me a gift like this."

"Julian?" I thought back for a moment. "The blond vamp from 'Ecstasy'?"

Vanessa nodded. "We were sort of dating for a while. Well, we're still sort of dating."

"Sort of dating?" I muttered and then stopped. Hell, who was I to judge, I was sort of dating the Vampire Holder of Edwards. "So, what happened?" Why was I asking? Did I really want to know? Uh, yeah, it seemed I did.

Vanessa shrugged her shoulders. She flicked her ponytail back and turned her large eyes on mine. "Julian's great. He's gorgeous…" She grinned at me. "You know that, you saw him." She continued when I nodded in response. "His touch is magic, and his bite, well…it transports me." Her eyes went dreamy and then dead, all in two seconds flat. "He needs more than me though."

"What?"

Vanessa swallowed and began to fuss with her hair. "I understand. I mean, I should not expect that he would only want my blood…he needs variety. But lately, his bites have become less and less frequent. I think that he's tiring of me."

Was I hearing right? Vanessa was upset because she wasn't getting bitten more often? Now I had heard it all. I suppose I understood Vanessa's point, maybe just a little, it was sort of a vampire's way of cheating, and who wants their boyfriend to cheat on them, whether he be dead or not. But jeez, at least this way she wouldn't have to worry about becoming anemic or, worse still, dead. "I'll wear the damn dress." I saw the relief that overwhelmed Vanessa at my words. I'd done my good deed for the day. I should be given a damn medal for this.

"Let me fix your hair."

Well weren't we just having a girl's night? Without the prospect of being surrounded by hungry vampires, possibly losing blood and flesh, and having to wear this reject from Cher's closet we might just have been able to have a nice night of bonding…or not, definitely not. "Go ahead, have a ball."

"Do you have scissors and some yarn or twine? Perhaps colored?"

Oh, hell, what had I gotten myself into?

One hour later we were good to go. After I had convinced (by the way of threatening to take her apart piece by piece) if she even cut a strand of my hair, and some agile manipulations on her part, to perfectly coif my hair. The final result had me two steps away from a nervous breakdown. Oh my god, did I look like a hooker?

"You look fabulous. Okay, we've got to go."

I guess Vanessa didn't think so. Or perhaps she liked how hookers look.

"Uh, okay, I'm going to grab a shawl." I began to leave when Vanessa grabbed my arm.

"No, you'll ruin the effect. You can't wear anything else, and don't cover that bodice whatever you do." She continued to tug at my arm. "We've really got to go." She looked at the clock. "Julian and Nula are probably outside right now."

"Our escorts, I'm assuming."

"Yeah."

"You could have driven me."

"No, I couldn't have. We're going to the lair tonight."

Well, that explained it all right. "Who's Nula."

"She's new to the Hive. She moved here from Alabama about four months ago." Vanessa's face fell. "I think Julian likes her."

I hated to be the bearer of bad news, but I really thought our over hungry friend Julian liked everyone. "Okay, let's get a roll on. The sooner we leave and get this over with the sooner I can get home to a hot bath and comfortable bed."

"You are so lucky to be invited to the meeting."

"Yeah, I'm just rolling in good luck lately." Luck along with dead bodies.

It was positively sickening to see. Vanessa sat in the back of the car along with little ol' me. The awe and adoration in her eyes when she looked at Julian made me want to puke up my dinner.

Julian sat in the front, along with the most stunning African American girl I had ever seen, correction, the most stunning dead African American girl I had ever seen. With a coffee colored complexion, unbelievable dark green eyes, wide full lips and a statuesque frame, she was simply gorgeous.

And Julian was positively drooling, Vanessa had been right.

Vanessa sat, staring at the back of Julian's head as Nula drove the SUV. Her eyes were consuming him, drinking in every detail. It hurt me to see how much she wanted him. Vampires could not sustain 'life' from drinking the blood of their own kind, which is where we humans come in. It was obvious to me, if not to Vanessa, that Julian still needed her. But was he using her, hell yeah. Julian would drink Vanessa dry, all the while flirting with the beautiful new vamp from Alabama. God relationships were never simple, not even if you were dead. And men were dogs, dead or not.

"Hey…" I called out, getting no response in return. "Hello…anybody home?" No one blinked an eyelash. "Hey, I'm talking to you!" Okay, now I was just annoyed. I reached into my small purse and pulled out a pen. Taking aim I flicked it at the back of Mr. Blondie's a.k.a. Julian's head very pleased when it hit him squarely in the back of his head.

Julian effortlessly turned around in his seat. His large cold blue eyes stared unwaveringly at me, and his mouth curved up in a smile. "There are other ways to get my attention." He said suggestively.

Yeah, a vampire lothario, just what we needed. "What, no blindfold this time?" I asked.

Julian shook his head, causing his blond hair to fall over his shoulder. "Our Master is showing great trust in you this evening. He tells everyone, especially the Council of Southern Night Leaders, that you are his companion, that, you are to be believed and believed in. And Vanessa, although she does not know the way, has been to our lair before." He smiled wider and turned those big eyes onto Vanessa. "Haven't you been to our lair, Vennie?"

Vennie? Well they even were on a nickname basis, how cute.

"Yes Julian." Vanessa's face was brilliantly happy. She could hardly contain her obvious joy in the fact that Julian was speaking to her.

"Vanessa has such supple skin and…her blood is quite good. She delights everyone." Julian turned back to me, eyes feral. "But I think your blood would be beyond sweet…"

Now he was just being rude. It didn't even deserve a response. I turned my dark violet eyes to his and gave him a look that was so glacial that it would freeze hell over in two-second flats. Vampire Julian's face stiffened and the skin from his cheeks seemed to pull and tighten over his face. His breaths quickened and he began to glow. Oh boy, the glowing. I stood my ground and continued to give him the eye. Eventually the glow subsided and he seemed to fall back to his normal self, or however normal a vampire can be. He gave me one last look before turning back in his seat.

I turned to look at Vanessa, I wanted to see if she had been bothered by the 'display', Vanessa's expression was unchanged, she wasn't fazed…nope, there just wasn't much upstairs. Oh, yeah, it was always a treat riding in cars with vamps.

Chapter Twenty-Six:

I was back in the black room. Same black bed, same familiar black furniture, same black walls, floors and ceiling.

Vanessa had left me not two minutes after I was secured in the black room. She had fiddled with my hair for a moment before departing. I swallowed, I was sassy and great at bullshitting but I felt fear just like anyone else. Dressed as I now was, and facing what I was about to face I was more than just a little afraid, I was terrified. But I could deal with fear; I had dealt with it before, and would deal with it again. If I had managed to fake out the human world I could fake out the vampire world. Conquer one more world; it was all in a days work.

I felt the hairs on my arm prickle and stand on end. There was a cool wind that suddenly wrapped itself around me, embracing me, caressing me. I sucked in a deep breath and closed my eyes, reveling in the beauty and the sensation that it evoked in me. The moment was perfect; there was hardly a need for words. The wind picked up and rushed through my legs, tossed my hair and seemed to linger and whisper in my ear.

"Magnificent now, magnificent always…you are truly beautiful Holly."

The voice was low, hypnotic, sensual, all things wonderful and unreal. The words were whispered directly into my ear and two strong hands were now resting on my shoulders. I was tempted, and for once I would not resist. I leaned back and let myself rest in his embrace. It tucked my head comfortably into his chest and let myself indulge in the sensations and the need he invoked in me, a need that for once I wished to wash myself in. "Can't we just stay like this?" I asked.

"If we only could. I would like nothing better…but it is not possible." Lucien smoothed a hand down my side. "We must enter together, as protocol would dictate."

I felt Lucien's cool fingers playing with the ties at the back of my dress and frowned. I moved away from him and he dropped his hand.

"I like this dress Holly, I like it very much."

I rolled my eyes. "Yeah, you should, you picked it out for me. And by the way…how could you imagine that this was a dress…"

Lucien's eyes gleamed and he smiled. "I could only imagine what it would look like on you, but now, now I am getting to see it on you for myself, and you look even more beautiful than I could ever have imagined."

"Thanks." My reply came out dry, I couldn't help it, it was the best that I could manage under the circumstances.

"Are you nervous my Holly flower?"

"Me, nervous? Of course not."

Lucien gave me a knowing look and nodded. "Of course not." He held out his hand. "Shall we go, Holly flower?"

"Yeah, lets. Why the heck not?" I placed my hand in his and gripped it. "Okay…" I muttered under my breath, "Okay."

The throne room was still stark but tonight it was filled, near capacity. The large table in the center boasted a huge silver server filled with, what looked an awful lot like blood to me. I swallowed back nausea, hey it was a vampire meeting, I suppose there had to be vampire refreshments.

When Lucien and I walked into the room everyone stood. It was like being in the presence of royalty, not that I had ever been in the presence of royalty before. He had made his way, with me on his arm to the dais, where he took his place on the throne. There was now a smaller seat placed beside the throne and I just took a wild guess that this was where I was supposed to sit.

Once seated, the rest of the room sat. The smaller seats on either side of the room were now all filled. Each one occupied by a strange array of very strong vampires. By the side of most of the vampires there stood a female or male human, companions I was guessing, who else? I closed my eyes for a moment and tried to imagine steel doors and double fortified walls. They would be heavy, and strong and unbreakable. They would be…

"Are you well Holly flower?"

My eyes popped open and I turned my startled gaze onto Lucien. "Excuse me?"

"Are you well…your coloring is a little pale."

I gave him a pointed look. "You're joking right?"

Lucien sighed. "You look unwell."

"I'm fine." Another barrage of strong mental pushes flew my way and I flinched. I swallowed back a frustrated scream and steeled myself. I let the mental streams pass over me and imagined them running off me much like water would.

"You are being tested." Lucien said.

It was pointless to deny it. "Yes." I cleared my throat before going on. "It's why I'm so uncomfortable…" That along with a couple dozen ancient bloodsuckers was definitely why I was uncomfortable.

"I am sorry. However, it is to be expected."

"Oh?"

"You are my companion. And you are strong, very much so. You are here tonight for your formal introduction into our society, for lack of a better word. The other city leaders are seeing for themselves how much power you possess. Some do it inadvertently, but most are here to gauge you and your abilities for themselves."

I gasped as my mind was suddenly penetrated. I gritted my teeth and shoved the intruder out. I turned angry eyes to Lucien. "Yeah, well couldn't you have told them to do their gauging one at a fucking time?" I clenched my hands. "This is ridiculous!"

Lucien nodded. "I cannot say anything, it would be considered an interference."

"Hell yeah it would be an interference. A necessary one, I'm being attacked here Lucien. If you don't want me passed out on the floor you'll tell them to behave themselves."

"I cannot tell them anything. We lead, we are not lead."

I groaned. I took a deep breath and tried to push everything back. I concentrated on the room, the inhabitants the gorgeous dead guy by my side, anything, absolutely anything but the mind probing that was occurring. "You'll have to deal with the consequences." I muttered under my breath.

"We all will." Lucien replied. Lucien stood and bowed his head. He then passed his forest green eyes around the room, drinking each 'person' in, one at a time. "Welcome to my territory, thank you for attending. May we be blessed in darkness." He paused for a moment, I think for effect, before continuing. "Tonight we are here for a two fold reason. The first being, your first contact with my new companion, I am sure by now each and every one of you has tested her mental guards for yourselves. I am sure you will find them more than adequate." Lucien swept his gaze around the room meaningfully. "As I am sure you will find her more than adequate, and more than up to your challenges. The second reason is an exchange of information and a pooling of minds. We have recently come across an opponent that has tested our resources greatly. This adversary has killed both humans and vampires and blatantly challenges our authority. With help from my companion we have established that our adversary is a demon…"

I watched as a number of expressions flickered across the vampires faces. There were murmurs and whispers and exchanges of looks. Obviously the mention of demons affected the other bloodsuckers in much the same way it had affected mine.

"We will begin now, as we obviously have much to talk about." Lucien sat then. He looked at me with an amused expression when he saw that I was fiddling with the folds of my dress, trying to cover my very exposed legs, damned slits.

"How many vampire victims are we talking about Lucien?"

This came from a very pale (hell they were all pale) very slender vampire on the right side of the room. He had dark hair and dark blue eyes and was dressed elegantly in black pants and a black silk shirt. His features were sharp but not unattractive and beside him stood a young woman.

"Three of my Hive are now gone, does that answer your question Yanos?"

The vampire named Yanos nodded. I could see something in his eyes, and what I saw I didn't like. It was obvious that Yanos considered losing three members of one's Hive, an appalling blunder, and perhaps it pointed to a serious lack of control and authority. I swept my eyes around the room and could see similar expressions on the other vamp's faces. I was furious. It wasn't Lucien's fault. It wasn't as if he had called forth the killing demon.

"This demon could get to any of you and yours." I blurted out before I could stop myself. I knew that if I looked at Lucien I would see dissatisfaction in his face, so I didn't look at him.

"Have you lost control of your companion much the same way as you have lost control of your Hive, Lucien?"

I immediately located the vamp that had spoken. He had a dark complexion and hair, which was streaked with white. His eyes were small and beady (I disliked him already) and his nose hooked, as if it had been broken several times and had never healed properly. His mouth was set in a sneer and his hand was curled possessively around the wrist of a very young girl, whose face was pale, and withdrawn, oh yeah, I really didn't like this one.

"I have lost no control Victor, and my companion speaks correctly. This problem does not concern merely me and mine; it concerns all of the Night Walkers. This demon is very powerful and has been summoned by a sorcerer who is only strengthening himself. He has managed to take unawares, incapacitate and kill three vampires, all of whom were over one hundred years in age. There has been nothing to indicate that these three vampires were chosen for a reason, other than the fact that they were vampires. There is nothing to indicate that Edwards is being specifically targeted. The sorcerer and subsequently the demon are here, in Edwards now, but for how long? How long before they decide to target…Savannah…?" Lucien pinned vampire Victor with a long look (I suppose he called Savannah home) before moving on. "Or Atlanta, Charleston, Charlotte, New Orleans…" He let his voice drift off and eyed the room. "How long before your Hive begins to dwindle…how long before you are where I am now, standing before you, asking you for your information, your ideas." Lucien's eyes were filled with fire and ice. His face had become nearly transparent and the delicate blue veins in his face were prominent and intimidating. He stood in all his glory and if he wasn't considered a scary sight, then I didn't know what was.

"And how is your pet involved in this?" Again, it was vampire Victor who had spoken.

I'm sure Lucien must have seen the barely disguised disgust and aggravation in my face. He looked at me with a very telling expression, one that screamed, 'do not say anything, and just control your temper.' He gave vamp Victor a terrifying look. It was hard, cruel and very, very, very cold.

I wanted to applaud. Lucien let his eyes and mouth soften into a taunting smile.

"I have no pet, do you?"

I saw vamp Victor stiffen and his mouth tighten. I pushed my way through, seeing an immediate opportunity I took it. His mental pathway was open. He was filled with rage and fury and was not taking care to fortify himself. I lasted only a minute or so before I had to retreat. The anger, and fury had nearly suffocated me and I couldn't have held out any longer. But in a vampire's mind, a minute is enough. Here was a vampire that really hated Lucien. His thoughts were twisted with nothing but evil and I knew, I just knew that if given the chance he would try and destroy Lucien.

Vampire Victor tightened his grip on his companion's arm. I gritted my teeth. He jerked her arm forward and faster than you could blink sank his fangs into her soft flesh. I watched in horror as trickles of blood ran down her wrist, pooling into her open palm. I looked around to see if anyone else was mirroring my shock, no one was. Indeed, I saw expressions of amusement, hunger and boredom.

I gasped when pain shot through my body. My wrist was burning. I looked down but saw nothing, not a bruise, not a cut, nothing. The pain continued to streak through my body, twisting my gut and causing me to grip the side of the chair almost painfully. I tried to focus my now cloudy eyes around the room and within moments located the source of my pain. Vampire Victor's human companion was now on her knees. Her wrist was still pinned by her master's fangs and he was still drinking her life's blood. Her eyes were pain filled, and I saw small tears gathering at the corner of her eyes.

Oh god, he hadn't put her under. He hadn't hypnotized her. It would be like going into surgery without any anesthesia, the fucking bastard. I made a move and instantly my arm was held firmly in place. I looked to my side and saw Lucien staring at me with those cold eyes of his. I began to open my mouth and protest but he silenced me with one look and a slash of his other hand. I beseeched him with my eyes, but he only shook his head before turning back to the display.

I tried to control my breathing but it was becoming harder. I could not construct decent walls against vampire Victor's companion's pain. She was scared and hurting and her mind was invading mine so completely I felt her feelings to my very core. I could feel the pressure building in my body, my wrist was burning and my heart was pounding. I felt a familiar migraine coming on and I was suppressing the nausea with all of my might. I wriggled my hand, which was still trapped under Lucien's and he turned back to me. I immediately read the concern in his face. He could see what this was doing to me, he knew. Lucien stood before I could say anything, I didn't want him to do anything stupid. What was I thinking? I was about to pass out, hell yeah he had better do something.

"Halt, you will stop your display now Victor, or I will stop it for you."

I saw; through a cloudy haze of pain vampire Victor release his companion, more or less thrusting her cruelly away from him. She knelt by the side of the chair, huddled and pathetic. I wanted to go to her, but I was just now regaining my mental facilities. Not to mention somehow I thought Lucien wouldn't appreciate my interference at this moment in time.

"You overstep yourself Lucien." Vampire Victor said.

"No, it is you that overstep yourself Victor."

"I am within my rights to take blood from my companion. That is what she is here for, is it not?"

Lucien narrowed his eyes and his body began to shimmer. I watched in amazement as that familiar glow began to surround him. I noticed that I was not alone in my awe; similar expressions were gracing several of the vampires in the room, not to mention most of their humans. Lucien took two steps down, away from the dais. He stood, staring at Victor with what could only be described as a really, really ferocious look. "What you do is unaccountably rude. You may take blood, yes, but they way you took the blood was an insult to me and mine." Lucien's skin began to stretch and pull and my eyes widened in horror, oh god, was he going to change right now? "You used no compulsion, and you know that my companion is Empathic. What your companion felt my companion felt. You clearly overstepped your bounds. What you did could only be an insult, and I took it as such."

"I did not realize the full extent of your companion's powers." Vampire Victor said with a sneer.

"You would have tested her when we entered the chamber. You knew."

"I say I did not." Vampire Victor stood from his seat and faced Lucien with an equally ferocious expression on his face.

My eyes darted back and forth between Lucien and vampire Victor. I really didn't like where this was going. I stood from my seat with the intention of joining Lucien, but was stopped by the quick motion of Lucien's hand. He had sensed my movement without looking and was telling me without words to do nothing, say nothing. I sank back into my chair but if things got ugly there was nothing he could do that would stop me from doing what I could to help him. There were enough inanimate objects in this throne room that I could 'toss' vampire Victor's way to keep him busy for a little while. A girl's got to do, what a girl's got to do.

I turned my attention back to Lucien and vampire Victor who were still standing perfectly still, staring at one another? I noticed that there was not a sound in the room. Each vampire was seated stock still and perfectly composed. They watched the display with not an ounce of my trepidation. Well, they were vampires, what did I expect?

"There are other ways to settle this Victor. You have been more than clear in your intentions for some time. I would choose a more private venue for our 'discussion' but if you would like to settle this now, we can." Lucien's aura glowed brighter. He seemed wrapped in moonlight. His pale face was brilliant and his eyes were blood red.

I saw vampire Victor hesitate. I probed and instantly fell into his mind.

He was torn. He wanted nothing better to tear Lucien limb from limb, but he knew that his powers were inferior. He feared Lucien, and, for once I was really happy that Lucien was a badass. I retreated quickly from vampire Victor's mind, less I sink too deep and find myself stuck in that evil mind of his permanently.

Within moments vampire Victor took a step back and sank back into his chair. He shook his head and gave Lucien a semblance of a smile (not that he didn't want to rip his heart out while doing so). "You take things too seriously Lucien. You must learn to relax. I meant nothing by my actions. Would you begin something over nothing."

"I will 'relax' and forgive your blunder when you apologize to my companion for your blunder and intrusion into her mind."

I held my breath. Oh jeez. I saw vampire Victor's eyes narrow ominously. He looked around the room but no one spoke nor moved. He cast rage filled eyes on Lucien, who still stood, glowing and perfectly still below the dais. He nodded curtly, his fury still apparent. "I fear that my actions caused you discomfort, companion to Lucien, and for that I offer my regrets."

I nodded. I knew that was as close to an apology as I was going to get from the scary vamp. I saw that Lucien realized that too. He moved back to his place on the throne and sat. The silence was deafening. Well, Lucien hadn't been wrong, this meeting was definitely enlightening...the question was what was it enlightening?

"We had murders, similar to those that you have described to us Lucien, in Charlotte." The voice pierced the silence and heads turned.

I located the voice. It belonged to a fair-haired vamp seated not far from the dais. The vamp was exceptionally handsome. With strange gray eyes and hair so pale it appeared white in the light, he was very striking. I observed that there was no human standing by him. He sat alone, formidable, with clear, intelligent eyes. "They occurred a year ago. We had only two victims, both human companions. Our Hive was not struck, but the loss of our companions hit us hard." The strikingly handsome vampire paused before continuing, "We deducted that magic had been used, but before we could solve the mystery, the murders stopped."

"But there were no vampire victims, you said." Lucien asked.

"No."

"I see, thank you Michele." Lucien cast his eyes around the room. "Have any of you, like Michele, encountered a similar M.O."

I saw the other vamp leaders shake their heads.

"Will you offer us aid if the need arises?" Lucien asked. He cocked his head to one side and let his words sink into the deep silence. I knew this was important. It was obvious that asking for aid from other vamp leaders was a nouveau experience. Area vampire Holders were the ultimate authority and they were obviously not adept at sharing leadership or power. I was awfully proud of my particular vamp for his initiative.

"Will you offer it to us?" This came from the handsome blond vampire Michele.

"My blood will be your blood as yours will be mine." Lucien said the words formally and bowed his head somberly. I knew that something big had transpired as I saw the entire room shake their heads approvingly. Everyone that is, except, for scary vampire Victor, who still stared at Lucien with hate filled eyes.

"I file my objection now," Vampire Victor said angrily, troublemaker, (yep, there seemed to be one in every bunch) "I still claim that this is Lucien's problem and his problem alone. We are not needed for this trifle, it is an admittance of weakness on his part that he convenes a meeting for this purpose...." He tossed me a look, now what was that about? "Among other things."

"Is a demon a trifle, Victor? I very much believe you thought otherwise...especially, oh, in 1899... or did you not have a slight problem with a demon yourself that year?" Michele's voice was soft and mocking and I almost spoke my thanks, but wisely held my tongue, perhaps I was getting better at this.

I smiled when I saw vampire Victor's face tighten and his posture stiffen considerably, oh yeah; he was pissed off big time.

"The matter was dealt with efficiently." He spat out.

"But not by you." Michele said snidely. This comment effectively shut vamp Victor up. I almost cheered, but again, I didn't think that would be appreciated by the bloodsuckers surrounding me. Michele cast his eyes around the room and then let them rest on Lucien's seated form. Something seemed to pass between them, what, I could not say, but I could feel the weight of it between them like an anvil. "So it is settled." Michele whispered.

"So it will be." Lucien said. He turned to me with those dark green eyes of his and gave me a small smile before turning his attention back on the room. "Shall we dine?"

There was a general murmur of agreement before the vamps stood from their chairs and began to mingle, yeah mingle (funny, huh, mingling vampires).

I turned to Lucien. "So they'll help us, right? That's what this was all about, right?"

"That and other things, yes. They will help us..." He smiled slightly, "If we need it."

"Who decides if we need help or not?"

"Why they do, of course." Lucien smiled at my annoyed expression. "It takes much to convince Night Walkers to aid other Night Walkers. We have accomplished much in this eve Holly, be at peace."

"But..."

"It is a victory."

I rolled my eyes. "Yeah, okay, whatever. But only because you guys are so damn stubborn."

Lucien laughed, a genuine rolling laugh. "Yes, we have learned to be, over many, many centuries of life." I saw Lucien turn his attention to the center of the room where the handsome blond vamp, Michele was pouring himself a 'refreshment' (ugh, totally icky). "Come..." He practically dragged me down the dais.

I stood stiffly beside Lucien. I didn't like being this close to this many vampires. I eyed them through my peripheral vision and was just getting more and more nervous as the minutes went by. The probing hadn't stopped, just subsided a little, so I wasn't being bombarded. I could see some of the vamps looking at me with what could only be hunger in their eyes.

"Michele." Lucien said the blond haired vamps name.

"Lucien." Michele answered the same.

"This is my companion, Holly, Holly, this is Michele, and he is the Holder of Charlotte."

I nodded, I sort of figured that one out already. But I bowed my head respectively, just to be on the safe side. When I cast a sidelong glance in Lucien's direction I noticed he was looking at me with and approving smile on his face.

"She is indeed as they have said."

What? Okay, huh?

"She is, and more." Lucien answered.

Now, I was annoyed. Were they talking about me? "Hey, hello boys, uh, like what's going on?"

Lucien grinned and turned to Michele. "She is also easily annoyed."

"*She* is also right here." I said tartly.

Michele laughed. "Indeed. I apologize for my lack of manners, companion to Lucien. I had received reports of your…beauty and talent, it was a pleasant surprise to see that the reports were not exaggerated."

I rolled my eyes. Oh yeah, right. "I'm supposed to believe that you heard about me all the way from Charlotte." I laughed. "Boy, good news travels quickly." I said sarcastically.

Michele and Lucien stared at me until I thought they were going to bear a hole in my head.

"You are a PSI talented human, you would make an ideal companion, so yes, news travels quickly as you so quaintly put it." Michele said.

I saw by his look that he really wasn't kidding. "Are you trying to tell me that you were like, keeping tabs on me?"

Michele shrugged his shoulders and turned to Lucien. "Have you not explained this to her?"

Lucien laughed. "You will learn that Holly is sometimes…difficult to talk to."

"Hey!" I said.

"Is it not the truth?" Lucien asked, giving me a wide-eyed look. Damn, could I lie in front of the vamps?

"Well you're no picnic yourself." I grumbled. I chose to ignore the amused expressions on the vampire's faces. "So, like, back to the subject…were you spying on me?"

"I do not need to spy" Michele said tightly. I rolled my eyes.

"So, did you have anyone of your goons spy on me?"

"Goons?"

"Your people" Lucien supplied. Michele nodded and I sighed. Jeez the vamps needed modernization almost as much as the Edward's police force did.

"It is necessary to keep abreast of the news. You, companion to Lucien are news."

"Can you like, stop, with this 'companion to Lucien' stuff, I'm Holly, just Holly."

Michele turned to look at Lucien. I saw Lucien give a brief nod and Michele then turned back to me.

"As you wish, Holly. As I said you were, still are, news. Your appearance, quite unexpectedly, at one of our establishments caused quite a stir."

Boy, oh boy, how did a girl get so lucky? I had flaunted my power and caused a stir, yeah great, that's what got me into this entire mess in the first place. "But how did you know about that night?"

"We are council, we know everything…" Michele turned slightly amused eyes back to Lucien and added, "Eventually."

"Because you spy." I said.

"Because we are attentive." Michele corrected.

"Fine, fine, so you're like a vampire grapevine." I didn't even try to explain that last to them, let them figure it out. But what Michele said next stopped me.

"I was waiting, as we must, by law. But Lucien claimed you, as is his right, so…"

"Uh, what?" Claiming? Rights? What the hell was this about? I turned narrowed eyes on Lucien and noticed that he was not looking at me. He was staring at Michele.

"Michele…drink, you let the blood grow cold." Lucien said almost urgently. I planted my one un-slinged arm on my hip and glared at Lucien.

"Okay, what the hell is he talking about Lucien?"

"It is nothing."

"Uh, huh, like, why don't I believe that?"

Michele was watching this exchange with interest. His eyes widened and his smile grew. He turned eyes, which were filled with mirth in Lucien's direction and said quietly. "You did not tell her?"

Lucien shrugged. "There was no need, nor time."

"Tell me what?"

"Again, it is nothing."

"You'd better tell me what's going on before I throw a total hissy fit, and believe me I will."

"Hissy fit?" Michele asked.

I threw up my hand in exasperation. "Basically I bring down the damn ceiling with a major tantrum if one of you don't tell me what the heck is going on, what you're talking about."

Michele smiled. It made his already handsome face, stunningly beautiful. "Please, allow me the honors." He ignored Lucien's protest and continued. "We are all permitted companions of the human persuasion…"

So far, so good, already knew all this. "Yeah, okay."

"It has long been said that humans with PSI talent have sweeter blood, and pliant flesh. They are considered the most…desirable of acquisitions. In addition, the abilities that they have, added to ours prove a formidable power. If you have a strong companion, then your strength is compounded, lucky is the vampire who acquires a PSI talented human." Michele paused and I saw him toss Lucien another knowing smile. "The council long ago decreed that we were allowed to seek out and to bind a PSI talented human to us. In Lucien's case, you were in his territory, more the pity to all of us. It was Lucien's right to claim you as his companion, if he so wished it. He took longer than some to announce you, thus, some of us believed that he would throw you over, and that we could claim you for ourselves. I have been keeping watch over all the developments...If Lucien had not claimed you, I would have struck a bid for your companionship. You have an exceedingly fair face and your power is such that would tempt any vampire Holder." Michele paused. "But it is all moot now, Lucien formally claimed you tonight, and the Southern Night Leaders have accepted his claim."

I was mad enough to spit. Maybe I would. I felt my rage boiling and churning within my entire body, especially my head. I desperately tried to hold onto the reigns of my anger, I remembered what happened to Detective Marcus the last time I felt such rage in my mind. Somehow I just didn't think it practical to let lose in a room full of really, really, ancient and really, really unfriendly vampire leaders. I did, however, think it was okay to give Lucien a little piece of my now furious mind. I turned my eyes, which were filled with wrath, in Lucien's direction. He was staring at me with what I recognized now as arrogance. He obviously was going to try to bluff his way out of this one. No damn way was he going to get out of this. "So this was like a plan from the beginning." I said, pleased that I hadn't hit him yet.

"Michele speaks the truth. But there was no plan. You were an unexpected surprise. However, if I had not claimed you, someone else would have." He gave me a penetrating stare. "Would you have liked that my Holly flower? Someone else claiming you?"

"Considering you're a lying, sneaky, Machiavellian asshole, yeah, maybe being 'claimed' by someone else wouldn't have been such a damn bad idea!" I stood my ground, giving him the most ferocious look I could muster under the circumstances (I mean I was surrounded by two dozen or so fang tooth fiends and I was sporting a sling and was minus the use of one hand...how ferocious could I be?).

"You are merely upset because you are continuing to learn our rules."

"No, you shithead, I'm upset, and there is nothing merely about it, because you have been manipulating me from the beginning. Making me think I had a hand in all of this, making me believe that you were just 'dating' me, when all along you planned this little vampire get together in order to put some archaic sign on my chest that reads 'I belong to Lucien.' And hey, when were you going to tell me about this little testosterone filled bidding event and the fact that someone else could claim me if you didn't. By the way, I fucking hate that word, 'claim' I'm not some lost puppy you're picking up at the damn pound." I was clenching my one good hand so hard that I was digging nails into my palm. I could feel the blood pounding in my ears and had never wanted to hit anyone so hard as I wanted to hit this dead hunk of flesh right now.

How fucking dare he! How dare he use me and manipulate me for his own greedy, selfish needs. He had totally lied to me. If Michele, the Holder of Charlotte hadn't informed me about all of this, would Lucien have ever told me? Well, duh, obviously not. The asshole.

"You are once again, misconstruing the entire situation my Holly flower."

"Don't you Holly flower me, you, you…"

"Shithead?" Michele supplied with an enigmatic smile.

"Yeah, you shithead." I said. I ignored the look Lucien threw in Michele's direction and continued to glare at Lucien. Oh, damn, if we weren't totally surrounded by all these vamps I'd totally give Lucien a little demonstration of my powers…a demonstration that would knock him on his ass, literally. "I hate you."

"We have been over this before Holly," Lucien said.

"Yeah, but that was then, this is now."

"Holly." Lucien sighed.

"I believe we should speak of other things" Michele's voice broke into our argument. "Victor is deigning his attentions upon us."

I quickly looked around and sure enough scary ass vamp Victor was staring at the three of us with pure malice. I quickly remembered about sensitized vampire hearing and swallowed back swearing. Damn, I had really wanted to nail Lucien some more. But I wasn't about to get us all skewered (figuratively and literally) because I couldn't hold my temper…just until we were in a more private setting. I choked back what I was going to say to Lucien and just glared at him, he'd get it.

I forced myself not to shrug off Lucien's arm, the one that he placed around my shoulders. I stiffened when he leaned into me and brought his lips to my ear.

"You are beautiful tonight my Holly flower, a rare jewel. You have impressed the Southern Night Leaders."

I grit my teeth. I leaned up and whispered into his ear. "Don't think you're getting out of this with a little flattery you jerk, you're still a dead man."

Lucien smiled. "That I am. At least I was at my last account."

Ahhhh I hated it when he one-upped me. "I'm going to kill you." I murmured.

"And how do you plan to kill a dead man, my holly flower?"

"A sword and steak will suffice for now." I grinned at Lucien's unfeigned surprised expression and Michele's gleaming eyes (obviously the vamp had heard what I had said, guess I hadn't whispered low enough).

"So bloodthirsty," Lucien said.

"No, that would be you."

Michele couldn't quite stifle a laugh. "I believe, she has you there, Lucien."

I grinned, point for me.

"We will talk more on this later Holly."

I nodded, suddenly very serious. "You bet we will, oh yeah, we'll talk about this." I suppressed a shudder when vampire Michele smiled a large fang toothed smile and downed the entire glass of blood he had been holding. But I couldn't suppress my disgust when remnants of that metallic, dark, wine red substance stained his teeth, yuck, totally gross.

Chapter Twenty-Seven:

When the last of the bad rejects from B movies had left, I allowed myself, for the first time during the evening, a real sigh of relief. I sat in the chair on the dais and allowed my eyes to sweep around the cold stone room. The serving bowl on the table had not yet been removed and there was still blood sliding down the side of the bowl and pooling onto the table.

I had been hard pressed not to scream out my disgust when the vamps had begun their 'meal.' Many of them had simply sunk their fangs into their companions, not even bothering with the niceties (whatever those would be). Some, like Michele, the Holder of Charlotte, had sipped, or greedily gulped down the blood in their cups, which they filled from the now nearly empty serving bowl. All in all, it had been a very enlightening evening, one that I didn't want to repeat anytime in the near future. "I thought you were all like equal." I blurted out. I watched Lucien turn around slowly. He was standing at the bottom of the steps, where had had been standing absolutely still and silent for at least fifteen minutes. His penetrating green eyes bore into mine, I blinked first, damn.

"We are, in some ways, and we aren't in others."

Yeah, yeah, why did vamps always talk in riddles? "Okay, whatever. Why do you get the completely cool chair, while they have to sit below?" It had bothered me from the moment we had stepped into the chamber and had taken our seats.

Lucien continued to stare at me. Okay, now he was making me nervous. "It is the way of things. If we attend a meeting in another territory it will be much the same. The design of the meeting chamber may be different, but the concept will be unchanged." Lucien paused before continuing, "We must show our authority, especially in our own territory. It is specific, so that we

216

have the advantage in our chamber. They must pay me their respect while they are on my lands, that they sit so, shows me that they acknowledge my power in my territory. Michele has a meeting chamber not unlike this one. But he has us seated at a table, where he is head. Again, to show us his power on his land, and for us to respect his power."

Why did vampires have to make everything so damn complicated? "All these stupid rules..." I muttered.

"What?"

"I said you have a lot of very stupid rules." I dared him with a look to argue with me.

"Our ways are very different from yours." Lucien said gently.

I was annoyed. I wanted him to yell at me so that I could yell back and possibly throw something in his direction. It wasn't helping matters any that he was being so damn complacent all of a sudden.

"Hell yeah, your way is different." I glared at him. "You should have told me about all this 'claiming' shit."

Lucien shrugged those beautiful shoulders of his. I watched the movement, drinking in the play of his muscles and the fold of the fabric as it molded his body. "We do not think to share things Holly flower."

"Yeah, you've told me this before."

"Then you realize that I have told you things that I would tell no other. I have given to you more than I have ever given to another. I did not think to tell you because to me, it did not matter if you knew or not. It is the way of things."

"Yeah, they're sucky ways."

"To you perhaps, because you are so stubborn." Lucien held up his hand to stop my forthcoming argument, he smiled. "You tell me that we, of the night clans, are stubborn, but you, you my little Holly human are fiercely so. Another human would not argue, would not fuss so about the claiming. They would merely accept it for fact, and they would enter our world eagerly, taking that which we offer and only that which we offer to them. No other vampire Holder has had to endure as much as I have endured with you." Lucien sighed, while I held onto my anger, thinly, held onto my anger. "I never thought to tell you about the claiming, as it is law, among the night clans. By the time I realized your nature it was too late, we were already engaged in a relationship, as you like to call it. Had I known it would distress you so much I would have told you."

"Yeah right." I skewered him with a cold look. "You would never have told me. If vamp Michele hadn't spilled the beans tonight you would never have told me, right? Admit it, you would have held onto all your little rules and secrets and let me be damned, isn't that he way of things?" I dared him with my eyes to lie to me. He didn't.

"I would not have told you…"

I was triumphant, the lying bloodsucker. "Yeah, I thought not."

"Because you need not have known."

Jeez. I dropped my head into my hands. I could have an easier conversation with a deaf person than I could with a dead one. "Is this hellish night over with?" I said instead.

"Pardon?"

"Are you done showing me off?" I said tiredly. Suddenly, I was exhausted. I felt all that fury and anger leave me, much like the sun after a storm. It fell away and left me bone weary and ready to fold it in. "If you're done, then I'd like to get home."

"You shall stay here the night Holly flower, you are too tired to return home."

Yeah that did it. Just try to make me do something I don't want to and see how fast I rally. "No way, absolutely not. I am not sleeping in this mausoleum. You can, like, take me home right now."

"Holly…"

"Uh, uh, no way, I came, I let all your vamp friends try to take a piece out of my mind, which by the way hurt like hell and was rude to boot. I didn't throw you across the room, like you totally deserved after that damn claiming bit, and I watched that vamp Michele drink blood out of a china cup…so, fuck it, I'm done. Take me home."

"You are being unreasonable."

"Yeah, so when have you ever thought me reasonable?" I watched Lucien ponder that one for a moment and smiled inwardly, another point for me. "So, point me to the door, I'm outta here."

"As you wish." Lucien's eyes were narrow and his mouth tight, like I cared. By now all I cared about was a warm bed and counting sheep.

I heard footsteps resonate on the stone and turned my face sideways. Vanessa was standing several feet away from Lucien below the dais. She had changed (guess she kept a spare set of clothing in the Lair, how practical). She was dressed simply in a tight tank and unbelievably short black shorts. I tried not to flinch when I saw fresh bite marks on her throat and on her thighs, marks, which were bleeding steadily. It seemed as if someone had gotten their fix tonight.

"Yes master" Vanessa's voice was low and oddly slurred. Obviously she hadn't shaken the after affects of the compulsion. Her eyes were glassy and gleaming with moisture as if she had begun to cry and had thought better of it. She was unsteady on her feet and began to fall, she would have if Lucien hadn't caught her arm and steadied her. I saw Lucien zoom in on the fresh wounds, which were still bleeding and his deep forest green eyes began to do that scary red haze thing that he did so well. He began to glow and he sniffed the air, much like a dog. He leaned in, as if to lick the bleeding wounds and thought better of it. He jerked back and composed himself.

I had found myself holding my breath the moment his eyes had bled to red. Disgust had coiled itself in my stomach when he had scented Vanessa's wounds and gone in for a lick. He had not done it though, he had not tasted Vanessa, and for some reason I was very glad of that fact. It wasn't as if I was offering to donate, but it wasn't as if I wanted anyone else to either. Yeah, fickle, maybe, but who ever said I wasn't?

I blinked when Julian more or less appeared out of thin air. I'm sure he had entered through a normal venue (a door, or something) but I hadn't seen him enter, it was that quick, that fast. Julian's color was good, in fact, if I didn't know better I'd say the vampire was flushed. His eyes were bright and strangely sharp.

Lucien spoke then. His voice was cold, frigid. The temperature in the room seemed to drop twenty degrees and I'm sure I had goose bumps up and down my arms. "I brought Vanessa here with the hopes that she would return Holly to her domicile, however, I find that she has been greatly bled, in fact, so much was taken that she will not be of her right mind for quite some time."

I looked at Vanessa, who by now was sitting on the cold ground. Her head was lolling to one side and she had a faraway look in her unseeing eyes. Bled mindless? I had never heard of such a thing. Bled dead, yes, but mindless? Fucking great, another neat little vampire trick I had learned of this evening. I gave Lucien an equally frigid look.

"Will she ever be the same?" I motioned to Vanessa who was as sharp as a lump of playdoh.

Lucien nodded. "In time." His hand shot out so fast that even Vamp Julian didn't have time to get away. Lucien held vamp Julian effortlessly by the neck. Vampire Julian hung, feet dangling off the floor, neck trying to swallow. He flailed his arms and soon, realizing it was futile stopped all movement.

Lucian smiled evilly; it was a smile that always chilled me, a smile I remembered from when he had tortured Laeticia. "You know better than to bleed a mind, Julian." Lucien didn't even give him time to try to answer. "You know what I do to those who abuse their companions as often as you do." Lucien threw Julian with one arm and I watched as the playboy vampire flew through the air and hit the opposite wall with a sickening sound. I shook my head in shock, when Lucien was suddenly beside him, holding him again in place with his hand, this time to the wall. "I have been very patient with you. I have allowed you your fun, your room. But you are playing a very tricky game, are you not? A game, which I am afraid I will no longer allow you to play. You have gone through too many companions in too short of a time to claim accident any longer. I have known of your proclivities, and have been more than kind to allow them to continue, and I am not known for my kindness, am I?" Lucien tightened his grip on vampire Julian's neck and I watched in horror as blood began to flow. Vampire Julian made strangled sounds but Lucien continued to ignore them. With his other free hand I watched as the skin stretched and pulled, and his fingers hooked and sharpened until they were razor sharp talons, as deadly as any weapon. Quicker than one can blink he had raked his razor sharp hand down vampire Julian's flushed face. Deep gouges ran red and vampire Julian whimpered. "One too many Julian…one too many. You and Laeticia, for all your age have so little in the way of sense. Both of you choose companions with little more sense than you yourselves have. And then, then you force me into these situations, situations where I must clean up your messes. I am the vampire Holder of Edwards" With those words he gleamed even brighter and his aura pressed outwards until I could feel it pressing against my carefully constructed shields. "Not a babysitter." Lucien released vampire Julian's neck and almost simultaneously snapped his wrist.

I screamed when I heard the bone break and covered my mouth in shock. "Oh my god." I whispered through the tense silence. I spared a quick glance for Vanessa, who was rocking back and forth and disgustingly, was wiping her wounds and licking the blood off of her fingers. My eyes once again found Lucien and vampire Julian. Vampire Julian was trying not to whimper, I was trying not to scream. I was fascinated in a terrified way as I saw the skin, bone and muscles in vampire Julian's wrist begin to reform and reshape themselves. Holy hell.

"You will take care of Vanessa, this one cannot die, it will raise too many questions, questions *I* would like to see you try to explain. I have dealt with your foolishness long enough. You will take care of Vanessa, or I shall take care of you." Lucien gave him a telling look. "Whichever you prefer…the choice is yours Julian."

I watched, as vampire Julian seemed to find his lost, nearly choked voice. His eyes were flashing a dangerous fire, but by now I knew that none of Lucien's Hive would ever defy him, or challenge him. He was, in every respect their Leader, and one does not defy one's leader. Not and live, anyways.

"It…will…be as you…say," Vamp Julian spat out.

Lucien smiled mockingly. "I thought as much." He waved his hand dismissively in the air. "You may take Vanessa away now, and remember, she is to be taken care of until she returns to her 'normal' self. And afterwards, well, afterwards…you shall treat her as a companion ought to be treated."

I watched as vampire Julian nodded and got up off the floor. His face had not healed and his hand still hung limply from his wrist, but the wounds looked remarkably better than they had only minutes before…a true testimony to vampire durability. He easily lifted Vanessa into his arms, (much like Clark Gable did for Vivian Leigh, except without any of the romance factor and, uh, soaring epic music). The only 'music' I heard was the sound of my own furiously pounding heart and the roaring in my ears. And I could do without that.

I sank back into the chair, limply, drained the moment vamp lothario Julian had left the room with Vanessa. I jerked back slightly when I found that Lucien was now seated by my side and holding my very cold and very stiff hand.

"Will you again reprimand me for something that had to be done, something that will most certainly be done again."

I didn't know what to say. It totally freaked me out to watch Lucien torture someone, yeah, even a vampire. But it also totally freaked me out and disgusted me seeing what had been done to poor, lovesick and naive Vanessa. I had seen with my own two eyes the recuperating powers of vampires, so, then, was it still wrong to punish them in this way, especially if they could heal as if it were merely a paper cut that had been inflicted upon them? I wanted to be all self righteous and angry, but I was saving it for Vanessa and every other poor fool that acted as a vessel. I may be dating a vampire but I was no one's meal.

"Does she let…other, uh, vampires bite her?" I asked of Lucien.

Lucien nodded curtly. "Sometimes, if they are short of…foo…" He stopped when he realized what he was about to say. "When they are short of blood.

She is a vessel. She carries the blood of life within her veins. It is her right to give and ours to take. However, she is Julian's companion. So noted before the Southern Night Leaders. They were, to use the human word, dating. But Julian, as you saw is not attentive, he takes too much blood and often his companions..."

"Die." I supplied the word for Lucien, tersely.

Lucien nodded. "Yes. Recently, it has become obvious that Julian does this not merely out of foolishness as I once believed, but out of cleverness. He is much like a greedy child. He sees something of beauty and wishes to have it, hold it...taste it. But once tasted he bores easily. Unless our companions break our rules, our 'Night Laws' or defy us we cannot kill them, but accidental death is of course...allowed."

"Of course," I said sarcastically.

"Julian has then, decided that all his companions shall die...accidentally."

My eyes widened in horror and shock. "How many has he had?"

"This year?"

"Oh god."

"Five, including Vanessa. They all died from loss of blood. Julian claimed hunger and inattentiveness. I have allowed him leeway, but no longer." Lucien's eyes narrowed into slits and he gripped my hand tighter. I winced and he released his grip immediately. "If Julian continues, others might get the idea that they, too, may rid themselves of unwanted companions by accidental blood loss. It is easy enough to dispose of human remains..."

la, la, la, la, la, la, la...I did not want to hear this.

"But to explain the disappearances to human authorities, that is different all together. We have been lucky in Edwards that most of the force is completely inept, and has no idea how to deal with the vampire community, however, how much longer can we hope that the authorities will turn away from human disappearances, especially, of their young ones?"

"And what of their families" I spat out.

"What?"

"What if the girls families get into it, what if they begin to ask questions, and don't you think they will, if their daughters go missing."

"Of course." Lucien gave me a blank look. "But they will not find anything, they have not found anything...there is, of course, nothing to find."

Oh god, I also didn't need to know that. "You're bastards" I muttered. "It's unbelievable how little you care."

Lucien looked into my darkening violet eyes and shook his head. "No, it's unbelievable how much I care for you, Holly flower. If not for you, I would not bother with all these trifles. It is because of you I deal with your, little, human community. I know you do not care for Vanessa, however, you would be hurt greatly, care greatly, if she were to perish, would you not?"

I nodded weakly. It doubly freaked me out when this dead guy admitted to caring for me, having deep feelings for me? "She may be foolish, but she's not food." I ground out.

"Everything that has been done to her, she has allowed. However, even she could not have known Julian's little game. That...that was my responsibility, and it was mine to correct this evening." Lucien gave me a look. "Do not worry my Holly flower, he will not hurt her too badly anymore...he fears me, as he should."

"Too badly..." I muttered, great, just great, how much was too much? "But he'll abuse her," I said.

"Some wish to be abused" Lucien said with a sigh.

"Some don't know what they want." I parried. I watched as Lucien's eyes grew strangely soft, moments before he placed a chaste kiss upon my cool forehead. I was puzzled by his reaction.

"You cannot look out for everyone Holly flower."

I shook my head. "Perhaps not, but I sure as hell am going to give it my best shot." I knew that sounded ridiculous. I mean, I was only one person, right? But the thought of poor Vanessa lying around just to be some vamps first course, or third course, or whatever made me nauseous. As long as I was in this relationship, or whatever it was with Lucien, and I had control over my actions and abilities, and a little over his, well then I'd do whatever I could to keep victims like Vanessa as safe as possible. She was only twenty-one, damn; she at least deserved a chance.

"You are not everyone's mother, Holly flower."

I thought back to my own mother, her cold face and even colder demeanor. The way she had looked at me as if I were nothing, would accomplish nothing. I remembered the beatings and the harsh words, and even worse the feelings of failure and hopelessness. My mother she had hated me, she hadn't cared one whit about me. She hadn't loved me, nurtured me or tried to rescue me from my inner demons. I would never be my mother. Perhaps I couldn't be there for everyone, but I would go to my grave knowing I had given it my best shot. I would not be my mother. "You won't win mother." I whispered to myself.

"Holly?" Lucien looked at me questioningly.

I shook my head. "Nothing, it's nothing Lucien." I saw, in my mind, Vanessa's blank face and her glassy eyes and, vamp Julian's smug smile and pleasure at her pain, and I turned to Lucien. "Thank you, Lucien."

"For what my Holly flower?" Lucien looked genuinely confused.

"For Vanessa. Thank you for helping Vanessa." Right now it didn't seem to matter that perhaps he had done it out of selfishness or self preservation, it only mattered that he had done it, that he had kept vampire Julian from destroying another innocent life.

"You are thanking me?" Lucien was obviously shocked, obviously he had been expecting something very different than a thank you from me. "You continue to surprise me Holly flower." Lucien murmured. "And believe me, it has been a long time since I have been surprised."

I believed him, somehow Lucien didn't seem like the type to let someone takes him unawares. "Glad I can keep you on your toes."

"You do that, you do indeed." Lucien suddenly shifted in his seat. He released my hand and scented the air. His eyes narrowed a moment before he pulled me quickly to my feet. "The dawn is coming soon. If you are to go home, then you must go home now."

I began to protest. I mean how the heck was I going to get home. "Lucien, I would, but…"

"I will take you home." Lucien said.

I stared at him open mouthed. "Uh, excuse me?"

"I said I shall escort you home."

"Why?" I saw his expression and quickly added. "I mean, that's fine, but uh, weren't you going to have someone else drive me home?" (Uh, wasn't it like getting way to late for the vamp leader to be taking chances with his…being?)

"Yes, but plans change."

"They do indeed." I muttered. "Listen, it obviously doesn't have to be Vanessa or Julian…how about…"

Lucien was smiling at me. His eyes bright and his mouth curved upwards. "Do you object to me taking you home, Holly flower?"

"Uh, of course not, I just thought, perhaps, that you…well that you…" I was stammering, god I sounded like an idiot.

"I will take you home." Lucien said firmly, and the discussion was effectively ended.

Once we reached the front of my apartment Lucien pulled me into a tight embrace. My heart was pounding and the blood was rushing to my head, just with the touch of his body against mine. His arms were wrapped around me and his face was a mere inch away from mine. Those forest green eyes of his bore into my violet ones and he whispered,

"Would that I could do more...than this, but time...time is limited"

"What?" I whispered back just before Lucien's lips claimed mine in a searing kiss. How cold lips could cause such heat was beyond me. But I felt my body simmer and then burn as his mouth continued to ravage mine. His tongue twisted with mine and I opened wider to accommodate his questing tongue.

My head jerked back when I felt the sharp tang of blood in my mouth. I felt around with my tongue and located the source of the flow; he had nicked me with his sharp fangs. I frowned, it was only a small nick, but he had nicked me nonetheless. I looked into Lucien's face and could see that he looked contrite (not that I wasn't sure he was enjoying the taste of my blood).

"I apologize, it was a mistake." Lucien's eyes were glassy and wide. His breathing was a little heavy and he stared at me with unveiled lust and huger.

I nodded, yeah I believed him, and we *were* going at it pretty hot and heavy. However, I wasn't in the mood to lose any more blood tonight, "You should go." I murmured.

Lucien nodded. "Yes, there is little time before the dawn." Lucien backed away from me and regarded me through those beautiful eyes of his. "I would kiss you again, but there is no time."

I shook my head and rolled my eyes. "A kiss isn't worth frying over, for god's sake get going...go."

Lucien grinned at me. "We shall see one another soon Holly flower."

"Yeah, yeah, that's what I'm afraid of. Go, Lucien, now." And just like that, he was in his car and gone. Hope he didn't get a speeding ticket, worse yet, get stopped...wouldn't that be inconvenient...for the policeman that is.

Hadn't I just gotten to sleep? It sure felt like it. I rolled out of bed and flung the beeping alarm clock across the room, effectively shutting it up. Wincing I looked at the clock and curled my lip in disgust when I read the time, *7:30 a.m.*, god, what an ungodly hour, who the hell wanted to be up at 7:30 a.m. in the damn morning. I haphazardly threw on some clothes and waded through my unbelievably messy closet in search of a pair of shoes.

Making my way to the living room I set the coffee maker and spent the next several moments eyeing my bathroom with undisguised longing, god I wanted a shower. Just then my coffee machine beeped, signaling the finish of my brew. I looked between the coffee and the bathroom, which did I want more, caffeine or a hot spray of water...god that was an unfair choice. Padding into the kitchen area I pounced on the coffee and took in the delightful scent that could only come from a cup of steaming hot coffee...nothing could compete with caffeine, not even a hot shower.

Downing the entire cup I felt perkier already. Okay, not terribly perky, but a little perky, and a little perky was going to have to do, hell it was Thursday morning, what did you expect. I swept my books into my backpack and gave my apartment one last cursory look before I left, locking the door behind me. God, I had Latimer's class this morning, was I being punished? I hopped into my Volvo and prayed that it would start. Hell, after last night's excitement I was ready and willing to deal with anything, and anybody. Spitting Professor...do your worst.

It was pretty bad this morning. Latimer had gotten me not once, but three times straight in the face. Talk about a shower. When class finished I gratefully and hurriedly rushed out of the room, mindful of the other students sympathetic expressions...oh yeah, they had all gotten sprayed at one time or another, I just had the misfortune of being in the front line of fire.

My right hand was itching again and all I wanted to do was fling my books down and tear the damn sling off right now, however, I didn't think my doctor would approve of this course of action, especially since I was getting the damn thing removed today, after classes. I eyed my watch and sighed ruefully, only about seven more hours to go.

I ran right into Detective Marcus as I was coming out of the hospital. My eyes widened, he was the last person I expected to see. However, in light of recent events I don't know why I was so surprised. His keen eyes took in my arm and hand immediately, noticing the lack of the sling or bandage. He reached for my hand before I could stop him and began his own examination. I snatched it away. "Do you mind?"

"Just wanted to make sure everything was okay."

"How'd you know I'd be here?" Perhaps it was a stupid question, that didn't mean I didn't want him to answer.

"The doctor told me when you'd be getting the bandage and sling removed when we admitted you. You're sure you're all right?"

I nodded, yeah that made sense. "Everything's fine. No infection, no nothing…and the doc told me it's healing very nicely, that I'm a very lucky girl." I said this last, mimicking the doctors patronizing voice.

"You were lucky."

I shook my head. "Perhaps, but somehow I think luck had less to do with things than you and everyone seem to think."

Detective Marcus's eyes narrowed and he seemed to be debating whether to tell me something or not. I took the decision out of his hands. "Okay, what is it that you're not sure you want to tell me." I laughed at his expression. "No, I didn't read you, no I didn't have to. Your face is very expressive today Detective."

Detective Marcus's frown deepened. "Come on, let's go someplace and talk."

By the look in his eyes this wasn't going to be a pleasant talk.

Back at my apartment Detective Marcus was staring moodily into his coffee mug.

"The DNA came back on that hunk of flesh we found at the last crime scene."

"Yeah?"

"It matches Pamela Courtland's."

I nodded. Okay, I could buy that. I'd been buying at lot lately (Probably would buy the Brooklyn Bridge, if you knew someone who would sell it). "So, Pamela…or should I say, evil pod person Pamela, was there that night, actually she was directly involved in the murder." I ran the many scenarios through my head. Pamela had enticed Yarbrow from club 'Thermal' to a deserted place in the woods, with the intent of killing him. She then incapacitated him and somehow carried out the deed. She was a shifter so obviously it would not have been as difficult as some thought. But why, that was still the question on everyone's mind. It was obvious to me that the sorcerer to lure his prey to the designated ritual site was using Pamela. I knew that all of this was directly linked to the demon. It had to be.

"I can see the wheels in your head turning Holly. What are you thinking?"

I shrugged. "I'm thinking that the demon is the source of the evil, but the sorcerer, well the sorcerer is the key."

"What?"

"If we find the sorcerer, then we find the demon and we find Pamela. No one has spotted the demon, so obviously the sorcerer hasn't been able to release it yet. It has to be a powerful one that it requires so much sacrifice, in a way that's good for us because it gives us more time to figure out exactly which demon is being summoned and who is doing the actual summoning." I looked at Detective Marcus with worried eyes. "But the demon will eventually be released, no sorcerer will summon a demon merely to keep it contained within a binding circle, they call them for a reason. We don't have much time left. The demon gains strength with each sacrifice and the sorcerer gains more power. Since he's brought back Pamela and is using her to procure his, uh, food, well it's only going to get more difficult. You saw how easily Pamela tempted that vamp into leaving with her. All she had to do was promise him a little taste and bam wham thank you ma'm he was ready to go. We've got to get the key, which is the sorcerer, if we get him, well everything else will fall into place. He's the ticket to cleaning this all up." I leaned back in my chair and gave Detective Marcus a tired smile. "Of course I'm sure the sorcerer isn't going to put up road signs that read 'this way to my hideout'"

"I really want to nail this sonofabitch. God this guy is going down." Detective Marcus's voice was rough and filled with seething fury. I nodded.

"I couldn't agree with you more Detective. However, there is something you seem to be forgetting, this is no ordinary man. This sorcerer is extremely resourceful and very dangerous. He's powerful and knows the ways of the occult. We're not just up against anyone."

"Fuck, I know that, don't you think I know that by now."

I ignored his outburst; I couldn't blame him one bit. "We'll stop him Detective."

"Yeah, yeah." He turned his tired eyes to me. "He always seems to be one step ahead of us. I'm busting my ass, without, may I add, any help from the rest of the force, and still this sonofabitch is a step ahead."

"Have you spoken to your Captain about needing some more men on the case Detective?"

Detective Marcus laughed mirthlessly. "Hell yeah, but she says we're stretched to the limit and we'll have to make do. Truth is, just between you and me; I don't think she's buying into this demon theory. Hell, she still thinks that I'm like one of those psychic phone line operators."

I read the worry, fatigue and anger on Detective Marcus's face and felt pity flood through me. No wonder he was exhausted. He was doing everything that he could and still it wasn't enough. And he was doing it alone. I opened my mouth to tell him about Yarbrow and Lucien's Hive when I felt a cool wind blow the hairs from the nape of my neck forward. I quickly snapped my head back, afraid of what I would possibly find behind me, there was nothing, we were alone.

I noticed the window was open and I sighed, obviously that accounted for the chill I felt, just an open window, nothing more. However, I felt as if my tongue had suddenly become a piece of lead. I couldn't tell him, I couldn't reveal Lucien to Detective Marcus, not now, not right now. "Tomorrow's Friday Detective, I'm hitting the library for a study session, I'll be in the mystic wing all night, perhaps I'll find something helpful to us there."

"Perhaps..." Detective Marcus murmured.

"Make sure someone is covering the vampire joints tomorrow evening...just in case Pamela comes in cruising for some action."

"Yeah, I've got it covered."

I took Detective Marcus's large callused hand into mine and looked him straight in the eyes. "We're going to stop this thing Detective, I know we are. Like you said, this sonofabitch is going down."

Chapter Twenty-Eight:

I had checked every good reference that I knew of and had come up completely empty handed. There was nothing in any of the books about demons that required vampire sacrifices. I was damn fed up with this entire business. I had looked for any mention of vampire blood and vampire flesh in connection to any known demons and had found absolutely nada, zilch, zero. All I had uncovered was some obscure mention of more than human blood, in connection with some ancient Judeo-Christian demon and a small reference to the Dead Sea Scrolls. It was nearing ten o'clock and I was as clueless as when I had first entered the library, not to mention absolutely starving, seeing as how I had skipped and forgotten about dinner.

I packed up my bags and shoved a few photocopied articles into my folder. I made my way outside and I couldn't help but pause for a moment in the direction of Freidmont Hall, unwanted memories assailed me. It was Portia Whitney's body I had, had the misfortune of discovering on campus, I later learned. Portia Whitney, a pretty and shy sophomore from Ashville, North Carolina. She had been majoring in music, and played the clarinet. Her memorial service had been filled with tears and cries of 'why' and 'she never hurt anyone.' I had lit a candle for her in the campus chapel. Now a startling and horrifying thought came to me. I shuddered. I did not want to go digging up any more graves. But what if, like Pamela, Portia's body wasn't resting six feet under, what if she had been brought back? I wondered if Detective Marcus had thought of this possibility and decided that he probably had too much on his mind to put those two together. I'd ask him about it tomorrow when I got in contact with him. Tonight, well tonight I had a party to attend.

Midnight found me wearing the very dress I had proclaimed I would never wear again (Lucien's choice for me at the vampire Council Meeting). Sitting at the bar I cast my eyes around the crowd searching and probing gently. I declined another drink from yet another 'admirer' and continued my undercover mission. 'Ecstasy' was exactly as I remembered it. The bar was rowdy and filled with a mixture of vampires and humans and the dance floor was occupied by inebriated coffin bait. There was the odd tourist or two, but mostly, mostly these all seemed like locals.

"What's your poison?"

"Huh?" I turned around. Came face to face with a leering vampire with a vicious smile on his face.

"What would you like to drink?"

I gave him a cool look. "Nothing, thank you." I turned away. I stiffened when I felt a hand grip my upper arm. I faced the leering vampire with a warning look on my now cold face. "I suggest you let go of me."

"Too good to have a drink with me."

"Definitely, let go, now." I was considering my options, in the case that he would decide not to let go of my arm when a familiar voice broke the tense silence.

"She's obviously not interested."

I knew that voice. It was Ryan. Ryan Maloney was standing right behind the angry vampire. I knew that I had to be staring but I couldn't help myself, what the hell was Ryan doing at 'Ecstasy'?

"Puny human, think you can take me." The vampire's voice had dropped lower and his eyes were narrowing.

"Would you like to give it a go?" Ryan asked. His voice was equally cold and his stance had turned menacing.

This could all go to hell in one more minute. I turned, and leaned into to the irate vamp and said quietly, for his ears only. "I am Holly-Anne Feather, companion to the Holder of Edwards…would you like to explain to Lucien why you accosted me this evening…I am sure he would be more than interested in the story." I watched, with much satisfaction as his face, already white, paled several times over. His mouth tightened and he forced a small smile.

"I meant no harm."

Ryan stepped forward. "Listen buster…"

I grabbed Ryan's sleeve and shook my head. Was he crazy, or just completely stupid? Oh, I forgot, he was a country boy, who didn't believe in magic, yeah, that explained it. "Don't Ryan, forget about it. He won't bother me again."

Ryan backed down and turned accusing eyes towards me. "What did you say to him?"

"Nothing."

"You said something."

"It doesn't matter, it worked didn't it?"

"I could have dealt with it."

I couldn't believe what I was hearing. I wanted to know if he really believed what he was saying? It didn't matter that he was several inches taller than the departed vampire and probably outweighed him by fifty or sixty pounds, the vampire was a fucking vampire. He would tear Ryan's heart out and eat it for dinner, along with a nice glass of warm blood. I settled for something else. "What the hell are you doing here?" I pinned him with my eyes. "This is the last place I thought I'd run into you at."

"I could say the same for you." Ryan said. I think I heard accusation in his voice.

The fuck with it, "I'm majoring in this shit, what's your excuse Mr. Non-believer?"

Ryan had the grace to blush. "I'm here with a friend."

"Oh?"

Ryan's 'friend' took that very moment to appear by his side. I knew I was gaping but how could I not. I looked over at Ryan who was still blushing. His face was bright as a tomato and he was shifting uncomfortably from one foot to another. I turned my attention back to his 'friend' and held out my hand. "Holly-Anne Feather."

"Brooke Hewitt," she answered.

Brooke? This girls name was Brooke? What sort of name was that? I pushed back my uncharitable thoughts and plastered a false smile onto my face. "Well, are you guys having a good time?"

"Well, it took a little arm twisting but I finally got Ryan to come with me. I told him that he'd have the time of his life." Brooke placed a hand on Ryan's arm and I tried not to flinch. It didn't matter, it didn't faze me, and I didn't care…yeah right. "He's so stubborn when it comes to these things."

Didn't I know it, "Well, it looks as if you two are having a good time." (I wanted to hit that perfect nose of hers and twist that smile right off her face).

"Oh we are," Brooke answered.

I looked at Ryan, he looked positively miserable, in fact, he looked positively ill. I wanted to throw something large and hard in his direction but knew that I couldn't afford to lose my temper. "Somehow I never thought this was quite Ryan's scene." I directed my words towards bubbly Brooke, but my gaze never left Ryan's.

"Well, he said he wanted to try new things, so I told him he'd never try anything as new and cool as coming to a vampire club, and wasn't I right, isn't this cool Ry?"

Ry? Ry? I was going to kill the skinny bitch. I calmed myself, I wasn't going to kill anyone, just then she smiled again, well maybe I'd just maim her a little (did that count?).

"Brooke and I are in computer science together." Ryan finally spoke. His voice was hoarse and I could see that he had to force the words out past his stuck throat.

"Oh…" I said.

"Uh, well, she…"

"Don't bother, I get the picture." I clenched my hands into fists and gave them both another wide smile. "Well please, don't let me keep you, have a great time, both of you." I gave Ryan a crucifying look, "I'm sure you'll see and do a lot of *new* things tonight." I turned my back then, effectively dismissing them both. I had better things to do than deal with this shit (or this shithead).

After several rum and cokes and a couple dozen more tacky pick up lines I was nearing my limit. I hadn't learned anything, except that vampires used come on lines much like humans, everyone seemed to think that wearing black would cement them into the community of the undead, and that Ryan was two-timing on me with some blond, cheerleader, Miss. America, floozy type. It didn't seem to matter that I was also dating the dead guy, or knee deep in a homicide investigation, all I could think of was blond Ryan with blond Brooke, and the little blond babies they'd produce…it was enough to make me want to puke. It was then that something caught my eye. Craning my neck to get a better look I was rewarded with exactly that which I had come to the club to obtain. I fished out my beeper and typed in the number for 'Ecstasy' into the hunk of machinery. I took a couple of moments to type in a brief text message and then I pushed the large black button at the bottom. When the message went through I let out a sigh of relief, perhaps this thing wasn't as useless as I thought it was.

I jumped off my stool and mindless of the large amount of leg I was flashing rushed over to the opposite side of the bar. I dropped my shields and sought out an open path, I was rewarded when I found one. The vamp in front of me was hungry and primed for action. His thoughts were disorganized in his hunger but they were strong and penetrating. I felt my body heat up with the warmth of his thoughts and the feelings they began to invoke in me. I let my eyes drift over to the woman in front of him. Her blond head (which was now conveniently streaked with red) was bent and she was whispering seductively into his ear. Her slender, perfect hands were stroking up and down his bare arms and her nails were lightly raking his skin. I shivered. I took a deep breath and prepared myself to do battle.

"Unless you want to end up minus a few vital organs I'd stay away from this bitch." I let my words pass over the huddled couple. They jumped apart. The vampire was facing me in a blink of an eye, sizing me up. His face held a mixture of shock, and delight. His companion wasn't nearly as delighted to see me as he was.

Pamela Courtland, a.k.a. scary shifter girl was staring at me with undisguised fury written all over her face. She had moved away from her prey only slightly, her hands now at her sides. I watched those hands, keeping an eye out for any abnormal movement. No more holes in my hands, thank you very much.

"Your appearance is most untimely..." Pamela Courtland hissed.

"No kidding?" I shot her an innocent look.

"I do not suppose you would leave and come back later...once I was through?" She asked. Her eyes were still wickedly cold, but her mouth had moved into an evil grin.

I shook my head. "Not on your life..." I laughed. "I forgot, too late for that..."

Pamela's eye twitched. I was definitely getting to her, goody for me. "Somehow I didn't think you would be a good little girl..." She said tightly.

Good? Me? Nah. "Back off Blondie...and leave the nice little vamp alone..." I was desperately searching my head for a course of action, something I really should have had before I stormed the fort, so to speak. I couldn't very well take her on right here, could I? I looked around quickly, was there enough maneuvering room? Would we hurt anyone in the process...damn right we would. I couldn't take the chance.

"You are becoming quite the problem..." Pamela said, coming a little closer.

"Yeah, you're already a problem."

"There is no need for this, I can pleasure you both." The vampire's voice interrupted us. The vampire was grinning widely. His razor sharp fangs were glinting in the light and his pale skin looked like alabaster. I rolled my eyes. God, it was the vampire equivalent to Vanessa.

"Listen, shut up. If you know what's good for you, you'll like, take off, right now and let me deal with this." I watched as the vamp eyed me now in anger…yeah I knew all about the short fuses of vamps and their egos. I wasn't about to stroke this one's.

"We were just going to complete some business…*pleasure.*" Pamela's voice purred. She once again placed a perfect hand on the vampire's arm, stroking his skin with her slender fingers. "You would be well advised to leave us to our…fun."

"Yeah, well I never did take advice well." I wrapped myself up, mentally, again, imagining those secured, impenetrable iron walls. I'd need some armor for what I was about to do. I thrust out one strong, single mental probe in Pamela's direction and was relieved and satisfied when it hit its mark. Pamela visibly shook. Her eyes grew bright and feral and suddenly began to turn. I swallowed when I saw those strange yellow irises and that unholy gleam. She released the vampire's arm, shivering. Her nostrils twitched and her mouth curled up into what resembled a snarl. Her hands, which were now at her sides, began to shake and I knew she was trying to restrain the beast. "Having a little trouble there?" I asked innocently, knowing full well what was wrong with her. I had just thrown, the equivalent of a mental arrow at her, it was painful, abrupt and obviously an attack. It wasn't as if the bitch didn't deserve it.

"You are playing a tricky game, pretty…" She was staring at me with an odd expression on her face.

"This is no game," I said.

Her eyes widened and were now completely yellow. The skin on her face was stretched taut and her hands were quaking with the obvious need to shift. "You are right…I play no game." She snarled. "You'd best remember that pretty…that and other things…" She tossed a penetrating and pointed look at my hand, which was now almost healed. I felt an almost palpable burning sensation shoot through my arm. I ignored it. It was all in the mind, she was trying to control me through my mind. I wouldn't let her. My hand was fine. It was healed. There was no pain. It was merely an illusion. I took a deep breath and tried to calm myself.

"Try again bitch," I muttered at her. Her eyes widened in obvious shock, she apparently hadn't expected me to deflect her.

"You are determined to spoil my fun tonight pretty…" she snarled.

"Yeah, it seems that I am." I groaned when out of the corner of my eye I saw Ryan's head above the crowd. He was craning his neck to try to get a better look at me. This was the first time in at least an hour that he had tried to get my attention, what had happened to the blond bimbo? I gasped when a long clawed hand just barely missed my face. I jumped back but found myself pressed against a throng of sweaty bodies. Damn, damn and double damn. The vamp that had been the object of Pamela's attentions was now standing to the side, surprise had settled on his face and then anger.

I threw another mental push Pamela's direction. This one was stronger and more forceful. It was the safest thing I could think of right now to do. It would distract her and wouldn't cause any one else any discomfort or pain. Pamela reared back, she shook her head to clear it, yeah, and obviously I hadn't lost my touch. When she turned back to me though her eyes were burning bright and her claws were unsheathed. They were large and sharp and just as deadly looking as I remembered. I looked around wildly. There were too many people…I had to get this beastie girl outside, and I had to do it quickly.

Just when I was figuring out the quickest way to the exit the almost forgotten vampire jumped Pamela. I watched in shock and horror as the two fell to the floor in a tangle of limbs. Oh boy. The vampire had one strong arm around Pamela's slender neck, but Pamela, beastie that she was, was slashing his arm with her claws. I could see angry, gaping wounds on the vamps dead flesh and blood beginning to flow steadily. The vamp tightened his grip and Pamela slashed out wildly, catching him in the face. He released her with a howl of pain and I saw that she had gotten him in the eye. Pamela sank her teeth into the vampire's flesh and he grabbed her by her hair in a desperate attempt to get her off of him.

People were screaming and fleeing. I hauled myself onto a bar stool and from there jumped onto the bar to get away from the jostling masses. I had eyes only for the fighting creatures on the ground. I heard someone calling my name, screaming my name above the noise of the crowd. I looked up quickly to see Ryan and 'friend' trying to push their way towards me to no avail. It was better this way. No point in having humans to deal with as well as monsters.

Pamela and the vampire were both weakening. Both had lost blood. Pamela was bleeding from nasty gashes on her back and her neck, the vampire from his arms and chest. Both were still locked in a deadly embrace and bleeding dry. I picked up several glasses both full and empty from the bar and began to throw them at Pamela, the good old-fashioned way, with my hands. She looked up for a split second and that was all the time the vamp needed, he brought one taloned hand across her neck and effectively slit her throat. I watched in horror as blood spurted out in great gushes from her neck. The vamp had staggered to his feet and fallen back weakly against the bar. Pamela was wide-eyed and bleeding. She reached out a hand, it seemed towards me (whatever for, I have no idea) just before she slipped in her own blood and fell on a heap to the ground.

"Police! Freeze! Don't anyone move."

I looked across the room to see that the Edwards Police Force had finally decided to grace us with their presence. I sighed in relief. When I looked back down from my perch I was shocked to see that only the vampire was still leaning against the bar, Pamela had disappeared. It wasn't possible, how could she have moved in her condition? How did she escape? She couldn't have. I saw Detective Marcus, granite face and all striding purposefully towards me. He reached my side in record speed, considering the masses of people and helped me down from the bar. He took me in.

"You all right?" he asked.

It seemed as if he was always asking me that. I nodded. "Detective Pamela Courtland was just here one moment ago. She was injured really badly and bleeding profusely, she can't have gone far."

He nodded and shouted some orders out to some of his men. His hard eyes took in the entire scene within moments. They came back to rest on me. "What the hell are you doing here?"

"Yeah it's good to see you too Detective," I said with a small smile.

"I'm not in the fucking mood. What the hell are you doing here?"

"Detective work."

"You're not a fucking detective!"

"I'm working with you aren't I?" I retorted.

His face was turning a nice shade of red. "Come on, we're getting out of here."

I wasn't about to argue with that. Best idea I had heard in a while. "You lead the way."

I was in heaven, or at least as close as I was going to get to heaven at three o'clock in the morning. Both Detective Marcus and I were at Waffle House and I was devouring another plate of eggs, hashed browns and bacon while taking great gulps of sweet tea. God I was starving.

"So you were going to tell me what you were doing at 'Ecstasy' tonight."

"I was?" I looked up from my eggs and gave Detective Marcus a feigned look of innocence. He frowned, obviously not fooled by my display.

"You were." The way he said it brooked no argument.

I sighed. "I told you...I was doing a little detective work Detective."

"And I told you Holly, you're not a detective."

"Hey, you're the one that pulled me into this entire investigation. Are you blaming me now because I'm involved?" I shoveled another pile of eggs and potatoes into my mouth and watched him with intent eyes.

"You're supposed to be doing research...not field work."

"Listen..." I said in exasperation. "If some of your men would do their damn jobs perhaps I wouldn't have to do any field work." I watched as Detective Marcus's eyes narrowed...oops; perhaps I had gone to far. Well damn it, I was right, the Edwards Police Force was about as helpful as a tapeworm was to a cat, or a flea to a dog.

"You leave my men out of this Holly."

"No, I bloody well won't. I thought your men were supposed to be staking out the vampire joints tonight. Why weren't you alerted to Pamela's presence at 'Ecstasy' sooner? It was my message that got you there, wasn't it?" I watched the indecision cross over his face. Obviously he was a loyal man. He didn't want to admit the faults of the department. But it was time that he recognized them, because they were hindering this investigation, and that was very much apparent.

"Yeah I got your message."

"It was my message that made you come a running...wasn't it?"

Detective Marcus nodded. "I had some men patrolling 'Ecstasy', they reported that they saw no sign of Pamela Courtland."

"She streaked her hair, but basically it was our girl, I recognized her from across the bar." I sighed. "She was attempting to pick up another vampire, and there is no doubt in my mind that she intended for him to end up like the rest."

"Well, thanks to you she didn't succeed." Detective Marcus gave me a small smile. I detected admiration in his voice, and knew that he respected me, no matter what the circumstances were.

"Yeah, but she'll try again. And she's majorly pissed off now. I ruined her plans, and inadvertently ruined the plans of the guy who's pulling all the strings...so it's retribution time."

"You think she'll come back to pay you a visit."

I nodded. "I'd like to think not, but somehow, somehow I know she'll come a calling."

"I'll have someone watch the house."

I opened my mouth to argue but saw that by his look he wasn't going to change his mind. "Fine, thanks." I grumbled. I didn't like the feeling that my freedom was becoming more and more curtailed. "Detective."

"Yeah."

"I had another thought."

"Yeah?"

"The body I found on campus...the one belonging to Portia Whitney..." I let my voice trail off and saw by the look on Detective Marcus's face that he understood what I was thinking.

"You think her body's gone."

I shrugged. "It's a possibility. I mean, who knows, but I'm thinking it's a real good possibility."

"I think we're due to visit the cemetery again." Detective Marcus said grimly.

You know what I think? I think I'm due for a nice long vacation. Instead, I nodded somberly. "The cemetery it is."

Portia Whitney's body was gone. Her casket lay open and gaping, gently mocking us with its emptiness. It wasn't as if I hadn't been expecting this, but I still felt an icy cold chill take hold of my body. Since Portia's body was gone it could safely be assumed that she had ended up like Pamela Courtland. I tried not to think of how Portia had been alive, that sweet, round, smiling face, dimples and all staring back at me from the newspaper. It was over, that girl no longer existed. What's worse was that she couldn't even rest in death. She had been stolen and 'turned' and now, whatever had once been Portia was only a walking shell of evil.

I looked over at Detective Marcus. His face was blank as he stood staring into the gaping hole in the ground where the coffin had been. Only the whitening of his knuckles indicated to me how furious he was. The shovel he had used to dig the casket out of the ground was lying beside him and mounds of dirt surrounded us. He had dug like a man possessed and perhaps he was...possessed that is.

"She'll be cruising, Detective," I murmured. I didn't want to interrupt his thoughts but this had to be voiced.

"Yeah, I know."

"Two of them…" I muttered. God. I looked down at my raw hand. It was scabbing over. The long claw marks on my arm were red and irritable, but like my hand they were scabbing over nicely. I was healing, but at this moment I could vividly remember every detail of the attack that had taken place in my house. Those bestial yellow eyes, dark gold in the pupil with lightness around. A wide, ferocious mouth which, when opened had revealed wickedly sharp teeth. I could still feel the sharp, cutting pain as she had pinned me to the table, and see the blood as it had leaked out of me, slowly at first, then quicker the longer I was held down. Her words had been taunting, yet her voice oddly smooth and strangely soothing (as if she were trying to calm me) my stomach still twisted painfully at the memory.

"Hey, you still with me?"

My head jerked up. Detective Marcus was looking at me with those deep, thoughtful, eyes of his. I nodded. "I'm fine."

"You sure?"

I swallowed. I would have to be. "Yeah, I'm sure."

"So they'll probably be working as a pair."

I shook my head. "Not necessarily. They might accumulate their prey faster and more efficiently working alone…"

"Then why bring both of them back."

I face was grim. "Strength in numbers? I don't know. But it seems likely that this way you can catch twice the quarry." I sighed. "I don't think we can be too careful. You'll have to keep an eye out for them working together, and working alone." I paused before continuing. "Also…I really pissed her off tonight Detective. I ruined her kill. She was all prepared to lead him out and I came along and interrupted her. She's going to be mad and perhaps desperate, maybe she'll fuck up."

"Fuck up is good…" he muttered.

I nodded. "Yeah, it is. However, I'm more worried that she'll strike randomly, out of anger. I don't know if her next victim will be pre-chosen or if she'll even take the time to think things through…"

"Fuck, she's going to kill tonight. It doesn't matter that it's close to Dawn." Detective Marcus said. He struck his fist angrily against his thigh and then ran a hand haphazardly through his mussed hair.

"Yeah, I think so. I don't believe either she, or the sorcerer, are going to be satisfied with waiting. They'll take someone quickly and without much thought." I looked down, suddenly feeling an overwhelming sense of guilt flood through me. "I didn't think Detective. I just saw her picking out her prey and I couldn't let her do it. I interfered, but I didn't think about the consequences...damn I didn't think about the consequences."

Detective Marcus let out a sigh and shook his head. "Don't let it eat you up kid. You acted with your gut, and sometimes that's the only thing you can rely on."

"But if she kills tonight..."

"Then it's not your fault."

I heard the words but my stomach still felt tight and queasy. "Damn."

"You could have let her have the vampire though, it would have saved us the trouble...and the manpower" Detective Marcus suddenly muttered under his breath.

My ears perked and I turned startled and surprised eyes in his direction. "What did you say?"

Detective Marcus shrugged. "You did what you thought was right kid. However, they're not really worth saving..."

I couldn't believe what I was hearing...or perhaps I could. Hadn't Detective Marcus once mentioned how he and his team had 'cleaned up' Chicago? Obviously he didn't mean janitorial duty. "You really mean that?"

"About the dead?"

"Yeah, about the dead."

His eyes were flint cold and there was no hesitation. "Hell yeah. They're evil."

"Just like that Detective? Black and white?"

"It's pretty cut and dry kid. You haven't seen what they can do, I have."

I wisely kept my mouth shut.

"They're monsters Holly. They use us for food and when they're done they dispose of us. We have to protect our own."

"And what about us Detective?" I said quietly. "What about us?"

"Whadya mean?"

I gave him an unflinching look. "If it's just black and white where do you see people like us? The telepaths and empaths, psychics and PSI talented, we're mortal but more than human, or some say, how do you see us fitting into this little equation of yours?"

"We're human."

I heard the hard edge of anger in his voice. I knew that Detective Marcus had come up against this very point many times in his life, much as I had. I could hear the truth of it in his words. "You think so..."

"I know so." He gave me an inscrutable look. "We're human Holly. We may have been born with a little something extra, but we're still human…" His eyes grew cold and icy "They're not. There is nothing human about vampires Holly. There is nothing left. Dead flesh means nothing." He continued to eye me. "And you had better just remember that…if you don't you're likely to end up one of their meals."

I said nothing, really, what was there to say? He had made up his mind and obviously nothing I said right now was going to change anything for him. And truthfully, did I know any different? Just because I got hot and light headed over one of the dead didn't mean that I didn't hear and mull over the possibility of the Detective's words. It wasn't so long ago that I had thought much the same way as Detective Marcus. Perhaps not as cut and dry…hell, whom was I trying to kid; I had been as bad if not worse in my thoughts than Detective Marcus was in his. It was sheer stupidity on my part that Lucien made me want to forget all my prejudices against vampires. Sheer stupidity, and hey, we can't forget suicidal.

"Dating one of the dead, are you girl?"

"What?" My eyes opened in shock and my mouth dropped. How did he know, had he been toying with me?

Detective Marcus laughed. "Just wanted to see if you were still with me. You seemed a million miles away." He took in my worried expression and grinned wider. "Hey, don't worry, I know you're not a dead dater. God, an Empath and a vamp, you'd have a nervous breakdown even if you were able to get over the fact that he was dead."

I gave him a weak smile. My stomach was churning. (Maybe I had ulcers, yeah, that had to be it, ulcers). I knew, I knew this would be the time to tell him about Lucien, the Hive, the missing vampires and how everything was connected, but I just couldn't do it. I opened my mouth several times ready to spill everything, and each time I tried I felt my tongue stick to the roof of my mouth and my throat clog up as if I were going to choke. He was right. I was dating a dead guy. How had I forgotten that? How had I forgotten that Lucien was nothing but reanimated flesh? Just because he wasn't rotting didn't mean he wasn't any less dead.

I shivered. Each one of those cold kisses was imprinted on my memory. The feel of his hands on my skin and the press of those cold, dead lips to mine. How he managed to bring out and illicit heat from me was a mystery I still hadn't solved. God, oh god, I was letting a dead guy touch me, kiss me, caress me. I had let him into my life, shared my secrets with him, and helped him. But worse was the fact that I had let him into my heart…just a little bit, but a little bit was all it takes to destroy you. "The dead are being targeted." I murmured. I could give him that much, if nothing else.

"Huh?" Detective Marcus turned to me.

"True, there have been two human murders, but the girls, they've been brought back. The vampires, well the vampires—they're not coming back." I saw Detective Marcus scratch his head thoughtfully, I continued. "It's led me to the conclusion that the human girls are not what the sorcerer is after. They're instrumental in the plan, but they're not the intended targets…" I let my words sink in.

"The girls are the bait," Detective Marcus said firmly.

I nodded. "They're luring in the prey." I thought back on the first vampire victim. He had not been interested in women; in addition he had already had a companion (of sorts). Perhaps the sorcerer had realized how much easier it would be to target vampires with young, nubile women. In any case, I was certain that the vampires were the intended prey. The college girls, well, they were just bonuses.

"I shouldn't even fucking bother…" Detective Marcus said, running a hand over his weary eyes.

I narrowed my eyes. "Victims are victims Detective."

He laughed. "That's a laugh riot. Have you ever heard of a vampire victim before kid? Do they seem like victims to you?"

I quelled my rising temper. "To serve and protect…isn't that your motto?"

"I know my damn job," Detective Marcus ground out. "I'm not here to play babysitter to a bunch of hungry blood suckers." He towered over me. "Why do you give a shit what happens to them anyway?"

I didn't hesitate. "Nothing is black and white Detective, there is always gray. Something out there is slaughtering vamps and humans…both need our help and protection. We co-exist Detective, dead or not, it's a being."

"Death doesn't need protection."

I sighed. I wasn't getting through, I probably never would (hell did I even want to?). "I'm done arguing with you Detective, the longer we sit and debate what constitutes life someone or something is losing it." My eyes were stone cold. "I don't know about you but I'm going to do my damn best to see that that doesn't happen…"

Detective Marcus grinned slightly. "Fucking stubborn kid."

I snorted. "Don't I know it." I squinted, just above his head, not far off in the horizon I could see the sun rising. It was a damn pretty dawn.

Chapter Twenty-Nine:

Three hours of sleep, that's all I had gotten when the phone woke me the fuck up. I tucked my pillow firmly over my head. I was not answering the damned thing. It kept ringing. Realizing the futility of the situation I picked up the receiver.

"Hullo?" I muttered.

"Holly?"

Now I was wide-awake. Ryan, it was *Ry* calling. "Oh, *Ry*, is that you?" I could almost see him flinching on the other end.

"Holly…I…"

"Yes?"

"I just wanted to explain about last night."

"What is there to explain?"

"Well, about Brooke."

"Oh, yes…Brooke." (The ditsy bimbo, I was going to have to hurt her, right after I got done with Ry).

"Hell…listen, I just want to talk to you…"

"Isn't that what we're doing?" I said coldly. There was silence. I waited. There was no way in hell I was making this easy on him.

"Can I come over?"

I looked down at myself. Ratty t-shirt, old pair of boxers, tangled hair and smudged eyes. "Yeah, fine."

"Okay, uh, give me fifteen minutes."

"Uh huh, sure." I hung up. (Jerk!)

Ryan was prompt. Fifteen minutes later my doorbell rang and I trotted over to answer it.

Ryan was crisp, neat and looked fresh as a daisy in a white oxford shirt, dark blue jeans and sneakers (I hated him. No one was allowed to look so good at this godforsaken hour). His face was void of the shadows and bags that marred mine. I could see concern etched in his eyes when he took in my appearance. I chose to ignore it. He could save his concern for his blond bimbette.

I handed him a cup of coffee without asking him and sat down on the sofa with my legs crossed neatly underneath me. He sat opposite me in a chair.

"Thanks for letting me come over."

"Sure, whatever." My hands felt like blocks of ice. I rubbed them together, along with my icy arms.

"Are you cold?" Ryan's voice was thick with worry.

"Do you care?"

He looked hurt. "Of course I care Holly."

"Yeah, right." I couldn't block the hurt that permeated from my voice. I didn't want him to see how much he had hurt me, but it didn't seem like I could help myself. Fuck it, he had hurt me.

"Holly…I care, I think too much," he muttered.

I rolled my eyes. "You care so much about me that you show up at a vampire establishment with another girl." I narrowed my eyes, pinning him to the chair with my violet orbs. "You're full of shit Ryan." I didn't care how wounded I sounded.

"It's not like that Holly, if you'd just let me explain…" Ryan's eyes were bright with emotion and his hands were clasped together. His large, burly frame looked awkward and out of place in my small chair.

I threw up my hands and snorted. "Sure, go ahead…explain."

He looked at me suspiciously. "Are you going to let me talk…or are you going to interrupt me?"

I couldn't stop the telltale blush that crept up my cheeks. Damn him. "Go ahead talk." (He was still a lying piece of shit).

Ryan let out a large sigh and took a gulp of coffee. He swallowed and gagged and began to cough. I bit my lip to hide a smile. "Uh, yeah…good coffee…" he said and took another sip, his eyes watered and he forced down every drop. "Brooke and I, well we have computer science together…" He nodded. "Well, uh, she's been flirting with me since the beginning of the year and, well, I just sort of took it all in stride. I mean, hey, there's no need to be rude."

I rolled my eyes. "Dickhead," I said under my breath. I caught him staring at me and shut my mouth.

"But I wasn't interested...I'm not interested," he corrected himself. "Basically since the first day of class I haven't been able to stop thinking about this girl...I see her all the time, in my dreams, when I'm sleeping and when I'm awake...she makes it nearly impossible for me to get anything done..." He looked at me earnestly...I wanted to throttle him, like I gave a shit about Brooke. His next words almost had me falling off of the couch. "It's you. I saw you that first day and I couldn't stop thinking about you. Every day I would see you and every day I would want to say hello...and totally make an ass out of myself. I dream about you..." His eyes were wide and searching and I was too shocked to move.

"Huh?" I swallowed. "Me?"

"Yeah, you." He said this with a smile. After a moment his smile drooped and he continued, grimly. "You're like totally fucking perfect. You sit there, not noticing anything or anybody but your work. You're so damn beautiful you take my fucking breath away. You're smarter than all hell and modest and unassuming, basically you're the ideal." He sighed. "How does somebody like me even think to approach someone like you?"

"But you did..." I murmured.

He nodded. "Yeah, I just couldn't stand it anymore. I saw you sitting there, day after day after day...and each day I told myself I was a complete pussy for not approaching you, not asking you out. One day I just had enough. I told myself there was nothing to lose and I came up to you."

I smiled, remembering that afternoon. "I was glad you did." He went on as if he hadn't heard me.

"I thought I had died and gone to fucking heaven when you smiled at me." He looked down at his hands. "That first date...well, it was wonderful. I had a great time...you were everything I had expected and more. But, well, when you told me you were majoring in Modern Mysticism and Magic...I sort of paused. I guess I kind of freaked out a little when I realized how different we were."

I nodded, urging him to continue. It wasn't as if he wasn't expressing anything I hadn't been feeling myself. "Yeah..."

"But, well, everything else was so great that I thought...hell, it'll sure make for some interesting conversations." He smiled slightly, revealing those perfect white teeth. "When you invited me over for dinner I thought someone up there had to love me...I thought everything was going really well, but then, well then you got sort of distant on me and I didn't know what had gone wrong." He looked up at me as if searching my face for the answer. "I, uh, felt as if I had gotten run over by a freight train when we kissed, but you, you totally shut down on me. After that date we didn't really talk and didn't really see one another except for class. And then you got attacked and well, I was scared shitless. I was so goddamned worried I skipped my computer science exam to come to the hospital and see how you were doing. They wouldn't tell me a damn thing…I waited in that room for at least three hours until someone gave me an update. I had hoped that perhaps we could spend some more time together, but even after the attack you seemed so damn preoccupied it was almost as if you were on another planet. I kind of deduced you just weren't interested." He began to reach out a hand to me when he caught himself and pulled back. "Lately…well Brooke, she's been on me about taking her out. I kind of thought about how preoccupied you've been and well, she's pretty and she was available…so I said yes. When she suggested this vampire club I totally balked. But it was you that talked me into it."

Now I knew he was nuts. "What?"

"I kept remembering how you defended your major and, well your beliefs…and…" His voice trailed off and he had a sheepish look on his face. "That's bullshit. The truth is I had hoped by going to 'Ecstasy' I could get a feel for what it is that you're studying, what makes you tick. I realized that we had a lot of different beliefs and well I wanted to see if perhaps we could find a way to meet in the middle. It really had nothing to do with Brooke…it had everything to do with you Holly." He seemed to run out of steam then. He sat still, staring at me, as if willing me to speak.

I swallowed. I wanted to tell him that I understood, that I was frightened too. That we could work out any differences that we had. I wanted to tell him all this and more…but I couldn't. The cold hard truth was that I didn't know if we could work out our differences. I wasn't sure what I believed in anymore, and what was worse, I didn't know whom I believed in.

"Hol, please say something."

I shook my head helplessly. "I don't know what you want me to say Ryan…" I bit my lip. God, wasn't anything about my life ever going to be easy again? Just then my pager beeped and I said a little prayer of thanks for the interruption. I read the number; it belonged to Detective Marcus. I looked over at Ryan's tense, taut face and sighed. It could wait, Detective Marcus would have to wait, he had waited before.

"And then there's this…" Ryan murmured. His eyes held the cold glint of anger in them.

"What are you talking about?"

"All this crap…you're hiding something from me Holly. Something big."

I rolled my eyes. "I don't know what you're talking about Ryan." (It wasn't any of his business.)

"First that Detective shows up at your apartment. I didn't know Detectives made house calls."

"You're being an ass Ryan." But he ignored me and continued.

"Then I find out he's been visiting you at the hospital. And well, there's this…" He pointed to the beeper. "Want to tell me who the page is from?"

"None of your fucking business!"

"It's him isn't it?"

I was shocked. Ryan was jealous. The frat boy was jealous of the Detective. If it weren't so ridiculous it would be funny. Here I was semi-dating the Vampire Holder of Edwards North Carolina and Ryan was jealous of the fact that the cop was spending so much time with me. And how would he react if he knew how we were spending that time, rolling around in graves, digging up bodies, bagging chunks of flesh and discovering sulfur based ritual circles. I rubbed my weary eyes. I had always wanted an exciting love life…now, well now I take it all back. Now I wanted nothing better than to join a damn convent and live out my life celibate and cloistered. There at least I would have some damn peace and quiet. Not to mention I wouldn't have vamp leaders criticizing my fashion sense. "Ryan you don't know what you're talking about." I was growing real tired of this real fast. (God, men were nitwits)

"Oh I think I do." His eyes were bright with anger. His hands were clenched tightly into fists and he looked like a tightly coiled spring ready to be released. "How was I to know you'd even care if I dated Brooke…you're spending all your damned time with this Detective…God, he's old enough to be your fucking father." He sneered.

Okay, enough was fucking enough! I stood up quickly, hands planted firmly on my hips, eyes blazing and temper boiling. "You're being a total asshole." I had never seen this side of Ryan (what had happened to the sweet county boy?) "You're the one who wanted to come over to talk. Now you're sitting here in my apartment accusing me of things that I haven't done. You aren't listening to me and you're being a judgmental shit!" I saw Ryan's eyes open wide with surprise. His mouth dropped open. Obviously he hadn't seen this side of me either. Yeah, it was apparent we both had a lot to learn about one another.

"I'm sorry," he muttered.

"What? I don't think I heard you."

"I'm sorry." He said it a little louder but it was still grumbled out.

I nodded. "Fine, you should be. Listen, it's obvious we're not getting anything accomplished. I think you've made it pretty obvious that you want to see other people. Well, fine. We'll see other people, it wasn't as if we were exclusive anyway…did it have to be a frigging cheerleader?" I said this last under my breath.

"What?"

I blushed. "Nothing. Listen. It's over, okay? Happy?" The moment I said the words I felt a hollow ache inside me. I don't know why. Ryan was right. I hadn't spent nearly enough time with him. We had barely two dates, and the time in class didn't really count. I had been engaged in some pretty secretive shit lately. All of this was true. And it was true that I should let him go. Let him go and date blond bimbo Brooke, Ms. Cheerleader Fucking America. I should let him find someone who could give him the time and attention he deserved. But somehow, for some reason I didn't want to let him go. I didn't want to sever the bond, however tenuous it might be.

"No."

"Huh?"

Ryan shook his head firmly. He stood up and took my cold hands in his warm ones and looked straight into my startled eyes. "I said no." He made a baffled sound. As if he himself didn't quite understand what he was saying, "It's not over. It hardly even begun Holly, how can it be fucking over? No, I refuse to think that we aren't going to give this a shot. So I made a mistake. I know I did. I didn't even want to be with her…all I could think of when I was with her, was you…and she knew it. When I saw that vampire touching you I wanted to break every dead bone in his body. I knew then, just as I know now that there is something here." He brushed his lips gently over my forehead. "Are you going to give up?"

"Ryan…"

"Just tell me one thing." He stared at me intently. "Do you want to be with me?"

I nodded but felt my heart twist painfully with the admission. (I want my cake and I want to eat it too) "Yeah, I do, but it's complicated …there is so much you don't know Ryan."

"We'll work it out." He smiled. Suddenly he looked so much younger.

"We're intelligent human beings Holly. There is no reason if we want to be with one another that we can't figure out a way to see one another more often."

"Maybe we shouldn't, Ryan."

Ryan frowned. "I'm going to pretend you didn't say that."

"Ryan…"

"Quiet Holly. You've already told me that you want to be with me…"

Uh yeah, but I also wanted to be with the dead dude.

"So, we'll date some more, we'll keep one another company…and we'll take it one day at a time."

He made it sound so damn simple. "There is a question of magic Ryan."

Ryan frowned. "What about it?"

"You don't believe."

"Holly." His face was shut down tight. "I don't know what the fuck to believe in anymore." He released my hands and took a step away from me. "Last night I saw things I never thought existed, not really. Oh, perhaps somewhere I knew, but if I didn't see them I didn't really have to believe. But last night, well, last night…hell, you saw it, them."

"Them?"

"The dead."

"Yeah…well it is a vampire club Ryan."

"I know." Ryan swallowed. "But I saw that thing attack you Holly, and it didn't look like one of them, it looked like something totally different."

I knew what he was talking about, god I didn't want to open this can of worms right now, didn't I have enough to digest? "You mean the shifter."

"Is that what it was?"

"The woman with claws and fangs…that was more beast than human?"

Ryan laughed nervously. "Yeah, that would be what I'm talking about."

I took Ryan's hand and led him back to the couch. Now I seated him besides me and stared into those deep blue eyes of his. It was time that Ryan joined the real world. "Ryan, some cold hard facts…"

"Yeah?"

"They walk among us."

"Huh?"

"All the creepy crawlies that your mother always threatened you with as a child if you were bad, and didn't eat all your vegetables…they're not figments of somebody's overactive imagination, they exist, and they're out there." My eyes didn't waver from his as I spoke. "The dead live, the demons, ghouls, goblins, ghosts…witches, sorcerers, trolls, fae, even fucking mermaids…yeah, they all live, and cohabitate this world with us. This isn't fucking 'Alice in Wonderland.' It isn't a novel. Why do you think they offer 'Other World' courses at College? Why do you think I take them? It's to be better informed about the world that we're living in, the world that we all live in. I don't want to be unprepared one day and get my head bitten off by some overanxious vamp, or end up a third course to some ugly ghoul. Face facts, this is reality, what you've been living in is fantasy." I stopped. I had run out of words to say. If he didn't get it by now, well he wasn't going to get it, and it was hopeless.

When Ryan finally spoke, it was in a voice so low and quiet I had to strain to hear him. "My youngest sister, Rebecca, was murdered by a ghoul."

My mouth dropped open in shock. "What?" I was trying to process this new information. "I thought you said you had two siblings."

"I do, I used to have three." Ryan's eyes were cold and lifeless and suddenly things were becoming clearer (oh shit). "Rebecca was only five. We had all gone camping. My mother had been afraid that it was too early to take Becca camping but my father insisted... he wanted the entire family to be together. He reminded my mom that he had taken all of us kids camping, and we had all been younger than Becca. Mom finally relented. It was great. We set up tents, grilled and fished and, well, I'd never seen Becca so happy." Ryan's voice cracked and I felt my mental armor cracking too. I took a deep breath to strengthen myself. I couldn't lose it now. He needed to let this out. "It happened the fourth night out. We were singing songs around the campfire and my mother felt a chill. None of us felt it, but she did. She went to get a blanket, and while she was searching the tent it attacked us." Ryan's face had blanched and he was unconsciously gripping my hand so tightly that I winced with pain. I didn't say anything. I could deal with it. "I've never seen anything like it Holly. It was nearly transparent…I could see through its middle, but things were hanging off of it, like flesh. How does flesh hang off something that's transparent?? God, I never figured it out. Its eyes were sunken in and it had blood coming from its mouth and hands. My father tried to protect us but it swatted him away as if he were a bug. It…it…oh God, Holly, I've never seen anything like it…"

But I had. My body was a block of ice. I had ice water flowing through my veins and I couldn't breathe or speak less I lose control. As it was it was taking an extraordinary amount of power and control to keep myself from being invaded by Ryan's pain, hurt, fear and anxiety. I could feel the pulsations coming off of his body and they were already bombarding my fragile senses.

"My father had left the gun in the tent…I was crawling to get it, my father was unconscious and my sister and brother were screaming. My mom had come out from the tent then and was trying to get to my little sister Rebecca but the ghoul was between her and Becca. Becca…" His voice broke. "She was screaming and crying for my mom, for me and pop. We couldn't get to her…that thing, that thing…he…he…took her and he…God, the blood…there was…" Ryan broke down and began to convulse.

I was taking deep breaths, trying to get air into my starving lungs. The more I concentrated on keeping my armor in place the more lightheaded I was becoming. Ryan's pain was so acute, so sharp that it was nearly impossible to keep his emotions from overtaking me. I was beginning to slip into his skin and I couldn't let that happen. He needed me. I took a steadying breath and placed my arms around his shaking shoulders. I knew what he had seen. I knew what had happened. It was all so much clearer for me now. "Shhhh, I understand…I know…"

His eyes were red and filled with accusation. "How the hell do you know? How can you?"

I stared him straight in the eyes. My gaze didn't waver and my voice was strong. "I know." I nodded. "I do."

He held my gaze, and whatever he saw in my eyes reassured him. "You do know don't you?"

I nodded. "Yeah, I do. I'm not going into it right now, you don't need that, but believe me when I tell you I understand."

Ryan slumped down into the couch, as if his muscles wouldn't hold him up anymore. "After we lost Becca mom went nuts." He gave a mirthless laugh. "No, really, she went nuts. She was institutionalized for a while. We all had to go to therapy." Ryan snorted. "What the hell do they know? They couldn't tell us anything we didn't already know for ourselves, that we hadn't already seen. My father withdrew, my other sister wouldn't speak for over a year and my brother…he was like a zombie…and I, well I just snapped." Ryan looked at me. "I stopped believing in everything. It was easier that way. My mind couldn't make sense of what had happened…so well I made up a way for it to make sense…it hadn't happened. I tricked myself into believing that Becca had died in a camping accident, that the preternatural had nothing to do with it. And, well, since no one in the family spoke of what had happened, spoke of Becca, we were all able to pretend that nothing had occurred." He laughed; it was hoarse and filled with pain. "Can you fucking believe it? I fucking tricked myself into believing that nothing had happened. That it had been an accident. That nothing so awful, unexplainable and horrible had come out of the forest and eaten my baby sister. God, and all these years I have lived with my delusions."

I shook my head. "It's natural. What you did was natural. You couldn't explain what had happened, how could you? You were a kid yourself. You didn't know what was going on and you had never seen anything so terrible in your life. Your mind made up a way to heal you. It devised a mechanism for coping, and you did." I stroked his sweating forehead and pressed my head against his shoulder. "You have done more than merely cope, you've survived, lived and you've grown. You're an amazing person Ryan Maloney. Don't ever berate yourself, if you do I'll…I'll have to hit you." I breathed a sigh of relief when I saw a small smile crack his lips. "And perhaps now…perhaps now you'll be able to grow and learn even more…now that you've uncovered some things." I sighed. "Believe me, there are all things in our pasts that we would rather just forget, unfortunately, sometimes, those memories are important keys to learning about who and what we are." I smoothed back a lock of his hair. "And you, you I want to learn more about, Ryan Maloney."

Ryan's head snapped up. "Really?"

I wanted to cry, his face was so surprised so without guile. I settled for a small smile. "Yeah really. Like I said you're an amazing person."

He looked at me somberly. "You don't think I'm a failure?"

Huh? What the hell was he talking about? "What?"

"Because I couldn't protect her…because I couldn't save her." He looked down.

I choked back a cry of outrage. I tucked my finger under his chin and raised his head to look at me. "You are not a failure, don't ever call yourself that again. You did everything you could. You can't blame yourself because you're alive. The true testimony to Rebecca's life will be you going on with yours…don't you think she would have wanted that?"

He nodded jerkily. "God, Holly" He wrapped his arms around me and dropped his golden head to my chest. We sat like that, wrapped within one another's arms for what seemed like an eternity, but what I knew couldn't have been more than three or four minutes. The pager beeped again. "Ignore it." Ryan muttered from his place against my chest.

I smiled slightly. "I can't. It could be important." (Of course it was important)

I checked the number, of course, Detective Marcus. I looked down at Ryan's head and wondered how he was going to take this news. We had just made such an important breakthrough I was loathe to ruin this moment by calling Detective Marcus…but I knew, I knew that two pages meant it had to be crucial. "I have to make a phone call Ryan."

Ryan sat up and eyed me with keen, cool and now dry eyes. "Calling that Detective aren't you?"

"Ryan" I said his name warningly. He shut up. (Well hallelujah perhaps there was some hope after all). I dialed Detective Marcus's number and waited for him to pick up. He did, after two rings.

"Marcus," he said curtly.

"Hey, it's Holly."

"Where the hell have you been?"

I rolled my eyes. Hadn't we been through this before? "Detective." I gave him the same warning tone I had just given Ryan. Unfortunately this time it didn't work, he didn't shut up,

"I need you to come to the station immediately."

"No."

"Holly."

"I don't like the station house Detective."

Detective Marcus sighed, it was beleaguered sounding and was meant to make me feel like shit. It didn't work. (I already felt like shit) "Okay, does 'Espresso World' sound better to you?"

Yeah, I could use another cup of coffee after the morning I had just had. "Okay, one hour."

"Fifteen minutes." He barked.

"Forty five." I countered.

"Twenty."

"Thirty minutes."

"Okay, yeah, thirty minutes. Be there." He hung up. (I had forgotten what good phone manner he had)

I hung up the phone and looked over to where Ryan was studying me. I sighed. Now I really didn't have the time. "I've got to go Ryan."

"Yeah I heard." He didn't sound like he liked it though. (Yeah what a shocker that was.)

"It's very important."

"Are you going to tell me what this is all about Holly?"

I sucked in a breath. We had taken a huge step forward, in his life and in our semi-relationship, but I didn't think we were ready to make that sort of leap. I couldn't tell him, he wouldn't understand...he really wouldn't. He had just acknowledged the presence of ghouls, how would he ever be able to comprehend the intricacies of the varied PSI and preternatural communities. I couldn't tell him. It was out of the question.

"Eventually, but not right now Ryan, I really don't have time." I waited with baited breath, would he accept that?

"Yeah, okay Hol. But I am going to find out what is going on eventually, and I hope it's you that tells me."

I nodded. "I've got to get ready."

He pressed a fierce kiss on my surprised lips before striding towards the front door. When he reached the door he turned back, his eyes alight with deep emotions. "I don't know about anything else Holly-Anne Feather, and I don't believe in much these days...but I do know I believe in you." With those words he left. Shutting the front door firmly behind him. God when had my life become a fucking soap opera?

Detective Marcus didn't look any better than I did (that made me feel a little better). Dark, deep, smudges marred his chiseled face and a heavy five o'clock shadow obscured his mouth and chin. He was wearing wrinkled clothes and I was certain that he hadn't bothered to shower. I held out a cup of steaming hot black coffee, plain, just the way he liked it. He nodded his head in thanks and accepted it. I sat.

"I doubt we're here to talk about anything good, right?"

Detective Marcus grimaced. "No, it's not good."

I sighed. "How bad?"

"Bad."

"Does it involve someone dying?" I swallowed. I was pretty certain I already knew the answer to that question.

"Yeah."

"Do you need me to check out the scene?"

"This isn't the sort of scene you can check out Holly."

I studied Detective Marcus's sunken face and knew that this was serious, really, really serious. "Hey, it's going to be all right. Tell me."

He looked up, and the pain in his eyes struck me to my core. "We lost Donovan."

I shook my head not understanding. What did he mean? "What? Donovan?"

"Donavan's dead." His voice was flat and emotionless.

I felt my hands begin to quake. No, it couldn't be true. Donovan couldn't be dead. Not that young, flirtatious, fresh-faced kid, Donovan, it couldn't be true. "What are you talking about Detective?" I refused to believe it.

"Damn it Holly. Donovan's dead, I told you, he's dead."

I felt numb. Numb and hollow inside, as if someone had scooped out all my innards with a razor edged spoon. "How?" Was all I managed to ask.

Detective Marcus shook his head wearily, there was so much to that bone tired shake of his head. "It shouldn't have happened," he said. "It was so damn quick…I don't know what the fuck happened. One minute I was yelling at that damn boy not to do anything stupid. To stay put and wait for backup and the next minute he was dead." Detective Marcus's mouth was tight with fury. "That bitch killed him."

My eyes widened. "Pamela?"

"No the other one."

Oh my god. "Portia."

"Yeah, that's the one, Portia Fucking Whitney. Donovan spotted her, he recognized her from the photo I had faxed over to the station and had distributed to everyone. God, it was a fucking fluke. He was getting breakfast and he saw her coming out of the woods near IHOP. He radioed it in. But the damn kid was so green. He thought he could deal with everything, fuck…god, stupid kid." Detective Marcus's face fell and he took another gulp of his coffee before continuing. "He approached her…and well, you can guess what happened next."

"She killed him."

Detective Marcus shot me a cold and furious look. Every line on his face was stretched taut in anger. He was almost shaking in his fury. "Not before she fucking tortured him."

"Oh god."

"She pulled out his goddamn heart, as if he were a common vampire victim, severed his head, hands and feet and left him there on the ground behind the damn IHOP." Detective Marcus shoved a hand through his hair. "She probably would have bled him…but I don't think she had enough time. Just enough time to take the kid apart."

God, oh god. I couldn't believe Donovan was gone, Donovan, poor rookie Donavan, Donavan who had done nothing wrong but underestimate his opponent. Detective Marcus and I had been worried that Pamela Courtland would attempt another kill, I hadn't even considered that Portia Whitney would be up and about yet. "So...she didn't bleed him."

Detective Marcus made a strangled sound. "She bled him all right...just not like the others. He sustained massive blood loss when his limbs were severed. But...uh, she obviously didn't take any of the blood with her. She took off pretty fast after the kill." He dropped his head. "It wasn't a planned attack, or a planned kill, I'm certain of that. Poor wet behind the ears Donovan was just in the wrong place at the wrong time, and didn't have the sense god gave him to wait for his fucking back up."

I knew that the harsh words that Detective Marcus spoke were coming from sadness, grief and ultimately from anger. "No sign of Pamela or Portia, right?" I asked quietly.

"No."

"I'm sorry Detective." I sighed heavily. "I know it's not much, but I'm so sorry."

"He was a snot-nosed kid...seemed the only reason he joined the force was because he thought girls liked a guy in uniform." Detective Marcus said this with a small smile, which I couldn't help imitating. "She took the limbs first...left the heart for last" He said bluntly. (Fuck) I knew what that meant. It was just too terrible to think about. "He was still fucking alive when she dismembered him. Still breathing."

I swallowed. My heart was pounding and I felt the onslaught of a terrible headache coming on. "Detective...please..."

"Sorry," he mumbled.

"I...I want to see the scene."

Detective Marcus's head shot up and he looked at me through slit eyes. "Are you sure?"

I nodded. "Yeah, I...I've got to see it."

"It's not pretty. It'll be hell for you."

Again, I nodded. It never was, pretty that is. But I knew what he meant. This time, the body may be gone but the memory, and the stain would not be washed away. I would relive the horror, and not even my strongest shields would be able to hold under the terrible agony and pressure of what had happened. "I need to see it." I held out my hands in supplication. "Portia Whitney, this is new. I don't even know if she's the same thing that Pamela is..."

"She is." The way he said it was so final that there could be not doubt.

"All right. Nonetheless I've got to see the scene."

"Fine." He said tersely. "But if it gets bad...I'm pulling you out."

I smiled weakly. "If it gets bad you have my full permission to pull me out, Detective. In fact, please, please do."

"Lets go."

The police tape was still firmly affixed around the site where Donovan had been killed. Large pools of dark red blood stained the pavement and clung to the grass like molasses. It smelled like death, true death. I took several deep, fortifying breaths and pulled into myself, I was not going to leave until I found out something useful. I owed that to Donovan, to Detective Marcus…to myself.

I saw out of the corner of my eye Detective Marcus watching me intensely. I knew that he was keeping an eye out for any signs that I might be weakening, any signs that the emotions and depths of the pain sustained here were invading me too fully. I ignored him. Better to concentrate on what was before me, than what could possible befall me. It was then that I smelled it…not sulfur…something else.

"Detective…"

"Yeah?"

"Do you smell anything?" I motioned him forward, closer to the blood-stained grass. Detective Marcus was by my side in several strides. "Do you smell anything?" I repeated.

"I wasn't really…" His voice trailed off and he sniffed. His eyes crinkled and his nose twitched (under any other circumstances he might have looked quite funny). "Perfume…goddamn it I smell perfume!"

I nodded. I gave him a small smile. "Yeah, me too…the same kind."

Detective Marcus knew what I was getting at. "Yeah, it's definitely the same kind that we smelled at the last scene."

"So Pamela Courtland was here…or…"

"Portia Whitney wears the same perfume." Detective Marcus nodded in agreement. "Donovan definitely didn't wear perfume." He said this with a sad smile. "No, it had to be one of them."

"I agree Detective." I looked around, my eyes taking in everything about the scene. My eyes lingered on the indented grass where the victim had half fallen, the trail of blood, so different from the pools of it, where Donovan had bled out. My eyes fell upon something near the curb, where the cement of the pavement met with the outskirts of the forest. I pointed. "There." I said.

Detective Marcus bent down. With gloved hands he bagged what I had found and studied it. "It's flesh..." His eyes narrowed. "Just like the last scene."

"Not just like the last scene Detective, for some reason I have the feeling if you test this you'll see it belongs to Portia Whitney, not Pamela Courtland."

"What are you thinking Holly?"

"I think they're both losing skin." It came out blunt. How else could it come out?

"Huh?"

"They've been brought back, but like I said once, nothing is brought back well. They're moving, speaking...and have obviously developed some new 'talents.' But I think that they are losing their human flesh the longer they remain animated. I think that would explain the flesh found at the last scene, and the flesh found now."

"Couldn't their victims have cut them...gotten a chunk out of them?"

I shook my head. "It's a possibility, but it's highly doubtful. They're strong Detective, really, really strong...and they're powerful. It's something that everyone seems to be forgetting in their haste to believe they're still human...they're not. Donovan forgot it...he saw a pretty girl, slight, small of build and forgot what she really is...a shifter, unnatural, dangerous as all hell." I sighed. "The vampire would probably have had a better chance at taking a chunk out of his attacker than Donovan did...but I don't think either one ever had the chance. Pamela subdued the vamp with a spell...it was either her or the sorcerer who was waiting for her. And, well, Portia...Portia didn't need to use anything to subdue Donovan..." I let my words trail off. I knew that Detective Marcus would get the idea. Donovan had been young, small and exceedingly too cocky for his own good. The shifter had been stronger than him, faster, and much deadlier. He had never stood a chance against her.

"Can this be useful to us?"

"Well...it depends on how quickly they're losing flesh. It looks like when it comes off it comes off in a pretty large amount. However, I don't think they're losing enough to slow them down any. I don't think we can count on them falling apart on us."

"Damn...was hoping they would do the work for us." Detective Marcus said this with small smile and brisk voice.

"It would be nice, yeah," I murmured. I looked down and shuddered when I saw that the toe of my shoe was touching some blood. It was the blood that got me thinking. Suddenly a thought struck me...I couldn't believe how stupid

I had been. Had I been brain dead for the past month? "Detective…" My eyes great narrower and my mind began to churn. It was the blood. It was all about the blood. "Detective…we're dealing with a demon…"

Detective Marcus looked exasperated. "Yeah, I know, so what…"

"Shut up, and listen." I ignored his affronted expression and continued. "The dead respect nothing more than blood." I waved my hand to stop his argument. "I know…I know that we're not dealing with the dead…per say, but we are dealing with something that is not alive…something that is not human. A demon, in Greek Mythology was thought of as something that was a cross between a God and a man…over the centuries; in different cultures it has been best described as a more tangible evil spirit. A demon thrives on anger, hate, and all undesirable emotions…it takes power from the unsure, the weak…but it is summoned and sustained, in most cases by…blood." I stopped. I looked at Detective Marcus and tried to gauge his expression, his state of being. I would not read him. I would not invade his privacy of mind. But, god, right now I really wanted to.

"It's why they're bled."

I smiled triumphantly. He got it. He understood what I was saying. "Yeah, it's why they're bled."

"But the heart…the head, the dismemberment…"

I shook my head. "Don't you see, it's a distraction, nothing else…the limbs don't mean anything to the sorcerer, or to the demon…except perhaps for a…" I shuddered, "…snack. But it's not necessary, the real prize is the blood." I kept shaking my head. I was disgusted with myself. I was majoring in this shit. I was an Empath a high level PSI talent and I hadn't even put it all together until now, until I had seen poor Donovan's blood, sticky and red against the ground. "The sorcerer has called the demon forth, but obviously hasn't released it. If he had…well we would have encountered a lot more death than this. I'm assuming that the demon hasn't been released because the blood sacrifices have not been completed, obviously there hasn't been enough…blood for it to fully animate itself." I shuddered. "For that we should be thankful. But we don't have a lot of time left Detective. The demon grows stronger with every sacrifice, and the sorcerer gains ground with every kill."

"Why vampires Holly?" Detective Marcus asked thoughtfully.

I stopped. Why indeed? I thought back to something, something I had seen, something obscure, something I had thoughtlessly passed over. "I need to check something out Detective."

"Are you going to tell me what it is?"

"I want to make sure I've got it before I tell you."

"Fine. As long as it doesn't have you running around the vampire night clubs."

I laughed. "There is no chance of that..." I smiled. "Not right now at least. No, this has me hitting the library again."

He nodded. "Fine, good, how much trouble can you get into in the Library?" He snapped his mouth shut and his eyes drew together, troubled. Obviously he was thinking on the same lines as I was, I could get into trouble anywhere I went, trouble seemed to have a way of following me.

Chapter Thirty:

I wasn't prepared for Lucien, who was sitting quite gracefully on my front step when I arrived home that evening. His black jeans were quite a contrast to his blood-red silk shirt with its wide sleeves and deep V neckline. His auburn, mahogany hair was pulled back from his face with a leather tie and the long ponytail draped over his shoulder and fell down his front. He looked gorgeous, desirable and delicious. And I totally didn't have time to indulge.

"Lucien...I don't have time to..."

"Rollins has gone missing."

God. It was getting worse. "Part of your Hive?"

"Of course." Lucien's tone was chilly and very controlled. I felt my skin freeze under the weight of the ice dripping from his voice.

"Okay, come in." I ushered him into my apartment and settled him on the couch while I changed quickly into a clean pair of jeans and threw a sweatshirt over my head. When I came out of the bedroom, it was to find Lucien studying the few photos I had scattered around the small living room and dining area.

"Who is this?" Lucien was pointing to a photo of Mrs. Muller, one that she had given me at my request.

"Mrs. Margaret Muller." I sighed. "She was my teacher...a long time ago."

"Pretty woman."

"Yes, yes she was."

"Was?"

My eyes were flat and hard. "She was killed several years ago."

"How."

"Does it matter?" I stiffened when I saw his expression. He wasn't going

262

to let go of this. "She was assisting the police in a serial kidnap murder case…she was killed."

"Was she also Empathic?" Lucien asked.

I shook my head. "No, she was clairvoyant." I remembered Mrs. Muller. God, I had loved her, she was one of very few people I had trusted and relied upon during my childhood. I recalled how her smile would reveal a set of slightly lopsided teeth and how her hair was never content to stay in the bun she preferred, but would fall haphazardly, drooping down the back of her head, as if she hadn't secured it with enough pins. She had been newly married, and had always spoken of her husband with enough devotion and love to make me cry, she had been very much in love, and loved. And now she was gone. And it was her love that had gotten her killed.

"You…cared for this person very much?" Lucien asked.

"Yeah, she was a good person." I snorted. "Always wanted to heal the world." I felt tears gathering in my eyes, despite my attempt to keep them at bay. "Can we not talk of her right now Lucien, please." I added.

"But you keep her photo out?" It seemed to baffle him. "Even though it causes you pain?"

I sighed, he wasn't human, I had to keep reminding myself that…dead, he was dead, and the dead don't feel, right? (God, I was a schmuck) "Yeah, it hurts to see her face, and to remember, but sometimes it's a good pain, okay?"

"But…"

"No, no more, okay, Lucien? No more."

Lucien bowed his head. "As you wish." His eyes went flinty cold again. "I warned my Hive about this girl, Pamela…I warned them…especially after that little 'spectacle' at 'Ecstasy.'"

I blushed. Shit. Caught, I should have known that Lucien would know everything that happened in the vampire community. "So…you found out about that."

"Holly, Holly, Holly…my Holly flower…you seem to forget that I know everything." There was the warmth of affection in his eyes now, and I preferred it to the cold ice that had been there moments before.

"I had a…thought, and I needed to test it. It required me going to 'Ecstasy' for a bit."

"And so you entered 'Ecstasy' without me? Or an escort?"

I rolled my eyes. "I'm not a child Lucien, I don't need a fucking escort." I sighed. "And it's not like I haven't been there before."

"Ah, yes, and do you remember what happened to you last time you went

Holly flower?"

How the fuck could I have forgotten? "Yeah, yeah. But I'm still not going to ring you up every time I need to go out Lucien...forget about it."

"We will talk more on this later."

In my mind we had already finished talking about this issue. No way was I letting the vampire think he could and would baby-sit me. "Pamela might not have been the one to abduct your vamp."

I shuddered when I saw the gleam that entered Lucien's eyes. I had seen what had happened to those who provoked that gleam.

"Who else would have dared?"

I took a deep breath. I really hated being the bearer of bad news. I especially hated bearing bad news to a vampire. It really didn't bode well to one's health. "We have another one Lucien."

"Another one."

"Yeah, another freaky shifter." I paused before continuing. "It seems that the sorcerer has been digging up all sorts of bodies. He brought back both Pamela Courtland and Portia Whitney...the girl whom I discovered on campus." I added.

"So you believe it is this Portia Whitney that abducted Rollins?"

"It's a thought. I mean, if you warned your Hive about Pamela they would have stayed clear of her, right? Especially since they saw that little display of hers at 'Ecstasy.' But you and they didn't know about Portia Whitney...so, well, she would have had an easy shot at any vamp she chose."

"It is still unclear to me how this...woman can defeat one of mine."

I sighed. Yeah, some things vamps would never see. "Portia and Pamela are preternatural beings Lucien...much like you."

"They are nothing like us." His voice was cold and final.

I shrugged. "Fine, they're not vampires, but they are Shifters. They are preternatural. And they can take you down. Plus they have the skills and talents of a damn fine sorcerer on their side. All in all they're a pretty deadly team. I would suggest that you warn your Hive to abstain for a while."

"Abstain?" He looked confused.

I rolled my eyes (jeez). "You know, like...not take blood from humans for a little while, until we stop this thing. Or at least not take it from pretty, young girls."

Lucien looked horrified. Under any other circumstances I would have laughed. "You wish me to tell my people that they cannot take blood?" His eyes narrowed. "And what do you suggest that we do instead...Holly flower?"

"Fuck, Lucien. Haven't you ever heard of Synthex?"

Lucien looked, if possible, even more horrified than he had a moment before. His face twisted up and his eyes widened. This time I couldn't help the small giggle that escaped me. "You wish us to drink Synthex?" His face was still screwed up into that twisted look which had me laughing. He was rather adorable. (Jeez, now I knew I was losing my mind, adorable? A vampire?)

"Hello...that's why Synthetic blood was developed, you snob, you."

"Synthetic blood is undesirable. It is also...a plebeian's drink."

Oh for fuck's sake, I was dating a finicky vampire, it figures. It was obviously time to pull out the big guns. "Would you rather have your Hive suffer through drinking Synthetic blood for a little while, or would you like to see them have their heads cut off, their hearts pulled out and their blood completely drained from their bodies...hey, you choose."

Lucien's face grew cold and tight. His skin paled significantly. I could see those small blue veins pulsing underneath his porcelain-tinted flesh. I didn't flinch. I had been through this before. I knew by now that his 'bark' was much worse than his 'bite.' He wasn't about to intimidate me into backing down. If he wanted his Hive to survive he would order them to abstain from biting any humans. It was simple, why did he have to make it so damn difficult. God he was an arrogant blood-sucking bastard. "Synthetic blood, or true death...what'll be Lucien?"

Lucien's face returned to normal, except for those eyes, those cold, hard eyes. They fixed themselves on me and I began to shiver. After a moment he spoke. "I will advise my Hive to take a brief diet of Synthetic blood, until this Shifter has been stopped." He gave me a pointed look. "However, they will not be content."

"Fine...but at least they'll be alive..." I ignored his amused expression, no; I wasn't about to argue with him about the 'animation' and 'life' of a vampire, not now.

"What were you doing this morning my Holly flower?" Lucien asked, changing the subject.

"Why?"

"Can I not wonder what you do when you are not with me?" He asked with a smile.

I shrugged. "Nothing wildly exciting." (No need to mention I had checked out a crime scene and had seen two men whom Lucien did not have an affinity for.)

"Do you lie to me Holly?"

"Is that a rhetorical question?"

He cocked his head to one side and gave me a steady look.

"Fine, if you really need to know I went with Detective Marcus to look at a crime scene." My expression became somber. "Our kill-happy shifter girl took down a rookie cop, Donovan."

"So she struck twice."

"It would appear so."

"She's getting stronger, or merely more sure of herself." Lucien murmured.

I shook my head. "No, Donovan was a mistake. She wasn't looking for him. He was getting breakfast and saw her…tried to take her himself, which was stupid of him and she killed him. But she didn't have time to bleed him."

"A mistake?" There was the warm edge of anger to his voice.

Shit. I guess I was going to have to tell him. "I think that they're targeting vampires Lucien."

"Oh?" Was all he said.

I swallowed. "I think everything else has been a ruse, or a red herring, something to confuse us, to throw us off track. The girls, well, they're useful, they lure the vampires out, but I think that the vampires have been the true targets all along. Donovan, well Donovan is a further example of that fact. She was threatened and so she killed him. But she didn't stake him out, didn't follow him, didn't lead him to the kill spot, and she didn't bleed him…" I whispered this last.

"What?"

"Detective Marcus said that she didn't have time to bleed Donovan, that that's the reason she didn't take the blood with her." My eyes grew thoughtful. "But I think that if she had wanted the blood, well nothing would have stood in her way. She would have figured out a way to take his blood." (Fuck, of course!) "She didn't need his blood."

Lucien's eyes grew dark and his mouth thinned into a taut line. "Vampire blood."

"Yeah, it's gotta be. It makes sense."

"But was not your second human bled?"

I shrugged. "Yeah, but she was reanimated…she came back as a shifter. She was probably bled at the time to throw us all off the track, make us think that humans and vampires were being targeted so we would not look towards the truth…that vampires have been the target all along…more than human blood." I muttered the last. "I need to get to the library, Lucien." I gave him a pointed look. This was where he was supposed to leave. He didn't, I sighed. "Lucien, you've got to go, I have to get to the Library to check something out."

"Does it have to do with the case Holly flower."

"You know that it does."

"Then I shall come with you."

"Absolutely not, it's out of the question."

Lucien smiled. "Why? Are you ashamed of me, my Holly flower?"

I blushed. "No, it's not that. You just can't come with me to the Library Lucien. You can't be seen on Campus with me."

"I promise to curb...my appetite."

I stared at him, horrified, until I realized that he was joking with me. I rolled my eyes. "You'd be totally out of place on Campus...you can't come."

Lucien's eyes grew cold and he was suddenly standing behind me, one cold, slim hand was wrapped loosely around my neck, I shivered. "This has to do with me and mine. I shall do everything necessary to secure my Hive."

I extricated myself from his loose hold and turned around to face him. I raised turbulent violet eyes to forest green ones and said quietly, assuredly. "I want nothing more than to stop this thing from taking anymore lives. I will do everything in my power to protect your Hive, Lucien, everything. I cannot let you come with me to the Library. You would be detected and would be in danger. How much protection could you offer your Hive from prison." I continued when he would have argued. "No, think about it. The security guards are extra cautious, as they should be, since both Pamela Courtland and Portia Whitney were murdered. They are not that open minded." I rolled my eyes. "We're in *The South* boy..." I said this in a thick drawl. "And they would like nothing better than to pin these murders on vampires, hell, everything is pinned on vampires nowadays...and you know it." I saw the truth of my words in his eyes. "The guards would spot you and call the cops quicker than you could say 'you'll have no trial' and if it's not the guards who see you it'll be someone else." I gave him a pointed look. "I mean you don't exactly blend in."

Lucien looked down at himself and a slow smile dawned on his face. It was magnificent to see. "You worry for my safety, Holly flower."

I shook my head. "No, I worry that you won't be any help to your people from behind bars. And I doubt prison stripes would be acceptable to someone with your high fashion taste."

Lucien was still smiling. He reached out and stroked my cheek. I let out a small sigh in spite of myself. "I am pleased that you worry about me. However, such worry is not necessary...I am the Holder of Edwards."

Yeah, yeah, yeah, blah, blah, blah, I had heard this before, and it wasn't going to change my mind about him not accompanying me to the Campus Library. "You're not going." He must have seen the resolution written across my face because he let out a small sigh and gave me a heart wrenchingly beautiful smile.

"It will be as you ask." He seemed to ignore the fact that I hadn't asked, I had told. "I shall not come with you to your human library. However, I shall be waiting for you afterwards."

"But..."

He gave me a look. "I shall be waiting. It is that, or I come with you, now, which do you prefer, Holly flower?"

I rolled my eyes. "Fine, fine, but I'll meet you."

"Corruption."

"No, back here."

"You wish me back in your home, I am honored Holly flower." He said this mockingly. Ah, the vampire could be so damn annoying.

"No, it's just easier for me this way. I'll probably have papers and books and well, I'd prefer to be in my own space, thank you very much."

"All right then, I shall meet you back at your *lovely* apartment."

I rolled my eyes. (Yeah, I knew the vamp didn't like my décor. Well, tough) "Great, fine. Okay, now go."

Lucien inched closer and within a blink of an eye had me secured within a tight embrace. I indulged for a moment (against my better judgment) pressing my head against his chest and basking in the strength of his arms. I stiffened when I encountered silence. It was the very lack of a heartbeat that had mine racing. His chest was still. There was nothing, no heartbeat, no breath, and no movement. I could feel my heart pounding, and heard it in my ears like a metronome. "If you are waiting for a heartbeat you wait in vain my Holly flower." Lucien murmured against my hair.

I sucked in my breath. It was as if he read my mind, every time. "I know. I know you have no heartbeat." I sighed. "It is just unsettling, when you realize how very still you actually are. When you hear for yourself...how there is nothing to hear."

"And can you accept this?"

I knew what he was asking was really, *can you accept me*? I didn't really have an answer for him. "I am trying, Lucien, I am truly trying." I bit my lip.

"I just need some time. Everything has happened very fast. I am still trying to make sense of it all."

"You have had a lot of time to make sense of what you are Holly. Are you sure that it is not something else that keeps you from me?"

"I don't know what you're talking about Lucien."

Lucien looked down at me and nodded. "No perhaps you don't. It will be as you say Holly. I shall meet you here after your appointment at the Library...do not keep me waiting overly long."

My mouth dropped open. One moment he had been standing there berating me, and the next, he had disappeared. It wasn't like the movies at all. There was no smoke, no fog and no strange whirlwind. He was just gone. Talk about totally creepy.

I was thumbing through another reference guide when my beeper went off. I ignored it. I couldn't very well leave the library now. And anyways I didn't have a phone to call Detective Marcus on. He'd just have to wait.

Ah ha. I had found it. It was so obscure I had totally rushed by it the last time I had been in here, *more than human blood.* I had been right. I knew I had seen that passage here somewhere. There it was, clear as day, an obscure mention in Hascall's, *Deciphering Demonology* about needing more than human blood to conjure and contain an ancient demon. Hascall? Hascall? There had to be more than one Hascall right? It couldn't possibly be our Library attendant, could it? I shook my head. This was just getting weirder and weirder by the moment.

The object of my mind's attention was standing not five feet away from me. Bent over a stack of aged volumes, Hascall was clearly studying the books. His hooked nose seemed even more prominent from this angle and his beady eyes were small and very intimidating.

I looked down at the reference guide and then back to Hascall. What the hell did I have to lose? I gathered up my books and copied pages, along with my bag and numerous other items and made my way to the library desk. I placed my stack of books in front of Hascall. He didn't even look up as he began to scan my books and stamp them. His hand stilled and then stopped completely when it came to a certain book. I felt a fission of relief and triumph when I saw his pock marked skin go pasty and white. He swallowed and his Adams apple bobbed up and down with the movement. He clenched his fist and brought his other hand down.

"Are you...interested in demons Ms. Feather?" His voice was rusty, like nails, and low.

I nodded. "I've found lately, that I'm quite interested in demons, Mr. Hascall." I pointed to the still unstamped book. "You wouldn't know the author of this book, would you Mr. Hascall? The text is quite fascinating."

Mr. Hascall grimaced and then forced a tight smile. "No, why would you ask?"

I gave him an innocent look. One that I knew worked well. "Well, why, since your name is Hascall, and the authors name is Hascall..." I shrugged my shoulders nonchalantly.

Mr. Hascall frowned and then narrowed his eyes. His face was still shockingly white. "There are many Hascall's in the world, I'm sure, Ms. Feather. Any one of them could have written this book."

I nodded. (Gotcha) "Oh of course. You're completely right Mr. Hascall." I waited a moment before adding. "Uh, can you stamp the book Mr. Hascall? I really need to be going."

He paused. Looking down at the book he jerked his eyes back to mine. "Are you sure you want this particular book, Ms. Feather. It is not very good."

Slimy sonofabitch. "Yeah, I'm sure." My stare was unwavering. After another moment Hascall nodded curtly and stamped the book. He stared at the stack for another minute before shoving it in my direction.

"They're due..."

"Oh, I know when they're due, thank you Mr. Hascall." I spared the frightened and angry library attendant only one more look before rushing out of the doors. If Hascall weren't somehow, even indirectly related to this entire mess, I'd eat my favorite pair of running shoes.

Back at my apartment I spread the books on my living room floor. I dumped my papers beside them and threw myself down in the middle of the mess. My phone rang. I ignored it. It rang again. Swearing, I picked it up.

"What?" I barked into the receiver. I let out a sigh and a shiver when familiar voice answered.

"Upset tonight my Holly flower?"

"Lucien." I rubbed my eyes. "Lucien, listen I really need to study these books, can I take a rain check on our...uh, get together."

"No."

"Lucien."

"I will be over in fifteen minutes my Holly flower. And then you can tell me what it is that you have discovered. What it is that puts such fear in your voice." He hung up.

Damn him, damn him, damn him…(Shit, somebody had already done that)

Lucien was as good as his word. Fifteen minutes later my bell rang and I answered the door. Lucien stood there stock-still. Wearing the same black jeans, he had changed his shirt. He was now wearing a black velvet top. The collar and cuffs were edged with red silk, just to give it that certain something. His color was good, almost too good, I knew he had fed, on what, was the question at the foremost of my mind.

"Come in." I rolled my eyes when he suddenly appeared in the center of my room. "Show off," I muttered. He smiled. Obviously he had heard me.

"My, my, Holly flower, you are a messy girl." His eyes were sweeping over the open books and spread out papers. He turned laughing eyes in my direction.

"Ha, ha, very funny." I looked at him. Rosy cheeked and pink lipped I could feel the self-satisfied swell emanating off of him. "Who'd you bite tonight, Lucien?"

His eyes narrowed. "Excuse me?"

"You heard me, who'd you snack on?"

"Are you accusing me of something Holly?" He stepped closer to me.

I braced myself. I didn't flinch. "Your color is high, I can almost see a pulse in your throat, and your thoughts, well your mind is particularly open tonight Lucien. You ate, and you ate well. Don't try to deny it."

"And?"

The fucking bastard, I was furious. My eyes were bright with anger and I placed my hands on my hips before advancing towards him. When I was nearly nose-to-nose with the irate vamp I let loose. "After everything I said about the shifters, everything I warned you about. And after I specifically told you about using Synthex, you go and eat…you're a total idiot." (Oops, had I just called the Holder an idiot?)

"You go too far, Holly" Lucien leaned forward. His eyes were glowing and beginning to fog over. "I took your words to heart. I informed my Hive of the danger. They were less than pleased with the prospect of using synthetic blood. However, they agreed to abstain from pleasing themselves in another manner…until this business is dealt with. However…" He growled. His eyes had bled to red. I really hate when that happens. "I am the Holder of Edwards. I must be strong, for my Hive to be strong. I know of the dangers and I am aware of the threat to our people. I took but a little blood this eve, and I took from a reliable vessel. There is no need for this...this display."

I stepped back from him. "Nothing is 100% safe right now Lucien. You must treat everything and everyone as a potential threat."

"There is no threat from this vessel. He has been with us for quite some time. He is completely safe." Lucien licked his lips. "And his blood is very potent."

I shuddered. He? "You took from...a...a..."

"A what?" Lucien asked. Looking deeply into my eyes.

"A, uh, boy?"

Lucien laughed. "Does this bother you? Are you bothered by that prospect Holly flower?" Lucien smiled slightly. "It is just a feeding Holly flower. It means nothing other than survival."

Well, survival was a big thing. "It isn't sexual?"

Lucien's face turned somber and he stepped closer to me. He reached out and cupped my cold cheek in his hands. My breath caught in my throat. He leaned closer, until our faces were nearly touching and our bodies were nearly pressed together. When he spoke his breath caressed my face. "This...this is sexual, Holly flower." He nuzzled my face. "That is just blood." He looked back into my eyes. They were hot. "But make no mistake, it can be sexual...it is a very intimate thing, the giving and taking of blood."

I nodded. I knew that. That was why there were so many vampire groupies out there. So many young men and women desperately craved the touch of the dead, the bite of the vampire. But I knew the truth. It wasn't about sex. It was about control. The strong controlling the weak, the vampire controlling the meat, the give and take, ha, what a laugh, the human gives and the vampire, well, the vampire, just takes. "You took a big risk." I murmured.

Lucien shook his head. "There was no risk involved."

Fine, whatever, I wasn't about to argue with him (even though I really wanted to). "I found something tonight."

"I knew you had." Lucien smiled and wrapped a strand of my loose hair around his hand. "You are such a smart girl. My Holly flower...so very brilliant."

I flushed. "I'm not brilliant. Just tenacious." I muttered. I led him over to the mess in my living room. I picked up a book and pointed to one particular section. "Here, look. *In many cases, more than human blood is the main component in summoning forth the desired ancient demon. The blood in question is sacrificial. And if the demon be pleased by the offering, it shall be released on a blood debt. The one who summons forth the demon must be prepared to offer fresh blood at each calling. See: Summoning vii.*" I looked up and over at Lucien. "Well?"

"Yes?"

"Is that all you're going to say?"

"Obviously the sorcerer has interpreted the passage to mean that *more than human blood* means vampire blood."

I rolled my eyes. "Obviously."

Lucien's look was thoughtful. "But *more than human blood* is not necessarily vampire blood, my Holly flower."

"Whatever, this is huge. I mean this totally clears things up. Why the sorcerer is striking vampires, what the shifters are being used for and why human blood is being ignored." I turned my gleaming eyes back to Lucien. "Oh, and there's more."

"Is there?" Lucien asked. The expression on his face was one of obvious resignation, tinged with a bit of amusement to boot.

"Yeah, listen. I looked up the footnote on summoning. *Flesh need not be present at the summoning but may be used to further tempt the demon.*" I grimaced. "But the sacrificial blood will soon not be enough for the demon." I shuddered. "It'll be released soon."

"Yes, I believe you are correct in your assumption," Lucien said.

My eyes lit up. "I need you to talk to Michele for me."

"Michele?" Lucien's voice was frosty. "Do you now call the Holder of Charlotte by his given name?"

I rolled my eyes. "Get over it, Lucien. I just need you to ask him if the companions slain last year were, uh, more than human." I waved away his argument with a toss of my hand. "I know he said that they were not vampires...but did they have..."

"More than human blood," Lucien finished.

I nodded. "Yeah. Could you ask him for me?"

"Of course."

"Okay. So now all I need is a plan..." I murmured.

"All *you* need?" Lucien was now, very amused.

"Yeah, a plan, you know, to stop this sorcerer from releasing a really bad mother fucker into our midst." I saw an argument coming. "And if you think you can stop me from helping, then you're totally deranged."

Lucien smiled, that subtle, beautiful smile of his. He ran a hand down my arm and cupped my cheek with his other hand. "I wouldn't dream of stopping you from helping, my Holly flower. However, you forget this is not only your fight."

I blushed. He was right, of course. This was a preternatural being, and he had just as much right, if not more to deal with it. Not to mention, I could use all the help I could get. I was dealing with a fucking powerful sorcerer and a potential city destroying demon, yeah, I could use some help. "Sorry…uh, I kind of get carried away sometimes."

Lucien laughed. "Do not worry, Holly flower. I find it and you adorable."

I blushed harder. I tried to remain focused (even with his hand rubbing my back so deliciously) "So what are we going to do?"

"First, as you said, I shall contact Michele and ask him about his slain companions. Then I shall endeavor to find where these Shifters hide themselves. It is a smaller community than you think Holly flower, the preternatural one. We in Edwards will all be on the look out."

"Good, okay." I chewed on my lower lip nervously. I was debating whether to tell him about Hascall or not. Hascall was human. Lucien was not. If Lucien knew of Hascall's part in all of this (and not even I knew of Hascall's part in this) then I doubt anything or anyone could stop him from his own sense of justice. And we had already established that Lucien and I disagreed fundamentally on the justice issue. What would Lucien do to Hascall? I shuddered. Whatever he would do, it wouldn't be pretty, and I'd bet my last dollar it would probably be fatal. No, I couldn't tell Lucien about Hascall. This was something I'd let Detective Marcus deal with. Hey, if Lucien wants me to keep secrets from Detective Marcus, well then, it goes both ways, I can keep some secrets from Lucien and tell Detective Marcus…it's only fair.

"Is there something more you'd like to tell me Holly flower?"

"Uh, what?" I jerked my head up, meeting his forest green eyes with my own violet ones.

"Is there something more you'd like to say?"

"Uh, no, why?"

"Because you look particularly troubled." He smiled. "Or perhaps it is just because you are biting that delectable lip of yours…something I've noticed you do when you are thinking particularly hard…or are particularly nervous. Which one is it?"

I let go of my lip. Damn. I was going to have to watch for that. I turned away from him, so that he couldn't see my guilty expression. "It's nothing, really. I was just…thinking, about…the demon, that's all." I knew that he was mulling that over.

"I have books in the Archives that may be of some help…I shall look at them; see if I can find anything useful."

My head snapped around at the mention of archives, and books, so fast I think I got whiplash. "What archives?"

Lucien gave me a knowing look. "Mine of course. At one time every Hive had an Archive. Now, with the constant modernization of things…some leaders prefer to disassociate themselves with the old ways and look towards the new." His voice was tinged with disgust. "I, however, do not believe strictly in the new ways. There is only so much they can do to help us…those of us born and bred in a time that you have long forgotten. I believe in preserving the past, and it is for that reason that I have kept my archives intact. They are quite complete, you will find."

I was staring at Lucien in disbelief. He hadn't told me? Why hadn't he told me that he had a library? "You dipshit, why didn't you tell me you had a library?"

Lucien laughed. "Dipshit? Another of your lovely words my Holly flower. We must try to expand your vocabulary a little."

"Fuck that. Answer the damn question."

Lucien shrugged. "The Archives can only be breached by the Holder of the Hive. They contain many secrets of the old world. The Council long ago decreed that the old ways could only be entrusted to one of power and strength. Many of these volumes are of ancient lineage and contain many powerful secrets. It was a wise decision on the part of the council to decree that not just anyone could be privileged to them." He smiled at me. "I know of your love and fascination with your…research as you call it. But you cannot enter the Archives, therefore I found no need to tell you of them until now."

"Can I not just take a quick look Lucien?" I couldn't believe it. The Hive had a library. And could you just imagine the books that would be contained in such a library? Lucien had said so much himself, volumes of ancient lineage. Who knows how far back they went. Who knows what sort of mysteries they could reveal. What they could solve.

"No Holly, you cannot."

"But Lucien…"

"No Holly."

"Lucien, what if there is something you can't understand? What if there is something you come across that you don't know?"

Lucien laughed. "Do you think me so illiterate my Holly flower?" He placed a kiss on my nose. "I have studied these volumes for as long as some of them have been in my Archives. I have lived that long." He looked at me, as if to gauge how I took that bit of news. I said nothing, so he continued. "I know my work Holly flower, as I know my duty."

"Lucien."

"No, there will be no more talk of you entering the Archives. It is out of the question and completely not debatable. I shall, however, share with you my findings, if and only if I find something worth sharing." He studied me earnestly. "You must understand, this is more than I would do for anyone else…"

I nodded, resigned. "Fine."

"Ah, good. Now, my Holly flower you must get some rest."

I was irate. "Don't tell me what to do you…you…"

"Shhhhh…. I know that you could call me all sorts of names, however, you had best keep them for some other time when I do not have your best interests in mind." He played with my hair. Wrapping it around his hands and sifting through the silken texture. "You have run yourself ragged my Holly flower. Shhh, no, I speak only the truth. Your eyes are hollow and you have darkness marring that beautiful skin of yours. I see the fatigue in your eyes and in your body…fatigue that you cannot hide from me…" He smiled. "Even though you try. You need rest. You need rest if you are to find and fight this evil with me."

I hated when he used logic on me. "I'm fine."

"Yes, you would say that. However, you are lying to yourself and to me. You will sleep now. I will leave you to your rest, and you must promise me that you shall."

I rolled my eyes. "You want me to promise you that I'll go to bed."

"Yes."

"Don't be stupid," I muttered.

"I…I am never stupid." Lucien countered. "Now…will you promise me that you will sleep, or shall I stay here and watch over you myself."

Oh boy, having a vampire watch me while I slept…uh, no way. Jeez, I don't think so. "No."

"No, you will not sleep and I shall stay, or no, you do not wish me to keep watch over you."

"No, as in absolutely no fucking way are you staying here tonight."

"Then you shall promise me that you shall sleep."

Ah, I wanted to kick him. I would if I didn't know that I'd hurt myself a lot more than I'd hurt him. "Fine, fine, fine…I'll sleep, does that make you happy?"

Lucien grinned. Looking carefree and suddenly very boyish. "Yes, I believe it does." He wrapped his arms around me and leaned in close. He nuzzled his head in my hair. "You smell sweet…"

"It's the perfume," I muttered.

"No, my Holly flower, it is you, only you." Lucien kissed me then. It was sweet and tender, more so than it had ever been. His tongue skimmed along my lips and seemed to beg for an invitation to enter. I obliged. He swept inside the warm recesses of my mouth and my senses whirled. I tried to breathe but found my lungs clenched and closed. It felt as if I were losing oxygen to my brain…and it was strangely wonderful. I was lightheaded and flying all at the same time. (How did he do this to me?)

Lucien pulled away from me, with difficultly. (That pleased me) "You tempt me beyond reason Holly. But I cannot take what is not offered…not this night." He smiled at me, but his face was suddenly grim. "I will take my leave of you. Before it is too late."

I watched him struggle to regain control of his senses. "Use the door Lucien." I said. I just wasn't up to dealing with watching him disappear again, not tonight.

Lucien grinned. "Of course." He strode to the door and when he had reached it he dropped into a half bow. I rolled my eyes. He left, shutting the door firmly behind him. I slumped to the floor, exhausted both mentally and physically. How the hell was I going to get through another day? I fell asleep, right there, on the floor, with that thought single most in my mind.

Chapter Thirty-One:

I called Detective Marcus first thing in the morning. I had slept in. And subsequently missed my morning class. I was pissed at myself, but mostly I was pissed at Lucien for suggesting that I sleep. It was entirely his fault. If he hadn't suggested it, I would have stayed up, finished my research and gone to class in the morning. Sleeping when I returned. Damn the overly concerned vampire. Detective Marcus had been as delighted as I knew he would be with the information I had dug up from my research. He had also been very interested with my theories concerning Mr. Hascall, EU's creepy library attendant. He told me that there was little to be done now, since there was nothing that could link Hascall with the murders. But that he would keep an eye on him, and that he would do a full background check.

I decided since I had already missed my class, and since there was nothing to be done about it now I would luxuriate in a bath...something I rarely did. I poured in the last of my honeysuckle bubble bath and placed my steaming cup of coffee easily within reach and stretched out in my tub. Oh god, it felt like heaven. Who the hell would want to take a shower when they could spoil their body in a bath? I put my cold relaxation eye mask on, sipped my coffee and cleared my thoughts of everything. Right now, at this moment, I was just Holly-Anne Feather, EU student, Empath, and entirely grateful that I had missed my morning class.

Ryan was waiting for me when I entered Professor DeWitt's class. He was sitting at the desk next to mine. I dropped my book bag and slid my frame into the uncomfortable seat.

"What are you doing sitting by me Ryan?" I whispered.

"Is there something wrong with this seat?" he asked, entirely too innocently.

I sighed. "You know you don't sit there."

Ryan smiled. "I convinced Tim that the seat by the window had a much better view."

I scoffed. "A better view of what?"

"Freedom," he said with a laugh.

I tried not to smile. I failed. "Listen, Ryan…"

"Hey, Hol, it's just a seat."

"I know, but I don't want you to distract me."

Ryan grinned. That wide, white grin of his, god, he was so adorable. "Do I distract you Holly?"

I rolled my eyes. "Now I know you're just fishing for compliments. You know you do."

He pulled on my ponytail. Smiling at my annoyed expression. "I like knowing I can distract you." He grinned. "Oh-so-serious Holly. Nice to know it's possible."

"Ryan," I said in that warning tone of mine. This time it failed to shut him up.

"Hey, I promise I'll be good."

"Yeah, sure."

"Scout's honor."

"You were never a Scout?" I muttered.

"How'd you know?"

"What?"

"That I wasn't a Scout."

I looked at his face, now sporting a devilish grin and I rolled my eyes. "Just had a feeling."

He laughed. I sighed. God, it was going to be a long, long class.

Professor DeWitt, this morning, did not look bright and busy tailed. Actually, she looked pretty awful. Her skin was waxy and pale, and her usually neat chignon was messy and in disarray. Her fitted suit was wrinkled and she seemed preoccupied and for the first time ever, disorganized. She blamed her appearance and manner on the flu, claiming she had caught some sort of bug that was going around. We said nothing. But I wondered if anyone else was thinking what I was thinking, what flu bug?

After class Professor DeWitt called out to me. I hesitated. I turned to Ryan. "Go on, I've got to speak with Professor DeWitt."

"Are you sure?" Ryan asked.

"Yeah, positive." I smiled. "Want to meet me at 'Espresso World' oh, in fifteen?" I loved the look of pleasure that spread over his face.

"Yeah, sounds great."

"Okay, see you there." I watched as he disappeared in the crowd before turning back to Professor DeWitt, who was waiting at her desk for me. As I neared her I saw that her complexion was terrible and she looked haggard and for the first time ever, exhausted. I let down my shields slowly, gently. I pushed outwards and tenderly breached the outer surface of her mind. I felt resistance and I hesitated. I pushed a little more firmly, still not hard enough to alert her to my presence, but just enough to sequester myself within. I was shocked. It was murky and dark within her mind. There was confusion and terrible fog. I felt myself choking and drowning in the darkness and I quickly jerked myself free. Poor woman, something was obviously wrong.

"Holly." Professor DeWitt's voice was hoarse and scratchy.

"Yes, Professor?"

"I just wanted to tell you that I am delaying my paper. Therefore, the research that you are doing for me, well you don't have to do it."

"But Professor…"

"You see, I haven't been feeling too well of late. And I think I need just a little break." She smiled at me coolly. "But don't worry. I'm sure by next semester I will be back on track with my paper and I will have need of your services again." She looked at me. "You do understand, don't you?"

Did I understand? Well, not really. "Uh, sure, Professor." I bit my lip. "Listen, uh, is there anything I can do for you Professor?"

She gave me a long appraising look. Her expression softened then and she smiled, what appeared to be a genuine smile. "No, nothing, but thank you Holly."

"Okay…well, if you need anything Professor."

"I'll be sure to ask," she said, again, cool and reserved.

I turned and began to walk away. "Oh, Professor…one question."

"Yes, Holly?"

"What scent do you wear? It's lovely."

Professor DeWitt gave me an odd look before answering. "It's called 'Hypnotic Poison,' it's by Christian Dior."

"Thanks," I said. At the door I added. "Again, it's lovely…really…unique."

Twenty-five minutes later I found Ryan sipping coffee and munching on what appeared to be biscotti. I smiled.

"Hey there, you."

Ryan smiled widely when he saw me. "Hey."

"Sorry I'm late, I keep forgetting how long it takes me to navigate through busy hallways."

"No problem." He blushed. "Sorry, I ordered without you, I really needed the caffeine."

"Don't worry about it." I held up the cup of foaming coffee, double espresso with a shot of caramel flavoring, just the way I liked it. "I got my coffee, it's cool." I sat down opposite him. "So…" Suddenly I felt awkward and shy. (Not like me, not like me at all)

"So…" Ryan grinned. "What do you make of DeWitt? Freaky or what? She was completely out of it today."

I stiffened and my grip tightened on my coffee, it sloshed over the rim, burning my hand. I let out a little gasp. "Shit."

"Hey, careful." Ryan gently ran a napkin over my skin, wiping away the spilled coffee. He studied my hand. "It doesn't look too bad. You might want to run it under some cold water in the rest room though."

I shook my head. "No, it's fine. I was just a little stupid." I steadied myself. "Sorry, what did you say?"

"Oh, nothing, just that DeWitt was in a strange mood today."

"Yeah, strange."

"And what was that whole bit about the flu? I didn't know the flu was going around."

"It isn't," I said quietly.

"Well she sure looked sick, or something."

"Or something," I muttered under my breath.

"What?"

"Nothing." I forced a smile onto my tight face. "How about I cook you dinner next week?"

"Next week?" Ryan grinned. "Can't see me sooner than that?" He put his coffee down and took my hands in his. "Your schedule too busy?" He said this with a smile.

Shit, he could never know how busy. "Uh, well…its just with all this school work…"

"Yeah, I get it…" He laughed. "Oh-so-serious Holly has struck again. I know how seriously you take your work Holly. If you can't see me until next week, fine, but I wish you'd let me take you out this weekend."

I looked at his earnest blue eyes and kicked myself internally. What was I doing? I was completely ruining all my chances with this gorgeous, smart, sweet and best of all, this living guy. I shook my head to clear it. "Okay, I'll cook you dinner this weekend, how does that sound?" I smiled. "You can come over, no homework, no studying, just you and me and…well…" I let my voice trail off.

Ryan tightened his grip on my hand. He nodded and smiled tenderly at me. "Yeah, I'd really like that Holly. But, I've got an even better idea."

"What's that?" I asked.

"How about I bring over some take-out?" His eyes gleamed, full of mischief.

My mouth gaped open and I let out some choking sounds. I began to laugh, a full deep laugh that warmed my insides. I swatted him on his shoulder with the palm of my hand. And we both laughed together.

When I got home I had two messages waiting for me on my answering machine. I pushed the little black button and listened. The first was from Lucien, telling me that he had spoken with Michele and that Michele had informed him that the two companions slain in Charlotte last year, had indeed been of more than human blood. The second message was from Detective Marcus telling me, in his usual gruff voice to call him ASAP. I groaned. At one time I had wanted more of a life. Now all I wanted was my life back.

I picked up the phone and dialed Detective Marcus's private line. He answered after the perfunctory two rings.

"Marcus."

"Hey, it's Holly."

"We've got another one."

I felt my heart trip. It had to be; it couldn't be anyone else but Lucien's missing Hive member. "Do you need me to come?"

"Only if you're up to it." There was an audible sigh on his end of the line. "It's pretty much the same."

"Pretty much isn't exactly."

"Hell, it's exactly the same Holly. The same pentagram, the same damn circle. I'm sure the same sulfur, and damn it if it doesn't stink to high heaven."

"What? Say that again Detective?"

"About everything being the same?"

"No, did you say it smells?"

"Yeah."

282

"But you can't smell the sulfur, right?"

"No, but I'd rather smell the sulfur over that damn perfume."

My breath stopped. I felt myself getting lightheaded. Fuck. "Is it the same?"

"Same perfume?"

"Yeah."

"It's Dior."

"What's Dior?"

"The perfume, I was right...the first time. It's Dior, it's called 'Hypnotic Poison' and you were also right, it's a fancy kind."

"What the fuck are you talking about kid? And how do you know the name of the perfume?"

I thought back to early this afternoon. How the scent had clung to her skin and invaded my senses. How unique it was, and how it had entrenched itself in the space around her. "Because my Professor wears it. The same brand, exactly the same fucking brand."

"Listen Holly, if you thinking what I think you're thinking...then perhaps you should think again." He paused and snorted. "I mean, thousands of woman, no hundreds of thousands of woman have to have that same scent."

I shook my head, and then realizing he couldn't see me said. "No Detective, it's very unique. It's also very, very expensive. And don't you find it a little coincidental that my professor wears the same perfume that we've smelled at the last three crime scenes?"

"We don't know that it's the same scent for sure Holly?"

I remembered. "I know Detective. I know for sure. It's Dior and Professor DeWitt wears it. I can't believe I didn't smell it earlier and I didn't put it together before now. My only excuse was that I wasn't looking at her as anything but my Professor. I'm telling you Detective, Professor DeWitt wear's 'Hypnotic Poison.'"

"So what the fuck do you want me to do about it?"

I couldn't believe I was hearing this. "Well do something."

"Listen Holly, I can't arrest the frigging woman for wearing perfume."

"For wearing the same perfume that was detected at the crime scenes."

"Even for that." He snorted. "What'll I tell my captain. 'Hey cap, I picked up a respected University Professor because I got a tip that she wears some expensive toilet water?"

My temper was rising and I was quickly losing my patience. I couldn't believe this. How could he not see what was going on? I remembered Professor DeWitt that day I had run into her outside of 'Espresso World' I remembered her pleasure and her strange mood. I also remembered how she was carrying a copy of Zuri. Zuri? Oh my god, the 'Dead Sea Scrolls', I needed to know what was in those books. I needed to get my hands on a copy of that book. "Fine, okay."

"What?"

"Fine, you're right. I'm sorry I snapped at you," I said quickly.

"Okay, what's going on kid?"

"What do you mean?"

"Why are you agreeing with me all of a sudden, why aren't you arguing?"

"Perhaps because I've realized that you're totally right. That I'm being unreasonable." (I bit my tongue).

"Yeah, and the Pope's an atheist."

Shit. I needed to get off of this phone. "Listen, Detective, I was wrong, you were right."

"What aren't you telling me Holly."

I sighed, totally exasperated. "Nothing, I've got nothing to tell you that I haven't already told you." I waited with baited breath.

"Fine, I'm coming over."

That was fine with me, I wasn't going to be here, "Okay, sure. Say half an hour?"

"I'll be there in ten minutes."

"See you then, Detective." I hung up the phone and prayed that I wouldn't be struck down dead for all the lying and deceiving I had been doing lately. If God were merciful he'd realize that I was doing all of this for a greater good.

Back at the library I was digging through mountains of books I had subsequently pulled off the shelves in my search for Zuri's three volumes. I was ready to tear my hair out. There was nothing.

"Shit." I slumped down and cast my eyes around. I was alone. It was late and the library wouldn't be open much longer. God knows I didn't have much time left.

"Looking for something in particular Ms. Feather?"

My head snapped around. "Mr. Hascall, god you scared me."

Hascall was wearing that same lemon-sucker expression that he always wore, but tonight his eyes gleamed brightly. "I tend to have that effect on people."

I didn't say anything.

"As I asked before, are you looking for something in particular Ms. Feather?"

I shook my head. "Uh, not really."

"Oh?" He came closer. When he was standing only a foot away he knelt down besides me. He eyed the stack of books around me and smiled a lopsided smile. Now I was getting weirded out. "It just looks like you're searching for something."

My eyes narrowed. My mind began to churn. It was becoming increasingly obvious that the only way I was going to get the information I needed was by just going for it. "Actually, I was looking for something."

"Oh?" Hascall's eyes narrowed even more, now they were but tiny slits.

"You wouldn't know what happened to Zuri's three volumes on 'The Dead Sea Scrolls' would you?" I knew I hit pay dirt when Hascall's face blanched and he swallowed audibly.

"I don't recall those particular volumes, Ms. Feather."

Bullshit. "Really?" I gave him a brilliant smile. "Well, I ran into Professor DeWitt." If possible Hascall's face whitened even more. "She was carrying one of the volumes..."

Hascall's face was impossibly cold and the lines near his eyes stretched so far that they appeared to fall off his face. "Now I know you can't be right Ms. Feather, those volumes are strictly for Library use, they cannot be checked out."

I shook my head. "Oh, I know. But I spoke with Professor DeWitt, and she told me that you and she had an arrangement." I gave him a tight smile. "And I'm definitely not mistaken, it was definitely Zuri."

"I fear you must be wrong Ms. Feather." Hascall had moved away from me. "As I said, those books cannot be checked out, and Professor DeWitt knows better than to take one of those books out...now, if you don't mind I have a lot to do before closing time." Hascall couldn't get away from me fast enough.

I watched Hascall scurry away, now more than ever I was certain that Hascall was involved and that he had to be stopped. I fished out my beeper and wrote a brief text message to Detective Marcus, not bothering to apologize for 'standing' him up, he'd understand. I took one more look around, but I knew that Hascall had to be aware that I was onto him, and therefore I was certain he had a hand in the disappearance of the three volumes that I needed. I gathered up my shit and made my way to the front of the library, casting my eyes around, basically making sure that Hascall wasn't around, or up to anything.

Once outside the Library I inhaled the night air and took in the ink black sky, and for the first time in my life wished I had a vampire near. More to the point, I wished I had my vampire near. I felt a chill crawl up my spine and I turned, there was nothing and no one there. I exhaled and began to make my way across campus. There was nothing left to do now but make my way home and contact Lucien. I needed some information on the shifters and I needed to know a little bit more about the vamp victims.

"*Pretty...*"

I spun around. The slivery voice came out of nowhere and had me stifling a scream. I recognized that voice. Oh god, I recognized that voice. "Hello?" I took another deep breath and began to walk faster. I was past Friedmont Hall and well on my way to the parking lot...just a little further and I would be safe. Safe? I didn't really know the meaning of the word any longer.

"*Pretty...Pretty...Pretty...I see you.*"

"Okay, if you're going to do something, you might as well show your fucking face." It wasn't the smartest thing I had ever done or said, but I didn't know what else to do. I didn't have a chance in hell of outrunning her, and if it came down to strength...well, you get the picture. The only thing I knew to do was to boast and bullshit...and to keep her away with my PSI abilities until the cavalry came to my rescue. I had already typed an SOS into my beeper (God bless Detective Marcus for it) and was praying that he would get it. "There's security everywhere...you can't start anything here." I yelled out.

"Ms. Feather?

I squinted, what? "Mr. Hascall?" I took several steps back. Hascall had literally stepped from the darkness and was now standing as if welded to the shadows.

"Who are you talking to Ms. Feather?" Hascall continued to move forward as I moved back.

"No one in particular Mr. Hascall."

"It's quite late Ms. Feather, don't you think you should be home?" Hascall smiled mockingly.

"That's what I'm planning on doing right now." I gave him a tight smile and braced my arms in front of me as if to warn him about getting too close.

"Allow me to walk you to your car."

"Oh, that's really kind of you Mr. Hascall, but I can get there on my own." I was slowly backing away.

"It's quite late Ms. Feather, and very dark…don't you know what happens in the dark, when you're alone?"

Was he joking? I watched as his eyes began to bleed to red, oh shit, I really hate when that happens. I turned to run, but found that my feet were firmly affixed to the ground. Subsequently I ended up flat on my ass staring up at the scary ass library attendant. By now Hascall was standing but a foot away, grinning down at me, eyes red, skin pale and shit, he was holding the very book I had been looking for.

"I believe you were looking for this." Hascall's eyes were still blood red but I knew that he was no vamp. I had seen vampires before. Hell, I was dating one…Hascall was no vampire. But he was definitely something I didn't like.

I leaned back, swearing. "You won't get away with this." The moment the words had left my mouth I realized how ridiculous I sounded. He'd already gotten away with it. "What did you do to my feet?" I asked.

Hascall grinned. He was obviously proud of his handiwork. "A very simple spell…any amateur could accomplish it…I, myself, am not an amateur." He knelt down in front of me, and stroked my hair, ignoring my growl and flailing arm. I was doing my best not to fall flat on my back. I had one hand braced behind me on the wet ground and one arm in front of me, trying to ward Hascall away. It really wasn't working. "You, Holly, are full of surprises, are you not?"

I gave him my poker face. "I don't know what you're talking about."

"PSI, you're PSI talented…such a nice surprise."

Oh boy, I really didn't like the sound of that. I began to struggle but it was getting me nowhere and proving only to exhaust me. I tried again, "This doesn't have to concern you, and it doesn't have to concern me." (Bullshit!)

"Oh but that is where you are wrong Holly. You see, this concerns me, but it is dependent on you."

I didn't have more than a moment to ponder those ominous words before my chest became tight, my airway became constricted and small white lights began to dance in front of my eyes. I blacked out.

Chapter Thirty-Two:

Blast and damn, hadn't I been through this before? My brain was just beginning to clear and my eyes to focus when I realized I was flat on my back on a slab of what felt like very cold stone. I let my eyes wander and all I saw was darkness, yeah, definitely déjà vu. Shit, it was cold. My eyes grew as large as saucers when I took in my state, my very naked state, well fuck, no wonder I was freezing. I lay up looking at the night sky when a face leaned over me, smiling. It was Hascall, yeah, my fucking favorite person in the world.

"Ah, Ms. Feather, so good of you to join us."

"Us?" I muttered.

Hascall grinned. He looked happier than I had ever seen him before. That was certainly not a good sign. "You see, I had worried that all our labors would amount to nothing...time has been drawing near for some time, but we have come up short...until now." Hascall knelt down beside me and began to pet my hair. I flinched. "You are perfect, and you have been here all along..." He frowned. "It was very remiss of you not to warn us of your talents..."

I glared at him. "So sorry to mess things up for you," I muttered.

"Oh no, don't worry. You but delayed our business...now, now we are ready to complete what we started."

Oh boy. I was naked, staked to the ground and there was nothing, absolutely nothing to toss in his direction, shit. "You keep mentioning a 'we,' who is we?" I watched as a second figure emerged from the shadows. Well, well, well...look what we have here.

Portia Whitney was as beautiful tonight as on the day she had died. Her long hair was shiny and had the health of 'life' to it. Her eyes were bright and

288

hungry and her complexion, well, her complexion was rosy and pink with life. My eyes went to her hands, no, they were still normal, but for how long? The hell with it, I obviously wasn't going anywhere. "Hey." I gave her a bright smile. I would have laughed at her confused expression if I wasn't so damned uncomfortable, what with being naked and all.

"*Pretty*...so glad you could join us." Portia's voice slithered through the night and affected me much like a thousand needles piercing my skin. I narrowed my eyes and studied her; there wasn't much else I could do. I knew that voice, I knew her.

"Pamela..." I murmured. Somehow, Portia was Pamela. I knew this as certainly as I knew that my death seemed very imminent.

"Oh yes, you do know me by another name..." Portia flipped her hair back (a very human thing to do) and came to stand by Hascall. She studied me much as a scientist would a bug under a microscope. "You are more than fitting for our master." She ran a hand down my side and I shivered. "Such pliant, pretty skin. You are perfect." Her eyes glowed feverishly. "Your death will signal life for our master...life for all those who have served him faithfully."

Well, guess I was right on my imminent death part. Now, now I wanted answers. If I was going to die, I was going to my grave with answers. "So...where's the sorcerer?"

Portia let out a giant roar of laughter. Followed by Hascall, I didn't like being in the dark. "For such a smart girl you are unbelievably stupid."

"For a dead person you look remarkably well..." I muttered.

"There is no sorcerer, if you have been looking for one..." Her smile widened, "Then it is no wonder you have not figured it out."

My heart began to pound and blood began to rush to my face. I watched in disgust as Hascall began to caress Portia's body. He ran his bony hands through her hair and over her shoulders. His eyes were bright with desire and hunger and hers, well hers were fixated upon my naked body. Oh boy, oh boy, oh boy. Great, I was going to die and the semi-dead girl and lemon-sucking library attendant were going to go at it in front of me. Perfect way to go out. "There has to be a sorcerer..." I said through grit teeth. "For a demon to be involved."

"And how do you know there is a demon involved?" Portia asked snidely.

I rolled my eyes. I was staked to the ground, not stupid...then again..."Pu-leeze..."

Portia laughed. "You are right...about the demon." She looked over at

Hascall who nodded and slipped into the shadows as seamlessly as he had emerged from them. Several moments later he returned holding a wicked looking knife. Fuck, this really didn't look good. "Well, *pretty*, I think we have dawdled long enough." With one downward movement she slashed me from side to side.

I screamed. Sure, I might have known she was going to do it, but it was a far cry from being prepared for it. I looked down and saw my blood pooling in a steady stream down my side. (Fuck, this hurt) "So…you going to take my heart and head too?" I ground out through the pain.

Portia shook her head. "Oh no, that really isn't necessary…" She dipped her hand (the one not holding the knife) into my blood and smeared it across my belly. "This…" she said, holding up her bloody hand, "Is all that is necessary" She licked her fingers. (Oh gross!)

"So…you're just going to bleed me…" I was beginning to sweat.

"Bleed, oh yes…you shall definitely bleed…" She slashed me again. This cut was even deeper and my blood ran thick and red immediately. Portia turned to Hascall and caressed his weathered face. She leaned into him and placed a kiss on his forehead. "Begin, let us finish this."

I watched through pain filled eyes as Hascall began to light candles. The dark was illuminated and I could suddenly see the ever-familiar pentagram around me. Yeah, I was smack in the center and obviously the sacrifice. Breathing was becoming difficult and I could feel my limbs start to go numb. Blood loss, massive blood loss, I knew the signs and I was certainly experiencing all the obvious symptoms. I couldn't black out now, I couldn't. I had to hold on. I might be set up for sacrifice, I might die, but I sure wasn't going down without a fight, fuck them.

"Her death with bring about the rise of our leader…" Portia seemed to be speaking to no one in particular. She walked the circle and spread what I assumed was sulfur around the outside of the circle.

"I'm not dead yet bitch…" I muttered. I felt my breath coming out in short pants and I knew that I had to slow my breathing down. I had to remain conscious. I had to. I grimaced as I saw my blood seeping into the ground. My eyes widened when I noticed that my blood was disappearing into the dirt as soon as it hit. It didn't congeal on the grass and it didn't linger, it was being sucked up and imbibed…and I had a really bad feeling I knew by whom.

I lifted my eyes to the sky and said a short prayer. I saw that Portia had stopped at the far corner of the circle and was kneeling with her hands held out in supplication. She was rocking back and forth and chanting. "So what the fuck are you?" I shouted. Good, I hadn't yet lost my ability to speak. I had to be coherent. Portia didn't look up. "I'm still here bitch." Well that got to her. Portia got to her feet daintily and came to tower over my naked bleeding body.

"Not for long, *pretty*...not for long." She smiled evilly. "I could slit your throat and just get it over with." She leaned down by me. "Would you like that?" Portia brought the knife to my throat and pressed it against my soft skin. I felt a pinprick and knew she had nicked me.

"Fine, go ahead. But I'm betting...my last...dollar that you don't do it." I ground out. I watched her with hostile, defiant eyes. She wouldn't slit my throat. She wanted to see me suffer. If she had wanted to kill me quickly she would have done so immediately and I wouldn't have awoken at all.

Portia sighed and then smiled. "You are right...this is much more fun." She ran a hand through my hair. "You asked what I was..."

"Yeah, I'm just dying to know."

Portia grinned. She motioned to Hascall, who like a lapdog came running. When they stood side by side, her hand resting lightly on his shoulder she turned to me and spoke. "It does seem fitting that you know your part in this."

I watched Hascall grope her and wanted to gag, but that would have to come later. I was concentrating too hard on remaining coherent right now. Portia flicked Hascall's busy hands away and in the flash of an eye held the knife to his throat. She turned narrowed eyes to his face, smiling at the fear she read in his beady eyes. "Did I give you permission to touch me?"

Hascall swallowed, that movement alone caused the knife to dig into his skin and he bled. "No mistress."

"Then you shall not touch me again without my permission..." Portia smiled and removed the knife from Hascall's bobbing throat. She placed a chaste kiss on his cheek and began to pet his hair much as a master would a dog. "Now..." She turned back towards me. "Where was I?" She smiled, "Oh yes, it seems that we have a little time to kill..." She giggled, "So I will enlighten you. For my smartest student you have been woefully neglect in your studies..."

Her student? What the hell was going on here? "Huh?" It was all I could manage. Her face was beginning to swim back and forth...yeah; this was a very bad sign.

"You see...I am a shifter..."

"Uh yeah…" (This I knew all too well).

Portia laughed. "Of course you know that. But how is it that I have gained this particular power? Have you asked yourself that?"

Many times. I had come up empty each and every time. I was indeed beginning to feel very stupid.

"Oh Ms. Feather, you should have studied your demonology, now look at the predicament you are in…"

I gasped. Portia's voice had changed. The cadence the tone, everything, and once again I recognized this voice. Professor DeWitt…but how? "I…I don't understand." I gasped as my stomach began to cramp painfully.

Portia, no, Professor DeWitt…began to cluck her tongue, "That much is clearly evident. But then again I cannot fault you entirely. The books that you needed for your research were unfortunately not available once you began to put the pieces together, were they?" She reached out her arm to Hascall and he placed the familiar large volumed book in her hand. "You recognize this of course…" She smiled. "Of course you do. It's Zuri's insights on the 'Dead Sea Scrolls,' you initially uncovered it much to my dismay, however, you had the misfortune of underestimating your opponent, *pretty*." Portia shook her head. Long waves of hair fell over her shoulder and rested against her face. "You see my dear, if you had read Zuri's volumes as carefully as you should have the first time you would have uncovered all you needed to know. Do you not remember a passage that made mention of *Onoskelis*?"

I was fading fast. I shook my head. "No," I murmured quietly.

Portia sighed. "You see the problem with youth today…they do not take their studies seriously." She smiled at me. "You, you I had hopes for. I was much impressed with your knowledge in class. I was going to make you my next shell."

"What?"

"You see…I do have the ability to shift, but my power revolves around the fact that I can change forms." She knelt down and leaned close. "Can you not see it now?"

I looked closely and blinked my eyes several times to clear them. Her eyes, her eyes were a soft dove gray, beautiful, clear, and filled with purpose and venom, shit, oh shit. "Professor DeWitt…you didn't just shift, you changed forms completely."

Portia laughed. "Finally." She tapped me against my head and I winced. "Finally you are seeing things a little more clearly." She turned those dove gray eyes on Hascall and smiled. "You see my pet…I told you that it merely takes death to make all things clear. Oh Holly, you are talented…and powerful. I didn't know until that night at the club just how powerful you were. You resisted me, blocked me…" She growled, "Indeed, you rather bothered me." She stroked my pale and cold face.

I swallowed. "How…how…" God it was becoming harder to speak. "How do you change forms?"

"Have you not figured it out by now Holly? I myself am a Demon…" What the Hell? It wasn't possible. "No…it can't…"

"Be? I assure you Holly, it is very possible." Portia smiled at me. "You see my pet Hascall summoned me…" She gave Hascall an indulgent look, "Poor man was quite lonely…and ever so bored of having so much power and no one to show off for. He, my dear, unlike you, had studied his Zuri, and he is quite a talented Warlock…I am rather proud of my little boy." She blew a kiss at Hascall. Hascall, in turn was standing obediently still, staring at her with unveiled adoration and admiration. It was starting to make sense. Too bad it was too late.

"The sacrifices in Charlotte…" I murmured.

"Indeed. Hascall needed more than human blood, the companions in Charlotte were easy prey and did the job nicely. I came out rather well, do you not agree?" She ran a hand down her hair and smiled at me with her stolen lips. "It is ever so simple, Holly. I merely devour the form that I wish to assume."

Oh gross. She was a demon and a cannibal, great, just great. "You eat your victims?"

Portia shrugged her delicate shoulders. "They are the shells, I am the soul"

"You have no soul." I countered.

Portia laughed. "Quite right my dear, quite right. But their flesh, all their flesh must be consumed if I wish to harness their…bodies." She frowned. "You destroyed my last lovely body at that club, thus, I had to make use of another form." She tilted her head. "This one was quite nice. Almost as lovely as the last one, and oh, how the men loved it."

"Yeah I noticed you made use of your stolen feminine wiles, bitch."

Portia whipped the knife down in a movement so fast I couldn't follow it and blood ran down my arms, both of them. Fuck, guess I pissed her off.

"I am *Onoskelis*, seducer of man and sworn follower of *Belial*."

My eyes were beginning to close when she spoke the name. They quickly snapped open. "Belial? Leader of the 'Sons of Darkness'…Chief of the devils?" (In other words we were dealing with Satan himself)…yippee skippy, Armageddon and the Dark Prince. Great, I was going to bring about the end of the world, just what I needed to know.

"Ah, you know the name of our Lord. Yes, *Belial*, who should have had his place on the right side of the Earth, as it's Leader."

"Mmmm, I'm guessing that didn't happen."

Portia's face contorted. (Yeah, now I could see about that Demon stuff). "He is our rightful Master, our Leader, our Dark Prince."

Oh boy, another groupie.

"Hascall thought merely of his own pleasure, his own needs, but once I was summoned he quickly realized the scope of his actions, the grandeur of the plan he had set into motion. He resurrected me so that I may resurrect our Dark Prince." Portia moved away from me, she went to stand back on the opposite side of the circle. She knelt and locked her fingers together. Her eyes were no longer dove gray, they were now solid red, much like Hascall's had been when he had taken me. "It is our Dark Prince's time…"

As Portia began to chant the air became thick with the smell of sulfur and heat. The humidity in the air was choking me. That along with my severe blood loss was enough to put me down. I knew that there wasn't much time left, and I didn't have many options. With the knowledge of what we were dealing with firmly in the front of my head I knew I had to do something, anything. I would gladly trade my own life if it would stop the opening of the Hell Gate. But I knew that my life, my living was the key to stopping Onoskelis's plan. I couldn't die, my death would signal the end for humanity and the beginning of Belial's reign. My more than human blood was obviously the last needed to resurrect Belial, and it was now soaking the ground in great red waves. "Oh my God!"

I felt my eyes burn and water as the air became hotter and thick with evil. I could clearly see the particles in the air as they began to float and form. Within moments I could see a clear membrane like substance beginning to take root within the circle. The structure of limbs began to clear. I could see an outline of a being, a thing. Shit, I didn't have much time.

I closed my eyes and began to concentrate. I tried to take myself away from the pain, the clear presence of evil. I only had this one chance. I didn't have enough strength to try again. When my eyes opened I saw Hascall holding another ceremonial knife, but this one wasn't aimed at me directly. He was walking as if in a trance towards my staked down body. When he had reached my prone form he deftly cut my binds and unwrapped them from the stakes ground deep into the pliant dirt. Within moments of my release he was walking assuredly towards Portia, who I now knew as Onoskelis.

Onoskelis had already broken down Hascall's mind in order to control him. His defenses were breached and his mind was pliable as Play-Doh. With her concentration focused on performing the last rites of the resurrection spell she wasn't aware of my probe into Hascall's busted mind. Once the probe was successful I knew that I could control him much as a puppet master would his puppet. Onoskelis had unknowingly made my work much easier for me. I knew the knife would do damage but probably wouldn't kill her. She was a fucking demon. But what other choice did I have.

I took a deep breath and focused myself. There was nothing but Hascall and the knife, nothing at all. With the first thrust of the knife into Onoskelis's 'shell' the spell began to waver. Onoskelis let out an inhuman roar and with clawed hands ripped the knife out of Hascall's hands. Turning on him she allowed her jaw to unhinge until it was three times its normal size. Fangs gleamed bright in the candlelight and blood ran red as she sank her teeth into Hascall's neck. Even his scream did nothing to deter her.

In the back of my head I heard noise, a fluttering of wings perhaps. But my vision was so blurry and my body so broken I couldn't really be sure of what I was hearing. I crawled to the edge of the binding circle, nearly choking on the scent of sulfur in the air. I reached out and stifled a scream when my hand was scorched by the warded parameter. I turned my head back, the wavering demon form was growing more substantial, Hascall's blood had inadvertently, (or perhaps it was the demon's plan all along) strengthened Belial, and he was beginning to take a tangible, scary as all hell form.

I had to break the circle. I had to get out. If the sacrifice escaped the pentagram the circle would shatter. However, the chance that the Demon would escape would also occur. I just prayed (and I really was praying) that Belial's form was not enough to escape. How much blood had I lost?

I reached out again and felt my body burn from the inside out. Oh god, oh god, oh god.

"Holly flower you much cross the circle for I cannot..."

I lifted my head...was I hallucinating? It couldn't be Lucien, but at that moment I felt a familiar cool breeze brush my cheek and caress my burning body. "I hurt..." I ground out, "It's too much."

"No Holly flower, you must do this...she will not be distracted much longer. Cross, you must, I promise you that you needn't do more than this.... Cross."

I wasn't hallucinating, I wasn't. It was Lucien's voice I heard and he would help me, I just needed to cross the damn circle. I took a deep breath and with nearly the last of my strength I hauled myself to my knees. I was aware of a roar of anger and rage from behind me and could feel my mind suddenly being invaded, torn apart at the seams. I heard Lucien's cool voice urging me on and with a scream of pain, horror, and sheer determination threw myself over the warded circle.

I couldn't do anything but lie there. There was nothing left. Out of the corner of my eye I saw a dark figure hurl himself at the semi-apparent figure of Belial. Screams echoed in my ear. Those screams belonged to me, Belial, Onoskelis and Lucien. Everything bled red. And the scent of blood permeated the air and hung on me like a blanket of death.

And as suddenly as Lucien had appeared I saw lights in my peripheral vision, lights and movement, a lot of movement. I could barely move my head but suddenly there was movement all around me. And then it began, gunfire, the roar of gunfire. The last and only time I had heard a gun discharged was when my mother had slain the ghoul who had tried to eat me; this sounded nothing like that time. This gunfire was constant and extreme, the shots echoed and cracked through the night like a whip. I felt like a broken doll and I lay twisted and bleeding.

My whole body screamed in protest as I turned my head to see what was happening. Onoskelis was down. Her stolen body was ripped and torn and shot full of holes. She was bleeding and gasping for breath as she flopped on the ground like a fish out of water. Belial, too, was injured, his body had never completely formed and therefore he was vulnerable. However, because of this state the bullets were not doing as much damage as they had to Onoskelis. I saw Lucien, half shifted, tearing deep gashes into Belial's misshapen head. Belial's arm flailed out and Lucien easily sidestepped the panicked demon. I watched as Onoskelis's human body bled and bled well. Her human body was dying and she didn't have another 'donor' to occupy, therefore she had no place to go but back to the hell she came from.

As I watched her bleed it all became clear, so perfectly clear. She had human blood in her. It was the mortal blood in her mortal body that was her undoing. She could not sustain her existence due to the mortality she had incurred when taking over Portia Whitney's body. Belial had my blood within his body. My blood was a key to his mortality. It wasn't my death which would bring on his resurrection it was my life. Onoskelis had tried to trick me, and she had almost succeeded in her plan. She had led me to believe that she was keeping me alive merely to torture me, when the truth was that she couldn't fully resurrect Belial without breath in my body. My life, my blood triggered his life and his blood. Once Belial had been fully restored there is no doubt in my mind that she would have let me bleed to death, but she had needed me alive, god I was stupid. The longer I lived the longer Belial remained on the earthly plane. I knew what I had to do.

"Lucien...I'm sorry." I murmured, casting only a brief glance in his direction. He was still fighting the demon. I remembered how he had spoken of his inability to kill a demon, and yet, yet he fought on for my sake. This, this I would do for his sake, and for all the others who would be saved by my true sacrifice.

"Holly...NO, NO Holly, do not..."

I heard Lucien's agonized words but ignored them. With strength born from determination I telekinetically transported the ceremonial knife dropped by the felled Hascall to my hand. I closed my eyes and blocked out everything, the screams, and the protests, the gunfire and the heart stopping heat, and plunged the knife deep into my receptive flesh. I felt my body spasm and my heart constrict and then I felt nothing.

I was awake...what was I doing awake? It had to be a dream, or, no, wow, there really was an afterlife, and it looked remarkably like the four white walls of a hospital room. I squinted, expecting, hoping to see an Angel, or possibly, if I was lucky St. Gabriel...what I saw instead was Detective Marcus's severe face staring down at me.

"Funny how you're showing up in my dreams now Detective...can't a girl catch a break?" I gasped as pain shot through my body. My voice sounded odd even to my ears, but what did I expect I was dreaming, wasn't I?

Detective Marcus came forward and with a couple deft movements of his hand raised the back of my bed so that I wasn't lying flat. He regarded me with those somber eyes of his and swept his gaze over my body. (Boy I hoped I wasn't naked in this dream)

"You aren't dreaming Holly."

I nodded. "You would say that."

Detective Marcus rolled his eyes. "I say it because it's the truth. You're alive Holly, against all the odds..." His eyes grew stormy and his mouth tightened into a straight stern line "And your own actions, you're alive."

I shook my head. "It's not possible. If you're here, and Belial isn't reigning over fire and brimstone that has to mean you defeated him."

Detective Marcus said nothing. I really didn't like that. "Detective. Only my death…" I didn't get to finish my sentence because Detective Marcus shushed me with a furious look. I swallowed.

"Yeah your death, thanks a lot for fucking letting me in on that little piece of information."

Oh, now I understood why he was pissed. "I didn't realize it myself until the very end Detective." I sighed, "I seem to be realizing a lot lately…like how much I don't actually realize." I gave a short, mirthless laugh. "How dense I really am."

Detective Marcus shook his head and clenched his hands into fists. "Shut up."

"Huh?"

"Shut up. Listen here, kid. Your act of total stupidity was what brought about that demon's destruction. The moment you…" He shuddered, "Did what you did, our bullets tore through him like a knife through butter. He was down and he wasn't getting up." Detective Marcus still wore that dark as death expression. "You, you weren't getting up either Holly. You were dead. Your heart stopped."

I frowned. "I…"

"I'm not finished," Detective Marcus growled. I shut up. "It was then that some godforsaken Night Walker, some vampire came to your side." He skewered me with an unreadable expression. I swallowed. Oh, this was so not the way I had wanted him to find out about Lucien, if he was ever going to find out about Lucien. "He wouldn't let me, my men or the EMT's near you." Detective Marcus's eyes were stormy. "And believe me I tried. He wrapped some strange field around the both of you, something impenetrable…something…" Now his look was accusing, "That a normal blood sucker would not be able to do. I watched as he sank his fangs into your chest and ripped open his own wrists and bled himself into you."

"What?" My eyes were wide with fear and shock.

"Yeah, fucking into you. He bit you and then fed you and coated your wounds with his blood."

"Oh my god…no" I swallowed. "Did everyone see…?" My voice trailed off when Detective Marcus shook his head.

"No, the field obviously protected you from prying eyes as well as from intruding hands. All those who aren't PSI talented couldn't see anything…and as you know I'm the only PSI talent on the Edwards police force."

I shook my head. I wouldn't believe it. I couldn't. "He didn't bite me." I said firmly. But my head was churning wildly.

Detective Marcus smiled grimly. "Believe what you want. I fucking know what I saw kid. And I have to say I don't like it."

"How did you find me?" I murmured.

He frowned, "The last message I got from you was an SOS. I had Hascall and Professor DeWitt checked out" He sighed, "After our little chat. Professor DeWitt spent some time in Charlotte, around the same time Hascall took a little vacation there himself."

I nodded. This I knew.

"In my research." He laughed mirthlessly. "You see I can do research too. It came to light that Hascall had a cabin within the Smokies. That, that was too coincidental, even for me." He sighed, "The rest, well the rest you know."

I gave him a small smile. "So you came to rescue my ass."

He nodded. His expression turned dark and he spoke. "Not that I'm not pleased as all shit to see you sitting here speaking to me…but a dead dater." He ran a hand through his hair, "God and I thought I was joking when I made the crack before…about…" His voice trailed off.

I shook my head. "The Vampire that you saw was the Holder of Edwards."

Detective Marcus's eyes grew wide and his mouth dropped open. "Holy shit."

"Yeah…" I muttered, "That about sums it up." I swallowed before continuing. "I didn't tell you about Lucien because I know how you feel about the dead…and, I didn't think you'd understand."

"Well you thought right," he ground out angrily.

I nodded. "I couldn't take the chance that you would do something stupid, like try to find him and, well…" I shrugged my shoulders, "do something stupid." I sighed, "So I didn't say anything. I am sorry you had to find out this way."

"I'm sorrier that you're hooked up with a corpse," he said flatly.

I winced. "It's not what you think."

"You don't know what I think."

I looked at him with light violet eyes. "I think I do."

Detective Marcus's face tightened and his stance stiffened. "No…" he ground out, "you do not!"

"Fine," I muttered. I shook my head. "I don't know what else to say to you, Detective."

Detective Marcus looked suddenly exhausted and so very weary. He looked at me intently before speaking. "Nothing, I guess there's nothing left to say Ms. Feather."

Ms. Feather? Shit, no, it couldn't end this way. "Detective…"

Detective Marcus held up a hand. "No, you're dating one of the dead and I'm protecting the living, there isn't anything to say." He sighed, "I wish…well it doesn't fucking matter what I wish." He began to go but then spun around before reaching the door, "Take care of yourself Ms. Feather." He nodded his head, almost resignedly, "Somehow I think you'll do just that." With those words he left. Leaving me wounded both mentally and physically.

When I awoke next it was to a cool and soothing pressure exerting itself upon my body. I sighed and leaned back into the pillows, allowing myself to bask in the comfort and strange consoling cradle of wind. I knew, without looking, who was in the room with me. "Welcome to my humble lodgings…" I said quietly.

"Holly flower." Lucien now stood by my bed. His beautiful face was still and calm. He reached out to place a hand on my shoulder and I flinched. He jerked his hand away and leaned back from me. "You know." It was a statement not a question.

I nodded. "Yeah, I know." I felt tears burning my eyes. I would not cry. "How could you Lucien? How could you do it?"

"I could not, would not, lose you," he said simply.

I hung my head. "You shouldn't have…you knew how I felt."

"Yes, I knew."

"And you did it anyway." I felt now familiar anger creeping through my body. It had been simmering, stewing for a while but now, now it was beginning to boil.

"You would have died." He looked at me with that unreadable face, "You did die. I could not stand and do nothing if I had it within my power to restore you to life."

"You blood-sucking bastard. You bit me, you fed from me," I ground out.

Lucien shook his head. "No, that is where you are wrong Holly flower. I bit you, yes, but I did not feed from you, nay, I fed you." He reached out, and as if remembering my earlier rejection drew his hand back to his side. "You had been bled dry. Your last…" his face shimmered with barely concealed fury, "act…caused your heart to stop beating. You were technically, by human standards dead for several long moments. Yes, your human doctors might have been able to revive and restart your heart…but what could they have

300

done for the other wounds? They were more than fatal Holly flower. I replenished your blood by giving you the most precious thing that a Night Walker can offer…his own. As for my bite, it was necessary to revive your vital signs. Otherwise, I would never have bitten you, knowing how you feel about such actions." He watched me—looking for signs of forgiveness perhaps? When he saw no signs of forgiveness he once again began to speak. "I do not understand your anger Holly flower…you are alive, you are still mortal. You have gained power and strength from my bite and vampire blood and yet you suffer none of the consequences of the 'change.' You will not be a Night Walker. You remain unchanged, the same."

I clenched my teeth. I drew my hospital gown down revealing the tops of my breasts and creamy flesh. Between my breasts, nestled within the valley were two perfect holes. The flesh was already puckered and it was obvious that it would leave a noticeable scar. "I'm not the same…" I murmured, "and I'm definitely not unchanged." I saw Lucien draw back, his face tightened and his skin pulled. He said nothing. Hell, what did you say to that? Suddenly there was a knock at my door, moments before it swung open to reveal Ryan's face. I looked from Ryan to the side of my bed. Lucien was no longer standing there.

"Holly, god, I'm so glad to see you're all right." Ryan came to stand where Lucien had stood just moments before. But Ryan took my cold hand in his and stroked my brow. His face was drowning in concern and fear. "The doctors wouldn't tell me anything. I'm sorry it took me so long. I was only allowed to visit now." Ryan gave me a tentative smile, which broadened when I grinned at him.

"I'm glad you came Ryan."

Ryan squeezed my hand. "I wouldn't want to be anywhere else Holly." He gave a nervous laugh. "You just have to promise me that we'll stop meeting like this. Enough with the bear attacks already." The look in his eyes told me that he knew very well that this hadn't been a bear attack. But I was heartened by the fact that it seemed as if he was willing to wait until I was ready to confide in him.

I smiled. "That's a promise I'll try to keep."

"Don't try, just do."

I nodded. "My best…I'll do my best." I held out my arms and Ryan shook his head.

"No, I can't, I might hurt you."

I grinned. "You'll hurt me more by standing way over there. Come on…"

I let out a sigh of pleasure when Ryan lifted my back away from the propped pillows and wrapped his arms around me. I ignored the twinges of pain and discomfort, basking in the feel of his warm arms holding me tight.

Ryan placed his warm lips on mine and I sighed. The pleasure was so intense. He deepened the kiss and now, now I felt as if I were glowing. My body came alive with sensations and my heart, well my heart was certainly beating. I felt his tongue, warm, smooth and soft, caressing my lips and tasting what I had to offer. He pulled back, looking at me with an expression of pure happiness and delight. I answered his look with one of my own. I was alive, he was alive, and life, well life was pretty damn great.

I felt a cold chill run up my arm and I turned my head sideways. Outside the window, hovering, nestled within the darkness of the shadows was a single, solitary figure. Auburn hair glinting fire in the moonlight, white face as smooth, perfect and beautiful as cut marble, was Lucien. His expression was unreadable, his mind impenetrable. But somehow, I felt him, knew him…longed for him.

I jerked my eyes away from the window and turned them back to Ryan's smiling, vibrant and very much alive face. Without another thought I leaned into Ryan's embrace and wrapped my arms tightly around his solid frame. I felt the heat of his body emanating off of him and seeping into me and smiled against his chest. Now, now I knew exactly what I wanted. I had found my way home. And I wouldn't be tricked into the darkness again. Not if I could help it.

* * * * *

Printed in the United States
24635LVS00004B/8